RETURN
TO THE
TEMPLE

AMANDA ROMANIA

BOOK 1 OF THE DIVINE ORACLES SERIES

RETURN
TO THE
TEMPLE

AMANDA ROMANIA

BOOK 1 OF THE DIVINE ORACLES SERIES

FLOWER *of* LIFE PRESS

FLOWER *of* LIFE PRESS

Return to the Temple
Book 1 of the Divine Oracles Series
By Amanda Romania

Published by Flower of Life Press
www.FlowerofLifePress.com

Interior Design:
Jane Scott Ashley, www.floweroflifepress.com

Cover Art:
Amanda Romania

Editorial services: Claire Trivax and Jennifer Kirwan

Library of Congress Control Number: Available upon request.

ISBN: 979-8-9878275-0-5

Gratitude to my spiritual sisters and mentor Isis
for opening the doorways of the temple
for our souls to remember.

CHAPTER 1

The rich, dark crimson ocean coaxed me along in the starless, onyx night. I felt I was floating, lost and alone. A faint beam shone in the distance, calling me toward it. The warm waters seemed to understand this and gently carried me closer until the brightness of the white light overcame me. Suddenly, the light plucked me from the waters, which were already retreating, and enveloped me completely.

I then found myself at the top of a hill on a warm, sandy shore, devoid of human life except for two women in hooded cloaks, one in black and the other in a deep violet; they were just down the hill. From my vantage point, I couldn't see their faces or hear exactly what they were saying, but I could tell they were in a hurry and concerned about something. They kept glancing furtively around as if they were expecting someone to come upon their tryst at any moment. I started to walk toward them to see what was going on and to understand why I was there. As I approached, I could see the one in violet protectively holding a small wicker basket. She seemed to be agitated with the woman in black, who was trying to get her to put down the basket. I called to them, but neither of them made any indication that they heard me. Almost at the bottom of the hill now, I called again, but still no answer. The woman with the wicker basket was crying now, and she handed the basket to the other woman. I tried to run toward them to stop her, but the sand had other ideas. I sank where I was standing, and the sand grabbed hold of my feet, cementing me into place.

Panic washed over me, and again I yelled to the women, this time for help. The muddy silt was starting to pull me deeper and try as I may, I couldn't break free. The woman who had taken the wicker basket from the crying woman was now fleeing the scene. She got into a small boat just down the shore and rowed away with ease. The other woman knelt on the ground with her face in her hands, sobbing. The sand was now around my waist, showing no sign of slowing down. I called again to the woman, and again, she made no indication that she heard me. She then got up and started to walk away from the shore. Only as the sand was groping at my neck and the last feeble cry for help escaped my lips did the woman turn toward me. Her hood fell, and I saw a flash of raven hair and the glint of a gold necklace with a familiar symbol on it before she quickly replaced it. Then, as the sand was swallowing me whole, I saw her big, emerald-green eyes staring at me, full of tears.

Monday, May 19, 3:33 a.m.

I awoke with a start, those emerald-green eyes lingering in my mind's eye. I was gasping for air and grabbing at my body, expecting to feel the quicksand all over me. After I tuned in to my heartbeat and took a few deep breaths, I was calm and aware of where I was. I leaned over my bed to grab my phone off a pile of books and check if I'd gotten any notifications, but there were none, which was another reminder that I was alone. As I leaned back over to place my phone back on the books, I undershot, sending the pile of books cascading to the floor. The sound was like a cannon going off. I looked around, worried the sound may have woken someone up, but soon remembered that I lived alone.

With a deep sigh, I switched on my nightstand light, peeled the warm covers from my body, and traversed out into the tundra that was my drafty bedroom. I knelt down beside the heap of books and picked up and inspected each one. Most of the books were self-help or how-to volumes, but a few were on history, spirituality, and metaphysics. I'd recently picked them up at the local bookshop because I'd been feeling lost. I suppose I'd felt that way for a long while, searching for something outside myself. I convinced myself that if I became the perfect person, it would make getting up each morning worthwhile. But recently, it was all coming to a head, and I was tired of not doing anything about it.

That was what made me so willing to get these books—that and the woman, Lucinda, with whom I'd recently started taking classes on spiritual, spooky stuff. In a few short weeks, I'd come to call her my friend and mentor.

One would think there were more interesting ways to spend a Friday evening than in the back of a café, hidden from the world and practicing spooky stuff with a group of like-minded women, all in middle age and none wearing a wedding band. I thought my thirties were for exciting times with friends or being married and planning the perfect weekend of romance. Sadly, I had neither. My life had drifted into a twilight zone where I sought truth and wisdom—or rather, desperately tried to find the meaning of my life (or any life, for that matter) with spiritual arts.

My path had crossed with Lucinda's a few months ago when I visited a local spa for a birthday treat. I went for a facial, which I was sure would return me to the world with perfect, glowing skin. Instead, per my usual sour luck, I had an allergic reaction to the products. I had to spend thirty minutes lying in the chair at the spa with cold cloths on my face, trying to calm the swelling while the esthetician hovered over me, profusely apologizing and making a scene. When she could see the cold compress wasn't working, rather than let me see a doctor, she called for Lucinda, a spiritual therapist. I held my breath, unsure of what this Lucinda would do, but then a surreal calmness wrapped around me in the same way it does for small children when they are told their mother is coming to get them.

Lucinda was older, approaching her golden years. She glided into the room wearing what could only be described as a fashionably bizarre ensemble comprised of red cat-eye spectacles, a purple housecoat, baby blue silk gloves, and a forest green tartan wrap dress. Her teased, curly, crimson hair fluttered behind her as she approached me and placed her silken-gloved hands around my face without any fanfare. She whispered a few words and closed her eyes. Slowly, the burning and itching subsided, and everything began to return to normal. When she finished, she gave me a small smile and left the room without another word.

I was so intrigued that as I left, I asked one of the reception girls who and what on earth Lucinda was. She smiled and said that Lucinda had come to work a year ago as a therapist and had quickly gained a following for her abilities. The receptionist didn't know how it was possible, but she had magic hands and words. Magic hands and words? I felt I had to learn more.

And so I did.

I found out that Lucinda ran a small teaching practice of spiritual and spooky stuff each week from out of a local café. Without thinking twice, I signed up for her twelve-week workshop, not even knowing what we would be learning. But I didn't care. Most of the time, we would meet in the main seating area of the café during business hours, but sometimes Lucinda would have us meet there late in the evening, well after closing time. I always found it strange and a tad unsettling. We came through a back door in the dark alleyway behind the shop.

I remember one evening, the spring equinox on March 21, when Lucinda talked about how it was a very powerful time when one leaves behind the winter and gets set to take up a new adventure. That night, we were to open and explore what we truly wanted in life and release the fears of the past. Part of the teaching would be through the use of tarot cards to help us see the future. The other women in the group found all of this to be intensely fascinating, which made sense, considering their other most exciting outing was to their Monday afternoon knitting circle. Their admission of this made me laugh when they asked if I wanted to share knitting patterns. Then I realized that my most exciting outing was grabbing takeaway at my favorite Chinese place after work, believing this was a surefire way to have some weekend thrills. I remember thinking, *Dear lord, my life has come to this. What will become of me?* On the plus side, the ladies had brought me gifts of socks and scarves that were so beautiful, soft, and warm. "Cashmere," they whispered in hushed voices as they handed them to me.

That night, Lucinda must have read my mind because she then remarked, "Be very careful of your thoughts, ladies, as they create our dreams and our realities." My cheeks flushed with embarrassment despite logic telling me there was no way she could have heard my thoughts—that I knew of. I decided to be mindful and laid out the tarot cards, pretending to know what I was doing, fanning them out in a flamboyant flourish. Of course, instead of behaving the way I wanted them to, my cards jumped and fell off the table in all directions. I quickly went to retrieve them, hoping no one noticed. Unlike me, the other women in the group seemed to have perfect spreads all in order, and they were already reading expertly for themselves and those around them. *Witches' coven at work,* I thought.

I went back to my own bubble with a messy spread and a confused knowledge of the various card meanings. But, somehow, I could actually interpret the cards that night and receive real messages. My card configuration was that of the Star, the Hermit, and the reversed Strength cards, all three from the Major Arcana.

Just then, Lucinda came over to observe my reading and whispered, "So tell me what you have here?"

"Well," I began, "the Star card has to do with hope, rejuvenation, and fertility, so maybe it means that I will have a renewed power or that I will have a blessed life going forward, that I have gone through or will go through something traumatic, but I am not to lose hope but have the courage to continue on. The Hermit card means that I am wanting to be alone? No, that isn't right. I think it means that I am searching for my inner voice and the truth of who I am, and maybe someone will come into my life to help me? The last card, Strength, is reversed and means that I am experiencing self-doubt and have a lot of insecurities. It also could mean that I am at a point where my life is stagnant, and I need to regain my confidence and harness my inner strength to get myself out of it."

"Very good, Anna," Lucinda remarked. "And what is the solution?"

I pulled a card from the top of the deck and turned it over. "The Fool—that's not good. I don't want to be made a fool," I said, furrowing my brow.

"No, Anna, it has nothing to do with being a fool. It's quite a good card for your reading. The Fool represents infinite potential, as symbolized by his number being zero. He is yet to find himself, and he will be shaped by the new journey ahead. Thus, the card means that you will have a new beginning and start to your life that will free you from your current stagnation, as represented by the reversed Strength card. Your stalwart hope and courage, as brought forward by the Star card, have helped sustain you and get you to this point, whereas the Hermit card has shown you that the need for inner guidance will help you complete this journey, the outcome of which will be attaining complete enlightenment of self."

That revelation cheered me up—that perhaps there was more to my life than working a dead-end job at a locally based magazine. It was also validating to know that I had correctly read and comprehended the messages from the cards. At last, my psychic gifts had returned. It was a strange thought to be supplanted in my mind, as I was never aware that I had lost or even had them in the first place.

I had forgotten that night; it had been months since I had read my cards. It was now May, nearly June. Even though that night had been a breakthrough in my eyes, I was still skeptical about how real all of that hocus pocus was. Anyone could have guessed I was unhappy and looking for a change; I didn't need cards to tell me that. And if I was about to go on this big journey of self-actualization, when would it start? This reading occurred weeks ago, and nothing in my life had changed. These books I was so carefully placing back in order were not helping me; if anything, they were always in my way, and constantly repiling them was preventing me from returning to sleep.

The books on the floor were the stories and tales I had carefully curated for myself. Most of them were available online in updated editions. Still, they couldn't compare to the feeling of the scaly leather binding, the sound of the paper coming back to life with every page turn, or the familiar, comforting smell of the dried ink and look of the swirly letters sprawled out on the parchment. These books have a soul, a consciousness, and a history that they can share with you, like a well-traveled friend. It may be old-fashioned of me, but I would rather carry around a thousand books in my bag than a million on my computer. Better yet, ten thousand scrolls, like the ancient Greeks and Romans did. I loved each and every one of them.

The most recent book I picked up was my current favorite friend, a memoir about a woman who, as a child, was able to regain full memory of a past life in ancient Egypt after she fell down a flight of stairs. Her story recalled her struggle in attempting to blend these two worlds she knew to be hers. In the end, she reconciled her two selves and made Egypt her home, where she could truly be at peace. I was not sure I could live like that, but all the same, what a wonderful thought.

It was strange. Lucinda had mentioned in one of the weekly classes that we all had past lives and that many of us had had one in Egypt. She believes the women who seek out the type of spiritual practice she teaches are doing so because they still have connections to Egypt. I think she thought this memoir would help convince me of that. She said we were either priestesses or oracles. The priestesses mainly attended to the temple by performing rituals, leading people in prayer, and performing simple magic. The oracles, who were few in number, had prophetic abilities and advanced magical abilities, and they were protectors of sacred texts and secrets of the temples. These oracles and priestesses were an essential part of Egyptian religion in helping to protect the Egyptian people by foretelling the future, performing rituals, practicing magic, and keeping Egypt's greatest secrets safe.

It was an incredibly intriguing notion that women could hold that much power and influence in an ancient society. Ever since I was in primary school, I'd always found Egypt so fascinating. So when the opportunity arose, I chose Egypt for my project topic. In fact, I'd dreamt I could, at some point in life, study Egyptian hieroglyphics, but there wasn't a program at any school I could afford. I always dreamed I would journey to the Great Pyramid.

Unfortunately, I had never even gotten the chance to visit it; my mother was unwilling to take me anywhere as a child, and all of my friends were too busy to go with me as an adult. So books would have to do for the time being. I did want to learn more about this little-known history of the oracles of ancient Egypt, but more from an intellectual perspective rather than a spiritual one. It didn't matter to Lucinda where the messages and information came from; she was more than willing to lend me some of her books if that meant I was exploring all avenues.

All of the past life stuff was really interesting, and I did wonder if it was real—and if it was, what my timeline would have looked like. Was I a slave building the pyramids and a scullery maid for Queen Elizabeth I, or was I the leader of an ancient mystery cult and a world-renowned explorer of exotic lands? Either way, it seemed taxing for the woman in the Egypt memoir to reconcile her current and past lives into one cohesive existence. Whatever my past lives were, they could wait. I had a life-changing journey to go on first.

I chuckled at the thought, and just as I was about to place the memoir on top of the pile, I was startled by a pair of bright green eyes staring at me. I shook my head and looked again. It was a book with a large picture of a black cat on the cover. The book was about cat worship in Egypt—another gift from Lucinda. I gave the cat a wide smile and placed the memoir over it.

I crawled back into bed, where it was warm and safe. I pulled the covers around me and asked for all the magic of the books to connect with me and give me magical dreams. Maybe they would also give me a new career and a new life, but that was placing far too much on them. Perhaps they would give me magical powers, and I could become a real witch or something like that. With that thought, I pulled the bed covers back and placed my mobile phone on the nightstand. It was getting late, and I had work tomorrow and needed to be focused. I looked at my phone: 4:44 a.m.

Wow, where did that time go? But by now, I had forgotten my scary dream; all was at peace in my world. And now I needed some sleep.

CHAPTER 2

Monday, May 19, 7:07 a.m.

My alarm went off, and I got this feeling that I was trying to wake from a deep dream, unable to lift my arms or legs. I wonder what my subconscious found so interesting about my dreams, I thought. Then I dragged my heavy legs over the side of the bed and slowly sat up. Unsurprisingly, I knocked all my books onto the floor. That's it—they can stay there. I threw a brightly colored pashmina scarf over the top of the pile to hide the mess from my tired eyes and alert my now-rushing self to the hazard of tripping over them again. It would be horrible to trip over them as I rushed to get ready and head out for what I was sure would be a pointless day at the office. I will say that one blessing of my job was that it was only a ten-minute drive. As long as the sheep were not crossing the narrow country roads, I would make it to work on time, maybe even a few minutes early.

I worked for *Visit with Style*, a local magazine company that produced a high-end monthly magazine about what to do as a tourist and visitor in the northern countryside of England. My role was to answer the phones and book the advertising from the local hotels, restaurants, shops, and tourist attractions. It was a humdrum administrative role coordinating with the community and assisting the managing partner and owner. The forty hours per week at just a bit above minimum wage were supposedly worth it for excellent promotion prospects. Sure. I've always dreamt of being a writer, not necessarily at a magazine but writing something that reaches others and offers insights to them. With this job, however, it was always the prospect of promotion but never the actual promotion.

The owner, Natasha, used the magazine to fund her shopping addiction and attraction to the good life, staying at the hotel locations and sampling the food for free in exchange for what she said was a promotion opportunity for the business.

When I first joined her business, she was beyond sweet and kind. I had started with her when she was working from her home office, but in my first few months, we had secured many advertising clients, and she had expanded to a stunning new location and fabulous converted barn. I had thought, *How wonderful. I am getting in on the ground floor of this amazing new independent magazine.* Natasha encouraged me to give feedback on the current issues and on local businesses that should be featured. She even told me I could have my own review section, knowing of my writing dream and exploiting it all of the time. "Anna, you should write this," and "You could write that."

But I never got to do any of that. Most of my job consisted of looking up places from which Natasha could get free stuff. She was particularly interested in the spas that could help her look younger. Natasha wanted to exude an air of luxury, so she always kept her cropped black hair in place, and her nails were freshly manicured every week.

Despite her efforts to look thin, posh, and young, she came off as more plump, gaudy, and tired. But not wanting to judge based on appearances, I always took her at her word. It didn't take me long to realize that it meant nothing. Like her promises, she was merely a false idol for me to believe in and trust.

For businesses, getting a visit from Natasha was like getting a kiss from a vampire. She would pretend to be one's new best friend and customer, and then she would demand free service in exchange for a feature story in the magazine and make a big deal out of it if the company refused. This scheme seemed to work well for her because I don't remember the last time she'd paid for a fancy dinner. The truth is that most people knew they were getting scammed by her, including me, but we went along with it anyway because she convinced us of the enormous favor she was doing for all of us.

As I was thinking about this, I turned down the lane toward the office. It's a stunning converted barn with windows that have picturesque views of the countryside. The rolling hills have such a calm beauty to them—another benefit to the job. When I pulled up, a strange sight greeted me. I saw a large removal van outside and two men lifting desks and chairs into the back. *One minute—that's my desk.* I sped up and pulled to a stop behind the van. I jumped out, not bothering to close the door.

"Hey, that's my desk! Put it down!" I shouted.

"Sorry, ma'am, I've gotta move it. I'm just doing as the lady asks," said the older of the two men in a gruff voice. They both looked uncomfortable. He nodded toward the office, and I raced into the building, stopping in my tracks in the doorway.

There was Natasha, clacking around in her stiletto shoes and carrying boxes to her car. She ignored my sudden appearance and continued to walk past me as if I was air. I grabbed her arm and, in the calmest and most even tone I could muster, asked, "Natasha, what is going on?"

"We're closing." She said nothing else and continued to load up. I stood there in shock for a moment.

What the bloody hell does she mean we're closing? How is that possible? I followed her to her car, wanting to ask what was going on.

But then I noticed that she had been placing my files into her car. I knew they were mine because they were color-coded, and she even had my computer that I had loaned the business a few months back on her back seat. *What nerve she has.* But I didn't think to argue; sense told me to be swift and thoughtful.

"That's a damn shame," I said.

She was in a hurry to avoid me because both of us knew I would not be receiving a wage for this week. Thank goodness I had insisted on being paid weekly. I had to think fast, and my intuition stepped in. "Let me help you, Natasha," I offered.

She stopped. "Your things are inside," she responded.

"Great, let's load you up first, then me."

"Yes, yes, that's a good idea," she said a bit too eagerly. I could tell she was trying to get rid of me as quickly as possible with the least amount of explanation.

"Okay, now why don't you go select what you want, and I'll load these heavy boxes?" I said, smiling my best assistant smile.

She turned and went back into the office. "I need to make a call," she yelled over her shoulder as she walked away. "You keep loading boxes!"

I looked over at the two men loading the van. The older one walked over to me, shaking his head.

"I bet you won't be seeing her or your money for a while," he said.

"And I hope you were paid in advance," I replied with a smile.

"Oh, yes," he answered. He pointed toward Natasha's office, "She's a slippery one, but I got the money." He then looked at her car. "Does any of that belong to you?"

"Yes," I said. He nodded and winked at me as I started to remove my belongings. I worked quickly, first opening the boot of my car and sliding out the computer and my files while pushing the boxes into place to cover my tracks. I opened the side door, and there on the floor was a curious white box. I opened the lid, and there were my personal belongings: my picture frames, makeup, and everything from my desk. I stopped and wondered what else of mine she had. I walked back inside the building.

When I got inside, I saw that the offices were totally bare and had been for a good few hours. Natasha was still on the phone; I could hear her talking to husband number two. She was telling him the business I knew he had invested in was going wonderfully, and if he could advance her ten thousand pounds, she could reach another fifty thousand readers. Suddenly, Natasha turned and saw me, and for a moment, I swear her eyes were red. I froze and motioned that I was going to the bathroom. She nodded and went back to her conversation. When I came out of the bathroom, she had closed the door, so I could not now see through to my office.

But that was of no issue to me now. Something about her, those red eyes, scared me. I knew I had to break free of her.

I went back to her car. Once more, I opened up the door and lifted out the white box. As I did, another box fell over, and the lid fell off. To my surprise, the petty cash box revealed itself. I was tempted to take my wage, however I knew she had a greedy way of thinking and would have claimed this as theft because her signature was not authorizing anything. I will say this of Natasha: she held the rule of law on everything. I guess I was saying goodbye to my wages and other expenses, but this was increasing her bad karma, not mine. I quickly hid the box back into the pile and ran to my car. I quickly placed everything into my boot and ran back to her car just as she came through the door.

"Nearly done!" I said. "Just those boxes at the door if you're bringing them over."

"Oh, I will," she said. "But let me make a quick call."

"Of course!" I smiled at her as she did her famous disappearing act.

By now the van men had finished loading the large items, and they stood watching me to see what I would do next. The younger one came over and began lifting the boxes from the doorway.

"This is the last of 'em," the older man said with a smile. "Did you get everything you need?"

Before I could speak, Natasha appeared. "Are we done? Because I have an urgent appointment at the bank," she snapped.

"Yes, ma'am," said the older mover, and he began to get into the front seat of his van. "I'll take this all back to the store right away." I remembered then that she had never originally bought this furniture, only leased it, although she had been claiming to her accountant that she had purchased everything and even lied to the local bank manager to get a bank loan to pay for it.

"Are all my things loaded?" Natasha asked, looking at me.

"Oh, yes, for sure. You should go to your urgent appointment," I said. "We can meet up later."

She faltered and then remembered another of her lies. I had gotten used to them by now. "Can you finish and lock up, my dear? Here are my keys."

"Oh, yes, leave the rest to me." She handed me the keys. "Natasha, will I be paid for this week?" I asked.

"Sure, sure. I'll make it all work," she said dismissively. "Give these keys back to the landlord. He will be here soon; I told him we were leaving, and you would take care of everything."

"Oh, I think I see him," I pointed at a car approaching us.

With that, Natasha jumped into her car, and with a hasty "I will call you," she was soon gone, driving down the road in the opposite way, followed by the men in the van.

I stood alone as the landlord, Tom, drove up and got out of the car. "So she's gone, has she?" he asked. I smiled and nodded. "Anything left?"

"Nope, I don't think so, but I'll check." We walked into the offices, now bare and empty. I felt bad but also thankful we had paid his rent for this month.

"I'm so sorry," I said with a sheepish look.

"Don't be," he replied. "You all did me a favor, actually."

I looked at him, not quite understanding. "I'm sorry, a favor? Aren't we liable for paying the rest of the lease till the end of the year—or rather, Natasha is?"

"Well, you would be, not her."

I thought I misunderstood him.

He continued. "I just sold the building, and the new owners have decided they want the current tenant out, which means I would have had to buy the rest of your lease to secure the sale. So you, my dear, actually just saved me a lot of money."

"Certainly, I'm so glad you saved money, Tom, but I just lost my job." I paused. "Wait…what do you mean, just me?"

In response, Tom pulled out a copy of the lease and showed it to me. Sure enough, my name, information, and signature were all at the bottom, signed until the end of the year—and that was another seven months away.

I began to panic. *There's no way this could be happening.* "Tom," I yelped, "I swear on my life I have never seen this document, and I would never, ever sign my name to a lease for her."

"Well, Natasha told me you were going to be her partner, and you had signed the lease as part of that partnership. I never really questioned it at the time. Come to think of it, I probably should have. Originally, she was on the lease for the building with one of her other husbands when he had a business here, but then last year, just before you moved in, she wanted to sign up for this new building alone without him. I told her we would be running credit checks, and then suddenly, she came back with your name, no husband, and said you were investing in her company. Don't you remember? She said she was bringing the business here, and you would cover the lease as partners. Love, your name was on all the payment checks."

I remembered now that I had joined her six months before the move to the converted barn, and she had said the expansion would be wonderful, and I had to sign for the keys and be a co-signer on the checks to pay bills. I had not read the contract; I just thought I was a key holder and was listed on the documents to be called in an emergency. I thought it strange that I had to give her my passport and identity details. Obviously, she had been using my credit score and stealing my identity.

I wanted to sink into the ground and disappear forever. "She sold me out, Tom. I had no idea!" I could barely get the words out as the fear hit me. I was starting to cry when Tom reached out for my hand.

"Ah, so you had absolutely no idea, I see," he said, a twinkle in his eye. "So does that mean you don't want the security deposit back?"

I sniffled and looked up at him in shock, "Security deposit? What do you mean?"

"Well, when 'you' (he put air quotes around *you*) signed the lease, you had to pay the first and last month's rent for the deposit, and the check already cleared for this month. The way I see it, as the person currently signed on the lease, *you* are entitled to that money. I'd normally ask for next month's as well because you improperly notified me, but you need the money more than I do, and I put an incentive payment in for you to leave before the new owners arrive tomorrow. That woman seems properly rotten and doesn't deserve the money. Besides, the new owners shelled out a small fortune for this ol' barn. Now, if you will sign this release paper, saying you are okay with me terminating your personal lease, then I can give you this check here." He added, "Oh, and the keys, miss. I'll need them, too."

I looked at him, shocked, and dumbly signed my name on the dotted line. Then I handed the keys to him, and he handed me an envelope with the check and gestured for me to open it. It was for twenty-two thousand pounds and had no name payable. He gently took the check from my shaking hands and wrote "Anna Harris" on the top line. *Oh, my god, did those books on spiritual abundance actually contain magic? What is going on? This is nearly as much as I make in a year. Wow.* He handed me back the check and smiled at me. I stood there stunned, and my sinking feeling subsided. Suddenly my brain began to work, and I came back to reality. I looked up to thank him, but he was already getting into his car and driving off.

Just then, I heard a meow. I turned and saw a waif-like black cat standing on the doorstep. *She must belong to the neighbor from down the way,* I thought. They always had cats running around the area, but I'd never seen this one before. How odd that just this morning, I was looking at that book with a picture of a cat on it, and now here in front of me was one. What was it Lucinda said? Oh, yes: nothing in this universe is a coincidence, so you'd better take notice. *Well, I've taken notice, universe!*

"Guess it's time to change things in my life," I said out loud. The cat looked up at me with an amused expression, as if she could understand what I had just said. Then she yawned and stretched out on the doorstep, and I walked off toward my car.

I looked down; twenty-two thousand pounds was in my hands. A disaster of a day had turned fully around. I had enough money to support myself for at least a year and go on holiday. *On holiday.* The words dawned on me. For the first time in my life, I could go relax on a beach off the coast of some exotic land. The thought was so all-consuming that I barely had room to think about the strange morning I'd just had. Whatever had happened, I couldn't wait to deposit the check and plan my trip. In fact, I would do that on my way home. Maybe I'd pick up some travel brochures to get a head start.

CHAPTER 3

My mind was racing as I got back to the house, so much so that I almost missed the car parked outside. It was Lucinda's, and it seemed to be still running. I parked behind it and went over to see if she was there. I knocked on her window, and she jumped at the sound. I must have broken her out of a deep thought.

Without hesitation, I asked, "Tea?"

"Yes, please." She nodded. I motioned her to follow, and as we walked up the steps, I briefly pondered why she was there. But with Lucinda, it was better not to ask questions and just go with it. I wondered if I should share this morning's adventure, but something in my gut told me she already knew.

Once the tea was made, we sat in the kitchen, and I waited for her to tell me why she had come to visit. She was silent for a while and then seemed to hesitate before speaking:

"I had a most auspicious dream last night. In it, a woman of an ancient time with long white hair came to me with a request—an order, really." At this, she nervously laughed. "She told me I had to bring you to Glastonbury to see her."

"Glasto-where?" I asked.

"Glastonbury, in the south, where all the spiritual people go. It's the home for the psychics and mystics I work with."

"Did she say why?"

"I didn't ask. I find it best not to." She shrugged.

"Well, that might have helped if you did!"

"Yes, it might have." She looked away, pensive.

"So what else happened in the dream?" I asked.

"I can't quite recall."

Something told me she did but was not ready to share.

"Lucinda," I countered, "Why would I go to Glastonbury just because you had a dream that told you I should?"

"It was the woman in the dream," she corrected me.

"Either way, it still doesn't mean I should go to Glastonbury."

"Doesn't it? Annie, what is keeping you here?" It was funny how she used my name like she was addressing a child.

"Nothing. I don't know. There's the flat …" I began to stutter as the reality that I had lost my job sank in. "Besides, I can think of many more exotic and exciting places to visit than southern England. And before you ask, I lost my job this morning."

"I knew." She smiled. "And not because of my gift. Natasha came into the spa yesterday and told everyone the landlord had gone back on his word and evicted her, and the magazine was closing. She sobbed like a spoilt child!" She clasped her hands together. "So! You know, something told me you would not be at the office all day. I was awaiting your return, and sure enough, at 1:11 p.m., you were right on time. Look, Annie. You can't run until you walk. It would be a mistake for you to go somewhere else first. You need to find yourself and figure out your life's purpose!"

I was starting to get frustrated, and I could tell she was too. "Lucinda, I don't even know if I will go anywhere right away. I just lost my job not four hours ago. Let me catch my breath." Those words sunk in. Just then, I really did need to catch my breath.

"You can do that. Of course you can, Annie," Lucinda said with a patience that must have taken years to master. "But when you do, I hope you will take my advice. I promise I would never steer you wrong."

I was about to tell her that I would consider it but that she shouldn't get her hopes up, but my phone buzzed.

I had several text messages from Natasha.

"My bank account is frozen."

A lie.

"I can't pay u right now."

A lie.

"Will send something each week, though, until you are repaid."

A lie, lie, lie …

"Thank you," was my response. I smiled because, obviously, the news from Tom the landlord had not reached her, and I prayed it never would. Then I blocked her number. Finally, I turned my attention back to Lucinda.

"Sorry, it was Natasha. The wicked vampiress." I laughed a hollow laugh. "I appreciate that you care so much for me, Lucinda," I said in a serious tone, "and that you want what is best for me. Few people in my life do, especially those who have been closest to me. I've only known you for a few months, and you have shown me so much love and kindness. You know what? I promise I will seriously consider going to Glastonbury, for you." I knew she meant well, but this all sounded like a waste of time to me.

Lucinda gave me a kind smile. "Good, that is all I want for you." She wrote down a number and name on a business card. "My friend owns this guest house in town. You should stay there and see what happens. Her name is Emilee. She's a lovely French woman and has been living in Glastonbury for years. I will warn you, though: she is a bit eccentric, and even though she's been in the UK for a while, her English still isn't that good. She says that people should learn her language." I gave her a strange look. "I don't know, darling. She's French."

She shrugged. We both giggled at that.

Then she got up from her seat. "Well, I must be going." She took my hands in hers and squeezed tightly. "There is so much more to you than you know. Go to Glastonbury, listen, learn, and write like you always wanted. Your life just ended here; it's time to live your true ones." That was a strange sentiment, but again, I never thought to question anything she said like this.

"Ah, like the tarot cards predicted, I guess," I mused.

"Exactly, Annie. Now you are getting it! Trust yourself and make movement in your life. The answer of who you really are will arrive in due time."

I got up, walked my friend to the door, and told her I would think on what she had said. She pulled me in for a hug. "Don't wait, Anna," she whispered into my ear. "We all have waited so long already." With that, she flew out the door.

After she left, I sat on my couch for what seemed like hours, just staring at the wall. I was unhappy and made no attempt to hide it from anyone. But was my life really that bad here? I got up and walked around my flat. It wasn't Kensington Palace, but it had a certain shabby chic aesthetic that I enjoyed. I didn't own a lot, but I wasn't desiring material goods. And my job wasn't really that bad, was it? At least I got to be part of the writing community. Better to be miserable on the inside and pretend to be happy on the outside, right?

Oh, my god. It was true: I had very little here and not much to show for my thirty-three years on the planet. Just then, I opened my door to my bedroom and saw the pashmina scarf I'd put over my books earlier. I knelt down to pick them up and organize them again. I had just gotten them back into a nice pile when a loud creak startled me, and I knocked them over again. It put me into a dizzy confusion, and I began to cry hysterically, the weight of the day finally catching up to me.

It was early evening when I finally pulled myself from my pity party. I could hardly remember the earlier part of the day; it seemed like it had happened a week ago. My stomach was grumbling, so I went to the kitchen to fix myself a sandwich. On my way back to my bedroom, I caught sight of myself in the hallway mirror. There were dried streaks of mascara caked to my cheeks, and I had dark circles around my bloodshot eyes. My hair looked like it had been housing a family of small animals for a week.

I went to the bathroom and straightened myself up, splashing cool water onto my face, removing the makeup from it, and combing out my hair. I had never much cared for the color, a dark brown with flecks of red that could be seen when I stepped into the light. I wished it was completely red, which would have complimented my blue eyes better. Oh, well. When I looked in the mirror to inspect my handiwork, a bout of dizziness overtook me. I tried to get to the kitchen for some water, but my limbs felt too heavy to move. The room was spinning around more and more, and the edges of my vision started to go dark.

With my remaining strength, I managed to drag myself back to my bedroom and hoist myself up onto the bed. There were strange noises coming from the roof and outside, or at least I thought there were. It was hard to tell if they were real or not. The only thing I could do now was sleep and hope that I would feel better in the morning.

I found myself back on the sandy shores with the two women from before. The dark waves crashed in the background, and no moon shone in the night sky; only the stars illuminated the beach. This time, instead of waiting on the hill, I rushed toward them so I could hear what they were saying. I tried to get as close as I could to them, but thick tendrils of sand shot out of the ground and grabbed at my feet as I barreled down the hill. I tried to shake them off the best I could and managed to gain a few more precious meters than last time before the sand wrapped around my foot and pulled me to the ground. All the while, the women took no notice of me. I was invisible.

From my position, I could make out that the woman with the emerald-green eyes and wicker basket was dressed in beautifully draped alabaster and amethyst silk, strategically placed so as not to highlight a trim figure. The part of her arms peeking out from the cloak were adorned with gold cuffs, and she wore many rings, one with a scarab beetle atop it. She appeared regal. Despite the pained expression on her face, she stood resolute and strong, maintaining control of the situation, as perhaps a royal upbringing might have taught her to do. I could see that she was not much older than me. She had very few lines on her sun-darkened skin, which glistened with beads of sweat not from the heat but from something else.

The emerald-eyed woman was arguing with the other woman dressed in a black cloak about where to go. She wanted to head to Alexandria, but the other woman argued that heading south to Philae would be safest. She argued it would be safer for her in Alexandria. The other woman simply would not have it and said that it was written in the stars for this to happen. The emerald-eyed woman nodded and silently turned away from the black-cloaked woman. Then she carefully set down the basket and knelt beside it. Only in that briefly private moment did she allow the glittering drops of liquid, which had threatened to betray her before, to fall from her bejeweled eyes. She looked into the basket and whispered something imperceptible to it. Finally, she sniffled, wiped her eyes, and with a resolve unmatched by the strength of anyone took out a small bundle wrapped in linen and handed it to the other woman. Just as she had before, the woman in the black cloak, who appeared much older than the other woman, took the bundle, replaced it into her basket, and went off to the small skiff waiting for her to sail away.

I then realized that the sand was still coming for me and had nearly covered me to my neck. I struggled, but to no avail. Then a thought struck me, and I wondered if that bundle was a baby. Apparently, I said that aloud, and the emerald-eyed woman immediately looked up at me and said, "Find her. Go and find her."

CHAPTER 4

Tuesday, May 20, 2:22 a.m.

I was violently roused from my strange dream by a loud banging noise that sounded as if the earth itself had torn open. I went to get up to discover the source of the noise but found my body unable to move. The room went deadly silent, and shadows surrounded my bed. Fear set in, and I tried to call out for help, but my body would not let me. My chest felt constricted, and it became hard to breathe; it was as if an invisible weight was pressing down on me. The shadows danced around me, seeming to mock my situation. I was fully awake but was helpless to fight off these malevolent entities. My breath was so shallow at that point that I thought I would die from lack of oxygen. I began to feel light-headed, and my eyes fluttered, fighting to stay open. Then very suddenly, everything went black.

I was awoken again a few hours later by more banging noises, which appeared to be coming from the ceiling. This time, I could move my body like nothing had ever happened in the first place. I quickly got out of bed to investigate, almost tripping over the heap of books I had left in a mess earlier. Once I got to the door, I noticed my feet were wet. There was water coming under the door, and quickly. I ran to place the books out of harm's way, but the water had already reached the other side of my bedroom. I picked up as many as I could. That poor book with the cat statue on it was ruined, and the Egypt memoir was completely soaked through. I hoped Lucinda would understand.

I then rushed to open the door, and everything was covered in water A large hole was in the ceiling, where it looked like a main waterline pipe had ruptured. I ran back to my phone and called the emergency number and then my landlady.

I managed to get to the shut off valve within a few minutes, but the damage had already been done. My flat was filled up with about ten centimeters of water, and it wasn't draining. I knew the furniture was ruined and any clothes and papers that had been on the floor wouldn't be worth keeping. I had fallen asleep with my laptop on my bed, so at least that was safe, even if the charger wasn't. When the plumber arrived about an hour later, he looked in dismay at my rooms. He told me that the whole system would need to be repaired and that special cleaners would have to be called in order to drain and dry everything.

After securing the pipes and ensuring they wouldn't rupture again, he said in a gruff, matter-of-fact voice, "I'll call Laura, miss. She'll handle all the insurance stuff for the building, but I hope you had coverage for your furniture and the like. Although judging from how quickly the furniture has deteriorated, I'm thinkin' you probably didn't bother. You should save what you can and be prepared to not live here for, oh, three months or longer. If your landlady or you have no insurance, well…" He paused, unsure of what to say next. "I guess you should call a friend and get out of here." He gave me an awkward pat on the back and left.

A friend? What friend would want me to stay with them for months? Who would want an unemployed, miserable secretary as a roommate? Who would hire this glorified "fetch me this, girl" with no references from her previous boss, because why would Natasha ever help me? Never mind that she'd used my name on the lease and god knows what else. Why was everything falling apart?

It then hit me. I needed to come off of my pity party loop. I wasn't being positive or productive. I needed to make a change.

I ran to grab my laptop and went to the café around the corner to do some research on Glastonbury. It looked beautiful; there were so many hills and gardens and wonderful places to explore. I was also fascinated by the history of the place. Perhaps Lucinda, or the woman in her dream, was onto something. The perfect place to stay and rebuild my life might just be Glastonbury. I fumbled around my bag for the business card Lucinda gave me and called the number.

The phone rang three times before someone answered. "Hello, Gables Guesthouse, this is Emilee," a woman with a heavy French accent said.

"Um, hi." I hesitated. "Um, yes, well, my name is Anna Harris, and my friend Lucinda gave me your number. She said that you ran a bed and breakfast."

"Oh, yes, she mention you, Ms. Harris. I think you want to come visit, oui?"

"Um, oui. What is the soonest you have available?"

"Well, it all depends on how long you plan to stay."

I hadn't thought about how long. "Oh, well, at least a month, maybe longer. I haven't decided if I want to travel anywhere else after."

"Ah, you are a traveler! Wonderful!" she exclaimed.

"Well, I'm not really, but I think I want to be—traveling, that is—at least for a bit until I figure out my next steps."

"The Gables Guesthouse is a great place for that. Would

you like a room with a private bathroom, since you will be staying for a time?"

"Yes, how much does that cost?"

"A single room with a private bathroom is three hundred pounds per week for you, if you like. That includes breakfast, cleaning, and laundry services. It will be available starting Monday, May 26. Sound good?"

Without thinking I blurted, "Perfect, I'll take it!"

"C'est magnifique! Let me have your full name, email, and credit card number. I'll send you confirmation."

"Thank you so much! Um, merci!" I said, and I gave her my email and card information.

"Je vous remercie, Mademoiselle Harris. I look forward to meeting you!"

We said our goodbyes, and then I put the phone down and looked around. Everyone was going about their business in the café, working, chatting with their friends, and reading books. They all seemed to have purpose in their actions, yet they also seemed miserable; not one person was smiling. I now had a chance to avoid that and change my path. I closed my computer and went back to my flooded flat to pack what I could.

It took a few hours before Laura arrived, but by then I had already packed what I could salvage into four boxes and two suitcases and loaded them into my car. She walked up to me as I was loading the last box.

"Oh, my dear one, I'm so sorry," Laura said. "Tuesday is my busy day collecting rents. Is much ruined?" She was the kindest lady, always thinking of others. She reached out and touched my hand. Laura was very petite in her features. Her hair, a white silver, neatly framed her face, and her gray-blue eyes were so pretty they seemed to sparkle. She always reminded me of a fairy godmother who would keep me safe. "I came over as soon as I could," she continued. "I must look a terrible mess, I do apologize!" She smoothed down her coat and pushed back her hair. Even though Laura appeared to be in simple clothing, one could tell these were expensively cut and designed to fit. Meanwhile, I was in pajama bottoms and an old jumper with a coffee stain I tried to hide.

"Well, the furniture has gone to pieces," I said while closing the boot. "But I never much cared for my secondhand checkered couch set. I've saved and packed what I needed. Now I just need to figure out what to do about cleaning up the place. The lease says I'm covered for all the damage and repairs, but not my own personal items, which is fine. But it will cost me a small fortune to pay a company willing to move the rest of my stuff out of a flooded apartment. What extra money I received as, uh, severance, from my job will cover the cost of the removal and new furniture, if I return, but it won't leave me much for living expenses to cover the whole period of the repair."

"Oh no! You lost your job *and* your flat flooded? That's a spell of bad luck, isn't it? Poor angel. Are you doing all right?" she said with a look of genuine concern on her face.

"Yes, I am fine. I wasn't happy at my job anyway. I got quite a nice bit of cash because the business was closing; I was just hoping to make it stretch a bit further. That's my fault, though, for not insuring any of the junk I had." I had to have a hearty chuckle to stop my tears from returning.

"Hmm, that is true. Without renter's insurance, you aren't technically covered for that." There was a glint in her eye I noticed as she continued. "I reviewed my insurance policy before coming here, which is why it also took me so long to find you. I think I can work it out to where you only pay a small deductible to have everything done, including removing, repairing, or buying new furniture. And it will even cover your living expenses while repairs occur."

"You can? How is that possible?" I asked.

"I have very good insurance, my dear," she said with an impish smile. "Now, what did you mean when you said, 'if I return'?"

"Well, it is a long story, Laura, but the gist of it is I am going to Glastonbury next week because Lucinda had a dream…"

I knew Lucinda and Laura were friends, and to my surprise, Laura had attended some of my spooky spiritual classes.

"Say no more," she interrupted. "If Lucinda had a dream, then you are doing the right thing. How long will you be gone?"

"At least a month, but now with your help, maybe longer!" I said with a sudden rush of excitement.

"Oh, that sounds so lovely! And it is the perfect time to head south!"

"Yes, I think so!" I then looked down at my phone to check the time. "Is that the time already? I need to get going to the hotel down the street and see if they have any available rooms!"

"Oh, nonsense, Anna. Stay with me. It is the least I can do; it was my water pipe that flooded your home, after all. Besides, I would love the company."

"Really? You are too kind, Laura. I'll get in my car and follow you out." I did not have to be asked twice.

C'est la vie. The bad and good fortune I've had the last few days are astounding. Seriously, maybe Lucinda and the books she gave me really do have something to them. And now I was speaking French. Bizarre.

♀

Staying with Laura those few days was a blessing. As soon as I walked into her cozy and warm home, I felt safe. A strange thought entered my mind. I didn't remember not feeling safe, and yet now here I was, wondering what wouldn't be safe about my life.

Her home was a beautiful one-story cottage on the edge of York's city center. The cottage had been built in the 1850s and still had its original interior features. The wood outside looked weathered by time and its many past owners. This was a place with a few stories. Laura actually had a book that contained all the details of every family that had lived there. It had become tradition that whenever the cottage was sold, the previous owner would provide a brief history of his or her family's time there for the cottage's book. There were even some photographs dating back to the original owner. Laura was kind enough to share all of this with me on my first evening there.

"And this was my grandfather." She showed me a photo of a very grand-looking gentleman in a suit. "He was the one who bought many of the properties I have today." She looked around the room as if looking for someone and then brought her attention back to me. "It's so good to have you here, my dear." She smiled, and her whole face softened.

I had never really paid much attention to her when I paid my rent each month. She would simply pull up in her car outside, and I would go out and hand her an envelope—very clinical. But now it was as if I were with family. I couldn't explain why, but my heart felt such a calmness, and also so much emotion that I wanted to cry.

"You know, I think we can become best friends in five days," she said with a laugh.

"You know, I think we already are," I said.

Over the next few days, we fell into a routine. Laura would go about her business during the day. Her role was a simple one, as she had explained: collect the rent, organize the repairs, and see to any legal matters. She had lost her husband a few years previously, and he was the one who had been in charge of the properties before her. She didn't mention her husband often, and I didn't want to pry out of respect, but I did notice his pictures everywhere, which made it feel like he was still roaming around the cottage.

We spent our days apart, she tending to her properties, and I reading about midlife career changes. However, when six o'clock in the evening came around, we seemed to find ourselves both in the kitchen preparing our meals and each enjoying a glass of wine. There was an inviting dining room in the back of the cottage, but for some reason Laura always ate her meals at the large oak kitchen table.

At that oak table, we would talk about any old thought that popped into our minds, and I would update her on what I thought I could now do with my life and the work I would like to try.

I had gone from considering shop work to being a legal assistant or secretary. At one point, I even considered being a medical assistant or massage therapist. Laura would always give me a warm smile and offer words of encouragement. On my last night, I found us doing the same, but my thoughts suddenly wandered to a topic I seldom thought about: my mother.

My mother had always had very clear ideas on what I should become in my life. She had wanted me to keep myself looking perfect and acting witty and charming, so that I'd be able to find a wealthy man to marry. She had always said, "Sit up straight! Cross your legs at the ankle! Put some blush on that sickly face! You'll never get a husband if you look like a slob!" Her words seemed so far away now.

My father had passed when I was barely four years old, so she had been the only parent I had ever really known. Now I could barely remember him, and it didn't help that my mother had hardly ever talked about him. All I was told was that he had been a police officer and had died on the job from a sudden heart attack. I think that created a big rift between my mother and me. We never saw eye to eye, and I often wondered if she had neglected to tell me that I was adopted because our lives seemed so different.

I was a mild-mannered child who always tried to blend in with the crowd. Mother was a gaudy and flamboyant woman from a family of moderate means who had always wanted more than she could have in life. While I was growing up, she had aspired to be a lady of leisure but lacked the fine breeding and class to be accepted by the high-tea crowd. It really affected her, and she took out all of her frustrations on me. Her words were so cruel, and I always felt like I was walking under a dark cloud. It wasn't until I was older that I realized she resented me for a whole different reason.

When my father died, my aunt Lydia, her sister, moved in to live with us. She was my saving grace and always defended me when my mother was being particularly critical of me. I remember so clearly, when I was sixteen, Aunt Lydia explaining to me why my mother was the way she was. Laura actually reminded me a lot of her. I think that's why I felt so safe in her home.

"Anna, you are loved," Aunt Lydia had said while we were doing laundry that day. We were in a small room at the back of the house where she and I would often go to talk, usually after a tongue-lashing from my mother about my hair or clothes. "Your mum and dad had plans for their lives and were looking to travel after they got married," she continued. Perhaps to even move abroad. Then your mum got pregnant with you, and your dad decided that they should stay in York, to be close to family. She wasn't ready to be a mother but knew that not keeping you wouldn't be an option for your dad.

"When you were born, your dad took to being a dad like a fish to water. He loved you so much, and I think she really did too, in her own way. But when he died, she resented that he had left you with her. That man was the love of her life, but she hated him for leaving her alone. You were a constant reminder that she had not only given up her plans to travel but also had lost the man with whom she had planned to travel. I guess she felt trapped and unable to leave the area. She once told me she felt chained to the city walls, trapped in a life that was not hers. So because she couldn't travel around the world, she tried to travel up the class scale. I know it doesn't seem like it, but she does care for you and wants you to have everything she couldn't."

It had been a shocking realization, but it made sense why she was so critical of me, and why she never talked about my father. Not a great image, however from then on, I knew that this was never really about my inability to be perfect but about my mother's imprisonment to a life she felt wasn't hers. I vowed to one day set her free.

When I was eighteen, I decided to leave home. Because my father was a policeman, he had a substantial life insurance policy, which supported all of my mother's endeavors of the perfect lifestyle. Luckily, there was a stipulation in the policy that if he died before I was eighteen, an amount of the payout had to be set aside for me to go to college and buy a car, which would be paid to my bank account when I turned eighteen.

On my eighteenth birthday, I remember going down into the kitchen to celebrate with my mother and aunt, all the while knowing my bags were packed upstairs and I would be leaving for York that night. My friend from secondary school and I were going to share a small flat. I left home the next day, leaving a note on the kitchen table. My mother never tried to find me or contact me, and I had never attempted to return home. Christmases and birthdays were often very lonely, but Aunt Lydia would always send a card and find out where I was living and working, and when she could get away, she would occasionally meet me in York for the day. We would shop, have lunch, and laugh together. But we never mentioned how my mother was; we never even mentioned her name. A few years back, Aunt Lydia died, and I was completely alone. To this day, I don't know what happened to my mother, and I don't know if I want to.

It had been such a long time since I had thought of my family. I hadn't meant to think back on that chapter of my life, because it was closed. But as it came back to haunt me, I couldn't help but cry.

"Anna," said Laura gently, her soft voice waking me from my reverie, "it's time to let the ghosts go and be free." It was as if she had read my mind and was seeing my pain and expressions. Her hand reached across the table. "This time tomorrow, you will be there. You will be all tucked up in your room in Glastonbury, and you will forget all about this other life you had.

"You being here over the last few days has been a gift. In just a short time, you have made me laugh and smile and remember what it is to be alive. When my husband David passed, I died inside. I stopped living for a while and simply went about being a property manager with no zest for life. It's a lot of money each month, I have to confess." She said this last part in a whisper as if she was ashamed of her wealth. "But you know what, Anna? I feel like it's chaining me to this place."

Suddenly I felt a chill in the air, and there was a large bang outside.

"Oh, that's just David." She shrugged it off.

"He's here in the house?" My voice sounded alarmed.

"Not in person, but in spirit. I made a promise to stay and carry on this work when he died. It felt like a sacred contract at the time, but now it feels like a binding curse." She stopped as if she had caught herself in another world that she was not ready to share with me. "Now, my dear," she said with a smile, "Glastonbury is a totally magical place, and you will find what you are looking for, I am sure."

"I'm sorry, Laura. I never thought to ask if you had ever been to Glastonbury."

She got up from the table and seemed uncomfortable with me asking. As she stood with her back to me, she started washing the dishes. "I went a few times after David passed," she explained. "I have known your friend Lucinda for a few years."

"When did you meet?" I asked her.

"Well …" She paused with her dishcloth in her hand, and then she neatly folded it and set it down. She sat back at the table. "With my husband gone," she continued, "I felt beyond lost and would sit for days listening to the executors of the will telling me how to handle the business and how not to. I had prayed for guidance from God. The next day, I saw a card in my hair salon; it's now the spa. You know that one?"

I nodded.

"The card said I could find my answers and reach those who had passed over." She seemed a little embarrassed, so I gave her a reassuring smile and encouraged her to go on. "Well," she said, "I called the number, and it was Lucinda. I told her about my circumstances, and she was kind. She even came here and made a house call."

"She came here?"

"Yes, my dear, and she knew at once my husband had not passed on. She described him before she even saw the photos. At first I thought she must have known from looking in the obituaries in the local papers. But, no, she knew things no one knew." She bent her head and began to whisper to me. I looked around, unsure of who she was afraid would hear her. "Anyway," she went on, "I told Lucinda I wanted to leave and sell everything. She read my tarot cards and said that I would do well to wait. I had unfinished business and karma with my home and property. She could not say when I would be free to leave, but she said that I should consider my next steps with caution. She said I still had a purpose and was to wait. She did tell me I could travel and invited me to come to Glastonbury. In fact, that was three years ago this month. My, how time flies."

"And what did you think of Glastonbury?" I asked.

"Oh, it was beautiful. You must go visit the Tor; it is the jewel of the town; it is a monument built high upon a sacred hill. The history behind it is fascinating. Even though it was challenging for me spiritually and emotionally, it was good for me, and I was very happy during my stay."

"So why did you come back?"

She looked around even more awkwardly. "I had to. My husband, may he rest in peace, still was here. I'm bound to this, Anna till my sacred contract is complete." Laura looked me directly in the eye, and I wondered if this was the wine talking. She seemed so serious as if she were afraid of something or someone.

She then smiled and changed the subject. "Well, anyway,

you will love your time, I am sure." She got up from the table again and began clearing the dishes and making herself busy. I went to go help her, but she stopped me. "No, I'll clear up here. You run along and pack."

I smiled at her. "Thank you, Laura. You have been a godsend, truly!"

"Oh, but before you go," she said, standing up and retrieving a box wrapped with beautiful lilac tissue and a large fuchsia pink bow from the kitchen dresser. "I have this for you." She handed the box to me.

"Oh, I'm so sorry. I didn't know we were exchanging gifts tonight!" I said with a panicked look on my face. "Laura, come with me to Glastonbury!" I found the words flying out of me.

She laughed a hearty laugh at my sudden outburst. "No, no, my dear girl. I have to make my peace here first."

I didn't understand what she meant, but suddenly it was as if my mother's face washed over hers, and my mother was speaking to me. I felt such a sadness and anger, yet compassion at the same time. I reached over and took her hand. "Well, if you do decide, you call me, okay?" I said, holding up my phone for effect. "I mean it, Laura. You call me, and I'll be there to help you."

"Then that's my gift." She smiled. "Thank you, dear."

Then she insisted I open my gift. I opened the box, and as I pulled back the paper, a beautiful, gold foil–covered notebook fell into my hands. She clasped her hands in delight and exclaimed, "Your new journal! Start writing, Anna. You have told me so many stories these past few days that are all so interesting. And how you described everyone! I tell you, I laughed so hard! Glastonbury will have great characters to describe, I'm sure. Write about them, even if it's just for me. Let me share this journey with you, even if it's from afar, although I have a feeling that many more than me will enjoy your stories. Write from the soul, my dear, and you will find peace."

I began to laugh and held the journal close to me. "Only for you," I exclaimed. "You know that I will. For you." I opened the first page and reached for a pen from my bag. On the first page, I wrote,

For Laura, who told me to write from my soul.

"There," I said, putting the pen down and holding up the book. "It's started. I'll use this journal to capture stories and characters and write them up each week."

"Perfect," she said as she raised her wine glass. "I'll drink to that! Cheers!"

CHAPTER 5

Monday, May 26

The next morning came around far too soon. My few days with Laura had been like being with family, and it crossed my mind that perhaps I should stay around and push back the Glastonbury trip. But I had already booked my room, and I knew that if I didn't go now, I never would. Soon it was my time to get on the road.

I decided I would go onto the motorway and head south. I figured I'd arrive by mid-afternoon and then start a whole new dawn and new day in my life. I had tied up my loose ends and created closure for my old world.

☥

Earlier that morning, I had checked my emails, and several had been from Natasha asking for login codes and email contacts. *Ah, so this is why she tried to take my computer.* We both knew everything was kept in detail on there, and she couldn't say I had stolen the computer because it was my property in the first place. I had repeatedly told her to back everything up in her computer system, but she always took the easy route and then complained later. She had been the one to tell me to use my own computer, and it all made sense now: she could never be liable for anything that went wrong. I thought about checking to see whatever else she had signed my name to, but I had been so happy enjoying my time with Laura that I decided to leave that for another day. I had blocked Natasha from my phone and thus had to block her from my life, as well.

Before I did that, I wrote her a short email.

Hi Natasha,

I'm now using a new computer, as it appears mine went missing in the recent move; I thought you must have taken it by mistake. Sorry to hear you misplaced it! No worries, I am sure it will show up. Unfortunately, I'll be disconnecting this account soon, so I might be a bit hard to reach. But don't worry; I'll update you; I know you hate being unable to reach me, so I'll stay in touch. Regarding your other accounts, if you contact them directly, they will help you change your passwords. Cheers!

Regards,
Anna

I laughed when I wrote this. I could now imagine her franticly looking for the missing computer. *Serves her right. I owe that vile and greedy lady nothing.* I was now grateful to be free.

It was 11:00 a.m. when I finally left, about two hours later than I'd wanted. It turned out that leaving was harder than I'd thought. I kept going back into the cottage to make sure I hadn't forgotten anything. After the third time, Laura walked me out and told me that if she found anything, she would post it or bring it herself.

Laura waved me goodbye, and I knew in my heart that although I had been acquainted with her for a long time, I had only truly known her for a short while. But I felt that she would stay in my heart forever.

I had about 250 miles ahead of me and needed to get going to avoid traffic. It would take four hours, according to the route-finder on my computer.

I then realized that my phone had not buzzed once with notifications all morning—a very welcome change. Perhaps I was now free and not chained to the walls, as my mother would say. I shuddered at the thought as a vision flashed into my mind of metal chains on my wrists. I shook my hands and my head to let go of that picture. I was on my way to bigger and better things; at least, that was what I prayed for.

Before I knew it, I had passed the halfway mark, and it was 1:11 p.m. I decided it was a good time to stop for lunch and fuel. At the service station, I watched all the cars and trucks pulling in, and I wondered where everyone was going. So many people were going about their business; it was time for me to begin going about mine. I grabbed a coffee, sandwich, and some snacks for the trip and was quickly on my way again. No time to drift—I had to stay on mission.

The farther and farther away I was from York, the more it felt like I was escaping something oppressive. I felt an urgency to reach Glastonbury like I had not experienced before. I was sure it was just about reaching a new place and feeling safe. But there was also something else.

I did not know whether it was fear, but I began my calming trick that I had learnt when I was a child. I imagined I was a guest on a chat show and telling the audience everything that was going on around me and what I planned to do. I began to describe my surroundings and then jumped into the future, talking about my life in five years' time.

I enjoyed this game as I described my career as a successful writer. I babbled on about the book I had written and how I was going to interviews and book signings. I thought about going down the path of revenge with Natasha when she would undoubtedly ask me to write a serious article for her new magazine.

I then rethought that chapter. I needed to close the door on that toxic relationship and focus on what I had learnt, which was how to write commercial articles and operate a business. Natasha was hardly ever available, so I'd had to self-learn the office skills. I prayed I would be able to use this and my twenty-two thousand pounds in the future. Just knowing that gave me a sweet satisfaction, which I'm sure was its own type of revenge.

I was reminded of the wise words of my friend Lucinda: "Karmic drama is something that holds onto us in this world. Remember the positive and stay in the light." I did not know what she meant at the time, but I was sure of one thing: if I focused on Natasha too much, it would take me down a dark path from which I may not easily come back. I decided to shift my thoughts and check my journey map, so I pulled over at the layby and called Lucinda on my phone.

She answered on the first ring. "Guess where I am?" I shouted.

"The M6, I would think by now," she responded.

"Wow, you are good!"

"Not really. You texted me when you left, Annie, and I did the math. As it's now 2:22 in the afternoon, you must be not more than an hour away."

I laughed. "Lucinda, I feel so excited! I really think this is a perfect move for me. I'm going to start looking for work straight away!" *I'm free!* I almost felt like singing out loud.

"Annie, calm yourself," my friend advised. "Give yourself some time to find opportunities, but also let the tide come to you, remember?" I remembered the story from her recent class about being in flow with the world and looking at life as an ocean. The tide comes in, and the tide goes out. Well, perhaps I would wait a little before jumping into this new ocean of life.

"Okay. Well, I wanted you to know I've closed the chapter with York and all the chapters of my childhood. I'm ready for a new chapter, and Laura gave me a journal. I'm going to focus on my writing. I'm even thinking of writing a few tourist pieces, especially from the spiritual novice perspective," I said quickly in an exasperated voice. "With no Natasha criticizing my writing and grammar, perhaps I'll get over my fear of expressing myself!"

"Ah, well, Annie, I'm holding space for you. And remember, Natasha has been an amazing teacher for you. Think of it as a tough-love school," Lucinda responded. I think she meant she was keeping me in her positive thoughts and I should stop complaining about Natasha.

"Thank you. I appreciate that. Now, wish me luck—I'm nearly there!"

She laughed, "Okay, luck to you, dearie!" She hung up the phone, and I got back to focusing on the road.

I saw the exit not far ahead. I turned off the motorway and found myself on a country road, which was narrow and winding. I turned around a bend and saw beautiful pastoral, rolling hills that were lush and green. All of a sudden, I felt a little dizzy. My stomach began to ache, and I wondered if I was getting sick. My skin felt clammy, and my heart beat faster.

I looked out across the hills, and there in the distance was the Tor. The statue on top of the hill in the center of Glastonbury was a famous tourist attraction. It was one of the things I was most excited to see, but while drawing closer to it, this weird sickness got stronger. Then it fell from view, and the sickness subsided, and it was like nothing had ever happened.

That was really weird, I thought.

The sign stated three miles to Glastonbury. Before I knew it, I was driving into the town. The buildings were mostly modern, with many new family homes. I must say I had expected to see more of a medieval-looking town, like what one sees in the films.

I turned down one more corner and was right on the main street in the center of town. To my delight, I was greeted by a treasure trove of old-fashioned and spiritual shops. I drove slowly so I could take in all of the wonderful sights. I looked into the windows of a bank, a coffee shop, and a bookshop. Then I had to laugh at the next shop, which had witches' cauldrons and broomsticks in the window.

People were casually walking around in modern clothes, but every so often, I caught sight of someone wearing fairy wings. I wanted to take photos so I could remember this for my writing. The spectacle of everything renewed my excitement to write about all I was experiencing. But that would have to be later; now I had to find the Gables Guesthouse.

☥

Soon I arrived. I pulled over to the right onto a dirt driveway that sat across from the house. A large wooden sign with curly script read, "Welcome to the Gables Guesthouse." I wound down my window and took in the vision in front of me.

The Gables was stunning: a two-story, stone-built, gray Georgian home. It must have been at least two hundred years old and wore its age. There was a small stone fence around the front yard and an open wrought-iron gate with peeling black paint. A crunchy pebble path led to the bright red front door, which seemed to have been recently painted. The shutters on the windows looked less so, being a long-since-faded cerulean blue. The common ivy had been allowed to climb with reckless abandon and was in danger of obscuring the view from the second-level windows. It was perfect, just as I had imagined.

Despite the slightly weathered and aged look of the home, the front garden was meticulously kept. A large oak tree stood tall on the left side of the yard. Rectangular beds of daisies lined the fence, and bright sunflowers greeted guests at the gate. Grey Witch daylilies displayed their gradient purple petals in a perfect line along the path. The porch was framed with five-foot crimson rosebushes with flowers as big as my face. Natasha always had a local florist heavily featured in the magazine, so I was well-schooled in English gardens. I was amazed at how I was describing them to myself in such a poetic manner. Perhaps my writing gifts were switching on.

The combination of it all created a spectacular sight. The old home, which felt so rooted in the past, was contrasted with the bright and lively gardens so reminiscent of the present. I could hardly believe that I was going to stay here for a whole month, and maybe even longer if all went well. Best of all, it was already starting to spur my creative thoughts.

This is my new home, was my only thought, and with that, I drove through the gateway. I parked in front of the quaint carriage house to the right of the home and grabbed my travel bag. I walked over to the main house, and as I looked across the lawn, I noticed a small fairy garden situated under the oak tree. I went up to the front door and reached for the brass knocker. As I did so, the door immediately opened. Again I felt an emotional pull within me. I did not know whether I should laugh or cry.

"Bien! Anna, I been expecting you! I'm Emilee, housekeeper and patron of the Gables Guesthouse. We spoke on the phone," said the woman with a thick French accent who was standing in the doorway. She was not the housekeeper I had imagined. I had pictured an older, traditional grandmother type, but that certainly wasn't Emilee. Her dark hair was swept up in a sophisticated twist, which revealed her bright eyes and warm smile. She wore a bright red dress, the same color as the door; it was tapered at the waist and had a knee-length A-line skirt. A large belt highlighted her tiny waist, and over the top of her outfit, she wore a white apron, which had big bright cherries all over it. On her feet, she wore black patent leather stilettos. Hardly the "quaint, little town" look.

"Lucinda, she call me and say you are not far," Emilee continued. She gave me a big hug and led me into the large foyer inside. It had all the trappings of a traditional Georgian home interior: dark wood floors, wainscoting along the walls, and ornate plaster medallions on the ceiling. We walked through a narrow hallway and through another red door into the kitchen.

"Sit down, sit down." She took my bag and pointed toward a large oak table that was well etched with years and looked original to the home. It was strange that I had found myself sitting around a lot of oak tables recently.

"I make you some tea, and you tell me about your journey," Emilee insisted. She was already flying around the kitchen, putting the kettle on the stove and gathering cups and saucers from the cupboard.

"Can I use the bathroom first, please?" I asked her.

"Yes, of course." She pointed toward a small white door in the hallway. I felt a little dizzy again and looked around; the room began to spin and change color. It was quite strange.

Once in the small bathroom, I washed my hands and looked

at my face in the mirror. *I must be daydreaming,* I thought. I saw myself wearing old-fashioned clothing—a dress with a white pinafore—and my head was covered in a white bonnet. *That's crazy. I am seeing things.* I must be fatigued from driving. I left the bathroom quickly and went back into the kitchen.

It was nearly June, but for some reason, Emilee had a blazing fire going. I noticed she had pulled out all manner of pots and pans and placed them everywhere. At first, I thought the kitchen was in complete chaos before I realized that she was actively using each of them. They were emitting a strange smell.

"Herbs. See?" she said, seeing the confused look on my face and pointing at the garden. I strained my head and could see behind her, through the modern windows, a large grassy area with seating. Around it were plants and pots full of lavender and rosemary and many other things of which I didn't know the names. "Elixirs, potions, salves, and remedies. I make for the local shops," she continued as she waved a hand toward the many blue glass bottles and soaps that were piled up on the far side of the kitchen. "Many come to the door for their lotions and potions. My grandmother was from Marseille in France. She was born in 1912. She taught me all I know. When I had my thirty-third birthday, I left her for Glastonbury. That was twenty years ago." She stopped a moment and smiled at me. "While I claim England as my home, France is still in my heart, the place of my true home." She sighed wistfully and continued working on the tea.

I smiled and took everything in. "Why thirty-three years old?" I asked her.

"I don't know; it just seemed the time to go. Now, your tea, ma chère," she said. She handed me a beautiful antique bone china teacup and saucer. "Give me a moment; I will just place this onto boil for me to make a lotion later, and I will join you to talk about your stay with us."

I watched how she carefully began to spoon a clear liquid into the large copper pan on the stovetop and then add tiny amounts of a golden oil substance. "Measurement and magic are everything," she piped in. "Can you pass me the angelica over there?" She pointed to a few bottles on the sideboard that were labeled in large white letters. There were blue and green glass bottles, all neat and in separate rows. I first reached for one of the green bottles.

"No, no, no," Emilee called out. "Not the green ones!"

"Okay, I'm sorry!" I looked at the blue bottles on the shelf below. "Ah, here it is." I passed it to her.

"Merci, mademoiselle, I'm nearly complete."

"Can I ask why not the green bottles?"

"The green is for poison, and the blue is medicine. All is in my garden," she said, pointing to the beautiful plants. "But some are deadly, so be very wary of an English garden." She winked at me, and I wondered if she was serious.

"Okay, thank you. I'll keep that in mind," I said. Then I heard a noise coming from the back door, like a slapping sound of some sort.

"Ah, Wallis, you are here to greet our guest!"

I looked around but could see no one. Then suddenly, a large black cat jumped up onto the table. Emilee introduced me to her. "This is Wallis. She lives with us, but she also lives in the wild. We call her the guardian to the Tor because she likes to greet visitors walking the pathway there."

The cat was sitting in front of me and staring at me with her deep green eyes, and I stared right back. Wallis then slowly lifted her paw and tapped my arm.

"Wonderful!" Emilee exclaimed. "That's her saying hello. She's really a bright animal, and I'm sure she is telepathic." I stroked her back, and she began to rub against me. "You like cats?" she asked.

"I suppose," I replied. "And apparently, this one likes me."

"Then you are blessed. She normally does not come close to the guests here. Maybe she thinks you are family now."

"Perhaps." I smiled. I then found myself wondering when I was going to see my room.

"Ah, your room. You would like to see it?"

Another telepathic lady like Lucinda. This should be interesting.

Emilee turned down the gas on the stove and went toward the back door to a picture frame that had many hooks and keys. "Well, you're my only guest this week, but more will arrive soon. The goddess conference and the solstice are only a few weeks away. You should stay longer, perhaps."

"Perhaps." I smiled again.

"So many, perhaps! Number eight shall be for you, my dear. Please follow me now."

As we entered the corridor again, I had another flashback. I asked Emilee, "Do you ever get déjà vu here in this house?"

"Always," she said with a nod. "I was here in 1786 with my husband and three children. He was a trader, you see. We came to escape the French Revolution." I was stunned that she said it so matter-of-factly. "This house was built in 1745, you see." She pointed to an old, framed map of Glastonbury on the wall with a large cross on the house location. Underneath, I could just make out the date. The place was much older than I'd thought.

"As soon as I saw this house when I first arrived in Glastonbury twenty years ago, I knew that it would be mine someday. I know every brick and every window." She smiled as she ran her hand lovingly across the wall. "And I know the secrets. Now, let us bring some of your bags in from the car."

There was no lift to the first floor, so we climbed the small narrow staircase and went into the north side of the house. There were five rooms on this side. I looked at all of the rooms and wondered where Emilee slept.

"I live in the attic," she chimed. "It's very comfortable; I will show you later. But now I think you need to rest."

"Yes, thank you," I said as she opened the door marked with the number eight.

"Here we go." We swept into a large and very grand bedroom. Based on the price, I had expected a small single room like in a dormitory with basic furniture. But this was truly a beautiful suite. "Your window." She pointed to a large sash white window with lattice framed glass. "Closet and bathroom over there." The bathroom had a modern shower and fittings, which was next to a gorgeous, antique claw-foot tub. It was pristine.

"And your bed," she continued.

"Heaven," I said. "Thank you."

"Here is your key, ma cherie! Oh, and welcome home. Rest and then perhaps come down later. I'll have some 'welcome home' soup ready, and we can become more acquainted." With that, Emilee turned and strutted out the door.

Once it was closed, I fell onto the bed, which was a double size with a four-poster canopy. I kicked off my shoes and relaxed for the first time in days. I looked at my phone and saw that it was nearly 5:00 p.m. *I'd best not fall asleep*, I thought. *But I could still nap a little bit.* My head and body felt heavy, and I slipped off my clothes and climbed under the duvet. The white linens were soft, and as I pulled them around me, I fell asleep.

Once more, I found myself on the sandy shores, but this time I was at the bottom of the hill, and only the emerald-eyed woman was standing there, looking out over the crimson water. I tentatively walked toward her, acutely aware that the sand could wake at any moment to drag me to its lair. I took care to gently place each foot down and watch for movement from the ground. So much of my focus was directed toward the sand that I had not noticed the woman had turned around and was watching me with a curious look in her eyes.

"What are you doing?" she asked, giving me such a fright that I nearly fell backward.

"Oh, I am trying to avoid being swallowed by the sand," I said sheepishly.

"Swallowed by the sand? What a ridiculous notion." She snorted.

I gave her a confused look. "Yes. Do you not remember the last two times I was here? The sand shot up, grabbed my feet, and tried to drag me under!"

"My dear, sand does not act on its own accord; you must be thinking of quicksand, of which there is none here. I just watched you walk across this beach with no issues. Besides, I don't know what you mean by 'last two times.' I've only just arrived on this beach." She stiffened as if remembering something horrible. "And you just intruded on a rather private moment, in a rather rude way. Why are you here?"

I wondered why she didn't remember me from before, but I let it slide for the moment. I responded, "Well, I don't really know why I am here. I was hoping you could tell me."

Before she could respond, the sky cracked open and turned the same dark crimson as the sea. The clouds rumbled, and we could see lightning in the distance. The emerald-eyed woman turned back to me. Her face looked different, less cold and formal, more worried and desperate. "Anna," she said in a hurried and hushed voice, "we don't have much time. I need to tell you something important."

"What is it?" I asked, mirroring the worried expression on her face.

She looked behind me and then back at me. "You need to find her. She is the key to all of it." The woman again looked behind me, and I turned to see what she was gazing at. Several shadowy figures had appeared atop the hill and had started to make their way down it.

"What are they?" I asked, suddenly very frightened.

"I am so sorry, Anna. I didn't think they would find you that quickly." Just then, the figures dove beneath the sand and rushed toward us, creating the very tendrils I'd dreaded. Before I could run, they had grabbed hold of my feet and were pulling me down with more force than before. "Help me!" I screamed. "Please, help me!"

"I am so sorry, Anna," the woman said again, her bright emerald eyes dimmed to a dark olive. "I am so sorry."

As the sandy arms wrapped their way around my body, pinning my arms to my side, I pleaded again. "Please, don't let them take me!" The woman shook her head sadly and turned away, not wanting to see what would inevitably come next. Just as the sand was covering my mouth, a thought popped into my head. She had balked at the idea of quicksand being on the beach, but wasn't this kind of what it was? I remembered something I had watched on a survival show: the more you struggle, the faster it will take you. So ignoring every instinct I had, I closed my eyes, stopped fighting, and let my body go limp.

Suddenly, I could feel myself being lifted up, the tight grasp of the sand loosening around me. I opened my eyes and found myself sitting on the shore. The clouds had parted, the waves had calmed, and the sky had returned to a normal color. The emerald-eyed woman was facing the water again. I got up and placed my hand on her shoulder. She didn't shudder at my touch or turn around. "Like I said," she spoke with a distant voice, "being swallowed by sand. What a ridiculous notion." Then she removed my hand from her shoulder and said quietly, "You must never let them get that close to you again."

"Pardon me?" I asked.

She turned around suddenly, her beautiful dark skin and regal form replaced with pallid skin and a haggard, gaunt appearance with a snake wriggling around her neck, its eyes as bright green as hers. "Run!"

Tuesday, May 27, 7:07 a.m.

I woke suddenly, not sure of my surroundings or where I was. My eyes adjusted, and I could see that I was in my room in the Gables Guesthouse. It was a comfort to know I was not buried in sand, as I thought might be the case. Then I remembered the woman's words: "Find her. She is the key to all of it."

I scrambled out of bed to grab my journal and write down what I had just experienced. At the same time, my other dreams seemed to flash in front of me, and I had full recollection of them. I wrote out as detailed of an account as I could, as well as a list of questions I still had.

Who was the emerald-eyed woman? Was she a queen of some sort? Why wasn't that other woman there? Did she have anything to do with those shadows that appeared? Whom was I supposed to find? Was it that baby? What did it have to do with anything? All of what? What is she the key to?

I crinkled my nose at the whole thing. It seemed so utterly ridiculous and dramatic, in a way that made me think it would be the perfect beginning to a book or movie.

I was roused from my thoughts as the smell of food wafted up from downstairs. It smelled like toasted bread, nutty coffee, and something pan-fried. My stomach spoke up with desire at this, and I was acutely aware that I was famished. I looked at the clock on the dresser, and it showed 7:30. I quickly realized it was 7:30 a.m.—I had missed an entire evening. I hurriedly opened one of my bags and pulled out some clean clothes. After that, I brushed my hair, cleaned my face of yesterday's makeup, and ran a toothbrush across my teeth. I walked downstairs and could hear voices in the kitchen.

"Yes, she's here. I'll have her visit soon." Emilee was on her phone, so I opened the kitchen door slowly. "Ah, Anna, you're here!" she said as she came over to hug me.

"I'm so sorry," I said. "I don't know where the evening went. I fell asleep and never woke up. I'm sorry I missed the soup!"

I think she could hear the remorse in my voice, so she rushed to comfort me. "No worries; you are here now. Coffee?"

"Yes, please!"

"And breakfast?" She pointed to two fried eggs atop some bean toast.

I nodded.

"Good. And on the table is cereal and juice; help yourself. You can eat in the dining room, if you like, or here at the table with me, since it's just us two. When more guests arrive, I can set up the formal dining room, but you may feel a little alone in there."

I was starving and sat down at the oak table and dived into the food before she finished speaking. Emilee didn't seem to mind and continued to move about the kitchen and chat about the weather and the farmers' market days. Once my plate was empty, she poured me another cup of coffee and poured herself one.

She finally sat down. "Now, Anna, there are many experiences in this town. It's a small place, and everyone knows everyone. The tourists come and go, but for those of us who live here or are here for a few weeks or months, we begin to see the world in a very different way. Do you know what I mean?"

"I think so," I said hesitantly.

"Well, you will come to meet certain characters you may think you have met before. There are no chance meetings. All is destiny."

"I am ready for a new destiny," I replied.

"Good, then I say you should unpack your bags. I can do laundry or ironing for you. The first week is already paid from your credit card, so anything you need, just ask. Also, if you would be kind enough to pay your future weekly bill in advance, then I can bill you weekly for any additional jobs you have me do. Now, if there is nothing else, I have a busy day, ma cherie. Oh!" She pointed to a large batch of blue glass bottles and whispered, "Love potions."

I laughed. "Perhaps in a few months, I may need some of that."

"Perhaps," she replied, winking at me. "Now, Anna, it's time to start your work." She held the red door open and motioned for me to get on with my adventure. She returned to her work in a flurry, and I became invisible.

This was wonderful, more than I had expected. I thought that this vacation was about to become a dream come true. I gulped down what was left of my coffee and ran back upstairs to quickly shower and unpack. There weren't many material items to show for my thirty-three years, and I had let go of many of my belongings while staying with Laura, but that was okay because I was going to start over. Once everything was put into drawers and closets, I made my bed and then checked my phone for messages, of which there were none. No surprise there.

Okay, today is going to be the beginning of an adventure,

I mused to myself. I grabbed my golden journal and a black fountain pen from my bag. Then I took out my computer and locked it in one of the drawers, out of sight.

Time to unplug and see where everything will take me.

CHAPTER 6

The prospect of going out and about the town for a day of exploration was exciting to me. Now that I'd decided to pursue writing, I wanted to approach my new life like a writer and see what would come of it. As I reached the outside gate of the Guesthouse, I had a choice of going right and into the town area or going left on a hike up toward the Tor. *What would a writer do?* The picturesque hills were great, but I needed to know more about the people and the history of the town if I was to write anything of merit about them. Besides, over breakfast Emilee had given me some suggestions of the best local haunts for mystic and psychic arts, which seemed a good place as any to start. So right turn it was.

My first visit was to an apothecary shop in a tiny corner of a building. The door creaked as I opened it, and inside were all manner of bottles and jars stacked on shelves. The walls and the floor were covered in old English oak wood panels, and pictures of herbs and flowers hung on the walls.

"Can we help you?" a voice came from the back of the store, and an old gentleman stepped out from behind the counter.

I wasn't sure what to ask for. "I'm just browsing," I stammered.

"Browse away," he said. He was very old and wore a smart white shirt with a colorful waistcoat. "They all have magic." He smiled.

"I'm sure," I replied.

"What's your heart's desire?" he continued.

I laughed. "A future with fortune and fame," I nervously said.

"Ah, then you need the four-leaf clover for fortune and fame, and the unicorn for a new future." He pointed to the tester bottles on the small table. "Go on, test them," he encouraged me.

I walked toward the table. At first, I was drawn to the smaller bottles with ancient symbols on the front. I wasn't sure what they were, but it did cross my mind that I'd seen these before in a dream.

"Not yet; maybe next time," said the man as if he had read my mind. "This is for you." He pointed to the bottles near the front with the clover sign and then the one with the unicorn. "Try as you please," he said, a curious twinkle in his eye.

There were all manner of strange and wonderful oils and potions and elixirs whose scents tickled my nose. But he was right: both of these scents really appealed to me. One was citrus fresh and uplifting, and the other made me feel dizzy, like I'd had an energy drink.

I decided to buy both the potions and trusted they would help me open my mind to all the new future possibilities. After all, I was in a new place, and neither could hurt to have.

My next stop was the Labyrinth Bookstore, which must have been there for many generations. One could tell that each new generation had added to the store with a new bookcase decorated to their liking. I was drawn to a really old, dark wood bookcase toward the back, probably placed by a founding book lover like myself, where I was drawn to a stunningly old book about Egyptian ritual. The book whispered to me the secrets of the oils and potions I had just encountered. A charge went through my body as I flipped through its pages, and something in my gut told me that this book could be the key to whatever was about to happen. I bought the book and a journal with an ancient Egyptian symbol on it to chronicle my thoughts. I was about to finish my purchase when I noticed a set of tarot cards with the words "Egyptian Oracle" written in gold. I added them to my pile of goodies and couldn't wait to get back to the Gables and play.

The last stop on my tour of mystic places that morning was the famed shop of the Goth, an ancient psychic whose family had been around since the medieval age, according to local legend. Well, that was what the tourist guide had said online when I had been doing internet research. I decided that it would be a good idea to get my tarot professionally read. Nothing had gone as I'd planned in my life recently, so what harm could it do?

Finding this place had been easy, but opening the door was surprisingly hard. The small shop doorway was painted a deep purple. A small, hand-painted sign read, "Enter at your own free will," and a small bell rang to announce that someone was crossing the threshold. For some reason, I kept resisting going inside and even wondered if anyone had seen me standing outside. *Could I make a quick escape? Perhaps.* With that thought, my hand instinctively reached out and turned the door handle.

The girl who greeted me was just as strange. Her hair was black and long, almost reaching her waist, and she wore an extremely tight black lace gown. I decided this was just for the tourists. She pointed to a curtain behind her, which was a dark, rich purple velvet with gold edges.

"Twenty minutes," was all she said as she pulled the curtains back to reveal a hidden room. I kept telling myself this was just part of the show.

There in the small back room, lit mainly by candles, was a man sitting and staring at a small table covered in rich purple velvet. As I sat down across from the archaic Goth—who, by the way, didn't look a day past forty—I wondered whether I should start the conversation. He also was in costume, and I felt as if I were in a TV show. I wondered if at any moment, a camera crew would leap into the room. He wore a black velvet waistcoat that covered a crisp white shirt. The shirt was pristine, and the cufflinks were mother of pearl with what appeared to be black snakes. His wristwatch was gold and stood out in the dim light. His head was shaved, and his skin showed no sign of aging. His eyes, however, were engaging and circled with black kohl; they really stood out against the room. Not what I'd expected, but everything I'd anticipated.

As he raised his head to look at me, it was as if he was blinking to focus. He licked his lips as if not sure how to address me.

I waited. It seemed only polite.

I felt strange pressure around my head and a pounding in my heart. He shuffled the cards three times and turned them over in a dramatic flourish. His voice faltered as he tried to find the words to tell me what the cards said.

The Goth was still unable to meet my eyes, as he had struggled to do when I'd entered the room. It was unnerving to sit there in abject silence, so I finally glanced at my watch and realized that we had been sitting there for ten minutes, and he hadn't even begun to tell my fortune. He kept turning cards and staring at them to understand the deeper message.

Finally, he broke the silence. "This is a moment of challenge," he whispered, pointing to a card that bore eight sticks. "You need courage, my dear." With raised eyebrows, he pointed to the Queen of Swords that appeared next. "This one tells me that a woman is about to enter your life. She takes no prisoners and has a purpose to connect with you."

"And once we connect, what will I find?" I asked.

He turned two cards; they showed the sun and the moon.

"You will find truth and enlightenment," he said, "but also a darkness and illusion. Your destiny will be revealed to you soon."

Once again, he looked away as if looking into the future, and he caught sight of me in a mirror located on the wall.

"I remember," he said, talking to himself.

"Remember what?" I asked quietly.

"Always and forever," the Goth said, obviously now in a trance. He shook his head.

I reached my hand across the table and patted his hand and smiled gently. "Thank you. This was wonderful. I'll take some quiet time to think now," I said.

He looked at me and smiled. "Yes, return on another visit."

But I think he was relieved I was going.

I handed over my twenty pounds to the girl at the cash desk. She pursed her red lips and flicked her long dark hair. She obviously had seen many people follow my path to enlightenment as entertainment. She stared intensely at me and then looked down at the magazine she was reading. I felt uncomfortable, so I tried to make conversation. "Now, on to my next adventure!" I smiled and went toward the door.

"Turn right at the street crossing," she announced. I was unsure if she was talking to me. I looked back at her. "I know what you are thinking," she said without looking up, "but now that you have heard the messages, you're about to step through a door that will open you up to a whole new world of possibilities.

Be careful, though, what you open in this lifetime." Then for the first time, she looked up and smiled at me. "So turn right and keep moving." She waved a long dark red fingernail at me, and I retreated out of the shop.

"But do I turn right out of the shop or at the end of the street to find this crossing?"

The woman ignored my question. I made a guess and turned right out of the shop and turned right again at the end of the street, but I could see no crossing of any kind. *This must be a joke,* I thought. *There is no way this woman is serious.* I went to turn left and found myself nearly crashing into a woman walking toward me, talking on her phone, and leaning on a slender black cane with the silver head of a lion.

"Watch out!" she cried, and she pushed me back where I had no choice but to turn to the right and almost fall into the doorway statuary of a café.

As I managed to regain my balance, the girl behind the counter had already watched my tumble and was able to catch me as I proceeded to fall in through the café door. "Are you okay?" She smiled at me. "There's no getting out of the way of ladies on a shopping mission," she said, and we laughed.

"That one has the strength of five men," I said.

"Well, you're safe in here. It's warm, and we have coffee and delicious desserts," she replied.

I finally looked around and found myself in another surreal Glastonbury experience. A large counter of cakes and treats with numerous styles of cups and plates surrounded a huge coffee machine, which appeared to make everything and anything one's heart desired. I decided to go for the classics and ordered a pot of tea and carrot cake. Then I went to find a small corner where I could reflect upon my morning experience. I chose a table with a bright, cheerful cover and matching cushions. It was in stark contrast to the room in which I had just been seated. The room was light and airy, and on the walls hung messages and positive affirmations. One read,

Love yourself. You are beautiful. Stay positive.

Perfect messages, I thought. *And not a tarot card in sight.*

I opened up my bag from the bookstore and also pulled out the journal Laura had given me. This was the perfect moment to start my writing and explore plotlines for my book. I sat for a while thinking of what to write when the words from the Goth raced back into my mind: *Courage, illusion, enlightenment,* and *destiny.* I wrote these words down and then focused on my other purchases.

It was so strange. I remembered being in the bookstore, but not why I had purchased these items. I was in Glastonbury; what did this place have to do with Egypt? But so much had happened that I decided to let that thought go. I opened up the cards and began turning them over one by one as I had seen in Lucinda's classes. Each one I fell in love with. Once I had turned each card, I opened up the small book that accompanied them. I decided to also open up the Egyptian journal I had purchased, the one with the gold symbol. I'd seen this symbol before but could not place it. I would use this journal to write about the thoughts I had and how I connected to the cards. That way, I might start to create characters.

I loved the Egyptian stories of the gods. I chose to read about Isis and Osiris first and wondered if theirs had been a love on a mortal level. I then shuffled the deck to find the two cards that bore their images. I held them together like I had my dolls when I played as a child.

"So, you two," I spoke to the cards, "was it love at first sight? Osiris, was it a date of dinner and lustful glances across the high altar?" I giggled at the prospect.

"Neither," said a sharp voice. For a brief moment, I wondered if the Isis card had spoken back, but out of the corner of my eye, I saw a woman to my left, standing while impatiently tapping her foot behind me—looking slightly annoyed. "You are speaking about the two most revered and powerful gods in Egypt. They weren't hormonal teenagers sneaking out at night behind their parents' backs. Their love had far greater consequences."

"Oh, I'm sorry," I said in a hushed tone, hoping that everyone in the café had not heard and was wondering why someone was reprimanding me like a small, naughty child. I went to collect the cards and place them back in their box, but in my haste, I dropped several to the floor.

"Horus," the woman said, picking up the card and handing it back to me. "A perfect triad." Her voice was then gentler, lower, and less conspicuous.

"Triad?" I asked and turned in my seat fully. Oh no! It was the woman who'd nearly knocked me over. Our eyes met, and I felt a shock go through my whole body. Her eyes were piercing blue, and her hair was a soft golden white that hung gently around her shoulders. She wore a blue shawl with golden flecks on it. She looked both regal and regular at the same time, to the point where I couldn't quite figure out her age or who or what she was.

I kept her gaze and smiled at her. "Thank you. I guess I should be more careful with these cards. My friend Lucinda told me they can pack some powerful energy," I said.

"Powerful and magical," she nodded.

"You know, I have been fascinated with ancient Egyptian mysticism ever since I can remember. It probably started when I read a book about the British Museum's Egypt exhibition in London in primary school."

"The museum has many important pieces, and they come alive at night, you know." She spoke with complete certainty. "Have you ever been to Egypt?"

"No, it's a dream for me to go. Perhaps one day. Have you visited there?"

"Oh yes, many times and in many lives."

"Many lives? Oh, my friend mentioned that once. What did you do in your lives in Egypt, do you know?" I could feel another Lucinda-type moment coming on.

"I have come to this world for many millennia wearing many guises in order to help facilitate the opening of hearts and minds to love and peace."

"Oh, wow, that's something!" I mused, intrigued and a little skeptical. Whether what she was saying about past lives was true or not, here was someone who had been to Egypt and who could perhaps give me some great travel tips. *Do I have the time?* I looked at my watch and then glanced outside. It was now raining; I wasn't going to be leaving anytime soon. I offered her the empty seat across from me, and she sat down with her cup. She stared at her drink for a bit, as if in a deep trance. I then wondered how she spent her days and concluded she must visit town daily for tea, cake, and conversation. Otherwise, why would she have been so eager to speak with me?

I lightly touched her hand so as to wake her out of her trance. "Excuse me," I said. "I was wondering if perhaps you would give me a few tourist tips in exchange for a fresh pot of tea? I am hoping to travel to Egypt someday. Also, it's raining so hard out." I pointed outside. "Only if you are not in any hurry, of course."

"Oh, I never hurry," she replied. "I find that is not a productive way to live. And you will travel to Egypt; I see it in your future before the year is out."

Oh, yes, I thought, *she's a fortune teller. Perhaps she will read my tea leaves.* But all the same, I was too afraid to ask.

She sat back in her chair, and I saw a glint of gold around her neck. She was wearing an ankh, similar to a necklace I had seen in one of the shop windows. The description beneath it said it was worn by the priestesses of Isis and was a sacred symbol.

"I see you are wearing an ankh," I said to open up connection.

She touched the necklace, and her fingers lingered upon the golden symbol. "Yes, this was given to me many lifetimes ago when I joined the priestesshood of Isis at Philae. It's very precious to me. The ceremony was the most beautiful time of a young woman's life and stayed with me forever."

Philae? Something sounded familiar to me about that, so I decided to listen and ask questions and not rant on about myself. After all, I was the spiritual detective now in search of a story. "Through every lifetime? You make it sound as though you have lived many lives and remember them all. Is that even possible?" I asked. She nodded her head. I watched as her eyes seemed to well with tears.

At that moment, the waitress approached the table. "Are we finished?" she asked the woman.

"This is all finished," I responded, "but we would like fresh tea for two at this table, please." I smiled at the woman, who hung her head so as not to show any emotion.

"Okay, coming right up, miss!" said the waitress, and she began to clear the table. I turned my attention back to the older woman, who had a wistful expression on her face and seemed to be holding back tears.

"Are you all right? Would you like to talk about it?" I asked, gently patting the woman's hand. The woman was about to open up; I was sure of it.

But she silently shook her head. "No, no, thank you," she replied in a very faint whisper. "You remind me of someone, and it just brings back emotion." The waitress had just finished clearing our table and had heard that whole exchange. She looked at me, and I motioned to cancel the tea and get me my bill. The woman slowly wiped her tears and then stood up and balanced herself on her cane. "Well," she explained, "I think it is time I make my exit whilst the rain has ceased."

"I'm so sorry," I said as she walked away. "I know I can be a bit too forward sometimes, and I don't know many people here, so—"

She stopped me by raising her hand and then pushing back her golden-white hair to reveal those piercing blue eyes again. For a moment, I swore they flashed green, but that could have been the light. "Not here, not now, but soon you will remember," she promised. "You will remember who you are."

It seemed like my life lately was full of cryptic messages from mystical women. Something was going on here. I then realized I had never introduced myself, and she had never introduced herself either. "Oh, how rude am I? I apologize! I never did properly introduce myself. My name is Anna Harris; I'm staying at the Gables Guesthouse."

"Of course, my dear." She smiled but still doesn't offer her name. "The day after tomorrow, Thursday, come to the temple on the hill, just past the Tor. Our place is called the Sanctuary, and your housekeeper will know the address. Be there at two in the afternoon, and you can meet the Oracle of Edfu."

"The Oracle of Edfu?" I replied.

"The Oracle of Edfu." She nodded and smiled again. "We will let her have a look at you, and then perhaps..." Her words trailed away, and she looked outside the window. "The rain has stopped. I have to get back." With lightning speed, she gathered her belongings and headed out the door.

"She's a strange one," the waitress said as she finished clearing the tables nearby, "but there's no one in this here town knows their magic like she does."

Magic. Now that had my interest.

"Mmm, yes, magic," she nodded her head. "Two in the afternoon. Don't be late." She must have been listening, which I thought was rude, but at the same time, the tone of her voice was strange and not her own. It almost sounded like she was momentarily possessed. I shuddered at the thought and gathered my bag and shopping goodies. Then I headed back out of the door and toward the Gables Guesthouse. Thank goodness the rain had subsided and the sun had come out.

On arrival, no one appeared to be home, giving way to a peaceful and quiet atmosphere, the effects of which had an instant effect. I suddenly began to feel very sleepy. I was grateful that no one was around to ask me about my day's adventures. I climbed the stairs to my room and lay down onto the bed. It was only 1:30 p.m., but I definitely needed a nap.

As I lay there, my body began to feel heavy, and I could sense myself sinking into the mattress. My skin began to feel like it was moving, and I was aware of every cell in my body vibrating with energy. At first, I thought it must have been an allergic reaction to something I ate or drank. Rather than grab medication for a reaction, I let the sensations and the heaviness completely overtake me and carry me off into a deep slumber.

CHAPTER 7

ind her. Find her, Anna. Don't let them get you!" Shadows swirled around her until all I could see were her bright emerald eyes. Then they were swallowed up in darkness.

Wednesday, May 28, 3:33 a.m.

I awoke with a start. I'd had another horrible dream. I grabbed my wristwatch off the nightstand to check the time: 3:33, so it must have been afternoon. However, the darkness, broken up by moonlight, in my window told me it was early morning. *How could I have slept for over twelve hours?* I was lost in days and timelines.

I went to the bathroom, came back, and drank some of my water on the nightstand. It was so strange; it was as if I was watching myself. I still felt like I was in a dream and out of my body, even as I changed for bed, removed my makeup, and crawled into the covers. I felt safe, warm, and peaceful as I drifted off to sleep again. Those feelings dissipated as soon as I sunk into slumber.

I was walking alone down the center street of a small village in the dead of night. By the light of the first quarter moon, I could see that the buildings were made of wood and had thatched roofs. The cobblestone street was lined with wrought iron streetlamps, though none were lit. The buildings, too, were dark and made no indication that they contained any life. All was still and entirely too quiet. The only sound that could be heard was the sound of my shoes clacking on the cobblestone, amplified tenfold because it reverberated off the buildings.

I passed empty carts and dark shop windows, which held no goods to buy. Then I passed what could have been a tavern, except there were no bottles of beer or alcohol on the shelves, no fire going in the hearth, and no rowdy bar patrons sitting on the stools. This village seemed abandoned, but I couldn't figure out why. It looked like everyone had decided to leave at the same moment, but they had also scrubbed the village of any unique sign of life. Perhaps a more accurate description was that this place gave the impression of a village that could have been part of any old town in the seventeenth century.

As I neared the end of the street, I saw a few lights appear on a distant hill. It was strange that they would appear now, near this vacant village. I stopped walking so as to observe them. They were coming closer quickly at first, but as they reached the base of the hill, where the road turned from dirt to cobblestone, they slowed their pace. When they were about half a mile away, a great gust of wind suddenly rushed through the street, nearly knocking me down, as if trying to push me out of the way as it ran from the lights in the distance. Something awoke inside me, telling me to get away, not to let those figures reach me. I needed to hide—now.

I went to a door nearest to me and knocked, thinking that perhaps someone might answer and let me in. Maybe the town was hiding from the figures; maybe they weren't all gone. I got no response, so I tried the next one—still nothing. I kept knocking on the doors. No one was here. The lights were close enough now where I could see that they were glass lanterns with candles glowing inside them. I could not make out who or what was holding them, but I knew I did not care to find out. Panic seeped inside me as I desperately tried to open any door or look for any object I could to break a window and get inside. Nothing worked. As I hurried from house to house, I checked behind me to see how close they were. Every time I looked, the lanterns with candles burning were closer.

I was still zigzagging across the street and looking for a door when the figures entered the village. I attempted to escape out the other side of the street, but they had come through there too, barring me from exiting. I froze mid-step and waited for them to descend upon me. They didn't; they simply stood at either end of the street, waiting. Now that they were so close, it became evident that the lanterns were being held by dark, shadowy figures seemingly made of thick, gray smoke twisting and writhing around the lanterns. The air around me smelt metallic, and I got a whiff of something foul, like sulfur. Whatever these creatures were, they were sinister—perhaps the reason this place had been deserted.

I waited another moment, but they didn't move, so I resumed my fleeting quest to find a door in which to hide. The figures seemed unable to see me, which was good, but I still needed to leave before they figured out I was there. I quickly and quietly went to a door I had not yet tried, which was made of older dark wood and had a gilt object hanging from it. I gingerly jiggled the tarnished brass knob. It was locked too, but it felt different than the others, more worn from repeated use and more likely to break, if I could just turn it a little harder. I tried to coax the lock to break by turning the knob clockwise while resting all of my weight on it. The door groaned loudly at the additional weight being placed on it. I looked around to check if the figures had heard me.

Like a rippling wave, the figures turned their hazy heads—or what I think would have been considered their heads—in my direction. They resumed walking, if one could call it that, toward me. Perspiration broke out on my face, and my heart beat loudly in my chest. My breath was shallow and quick, and my throat was too dry to cry out. They were almost upon me, and I was going to be swallowed up by them. "Don't let them get you," I heard a distant voice say. That motivated me to keep at the door. I knew it would break open; I just had to keep trying.

For a door seemingly so weak, nothing was making it budge. I changed tactics and picked up the key-like gold object, which had appeared that was now hanging from the knob, to use as a wedge to open the door. As I stuffed it between the door and the frame, I noticed that it was an ankh attached to a chain. There was something familiar about it, and I leaned in closer to get a good look. As I did, the figures surrounded me.

I suddenly awoke back in my bed at the Guesthouse. The sheets were twisted and tangled around me, and the duvet lay in a heap on the floor. I was probably thrashing around in my sleep. There were bright beams of sun streaming through the gossamer curtains, a clear indication that it was morning and that the time for sleep was over, not that I had any desire to close my eyes after that terrible nightmare. I looked at my watch: 7:03 a.m. *Wow, that was a crazy day and night.* For some reason or another, my feet were aching, and I could hear my stomach grumbling in protest from lack of food. I quickly detangled myself from the sheets, threw on some yoga pants and a light jumper, and raced downstairs to the kitchen.

It was the same as yesterday, the aroma of coffee brewing and bread toasting wafting through the hallway. Today, instead of eggs, the scent of breakfast sausage crisping in a pan accompanied the coffee and toast. It smelt like home; well, *a* home. Not *my* home. All the same, it was comforting as I imagined the fragrances of home should be. Plus, I needed to talk to someone about my crazy last twenty-four hours and keep me grounded in reality.

"There you are," Emilee said when I walked into the kitchen.

"Here I am, but to tell you the truth, I'm not quite sure where here is," I said.

She laughed. "The coffee shop girls told me of your encounter on Tuesday when I went into town. I saw your shoes in the hallway, so I knew you were back and did not need to worry. I heard you go outside a few times yesterday, and we had soup for lunch, don't you remember?"

"But it's Wednesday, Emilee, yes?"

"No, ma cherie, it's Thursday. You lost a day, perhaps. But I also think maybe you are having an astral travel adventure!" she chided.

"I…I lost a whole day? And I…*what* travelled?"

"Astral travel!" she exclaimed, as if it was the most common thing in the world. "It's when your body remains in a sleep consciousness, but your soul travels to somewhere else."

"How would I know?"

"Erm, let me see," she said. "Well, first you would feel heavy, like you have to sleep, like being hypnotized."

"Oh. I've never had that. What's that like?"

"Mmm, no one look you deep in the eyes recently?" she stated matter-of-factly.

"Oh, yes, someone did! Is that bad?" I asked as I remembered the lady in the café and her gaze and comments to me. A sudden grim realization washed over my face. "Emilee, do you think I was possessed?" I think she could see the panic in my eyes.

"No." She laughed again and began to pour some coffee. "Just connected to another world or state of being, where you begin to remember secrets locked away in you."

"Even scary ones?"

"Oui, especially scary ones," she replied.

I toyed with sharing my dream, but it was so dark, and even though she seemed understanding, I didn't want her to judge me. I wanted her to share more with me about this astral travel. "Any other feelings or sensations to look out for?" I asked.

"Yes, aching feet when you wake up. Like you walk many kilometers but not really doing that."

"Aching feet? But I thought you said the body was staying still the whole time."

"It does, but the energy from the souls of your feet keeps you connected like as elastic band, so your energy, body, or soul can return to home," she explained.

Now that makes the most sense out of anything from the last few days. I silently nodded.

"Also, you look like you have been in a warzone." With that, she went about the kitchen and begin banging pans and dishes. I went into the small bathroom to the mirror and, to my horror, saw that my hair was sticking out in seven different directions. The jumper I'd put on was severely wrinkled.

Oh, yes, not the look for the day, I thought while shrugging.

"I think not," Emilee called from the kitchen. "But do eat something first, and then perhaps take a bath before your adventure this afternoon." *How does everyone around here always know what I'm thinking?* She placed a plate of bean toast and fried sausage, and a hot cup of coffee in front of me. "Grounding food, Anna," she said rather brusquely.

"Thank you," I said, "I have not eaten much the last few days. I'm feeling all out of sorts. I have lost track of a lot of time."

"I know. Not to worry, though; once your body accepts the food and clears the energy, your other senses begin to come back fully. Then you feel better."

"Good because I'm supposed to be meeting with some oracle today, if it's indeed Thursday. Tell you the truth, I'm not quite sure of that."

She stopped and looked at me. "Some oracle?" she quizzed, raising one eyebrow and cocking her head to the side.

"Yes." I knew I was being rude by answering while eating, but I was so hungry.

"Do you know the oracle's name?"

"No, she didn't tell me her name, but she had a title. You know, like how knights were named for their city. It was some place I never heard of, something starting with an *e*, I think." I stopped and looked at Emilee. "Why? Should I be afraid? You make it seem like I should be afraid."

She had gone very pale, but she spoke in a measured voice. "Edfu. You must be talking about the Oracle of Edfu. It was an ancient city in Egypt that housed the Temple of Horus. The oracle always served the high priest of Edfu. She was his eye in the sky to see everything." Then she added in a hushed tone, "And often his slave." At the time I thought she said something different. But, on reflection, *slave* was the term she used. It still makes me shiver.

I chose to ignore this, though, and carried on eating and talking. "Oh, I got that card the other day, the Horus one, when the lady invited me."

"Yes, you told me," Emilee nodded, having regained some color in her cheeks. I didn't recall telling her that, but the last day or so had all been so confusing that it seemed entirely possible I had. All of this was giving me a weird vibe. *Is Edfu a place of good or bad energy?* I wondered. I was more inclined to think *bad,* but that could have been the lingering darkness of my dream influencing me.

"It is a mix of light and shadow, Anna," Emilee piped in. "We do not think of things in terms of good or bad but light and shadow. Much broader. Edfu, like most places, was a mix of both, but the shadow might have a bit more pull there. Please, try to stay aware and grounded. Now, I have to go get the other rooms ready for this weekend. Pardon." Emilee left abruptly, so I finished eating what was on my plate and took my coffee up to my room.

I closed my bedroom door and went into my bathroom to draw my bath. I noticed a small blue glass bottle on the stand next to the bath. How odd. I did not remember this being here earlier, but then again, my memory was a bit fuzzy. The label read, "Calm and Clear Emilee Blends." I opened the bottle, and the smell was heavenly: rose, lavender, and something exotic to my nostrils I couldn't quite place. Per the instructions, I poured a few drops into the warm water, and the smell began to fill the room.

Just before I climbed into the water, I had a déjà vu moment. The water appeared a deep red, and I could feel a cool breeze. I shook my head a little, and the water returned to its crystalline appearance. No window appeared to be open. I peered up at the mirror and pointed to myself. "Get a grip! This is all in your imagination. Those dreams aren't real, and they are messing with your mind. Take a deep breath and snap out of it! This is ridiculous!" That pep talk was all I needed to abate the ever-increasing anxiety I felt.

I gave my image an encouraging (albeit forced) smile and got into the tub. The bath oil continued to relax me, and I felt at peace again. I'd be ready for whatever this hocus-pocus woman and kooky oracle had in store for me.

☥

The walk to the Sanctuary took around ten minutes and, I have to say, was quite a soul-calming, beautiful journey. Emilee had left me a small map, but her advice was simply "go left up the hill when you go through the Gables gateway." So a left turn I took, and I was delighted with the view that surrounded me.

The English countryside was in full bloom. The snow-white and blush-pink blossoms on the trees floated around the streets like confetti. Greenfinches darted in and out of the hedges, and a hawk flew overhead. The cool breeze tickled my skin as the warm sunlight trickled through the tree branches. York wasn't exactly a congested city, like London, but the air here felt exponentially fresher, and the addition of pristine flora and fauna added to the whole experience. I felt I was in an oxygen chamber. Very soon I could spot the Sanctuary on the side of the small hill, looming not far in the distance. I felt slightly intimidated by its high, ancient-looking wall and recessed wooden doorway.

I ended up arriving at the Sanctuary doorway early and stood for a moment, wondering if I should enter or wait to my allocated time. My hand paused over the bell. I could not see past the old wooden door, and when I tried the handle, it opened easily. I paused to think for a second whether I should enter or turn and run, but curiosity got the better of me. I made a conscious decision that if for any reason things went slightly weird, I would give myself permission to leave.

Lucinda had said that was my divine spiritual right, that I had free will and free choice at any given moment. It was strange that I had been to so many of her events and remembered nothing until now. *But what if this really is some weird cult that will try to mind-wash me? Mind wash—is that even a real thing?*

Do I mean brainwash? Oh, my. I laughed out loud and could feel my entire body releasing tension.

I was now through the doorway, and what lay in front of me was the most beautiful sight. Green, lush trees and a lawn with a stone and crystal circle was to my left. To my right was a stunning koi pond that looked as if it was straight from a Japanese garden. The color of the fish swimming against the lily pads spanned the full spectrum of the rainbow. In front of me was a narrow white stone pathway. It curved slightly but led straight up toward the inner structure. The house in front of me seemed like a regular large home built in the 1950s. The large windows and white walls with red brick features seemed starkly out of place. It reminded me of my aunt's home that I had visited in York as a child before she'd sold it and moved in with my mother and me. *No way that is the same one. What was in that bath potion Emilee left me?*

As I reached the door, a woman with platinum blonde hair who looked fresh out of university opened a side door and peered out at me. "This way," she said. "You must be Anna."

"Yes." I smiled and followed her into the house.

"Leave your shoes there on the rack." She pointed toward a small wooden shoe rack. There were another three pairs of shoes, which indicated that I wasn't going to be completely alone in this place.

"No, not on the top," the woman said, and she placed my shoes on the lower rack. "The top row is for her ladyship!" She looked at her watch. "She won't be long now."

"Her ladyship?" I asked.

"Well she's not a real lady, she tells me, but you would think—" She stopped herself before she could speak out of turn, and she smiled. "I'm Lesley, by the way, staying here from London. Welcome to the Sanctuary." She motioned for me to move through into the corridor, and I was amazed to see such beautiful images that looked Egyptian. I was surprised.

"Excuse me, but exactly what is the Sanctuary?" I pointed to the art upon the walls.

"It's a healing center for spiritual retreats. People from all around the world come to heal and learn, even celebrities—" She'd leaned in closer, but she was stopped midsentence.

"Thank you, Lesley," the woman from yesterday said as she approached.

"Of course."

"Excuse me, my dear," said the woman as she swept past her. She was the lady from the café, but today she looked different; her hair was swept up, and she wore a beautiful deep blue dress and makeup. The woman turned to me and said, "Anna, thank you for coming." She held out her hand, and behind her I could see a doorway into what I guessed was a living room. "Come through, my dear." She smiled, and I followed her into the room.

At first, it looked like any normal living room: large windows looking out over the garden and into the street, plush sofas and chairs with a floral design, and antique lamps with large beige shades giving a soft, warm glow and bringing a certain calm feeling to the room. There were wooden shelves built into the walls filled with old leather-bound books, and a massive stone fireplace was waiting for colder days to be lit. There was even a TV veiled behind a large white silk cloth. *No, this must be a waiting area for conversation and relaxation. No way this is a spiritual room,* I thought.

The grandfather clock next to the door struck two.

I was expecting a door to open a secret chamber, but nothing quite as fantastic happened. I must say I was a little disappointed at the lack of fanfare. The lady simply told me to sit. "That chair, please." She pointed to a small blue and cream chair in the corner next to the window. I heard the squeal of brakes from a car outside. There was the slam of a car door. "Ah, the oracle!" The lady smiled at me and said, "I'll be back in a moment." She closed the door quietly behind her.

Once she left the room, I was aware of the silence. I lifted myself out of the chair to peer out the window over the wall at the car that had arrived, which I presumed was the car belonging to the oracle. I was surprised to see a bright red convertible sports car. *That's odd. Why would oracles have a sports car? Aren't they supposed to take a vow of poverty or something?* I heard footsteps and then conversation. The door, for some strange reason, began to open slowly. *The door frame must be uneven,* I thought. *Pretty common in older houses.* In the mirror on the wall in front of me, I could see the reflection of the first lady and now this new woman. What I saw was not what I had imagined.

From my view, she appeared petite and slender. I was a little shocked by the extremely high stiletto boots she wore; I imagine she wasn't more than five feet tall. As she approached the door, I could see she was wearing skinny black jeans with a fitted white button-down shirt and carrying a designer handbag—which I had just seen in the current issue of *Vogue*—in one hand and her mobile phone in the other. Her hair was jet-black, long, and so shiny it looked as if it were made of liquid glass. Her face was obscured by very large black sunglasses, but I could see she wore bright red lipstick. I couldn't quite gauge her age, but she seemed somewhere between my age and the older woman's, maybe in her mid or late thirties or early forties. I heard her complaining to the older woman about the traffic and the wind in her hair because the roof of her car wouldn't come back up. Certainly, she was not how I'd imagined her to be, and I became a little afraid. The woman seemed so glamorous and worldly, and I was sitting there in my ratty old jumper, ripped jeans, and mismatched socks. Would she judge me for my disheveled appearance and my lack of worldly knowledge?

I saw the lady point to the doorway that was now halfway open. "In there is Anna," she said. I straightened up and tried to make it look like I hadn't just been eavesdropping.

"Ah, yes," she said, her manner becoming very calm. "I'll go and introduce myself."

"Yes," said the lady, "please do. I'll be with you in a little while, and we can do formal introductions." Then she left from view. The younger woman—the "oracle"—turned to check her appearance in the hallway mirror. She took off her large sunglasses and placed them and her phone into her bag before pulling out a tube of lipstick. After taking the cap off, she gracefully swept the bright red shade over her lips in two swift motions. Satisfied with the results, she placed the cap back onto the tube and tucked it away in her bag. She took one last look in the mirror, smoothed down her hair, and walked toward the door.

At that moment, I was aware that Lesley was peering through the crack of a side door across the room. She looked at me and smiled, motioning to me not to say she was there. I motioned a finger to my lips and smiled. She nodded, mouthed the words "thank you" to me, and retreated back out of my view. Perhaps she and I could be friends.

The main door swung fully open just then. "I'm Naomi," the woman announced abruptly, and she held her hand out toward me to shake.

"A-Anna," I stuttered. "Anna Harris."

"So, Anna, Anna Harris, what brings you here?" She smiled at me, placed her bag on the floor, and sat down on the couch. She stretched like a large cat and brought her legs up to relax into the large cushions. It was then that I noticed she also had perfectly manicured nails that matched the shade of her lipstick. I hid my hands; perhaps I needed a makeover as well as a spiritual awakening.

I looked up at her. "Curiosity at first," I said. "I'm trying to find my way and part in the world. I'm not sure what that is, but a psychic in town recently told me my destiny was calling, and a whole new life could be waiting for me, which is similar to a tarot card reading I did for myself a few weeks ago. So I followed the advice and wound up here."

"Do you think this is the place?" she asked, looking and pointing around the room.

"I'm not sure, but I figure this is as good a place as any to start."

She nodded. "You're a writer, yes?"

How does she know? Does she have that mind-reading trick Lucinda has? "Well, I want to be one. You know, I always loved reading books as a child; it was an escape for me. I just loved the worlds you could experience in them. My mother was self-absorbed, to say the least, and books kept me grounded and safe. I never had a lot of friends growing up, but the ones I did have would tell you that I would tell them stories all the time. I have a great memory and can make sense of what people can't make sense of in their lives with the stories I tell. The problem is I haven't written most of them down or gotten them published, but I want to!" I was blabbering on like an excited child. I could not understand why I was sharing this with a woman I had just met less than a minute ago. In fact, I had not thought about why I wanted to be a writer for a very long time. I nervously bit my lip.

"No, you have not said too much." She smiled and was softer in her manner now, more relaxed. "People tell me their secrets all the time. I know everyone's secrets. In fact, I just came from London. I have many clients there, and their secrets would make your head spin. And by the way, self-absorbed mothers make us grow up to be independent and find our own way in the world. It's very liberating, so count your mother as a blessing." I gave her a curious look.

"I'm sorry; please forgive me," I started.

"Nothing to forgive! But you seem to be full of questions, so what do you wish to ask me?"

"So what really is an oracle? I mostly just picture an old woman wearing a hooded tunic, walking around, and spouting prophecies in the woods, but you don't look like you do that!" I pointed at her purse.

She laughed. "No, I'm not your typical psychic or oracle, that is for sure. But I am good at my work, and people do pay me very well."

"They pay you?"

"Yes, Anna, they pay me as much as their doctors and lawyers. Spiritual healing is just as important and valuable. My insight and advice can often save them a fortune in time and money, and it can save their souls much strife and anguish."

"Their souls? I don't understand."

"We can talk more about that later; don't worry about that for right now. All you have to know is that I see, feel, hear, and know things that many others do not. I've done this for eons of lifetimes and perhaps will for many more. Now, this is your time, so just relax." As she paused and stretched her body across the sofa comfortably, the door opened, and the older lady walked in.

"Isis, I think we are ready," Naomi said.

Isis...I stared at the woman from the café. It was no wonder she got offended when I had been playing with the tarot cards.

"Your name is Isis?" I asked.

"Yes, my dear. Did I not say that the other day?"

"No, I definitely would have remembered that."

"Well, you know now." She smiled and turned to Naomi. "Thank you, Naomi. I'm glad you and Anna have had a chance to talk and connect. I think you will have a lot to share with each other. Now tell me, dear soul sister, are you changing out of your costume?" She pointed to Naomi's high boots and chic outfit.

"Isis," Naomi said in an amused tone, "you know this is for the show and for my clients. My more eclectic outfits don't really work in London. Thankfully, I don't have to go back for a few weeks."

"Did they like the idea?" Isis asked her, and her eyes seemed to change to almost golden.

"They loved it. But we should talk about that later when we don't have guests," said Naomi, and she turned her attention back to me. "Now, Anna, how long will you be staying in Glastonbury?"

"About a month, but it could be longer, depending," I replied.

"Ah, it depends, does it?" enquired Isis. "Well, we can work with that, don't you think so, Naomi?" She nodded in response. "Then shall we take her back home?" Naomi smiled.

"Yes, I am ready, dear oracle," I said.

"Completely ready, Isis," said Naomi. Both women exchanged a knowing smile.

"Back home?" I asked. "To where, York? Do you need to know where I was born and what time, like for astrology?"

"No, no, my dear. To our real home, our first home, and our last home," Isis explained. "This is the reason why you're here: to connect to the sisterhood of priestesses. We are taking you back to the Temple of Isis at Philae."

CHAPTER 8

I sat very still, not knowing what to say or ask. Yet at the same time, I had a million questions in my head. The words would not come. I looked at both of these ladies who appeared to be in total control, acting like this was as easy as going shopping or swapping recipes for dinner. Taking me back to Philae? What on earth did that mean? I was about to find out. Upon reflection, I can truly say that journey changed my life forever.

"So, are we watching this on a video?" I asked.

Isis laughed. "No, dear. We will take you through a time portal of sorts in your mind's eye. You will be able to see, feel, touch, and experience everything that happened as if you were really there."

"Oh, just a simple time portal, of course. I use those all the time to get to work." I laughed nervously. I had no idea what this meant and suddenly realized I was probably in over my head.

"Have you ever had past life regression?" Naomi enquired.

"Not really," I replied sheepishly. "Would I be unconscious? You're not going to do something weird to me while I'm under, right?"

"No, certainly not. It will be for around fifteen minutes, and you will be totally safe."

Isis interjected. "Anna, your brain has many layers and areas not even tapped into. Do you ever get static shocks or find your hair stands up on your arms?" I nodded. "Well, what you are feeling is the electricity flowing through you, your electrical or energy body. Way out there." She pointed out the window to the sky. "Out there, there are many amazing things we don't even know, but they hold all this magic and energy that we can tap into using that electricity in our bodies. Doing so creates doorways into other realms, the past and the future, and when ready, we can step through these doorways."

Ah, now I was starting to understand, "Like the film *Stargate,* but not going for real, just like a video I get to watch. Like an amazing window to view life through."

"Something like that." She laughed.

"Okay, good." I took a deep breath and smiled at her and Naomi. Well, they did not seem like murderers or people trying to scam tourists out of money. I didn't really have anything to lose by doing this. I shrugged and waited for further instructions.

Isis looked at Naomi. "Well, my dear, would you like to do the honor?"

"No, my dear friend," she replied. "I think you should take her through first, as you did with me."

"As you wish," Isis remarked. She turned her full gaze onto me, "Now, Anna, I want you to sit back in the chair. That's it. Uncross your arms and legs and allow yourself to become really loose and get comfortable in the chair." She kept nodding at me as I did what she asked. I felt as if I was uncoiling in the chair, and a familiar feeling of drowsiness set in. I was aware of where I was, but everything was slowly shifting out of focus, like when a dentist used laughing gas on a patient to fill a cavity.

"And so we begin," said Isis. With a graceful motion, she pulled back her hair and tucked it behind her ear. Her blue eyes began to shift in color again, and I felt the temperature in the room begin to rise. She pressed the play button on some stereo I couldn't see, and I could feel this hypnotic melody surrounding me. I noticed my breathing oscillating between shallow and deep breaths.

"Let's start by taking a few deep breaths and relax," she cooed in my ear.

I tried to stay awake, but my eyes were becoming heavy and starting to close. I glanced across at Naomi, who was now sitting cross-legged with her eyes closed.

For a moment, doubt crossed my mind. *What if this is all a scam to get my money? Or maybe this is all an elaborate ruse to steal my organs.* At that moment, I had to let go of any fear I had. I gave into the emotion of the moment and surrendered to it completely.

"Begin to feel yourself becoming heavier and heavier," said Isis. "Relax and close your eyes. Begin to feel yourself being drawn into another time and place, and then allow yourself to drift into that time. Let your awareness flow to your heart and focus on everything in your life for which you are grateful. For gratitude and love will open your sacred heart, my beloved."

With these words, I felt my heart pounding, and I felt tears begin to flow. I was not sad, though.

"Now, Anna," she continued, "you are finding yourself drawn to Ancient Egypt, to Philae, a sacred site for many deities and temples. You find yourself drawn to one in particular: the Temple of Isis." The music picked up tempo and got louder; it was coming to a climax just as I was settling into a dreamlike state. "Now," said Isis, "tell me what you see."

What I saw and felt for that first time was something I wouldn't soon forget. It was as if I was in a dream but was able to speak. My mouth opened, and the words began to flow.

I am standing in front of a large temple made of limestone decorated with hieroglyphs. I turn to see that this temple is on an island in the middle of a lake. I am now walking through the first pylon and through the colonnade, lined with ornate columns. I am now at the second pylon and headed to the inner temple. Oh, I feel such joy here; my heart is full of happiness. But it feels as though it is fading, and I can't reach it for some reason.

I am now walking back toward the shore of the lake and see a ferryman. I shout to him, but I don't think he can hear me. I turn back around and noticed that the temple looks different and a little worse for wear, and that there are still no people around. Why aren't the other priestesses out? This temple should be bustling with people.

I suddenly have the urge to leave the shore and go back toward the temple, but my feet will not move. I try to turn around, but I can't do that either. Why can't I move? What is happening to me? Please, is there someone that can help me? I'm panicking here!

My heart was racing.

"Carry on, Anna," I could hear Isis telling me, but it seemed so far away.

I hear the voice: a deeper tone, almost an echo, off in the distance, asking me what is holding me here. Where is that voice coming from? I think it's from the inner temple. Hello? Is anyone there? I can't see anyone around me. Please, I don't know what is holding me here. Can you help me? Hello? The hot tears from my eyes are stinging my cheeks. Hello? Where are you?

I turn around and find myself inside the inner temple and in front of a large wooden door that's locked. Oh no, not another door. I can see a large round stone in front of this with strange writing, but this stone does not belong here. It does not belong here. I can hear my voice becoming hysterical. Why is the stone there? Why is the temple chamber locked?

It's not right; it's not right! I'm shaking like a leaf. I am becoming more agitated and confused. The strange voice speaks again and asks, "Can you go near the door?" No, it's forbidden. I don't even recognize the voice now coming from within me. I am losing control. My vision is fading.

"Something is going to break; they are going to break it," I hear myself saying.

"What are they going to break, my dear?" the voice presses on.

Everything is black, but I can hear shouting in the distance, and then I hear a singular, blood-curdling scream.

"What did they break, dear one? Anna, please answer me!"

I realized the voice was now Isis calling to me, but I was too afraid to open my eyes or speak. I didn't know where I was or who I was.

"Anna," said Isis in a calmer voice, "it is all right. Come back to us. Tell me what happened, please." I tried to regain my breath but began to sob even more uncontrollably. It took all I had to force the words from my lips. "You died. You, you, you… They broke you. They broke the sisterhood, everything. Isis, I know you were murdered."

The music had stopped, and all I could hear was silence. I calmed myself down a bit before I opened my eyes. As my eyes adjusted to the light, I saw that I was no longer in a temple chamber but back in the living room of the Sanctuary. I looked over at Naomi, who was now sitting with her arms wrapped around her legs and crying softly. She looked at me, and her mascara was running. I turned around to find Isis standing beside me and looking down at me with a somber look on her face. She was the first to break the silence.

"Move your fingers and toes," she said. Like a child, I did as she asked. "Are you present with us?" I nodded and tried to speak, but she held up a hand to stop me. "No words, please. Just keep breathing." She turned to check on Naomi. "Naomi, Naomi," she said her name a few times as if to bring her out of a trance. Isis paused. "Naomi?" A question hung on her lips.

"Yes, Isis?" she finally answered in a small voice.

"What do you think?"

Naomi looked at me with a small smile. She nodded to Isis. "Yes, I think she is special indeed."

CHAPTER 9

I felt like I was going to throw up. *What just happened? Did I go back in time? Was any of that real, or did they slip me something?* Either way, before Isis or Naomi, or whoever she was could say anything, I got up, grabbed my bag, and ran out the door. I could hear both of them calling after me, but I didn't care. As I neared the door, I ran into Lesley. She tried to slow me down, pulled at my arm, and asked what was going on, but I brushed past her. She grabbed at me again, and this time I really pulled away and ran.

I ran down the hill back toward town in a daze. I wasn't aiming to go anywhere specific until I reached the gate to a large outdoor garden complex. The sign above the gate read, "The Chalice Well."

I had seen this mentioned in some of the flyers in the shops but was not sure what it was. Strangely I had walked past this on my way to the Sanctuary, but for some reason, it had been invisible—veiled until now.

I got a strange feeling just then, like someone or something was following me, and I decided to stop and enter. My strange feelings of late usually had a reason for showing up, and I was beginning to trust them and follow them. The door was heavy, and I even wondered if I should be entering, but I decided it was better than being at the Sanctuary. I pulled on the handle.

As if the door read my thoughts, it opened, and a woman wearing a full-length blue cape stood in the doorway. She was an older woman with her beautiful silver-gray hair tied back, and she had what appeared to be strands of colored highlights like a rainbow in it. Another interesting character. She smiled. "Hello there. I'm Alice, the guardian of Chalice Well. This is the exit door; did you not see the sign?" She pointed to the wooden plaque, and sure enough, I had been trying to open the exit door. "The entrance is over there." She pointed to a metal arbor covered in blossom and a large sign that read, "Entrance to the Chalice Well."

I did not know what to say and stood still; my heart was beating so fast.

"Let's start with your name, perhaps?" She smiled at me.

I found my voice. "Anna. I'm staying here at the Gables Guesthouse with Emilee and covering stories for a new book I'm writing about the area and its spiritual teachings." That was the first time I had articulated the subject of my book. I was not sure where this had come from, but it appeared to spark some interest in my new acquaintance.

"Oh, a book? How fascinating," said Alice. "It's wonderful to meet you. The Gables is a beautiful property, and I had heard that Emilee was having long-term guests now."

I nervously looked behind me. I was sure I was being followed, or at least watched.

"Would you like to look inside?" she asked.

I nodded.

"Please know you can only stay until 5:00 p.m. sharp because we have a group coming over for a private ceremony. I am here preparing for them." She looked at her watch. "Oh, I see it's already four; maybe you should just come back another day." She saw me bite my lip and look nervously toward the door, and she seemed to understand I was in distress. "Oh, well, perhaps today is as good a day as any."

I sighed with relief. In my mind, I knew I had nothing to be afraid of. Isis seemed very kind, and Naomi was strange but not threatening. "That would be kind, yes. Just a little time, and it's still so light; the sun won't set for a while," I said to Alice.

Suddenly a large black crow landed on the tree next to us and began making the loudest noise, which made Alice smile for some reason. The crow squawked relentlessly, pacing back and forth across the top of the hedgerow. Even though he was really annoying, he had caught the full attention of Alice. She muttered something to herself and made a clicking sound with her fingers. I had seen Lucinda do this in a class before; she called it muscle testing. You can ask yourself a question, and by moving your fingers, you get your *yes* and *no* answers. She had tried to teach me in a pendulum class, but I was the worst student and failed because I kept dropping the pendulum, eventually breaking the crystal, much to the annoyance of the other students.

As I was thinking, I stopped paying attention to Alice, who appeared to accept whatever messages the crow was giving her and kept holding the door open for me. I followed her in and was amazed at the beauty. The gardens, the water, the trees—it was like something out of a dream.

"It's beautiful, is it not?" she asked.

"Stunning!"

"Come this way, and we will find a calming place. You look a little overwhelmed, so let's go beside the water."

How does she know this? But then I looked and saw she'd done the clicking with her hands again. She motioned for me to sit down on a small bench next to a pool with smaller interlocking circular pools at different heights.

"This is the Vesica Piscis Pool. See how the shape goes around, and then the two rings cross? The Vesica Piscis symbol represents the joining of god and goddess or heaven and Earth. It's sacred geometry."

"Should I do anything special?"

"Leave your troubles," she told me.

"Oh, I'm ready to do that, for sure."

I wasn't sure what to share, so I simply nodded, took a deep breath, and closed my eyes. The images I had seen of the Temple at Philae replayed in my mind's eye over and over: the door with the stone in front of it, the murder of Isis, the ferryman off in the distance, and the feeling of utter helplessness that washed over me as I struggled to open the door. I wanted to cry at it all.

Alice continued explaining. "The pools here were created to represent the chakras. This is one of the seven chakras of the world—Glastonbury, that is. Did you know that?"

I snapped out of my thoughts. "No, I didn't. What does that mean?"

"Well, within your body you have seven key energy centers," Alice said, pointing to each area on her body as she explained. "The root, the sacral, the solar plexus, the heart, the throat, the third eye, and the crown."

"Oh, yes. I remember I had a chakra balance session once."

"Did it work?" She smiled.

"I'm not sure, to be honest," I replied. Alice's kindness and warm smile put me at ease, and I started to feel more myself again.

"Glastonbury is often associated with the heart," she explained. "We have energy lines, known as ley lines, that converge here, as do six other places in the world associated with the chakras."

"What does that all mean?" I asked. "If it's the heart, is this the place to find true love?"

"You would think, but not necessarily. It means that your

heart can open when you find your truth and place in the world, let go of all your bad karma, and find your heaven on earth."

That sounds a little too optimistically profound, I thought. "I just came from the Sanctuary." I pointed up to the houses visible up the hill. "I don't think my heart was happy there. It felt like my heart was breaking."

"Then your heart needs to heal. This is a perfect place to allow that to happen."

I think this was the first time I'd actually thought about my heart. "I have been so concerned with my head, Alice. How do I heal my heart?" I asked.

"Well, think. What did you come to Glastonbury for?"

"To write." The words flew out of my mouth. "I want to be a writer. I want to tell stories, and I want to be published." I could hear the overeager tone in my voice yet again.

"That's good, Anna. This is your heart speaking its true desires. In the short while you've been here, you've talked about writing twice, and you speak with so much passion about it!"

"How does a heart speak?"

Alice pointed to my throat, then to my heart, and back to my throat again, "Your heart connects to your throat and speaks when it feels calm and happy. Do you feel calm?"

"Oh, yes, it's amazing. This place must be magic."

"Do you feel happy?"

I nodded my head. "Very, yes. I feel a happiness uninhibited by anything."

"Then you know your truth is coming to the surface, straight from the heart."

We both smiled.

She continued. "Glastonbury is an amazing place for inspiration, Anna. Work with her."

Something about the way Alice spoke made me trust her,

and her kindness made me like her all the more so. After the Sanctuary drama, I was afraid my time in Glastonbury would quickly sour, but Alice infused the sweetness back into me.

"Do you think the gardens can heal my heart?" I asked her. "I left a life just a few days ago, and I feel so lost and unaware of myself. You see, I just came from something called a past life regression, which I'm not even sure was real, but it made me question everything. Is it even possible to know about your past lives? I wasn't even sure they were real, and now I'm being told by the high priestess herself that I am special and can look back in time and see what other lives I had. I feel like I'm becoming something of a nutter here."

Alice nodded and smiled. "Did the regression show you images you wish you had not seen?" I nodded. I was not sure how much she would know about this. "Did the story that you saw, however impossible it might seem, feel familiar or true in some way?" she asked. Again I nodded. "These kinds of visions—regressions, if you will—are traumas from the past coming forward in an attempt to resolve themselves. You starting over and feeling lost, and the new visions you have seen are no coincidence, Anna." She looked up at the sky; it was clear blue and not a cloud in sight. "Let's keep walking. There is another place I want to show you before you go."

She led me up a few stone steps and farther along the path, which was surrounded by dark green bushes and towering ancient trees in their prime. The walk was so peaceful and the foliage was so beautiful that I felt transported to another world—one completely different from the one I had run away from an hour ago. We walked through a stone doorway, and there was a beautiful water feature that led to a stream.

"Come, Anna. Touch the crystal-cool water," Alice beckoned. I did as she requested, knelt down next to the crystalline pool, and placed my hands into the shallow stream. The water was so cleansing and pure that it felt like I was letting go of my burdens. "Let the water wash over you. Feel it ebb and flow, bringing in clarity and taking away any doubt and uncertainty. Feel the conviction of yourself come back and leave the past sins in the past, my dear," she said in a soothing voice. Alice then held out her hand to help me stand, and as our hands connected, I felt a huge electrical charge running through my body.

"Wow, I think I just got back in my body," I said with a laugh. I shook my hands to dry them, and my skin felt soft and smooth.

Alice was already climbing the next set of steps and pointing out the flowers, trees, and meditation areas. "That over there is a place of contemplation and peace," she explained, "but perhaps you can come back on another afternoon. I feel a strong need to take you somewhere else now." We turned right and walked over a small patch of grass to another fountain. "Here, let's stop at the Lion's Head Fountain." She pointed to her right.

At the far end was a small pond attached to the wall with a lion's head affixed to it. A thin stream of clear water spilled out of its large, fanged mouth and into a wider stream just thirty centimeters below it. The stone underneath the lion had worn away, and the iron in the water had stained it red. All of that gave the appearance that the blood of the lion, its life force, was seeping out of its mouth and collecting in the pool. Alice motioned for us to sit at the edge of the pool.

"This, my dear," Alice said, motioning around us, "is a place of great healing, so take a deep breath and let the calm energy rush over you. Now, hold out your hands again."

I did as she ordered and closed my eyes to take in a large breath. When I opened my eyes, I saw that Alice had filled a small glass with water from the fountain. The water was tinged with a faint crimson color from the rust.

"Drink," she said firmly.

I put the glass up to my lips and tipped it back. As the cool, metallic-tasting water filled my mouth, I felt a surge of strength growing inside of me, taking root in my stomach and radiating out. My whole body felt warm, and a pleasant euphoria settled in my heart. I was just about to refill the glass when Alice grabbed my wrist to stop me.

"Yes, I know the impulse, but it isn't good to drink more than you need. This water is for special use only," she said as she took the glass from my hand and gently placed it beside her.

"You know, Alice, since I came here, my dreams and thoughts have changed so much. I thought it was going to be fun—full of pretty crystals, sweet-smelling potions, and saying incantations from silly spell books. But so far, it's been full of uneasy feelings, ominous tarot card readings, and going on psychedelic-like journeys into the past lives. I'm not sure this is for me." I said all this in a flurry and could feel myself getting really worked up. Whatever the water had done for me was fading fast. I felt so bad for this poor woman, who had only just met me and now had to bear the burden of all of my issues.

However, Alice seemed to take everything I said in stride. She responded to my ranting with a cool and even tone. "This is the path of the initiation, Anna, the path to the goddess."

"Initiation? To what?" I asked.

"Well, into self-awareness—figuring out who you were, who you are, and who you will be, and your connection to a priestesshood that has been around for millennia. There are several trials that will come your way now that you are here. The first was getting through that first past life regression. Think of it as similar to passing exams for a subject in school."

"They don't teach the subjects you are talking about in school, do they?" We both laughed, which put me back at ease.

"I suppose not." She smiled. "But do look at your time here as being in a spiritual school or university of sorts. It's year one, you don't quite know how to find the classrooms or know the professors by name yet, and some of the lessons are new and intimidating, but you'll figure it out in time. Before you know it, you'll be year four and ready to graduate!"

That was an analogy I could relate to and an outlook to go by. It made me feel more confident in my decision to come to Glastonbury in the first place, knowing that I had a series of tasks to complete that would ultimately lead me to my goal of figuring out my life.

Alice continued in a resolute voice. "Anna, explore, ask questions, and write about all that you experience. The Sanctuary has master teachers. You have met and connected with them, and they are here to help you. Isis and Naomi's methods can be tough for the heart and soul, but they know better than anyone how to guide you through it all. You will learn more from them in your short time here than you did in all your years of school—that I promise you. When you are ready, Anna, go back to the Sanctuary, learn your lessons, and graduate into a higher consciousness of existence."

I knew she was right; it all resonated with me. And now I felt embarrassed that I had run off in a panic from them. Perhaps I had missed my chance.

"They will be open to you again," she continued. "Now, I have to prepare for an upcoming ceremony this evening, so it is about time you get going."

Alice reached down into her blue cloak pocket and pulled out a small vial. She took off the cork, leaned in gently, and filled it with water from the mouth of the lion. She placed the cork onto the bottle, shook it, whispered a few words into it, and handed it to me.

"Anna, this is now blessed, and I have placed a protection spell within it," she explained. "There is going to come a time that you will need all of the strength and protection in the world to get you through your trials. Drink this when you are at the precipice, at the moment you feel that going forward might break you, but you must go on all the same. Keep it with you always, lest you be caught ill-prepared for that moment. It could happen at any time. Let this small bottle remind you to stay calm in the face of adversity and be open to all the amazing possibilities and stories that are coming your way."

I took the bottle with gratitude. "I hope it does. Thank you, Alice." Holding up the bottle, I added, "This is so kind of you. Not only that, but thank you for all of your encouraging words today. I can't tell you how much this means to me and how influential it has been." I clasped my hands over hers.

Alice gave me a warm smile and took my hands in hers. Then she led us down away from the Lion's Head and back toward the exit. "Now, my dear, it's time you get going home to the Gables. Perhaps come back in the morning or in a few days' time."

"Or when the crow calls," I said with a giggle.

"Yes." She chuckled. "Listen for the crow. You know, he speaks very highly of you, my dear."

We both laughed again and finished our trek back through the gardens and to the gate. Once we parted ways, I looked in my bag to check my phone and realized it was still on silent from the afternoon. There was one text waiting:

Dear Anna, please do not be afraid of all you see at first in past life regressions. If you wish to continue, we are

*here at 9:00 a.m. tomorrow, and we hope you can join
us again. Isis.*

I decided to sleep on it before I replied. But once I was
back in the Gables and writing in my golden journal, I suddenly
realized I had more questions and wanted them to be answered.
With a deep breath, I opened my phone and sent a simple text
back to Isis: *Thank you. I will be there.*

CHAPTER 10

Friday, May 30

The next morning, I was wide awake at 7:00 a.m. The images of the day before still filled my head, but I felt more at peace with them now. I had a few hours before I had to be at the Sanctuary, so I decided to go exploring some more. I pulled on some layers of clothes and ran down the stairs. Emilee was busy with a guest who had obviously arrived the night before and was talking in the kitchen. I crept into the breakfast room and grabbed some of the rolls and fruit. I took out my water flask and filled it with coffee. Then I slowly crept out, opened the front door, and stepped out into the crisp fresh air. The sky was a dusty pink, still changing with the rise of the sun. It seemed like as good a time as ever to go explore, so I set off towards the road leading to the Tor.

As I left the Gables and stood on the pathway, I saw in the distance a stone tower rising above a great cloud of mist. It was the Tor, the famous landmark in Glastonbury that I had seen on my way in. Now was as good a time as any, so I headed off in that direction. It would only take me about ten minutes to walk to the base. I figured I could have breakfast there and gather my thoughts in solitude before heading over to the Sanctuary, which wasn't far away.

It turned out I wasn't the only one with that idea; other pilgrims were wandering up to the Tor. There were two women in their late twenties wearing large camping packs on their backs, hiking boots, and cargo shorts. One of them was holding a map for the other to see. They seemed to know what they were doing, so I approached them to ask for directions. As I approached, they greeted me with warm smiles. I suddenly realized we were near the car park of the Chalice Well gardens.

"Are you going to the Tor?" I asked the woman with the map. She nodded and pointed to a small narrow lane up twenty meters on the left from where we were standing. If she hadn't pointed it out to me, I would have missed it altogether. The path was marked with such a small sign that I had totally missed it the previous day. The pair wished me well and continued toward the path, and I followed not far behind them.

Although it was narrow, the pathway felt quite serene. Tall English oaks and wide ash trees shielded me from the rising sun, and the only sounds I could hear were the birds chirping from their perches on the trees and the rabbits scurrying around looking for food. Everything was just beginning to awaken to the day.

After another few minutes, I came to a small step way and could see the trail leading up to the high hill. *Great, I am on the right path.* I checked my watch and saw I still had well over an hour before I needed to be at the Sanctuary, so I made my way toward the first of two small gateways. *This should not take me much time and is just an easy hike to the top,* I thought.

When I reached the second gateway, I was painfully aware of how out of breath I was. *Wow, I must really be out of shape.* Just past the second gateway, I could see a bench. It seemed forever to try to reach it. I felt sick and dizzy again.

While looking up at the Tor, everything seemed so far away. It was as if the vision was pulsating. Everything in my reality felt unstable.

I blinked my eyes to try to focus, realizing the houses had all disappeared. I looked around and there were no signs of life—no birds, power cables, roads, or pathways.

I could smell the air and the grass, and I took a deep breath in. I felt as if nature were healing me, oxygen flowing within every cell of my body. Not far into the distance, I could see a small deer, slight and dainty. Its soft brown coat with tiny white markings stood out against the lush green grass background. It looked at me straight on. Its black coal-like eyes locked into my awareness, and it then went back to its breakfast of grass, totally undisturbed by my presence.

I heard a rustle of the bushes behind me and knew it was more than wind. The deer also sensed others coming and quickly scampered over the hill and disappeared.

I turned to see a group of women walking towards me, but they did not seem to see me. They walked in a procession, all wearing long purple gowns styled from a medieval time and carrying tall wooden staffs. Their hair colors were various shades of golden red, and one at the back had jet-black curls. Each one's hair was braided in different ways with feathers and colorful ribbon strands. It was as if they even had different skin tones and eye colors. I stood silently, taking into my awareness their various striking looks.

On their upper left arms, each wore different copper bracelets. One, I noticed, was circles while the other was triangles.

They walked slowly and gracefully, as if each step were sacred and timed to perfection. The first woman in the procession stopped a small way ahead of me. She began to speak words I did not understand, but they resembled a Welsh or Irish dialect.

The woman raised her staff and banged it three times into

the earth. I almost fell over as it seemed to shake the very hill I was attempting to climb. I looked back up the hill and saw that the Tor monument was not there and was now replaced by a large oblong free-standing stone, a monolith similar to those I had seen in pictures of Stonehenge.

The women then all proceeded to move. However, they did not move straight up the hill but began to curve around. It was then I saw the hill had seven marked circles draped around its grass surface—each circle within the next circle leading to the top tier. I watched as they passed by me. Totally fascinated by them, I felt a connection so ancient my heart wanted to follow.

The final woman passed and turned to me. She saw me.

"Will you join us?" she whispered.

She held her slender hand towards me, and I was tempted—so tempted—but something held me back.

"Not yet," I nodded, "but soon."

"We will be here," she raised her staff to point to the procession of women. "Always and forever."

She dropped her hand and turned to follow the others, and I stood silently watching as they drifted over the hill towards the other side.

☥

I was aware that the vision had faded and I began to look around to see that once again, houses, gardens, and life were as they should be.

While looking up at the Tor monument, I thought it seemed so far away, and then I looked down the hill to see if I could recognize any landmarks. Both the Sanctuary and the Chalice Well were much closer than I had thought. Both shared space on the bottom of the hill where the Tor stood. I thought I saw Lesley in the garden, her hair bright in the morning sun.

She looked in my direction, so I waved. She did not wave back and instead turned around and walked back toward the house. I tried to get a better look at the house, but suddenly I lost my footing, and before I knew it, everything went black.

☥

"Are you okay? Miss, are you okay?" asked a discombobulated voice. I suddenly came back to consciousness to find the young women from before helping me back onto the bench.

"Here, have some water," said the young woman who had been carrying the map. She offered me a blue metal canteen, and I gratefully accepted it.

"I'm sorry. I'm so embarrassed," I said between sips.

"Don't be," replied the other woman. "This is a very powerful place. It's been known to cause more than one person to faint. My name is Izzie and this is my girlfriend, Mia. Now, what did you say your name was?"

"Oh!" I looked sheepishly at them. "My name is Anna. Sorry about that. I think I'm okay now. Here's your canteen," I said, handing it to her and trying to get back up. I stumbled, and Mia went to catch me.

"Take a moment," she said. "We are in no rush. When you are ready, we can help you back to where you are staying. I'm assuming you are just visiting?"

"Yes," I replied, and looked down at my watch: it was nearly 8:20. "But I have somewhere to be at nine, so I really do need to get going. I have an appointment at the Sanctuary, at the base of the hill over there. Thank you for all of your help. I really appreciate it!" I tried to get up again, but I still felt a little light-headed, so I sat back down.

"Look," Izzie said. "You are in no condition to walk on your own. If you need to get there, let us help you." Then before I could protest, they both had me up on my feet and were guiding me back down the hill like a small child.

As soon as I passed through the first gateway into the lane, I felt completely fine. All of the light-headedness and dizziness had subsided. I smiled at them, thanked the women again for their help, and told them that I would be fine and that they should continue back on their way. Mia looked hesitant, but she said that the color was back in my cheeks. She told me to make sure to eat something as soon as I could. Izzie gave me her business card and told me to call them if I was ever in need of some company; they would be in town a few more days. That was strange: every woman I was meeting was kind, caring, and showed such compassion. I set off slowly toward the Sanctuary, scarfing down the sweet rolls I had packed in my bag and taking large gulps of my hot coffee on the way.

I got to the Sanctuary door with ten minutes to spare. When I knocked on the door, Lesley, with that eye-catching platinum blonde hair, greeted me. She asked me whom I was there to see. I told her I was there to see Isis or Naomi.

"So you returned for more torture? Based on yesterday, I figured you'd be running for the hills. Oh, wait, isn't that what you did?" said Lesley in a teasing manner.

"Haha, yes, you got me there. More torture, though," I chuckled wryly. "That's one way of putting it, yes," she responded.

I found this woman a bit direct, but I chalked it up to her being a Londoner. I wondered how much she had heard or watched the previous day. "Yes, I decided that this was the place where I'd learn about oracle work and take my lessons. So I'm back to start my schooling with Isis and Naomi; they are the ones to teach me."

"Hmm, and you are so sure they will?" Lesley asked.

"I hope so. It seems like that's what we are going to talk about today," I said, furrowing my brow.

"If they deem you worthy, of course," she said with a saccharine smile.

"Well, I think I have been, thank you. And now I'd like to see Isis if that's okay with you?"

Lesley turned around and flicked her hair back. As she began to walk down the hall, she said over her shoulder, "Well, you know your way to the living room, I'm sure. Wait there. I'll tell Isis her presence is requested."

"Yes, please do. Many thanks!" I smiled. Lesley gave me a curt nod and was gone down the hall. I went to the living room to wait for Isis.

I was trying to wait patiently, but it seemed like Lesley had been gone a while. My nerves started to flare up again, and my thoughts started to spiral. *What if Isis only called me here to tell me she doesn't want me to come anymore? What if I did some sort of horrible thing that messed up the ritual? She is going to want me to fix it, and I don't know how. Oh, my god, she is just going to yell at me and tell me how I shouldn't have come here. Or worse, she's going to want me to do another regression. I don't think I could handle another one so soon.*

The door suddenly opened, the sound pulling me out of my thoughts. To my surprise, Naomi, the oracle from the day before, walked in. Her clothes had changed from the previous day, and she wore soft white silk trousers with a matching blouse. Around her neck, I saw a golden ankh. She looked like an angel and was much more relaxed than yesterday.

"Anna!" She smiled and came over to me, greeting me with a kiss on each cheek. "I apologize; Isis was suddenly called away this morning and won't be able to make it. It works out perfectly, though, because I wanted to personally apologize for yesterday. Things became a little too intense, even for me. But all is normal, and today is a new day."

"Thank you, Naomi. Apology accepted," I replied. "And I'm sorry I ran out like that! I will say I was hoping to interview Isis. No matter, I can come back another time."

"Ah yes, Isis, but who is Isis? She comes in many shapes and sizes." Naomi chuckled and changed the subject. "So, Anna, she told me you have a passion for Ancient Egypt. Is that true?"

"Yes. I love anything connected to Ancient Egypt. I noticed all of the pictures on the wall have paintings of gods and hieroglyphs on them."

"Ah, yes, the wall of eight." She smiled. "Let me show you."

She moved out to the hallway, and as she did, her clothes seemed to magically transform into a long, black woolen dress, worn leather boots, and a white bonnet. She noticed me staring and gave me a curious look. "What's got you all stopped up and staring?" she asked. "Do I have something in my teeth? Or are you wondering how it's possible I'm pulling off this all-white ensemble so well?"

I blinked, and her white trousers and blouse reappeared. "Nothing, sorry. I thought I saw…never mind. Yes, you do pull off white better than most. I'd probably spill something all over myself, knowing me." I gave a nervous chuckle.

Naomi looked as if she wanted to press me further but decided to let it go. She stopped at the first frame, a piece of papyrus with the profile of a black cat on it. "A guardian cat, Bastet; she sees everything," she explained. We made our way down the hallway, with Naomi pointing out the various figures on the wall. I tried my best to pay attention, but I couldn't get that image of her in strange, old clothes out of my mind.

Suddenly, Lesley reappeared out of nowhere in front of us.

She interrupted right in the middle of Naomi saying something about the god Anubis. It was like Lesley could float through walls, I swear. She announced, "Isis is here."

Naomi gave her a rather exasperated look for interrupting her and then said, "Oh, then it's time for me to get on. Look, Anna, why don't we meet tomorrow around 10:00 a.m. at my social office in town, where I see my friends? It's actually in the back of that café where you met Isis. I would love to share some of my story with you, since you are a writer and all. It might be therapeutic for me to get it out there, and who knows? Perhaps, you'll be the one to tell it correctly."

She reached over and, to my surprise, gave me a quick hug. Then she looked at Lesley and said, "Thank you, Lesley. It's nearly 9:30 a.m. now, and Isis will be needing her morning tea. Could you put a kettle on?" Naomi gave a smug grin and left. Lesley did not look pleased, and she stormed off to the kitchen in a huff.

I quickly followed Lesley because she hadn't told me where to go. When I got into the kitchen, she was already filling the kettle with water. She looked up at me and said, "You know, she never hugs me."

"Sorry," I said. "I didn't know she was going to do that. It surprised me, actually." I watched Lesley fly around the kitchen, grabbing items for the tea. "Lesley, is there anything I can help with? I can take care of all of this since I'm about to go see her anyways."

"No, no," Lesley replied, a twinge of annoyance in her voice. "You'd just mess it up. There is a specific order to this. Just sit at the table over there and stay out of my way."

I did as she asked and waited for her to finish. The silence between Lesley and me was awkward, so in an attempt to make conversation, I asked, "Lesley, can I ask you something? Were you out in the garden this morning? I thought I saw you, and you saw me."

"I wasn't, and I didn't," she snapped, clearly annoyed I was talking to her.

I pressed on. "This morning, while attempting to walk to the top of the Tor—although I could barely make it past the second gate—I thought I saw someone who looked like you in the garden. Perhaps I was mistaken. My apologies."

She paused from her work and looked up at me. "Did you say that you were at the second gate?"

"Yes," I replied. "I got really dizzy and blacked out. After that, I couldn't go any farther."

"You know we can't go up there, right?"

"Why?"

"Because of the curse. Didn't they tell you?"

"The curse?"

"Yes, the curse. The sins of one woman cursed us all. It's been in place for nearly five hundred years."

"Now that sounds like quite a story, Lesley," Isis said, suddenly appearing at the doorway. "An old wives' tale, no doubt. Good morning, Anna. I'm sorry for the mix-up. I went early to see if I could meet you at the Guesthouse and have breakfast with Emilee, but time seemed to have gotten the best of me, and I missed our appointment."

"You know Emilee personally?" I asked, surprised.

"Of course, my dear. This is a small town, which is even smaller for our community." Isis motioned for me to follow her, and she and I left Lesley in the kitchen. "Tea can wait," she announced without turning to look at Lesley.

I could feel Lesley's fury with Isis, but like an obedient child, she followed as instructed.

We walked back into the living room. The energy in the

room felt different; it was now calmer and less manic. I had been so nervous waiting in there alone for Naomi, and I had still felt uneasy when we talked. Now, with Isis, there seemed to be a softness and a more positive energy to the room.

"Ah, yes, I know. It is a wonder how much the energy of a room can affect your state of being, and how much it can change in mere minutes," said Isis from behind me. I turned and saw her close the door, and she gave me a small wink. The words inside me were building up again, and I felt like I was going to burst if I didn't tell her what I was feeling. She sat down and motioned for me to sit down again in the chair opposite her.

"I wanted to apologize," I said in a loud and shaky voice. "I have never experienced anything like yesterday, I have been having these dreams, and it was just so scary. I thought I was going to get sucked into the earth like one of those horror movies. I didn't mean to run out and seem ungrateful. I was just scared, and I didn't know what to do. I am so sorry."

Isis gave me a kind smile and said, "It's okay. I remember my first time in a past life regression. The sensation is very off-putting at first. I was lucky; my first experience was in a very calm life. It was in the medieval period, and I was a child. I remember living on a large English estate in the country. I loved running through the gardens; that was what I experienced first. Then I started to experience the everyday activities of my life there. I found out I was the daughter of one of the servants there and would grow up to be one as well. My last vision was of me getting married to the stableman, and then I came out of it."

"That was it?"

"Yes, that was it."

"But you didn't really think that was actually you, did you?"

"I did. I felt it in my bones and knew it was absolutely true. Do you feel like what you experienced yesterday was not true?"

"I don't know. It felt so real and was so vivid in my mind. It shocked me. When I was experiencing it, I felt like it really was my life, and I forgot for a moment who I really was, or who I was going to be—um, am? This time-jumping stuff is confusing. It's giving me a migraine just thinking about it."

"Yes, that does happen. However, I must say you saw very clearly with all your senses. We have not seen many with your ability who can do so much in their first regression. It gives me hope for the future of our community." She looked around the room and over at the door, and her voice became a whisper. "Doors and walls have eyes and ears. I would caution you not to display your talent too much. There are forces that have been working hard to keep people like you away," she said.

"What do you mean?"

"Oh, you will find out in time, dear child."

I thought about it for a second. *Do I really want to be part of a community where there are forces working against me?* I wasn't sure I liked that bit, but I knew I was too deep to turn back now, and I wanted to know what was going on with me. "Will you teach me, Isis, please? I'm ready to figure out what is going on around here and discover who I am; I'm sure of it. I just need someone to show me the way."

"Of course, my dear. I thought you would never ask. Why don't we meet at the café where we first met, tomorrow around noon? I can start to teach you about Egypt and what all of this means."

"Certainly, but can we make it 1:00 p.m.? I have another appointment at 10:00 a.m."

"Busy already?" she replied with a smile. "I'm glad, but we don't want to waste too much time; the solstice is fast approaching, and we need to be ready."

"Ready for what?"

"You will see," she answered. "Now, I have some clients to see, so why don't you visit with Lesley or explore the gardens?"

I felt like she was being dismissive; we had not done any teaching, and I wondered if I was wasting my day.

"No, not a waste. Off you go, my dear." She'd read my mind again. Then she walked me to the door of the living room, ushered me out, and closed it behind me.

As I stepped into the hallway, I searched the images upon the walls for the picture of the oracle, but all I saw were the papyri with hand-painted ancient pictures of goddesses and gods. I felt I could gaze at these all day, but I became aware of someone watching me. I looked up the staircase, and there on the stairs was Lesley. She smiled and again lifted her hand to her mouth to signal to be quiet. She pointed to the kitchen door, and I went to it.

Lesley followed behind me, and once we were both in the kitchen, she closed the door. "Sorry, Isis likes us to be quiet when she has clients coming around," Lesley said. "You just stay here a moment while I bring Isis her tea." She walked to the counter, grabbed a tea tray, and was out the door. She was back a moment later and briefly looked out the door to check if anyone was coming. Then she turned around and excitedly asked, "Wow, what a couple of days. So tell me: what was going on in the living room yesterday?" She swept past me and walked toward the very old oak dining room table, indicating that I should sit with her. Her tone and manner had changed dramatically in the last few minutes. *Does she want to be my friend now? How strange.*

I looked around and noticed that there was a family room just beyond the table. It appeared to be like an old family room with wood units and a stove that would easily fit into a lifestyle magazine from the seventies.

"Old, isn't it? And aged, too. Not my idea of a healing sanctuary, but it works," she said. "It's got that family feel, and when we have gatherings, it's warm and cozy." She touched the wood on the table, slid her hand across it, and smiled. "Now, come on—sit down!" she said, and she took a chair at the far end of the table. "But come over to this side. This place has walls with secrets, and you can tell me your story!" I did as she asked.

"I'm sorry we did not get formally introduced," she continued. "I'm Cinderella to the two sisters." She laughed and nodded toward the other room.

"Do you really live here?" I asked.

"Not really, or at least not forever. I'm only here for three months more. Isis is my mentor and teacher. And I'm an oracle, too."

"And you're from London? How'd you end up in Glastonbury?"

"Sure am! I'm from the East end. I came here for research and ended up staying. We go to Egypt in a few months, so I am waiting for that and then heading back to London afterward. I assume you are coming to that?"

"No." I smiled. "I've always wanted to go, though."

"You should—it'll be awesome! I think we have twenty people going, which is the largest group we've had."

"Will the oracle, Naomi, be going?" I was not sure if I could ask, but Lesley appeared open, and it seemed a simple question.

"Oh, yes, she's one of the reasons many travel on these trips. She knows your secrets before you do." I wondered if she knew mine, but that could wait until tomorrow. "Why are you not staying with us, Anna?" Lesley asked.

"I didn't know that was an option. Frankly, I didn't even know about this place until I got here. I'm staying at the Gables Guesthouse."

"Oh, I know the owner there. She's a really kind lady, considering she's French. Good old Emilee."

I nodded. "She is kind and French."

"And she's a witch, you know."

It didn't surprise me. "Isn't everyone in this town?" I laughed.

"Yes, but she's a Salem witch!" Lesley responded.

"Salem, like in the States?"

"Yes," she said with an ominous voice and wide eyes.

I suddenly became cold, and a vision of a woman in a black dress stepping up to the gallows to be hanged passed over me. My hand reached to my throat as if I could feel a rope pulling around my neck.

"Weren't they burnt?"

Lesley shook her head. "No, you were correct the first time." She pointed to my hand and then my neck.

"Pardon?"

"Tell the truth, Anna: you saw her hanging, or going to be hanged."

My voice became hoarse. "How do you know that?"

"I guessed. But I was right, wasn't I? You saw her, didn't you? And I saw your hand reach for your throat!"

"I'm not sure what I saw. I saw gallows and a woman, but I didn't see her face. It was covered by a hood."

"Yes, that's correct; they covered their eyes. Those who sentenced them were afraid if they looked at them in the eyes, they would be cursed. You sure you didn't see who it was?"

"No, I told you, I only saw the hood." I bit my lip because I did not wish to share that I had seen the woman's face as they placed the hood over her head. She reminded me of Emilee. I didn't understand why Lesley was being so invasive.

"But you know what?" Lesley continued. "They were

cursed by karma anyway, and that's been carrying on for over three hundred years."

Wow, this woman can talk. "What do you mean?" I asked.

"Well, the people who sentenced those poor witches have had bad luck in their families ever since. Until all those curses are lifted, it gets passed from family member to family member through the bloodline." Despite her brash nature, I had to say she was captivating and knowledgeable, and she seemed more than willing to explain everything. I was getting tired of "we will see" responses.

"So what you're saying is that I could be paying the price for things my ancestors did?" I asked.

"Yes. One of my great-great-relatives, too many greats to mention, watched the trials. Her family was originally from England and had emigrated to that area. I recently did a search on my ancestors and learnt so much. That is another reason why I'm here, to learn about any of my families' and my own special powers."

"Your family had witches?"

"Yeah, but I'm not sure how good they were. Weird, right?"

"Yeah, but don't you mean how light or shadow they are, or whatever?"

She smiled at me and gave a hearty chuckle. "Yes, I suppose that's right."

"That's all sounding a bit confusing and a little scary," I remarked, but Lesley seemed quite happy with her statements. I think she saw that I was uncomfortable and decided to change the subject.

"So, Anna, when will you be back? You know we are having a 'Healing the Inner Goddess' workshop here on the weekend of June 7."

"Heal the Inner Goddess?" I said, intrigued.

"Yes, Naomi will be teaching it, and Isis will hold a ceremony for us in the Chalice Well. Or it's the other way around—I forget. Have you ever been to something like this?"

"No," I replied. "I'm really quite new to all of this."

"You will be great, I'm sure, and it's also a great way to meet people. I think we have around ten people signed up, and most of them are coming to Egypt, so this will be part of their preparation."

"Preparation? What's that?" I asked. "Isn't going to Egypt just going on holiday as a group of tourists with a good tour guide?"

"No, no, not at all!" she exclaimed. "When you travel with Isis, she teaches you how to open up the energy dimensions and portals to your past lives. You are supposed to experience the temples in a totally new and different way. Like in ancient times."

"Perhaps I'll think it over. In truth, it all sounds massively exciting, but I don't know if I have the funds for exotic trips just yet. Maybe next year when I am more established." I looked at my watch: it was nearly noon. "You know, I think I should be going back to the Gables to rest. Thank you for letting me know about the ceremony and the Egypt trip. I will be meeting with Naomi and Isis off-site in town tomorrow, but I am sure I will be back in the next few days. It's crazy: Naomi is letting me interview her for my book!"

Lesley went very still and stared at me. She made no comment, which I thought was odd. I decided to leave the topic there for the day. "I'll see you to the door, then, shall I?" she announced, and I guessed that was my prompt to leave. As I got up, Lesley caught me by my arm, the same grip as the day before. She whispered, "Don't mention the witches to anyone. I wouldn't want anyone to get the wrong impression about me, especially here. If you tell, I'll have to enact an ancient blood curse on you that my family used to use!"

As she said this, Isis opened the door with such strength that it crashed against the wall, and all the copper pans begin to clatter and fall off the shelf. We both froze. "Lesley, that's enough!" Isis said in a booming voice. "Anna is here at my invitation, and she doesn't need any of your speculation and spiritual karmic drama."

Lesley turned sheet white and said to me, "Anna, I'm sorry. I was just adding color to my day. It's not every day we get someone new around here. Just ignore me. I'm invisible." She smiled and winked at me, and for the first time, I saw a playfulness in her eyes.

"Apology accepted. Thank you, Lesley," I replied.

She looked back at Isis. "Isis, please persuade her to join the retreat next weekend. She would be such fun to have there."

Isis looked at Lesley and raised an eyebrow at her before saying to me, "I would love it if you could join us, Anna. It's a small group, but there are some very interesting people there whom I would like you to meet."

More characters. Great, was my first thought. "I'd love to come," I responded.

"I'll get the credit card machine," shouted Lesley, and off she went to the office.

"Let's go to the office," said Isis.

When we reached the small side room filled with papers and computers, Lesley was already there with the machine in hand and contract for me to sign.

"Here we go," she said. "Sign here, and I'll take the credit card." I hadn't even asked the cost; I thought it was an invite. She read my mind. "We aren't a charity, you know. That's £188. It's for two days with an excellent lunch provided each day."

"Lesley is quite the salesgirl." Isis laughed. "Is that okay, Anna?"

"Oh, yes, that's perfect!"

"Good. It's great to get the material business out of the way. Now, my dear, know that as you invest in yourself, the Lakshmi will follow."

"Pardon?" I asked. "The Lak-what?"

"Lakshmi," Lesley cut in. "The goddess of wealth and abundance. She will send you money when you need it."

"Ah, well, Lakshmi has been kind enough recently to cover my home and living expense for a few months recently, so why not put it toward my education?" I said as I handed over my card.

Once the transaction was complete, Isis shooed Lesley away. "Let's go back into the kitchen, Anna," said Isis. "I know we were meeting tomorrow, but perhaps now is the perfect time for me to share a bit of my story. Let's go back to the heart of the kitchen, where we won't be disturbed."

"Don't you have clients?" I asked.

"Oh, yes, but I just cleared a few entities from them and sent them on their way."

I followed her back the way we came and sat down at the dining table. "We can sit sixteen at that table, you know. A little tight, but we're all family here," Isis said. She went over to the kitchen sink and filled the kettle to make hot water for tea. Evidently whatever Lesley had made her was not enough.

"So how was your conversation with Naomi, my dear?"

"It was really good. She told me I could come for training, and I would love that."

"Good, good," said Isis, focused on preparing the tea tray.

"Isis, now that Lesley is gone, I'd like to ask about what she said about Salem and the witches."

"Lesley is just spouting nonsense, my dear. In time all of this will make sense, and you will bring clarity through for yourself, I am sure."

"Yes, clarity. I'm not sure what I'm seeing is that normal. I am seeing visions and people changing clothes. It is so strange, like I'm hallucinating."

"Who, my dear?"

"Well, just now I was sure I saw Naomi wearing clothes from the olden days, and I had an awful vision of Emilee—you know, the lady from the Gables…" I dropped my voice to a whisper, and Isis leaned in. "Of her being hanged."

"You are simply having a delayed vision, reading the latent energy off of someone. You are seeing something that may or may not have happened in the past. The mention of a place will sometimes trigger this. Your mind pulls together the movie, and you see it linked to the person you are around. Observe what you feel about this and then let it go, Anna. It's not healthy to dwell on such visions, especially if they are traumatic. Also, this may be something connected to only Emilee and Naomi, so it is not for you to interfere. And if you let Lesley be part of this, you can trust it will become a bigger drama than it needs to be. Now, let me find the scroll."

"The scroll?"

"Yes, the scroll. I forgot to give it to you earlier. It may have some answers for you." She motioned that we go back through to her office. "And do not forget the tea," she said as she pointed to the tray, ready and waiting.

I did as she asked and, as if in ceremony, picked up the tray and followed her back into her office.

Isis told me to sit down across from her desk while she looked for something. The office seemed small, even with the tall ceiling, but that could have been because there were so many bookshelves and books on them that they took up all of the space. She climbed on a ladder and looked around for something. She got down and returned with a scroll of light brown paper that was curled up and looked really old. She held it in her hand, whispered into it, and then closed her eyes.

When she opened them, she told me she was ready and that the scroll had given permission for her to share the story of the creation of the Philae temple.

"The scroll gave permission?" I asked.

"Yes, of course! This is the Scroll of Magic and Prophecy. It should shed some light on what is happening. The symbols contained within it will help you channel and focus your energy. Now, you must have many questions." Her voice was sharp and forceful.

"Oh, yes, please." I reached into my bag and pulled out my journal.

"Perfect. Then I will begin," she said, her eyes beginning to glaze over. She sat back in her large office chair and took the phone off its hook.

"Anna," she continued, "if you are going to continue on this journey and come to the gathering and retreat, you need to know certain things. A doorway appears to have been opened, and the time is shifting fast. You saw part of the destruction of Philae, and now I'm going to share its creation with you." With that, she smiled and opened her scroll. "Let's begin, shall we?" She motioned to me to pour the tea.

As I opened up my journal, Isis looked at me and laughed. "Darling, that will take far too long." She passed me a small machine and sat back into the chair. "Just hit record when you are ready. I'll be in a trance going into the Akashic library."

I looked around, but there were only the bookshelves. I gave her a questioning look, and she responded, "It's the library of everything. Didn't Lucinda tell you?" I was about to question this and how Lucinda had appeared in the conversation, but I simply made a note in my journal for questions to come later. If I kept interrupting, we would get nowhere, so I pressed the button on the tiny machine and placed it on the desk.

I could hardly breathe; I was so excited. My first interview! "Ready?" I whispered.

Isis then sat up straight and began to recite something in a language I didn't recognize. She looked like she was in a trance and held the old paper scroll close to her. "Okay, now I'm in the library. I've found the books I need, so now I'll begin."

CHAPTER 11

The temple to Isis was built under the rule of Egypt's last native pharaoh, Nectanebo I, in 380 BC, although worship of the goddess Isis had taken place there for millennia prior to that. It was known from the Emerald Tablets of Thoth that he and other Atlantean stargazers had come to Egypt to rule and share their magic and knowledge with the people. They had left instruction that, at all times, a sacred female should hold space for prayer and meditation. Originally, Philae was simply an area of caves and circles of rocks and crystals. When the wind rose and flowed through the site, the crystals would make noises like musical instruments. When the sunlight touched them, colors filled the sky. Here was a place where devotees to Isis and the sacred feminine energy could worship in peace, and it was a haven for those who wished to practice the spiritual arts of the day.

As time passed, the Nile created different levels of water, which created an island location. It could only be visited by boat, and only certain fishermen were allowed to carry those of holy intentions to the island. The pharaoh sent his workers to create a tribute temple to Isis, but no one would stay more than a few weeks; even the high priests who were chosen to visit from other temple sites left soon after, due to the nightmares and dark dreams they had. Only the pure of heart and soul could stay any length of time.

Then one day, during summer solstice, a time when the sun was at its fullest and the longest day of light, eight women came to the sacred site, drawn there by some unknown force. They all felt an emotional and spiritual connection to each other. Each of the women had faced adversity in their lives and had overcome it with an unwavering strength. The gods had seen their souls and deemed them the holiest of women in the land, and these women were chosen to become the Divine Eight. The gods and spirits had whispered to each woman and given her visions of many future realities. Each woman held a sacred value and unique understanding of herself and the world around her. The pharaoh heard of these women and consulted with the priests and his oracles.

The prophecies dictated that the women be left in peace for a year at the site, with no visitors whatsoever. Thus the eight women quickly grew close and settled into a routine of performing rituals to Isis and tending to their livelihood. They started to fish and weave baskets from reeds found by the riverbank. After a few months, they had built a high altar in the largest of the rooms created in the temple and painted symbols all over the walls. By the end of the year, they had built a small yet thriving community for themselves. They began to build smaller altars and places of worship around the temple; in time, these would become very powerful locations. Always they had the protection of the pharaoh, which created some unrest in the other temples over time.

On the eve of the summer solstice of their second year, the women were visited by outsiders. A group of thirty-three priests in a great procession could be seen approaching over the horizon. They had journeyed from Memphis to pay homage to the Divine Feminine and bestow their blessings on the Divine Eight. They brought tribute for the goddess Isis and for the Nile River.

The eight women were not frightened by their sudden appearance. They had collectively dreamed of the priests' arrival for the last year and had prepared for it. The eight women sat around their high altar, waiting for the priests to help them unlock their true divine energy and bring a new balance to the world. The priests arrived in six small boats and were silent and still upon arrival. Once all were on the island, they began their ritual.

As the priests walked, they wore white robes with golden sashes across their shoulders, each of them with head shaven and clarity in their eyes that had not been seen in this part of the world since the stargazers had left. They walked with a slow in-and-out breath in total unison, as if a cord of energy guided them perfectly on their journey.

As they reached the crystal beds outside the high altar, they began to snake around and create a circle. The last one of them walked around the inside of the circle, bowing his head and making eye contact with each of the priests. As he made this connection, each priest would close his eyes and kneel as if giving his permission for the sacred ritual to follow. The eight women remained perfectly still, focused on the altar of flowers they had prepared.

Night fell, and the eight women and the priests fell into deep meditation at the high altar. All remained silent, and nothing could be heard except the night owl and the occasional sound of the wild cats that roamed and hunted by night. When dawn broke, the head priest finally stood and silently walked around the women, gently touching each on her head and whispering a prayer in a strange language the women remembered from a long time ago. When he reached the final woman, he touched her arm and guided her to stand. He then placed a large golden ankh around her neck and pressed it toward her heart. He opened a box and handed it to her.

Inside, she saw eight scarabs of aqua blue, and each one had a different image. Next to them were eight small, rolled-up pieces of papyrus.

"These amulets, the blue scarabs, are a sign that you have been trusted with the wisdom of the gods. You have their protection, and all who you present them to will give you sanctuary. These scrolls contain the wisdom of the elders, those who visited our world in a time when gods still walked among us and wished to share their knowledge. With these eight scarabs and eight scrolls, you can create a truly sacred temple here on earth, a haven for those who seek the higher consciousness and the mysteries of times long past and yet to come. You have been chosen, and you can share only with those who hold and protect the sacred temples here in Egypt." He gently closed the box, and the woman held it against her heart.

Then the priest asked the other women to stand, which they did, and to look upon this woman he had chosen. With instinct, each woman felt her heart energy suddenly grow, and then they saw a bright light appear to shine upon the head of this one woman.

"Isis," the priest whispered.

"Isis," they all replied in unison.

"Isis!" the priest shouted.

The woman held the box above her head and in an otherworldly voice shouted, "I am Isis, daughter of the sun and moon, Divine Feminine and Mother Earth. May all be in sacred balance with life in this most holy of places."

☥

When the sun began to rise and the priest proceeded to lead the women out to the shoreline with Isis, the last in the line of eight. No one else stood on the sacred site except for the other thirty-two priests, still kneeling with heads bowed from the night before. They looked to be in perfect unity, like statues. As the eight women lined up at the water's edge, they joined hands and gently walked into the Nile's waters. When the water reached their waists, the sun was fully risen. They waited and watched the water around them turn to rose pink. In the distance, they could see the six boats making their way back to the island to collect the priests.

Behind them, the priest was now walking back to the altar and around the circle of thirty-two priests, touching each on the shoulder and allowing each of them to stand and meet his gaze. No words were given, only small nods and smiles. Then as he reached the last one, the circle broke, and the chain of priests began to walk in single file back to the shoreline and onto the boats to follow the Nile and travel back to Memphis. The women watched over their shoulders as the last of them left their sight.

Once the last boat had gone from sight, they heard a rumble, like an earthquake. The women raced out of the water and toward the temple, where they felt safe. The new Isis remained; she seemed in another world. She stood still in the water, held up her arms to the heavens, and began to chant and call. Suddenly the wind began to pick up, and for the first time that the women could remember, it started to rain. It rained so heavily that the seven women dared not step out of the safety of the temple. They watched as the raindrops bounced upon the temple courtyard and steps and formed pools of water around the site.

Slowly Isis rose out of the water and walked toward them. She was smiling and totally unafraid of this weather around her. As she reached the women, she chanted, "Ay Asher aya kan tu ay alum ah!"

The women did not understand the words but felt secure and protected by her energy. As Isis continued the chant, the rain eased, and the rivers ran calmly around the island. Suddenly the sky cracked open with a large bolt of lightning that shook the whole temple. When Isis returned to them, she was carrying the box, and she gathered them together. All of the women stood strong and formed a circle by holding hands. Isis placed the box in the center of the circle and stepped back to join them.

"Always and forever will we be bonded to this order. Always and forever will we serve the goddess, Isis," called Isis as she looked around the group and smiled, making eye contact with each woman.

"You are my high priestesses," she continued, "so full of light, love, and divinity. Together we will build and create a haven here on earth. We will bring balance to the divine world of masculine and feminine. We will surround ourselves with beauty and pleasure. We will embrace life and the lessons of the soul. We will support with truth, trust, and integrity. We will guard the past, present, and future. We are one heart and one dream collective. And so it is!"

The eight women then raised their hands, gripping the person next to them to keep steady and stay connected as extreme energy raced around them like a vortex of light. "And so it is!" they responded.

With that declaration, the land shook again, and to their amazement and surprise, the temple held. They began to feel a stronger energy than ever before.

"Mother Nile has heard our prayer and commitment. She

will protect us!" declared Isis. "Only those of true heart and life may visit and reside on this sacred land. We will keep balance for all of Egypt!" They all took a deep breath and began to gently let their hands drop. The sisterhood was now committed and their destiny in place.

After this, they returned to their own personal spaces and began to plan the expansion and life within their sacred site. Each woman would undertake a certain part of employment in service to Isis and her temple. They began to debate how temple life would be. Each voice was listened to in time, and all thoughts were embraced and welcomed.

As would be the protocol going forward, Isis would make the final decision. Her wisdom was channeled directly; only one other, known as Serket, had the total gift of prophecy and insight, as was common for temple protocol. Serket would serve as the oracle, the keeper of the high altar, and would help keep the balance between all creatures in nature. All could consult with her, even Isis, when they had questions or needed clarity. It was to her that Isis entrusted the sacred scrolls and scarabs in the box given to her by the priest. It contained many messages, and both women knew it would take many days and nights to learn and understand.

Serket gave great wisdom, and her first request was that each woman find a place within the temple that gave her great peace. She asked each of them to go within themselves and ask what destiny they needed to create within this temple. They were to return at midday, and Isis would agree on their roles.

The other six women wandered out from the temple, where the pools of water were already drying up; the island appeared safe to wander around. Each of the women took a deep breath in and waited, then as if by magical command, they all began to walk around in silence.

When the sun had positioned itself at the high point of the sky, all of the women felt an energetic pull back toward the sacred high altar. In silence, they each touched the ground where they had been most at peace and marked it with a signature from themselves. The women then made their way back to the altar and felt a leap in their hearts, a comfort that they were supported and never alone, when they saw each other again.

As they reached the high altar, they saw Isis and Serket waiting for them. Isis was now wearing a long white robe with a golden sash in the same fashion as the priests had worn. She greeted them warmly with humbleness and sincerity. "My sisters, this is indeed a great day," she began as she motioned around her.

Behind her and Serket, there was a beautiful sight on the high altar: fruits, leavened bread, and glass bowls with cool fresh water adorned it. "Go and eat, for you all will need your strength," Isis announced. This was indeed a feast, and each woman took her time to select her food, careful to be sure there was plenty to share and nurture the rest.

After blessing and giving thanks for their food, they ate and felt the essence of the land run through their entire beings. Once they had all finished, Isis once again gathered them into a circle outside beside the crystals. "Now is the time of our destiny and truth," she said. "Each of you will tell of what you discovered this morning, and what you will bring to this order of the Divine Feminine at the Temple of Isis. This is a time you were born to connect with, to anchor the Divine Feminine spirit. Proclaim how you will serve our Mother Goddess!"

The women each spoke up in turn:

The first woman proclaimed, "I will serve this sisterhood through Renenutet, and give her offerings so that the harvest will be bountiful and sweet. I will pray each day to the Earth that we are blessed with water and food with which we can feast. Our livestock will be sacred, and our grains will be blessed. I will bring forward protection and security. I will watch over this island with all the love and protection a mother has for her child. Each season we will honor the snake goddess with ceremony and ritual." Just then, a cobra slithered by outside the room, a sign that the goddess approved.

The second woman proclaimed, "I will serve the temple through Qetesh, and bring forward sensuality and the tantric arts. Every woman will celebrate her body and worship it as she does the gods. May the goddess bestow the knowledge of the power and sensuality of the feminine spirit upon each of you and empower all women to seek pleasure that befits her own needs."

The third woman proclaimed, "I will serve the sisterhood through the sky and sun, Hathor, and bring forward the knowledge of destiny and soul purpose. May all who reside in this temple be made fully aware of their potential. I will go to Dendara, establish a temple there, and serve as high priestess to Hathor."

The fourth woman proclaimed, "I shall take up the mantle of Thoth and watch over divine and mortal law and writing in our land. I will protect and inspire scribes to write the truth. I will bring forward love and compassion and balance between all creatures upon the earth. I shall help connect the writings of the underworld to the mortal one."

The fifth woman proclaimed, "I too will serve Hathor, as the Mother, and watch over birth and help to bring forward new children. I will assist women from the time of conception to birth. These children will be born into temple life and thrive within its sanctuary. I will create a birthing temple within the temple at Dendara and serve as its oracle."

The sixth woman proclaimed, "I will serve as Seshat's oracle at the Temple of Ra in Heliopolis and become the keeper and protector of our ancient wisdom. Never will be forgotten the stories of the ancients, of the ego, power, and greed that caused Atlantis to fall. We will learn from their mistakes and draw greater knowledge as a result. I will help facilitate learning and scholarship so that no one may fear the unknown. May the light rays from Ra's eye illuminate a path to true wisdom and understanding."

Once the sixth woman had spoken, Isis smiled; all was in total compliment and balance. Serket now spoke. "Dear sisters, this is great news. I would like to share that I see each of you already wearing this aura and mantle. You have stepped into your first initiation in realizing your truth and potential. I am here for you and will always speak my truth. It is my destiny to connect with our star mothers and fathers in the other dimensions and universe. I choose this space beside the high altar and will work with each of you to bless your space of choosing and to design a place of great importance and wisdom for us all. It is my honor to serve you all." She bowed to the women in front of her.

They now all looked to Isis, waiting with bated breath to see what she had to say. Slowly Isis stood and smiled at each of them. "Yesterday, we were just a tribe of eight women, guiding our destiny one day at a time. We were sacred in heart and soul. The gods above and below have bestowed a great blessing upon us and rewarded our consciousness with gifts. We are sisters, and each of us has found a way to share our gifts not only with each other but also with those who choose to come and live within our temple walls.

"Together we will build this temple and future temples to house those souls that are guided toward us. When our energy is pure and strong, we will attract those of similar consciousness. We will worship the Nile and the sacred mother who feeds and nourishes us; with that, we will bring great abundance and prosperity to Egypt, both upper and lower. We will build our values on justice and fairness. We will stand hand in hand with trust and respect. We are women and have a divine connection with the masculine energies of this land. By joining and creating life, we bring a future to this temple and way of beingness.

"Our choices will come from our hearts. Our words and wisdom will come from our hearts. No more will we fear secrets or any of the sad pains of human life.

"We are the Sacred Eight, and I have been appointed to nurture and guide you. I am not your queen, nor am I your mistress. When I pass, my soul, bound to the mantle of Isis, will carry on into the next generation and the next one, and so on, until the gods find another soul worthy of the challenge. You all have chosen to become the voices of your patron gods and will share the same honor of your souls being bound to your roles. Together we will oversee feminine worship in Egypt for thousands of years to come! We will step out from this high altar today and take our places. I will hold my sacred space at this high altar at the heart of this temple. As we leave this altar, this holy of holy places, we step forward, never again to hide our gifts, never again to be hidden and afraid of the gifts from the gods that come to us. More sisters will join us and brothers too in time, our numbers will grow."

As she spoke, the women felt her words run through them with truth, and they felt a sense of elation and joy. Isis then asked each of them to come once again to the waters of the Nile and make their contracts with the divine mother of the Nile and the gods themselves. The women all agreed, and as they once again stood waist height in the water, they saw the most magnificent sight. The water became golden, a rich, luxurious flow all around them. They stood in what appeared to be liquid gold.

At the moment the sun disappeared, each woman went into a deep meditation and made her personal contract and solemn promise. Each one thought about the gift she brought forward and how she could work together to bring ritual and harmony to Egypt. As the rays faded, each of them slowly made her way from the water to the temple, and the group began to light the fires and prepare their food. Night fell, and they fell into a deep sleep. They would each dream a vision that night which would inspire their destinies.

Isis stayed awake until the last of them slept, and then she took her leave to go the high altar. That night she would dream about the ceremonies and rituals of initiation. Serket would also dream of future things to come; for as the oracle attending Isis, she would witness both light and dark.

That night, Serket drifted into a peaceful state, but she had a nightmare. She saw the temple crumbling and everyone running in a panic. She knew no one and nothing was familiar, except for the space currently known as the high altar. From this space, she saw blood running down the temple stairs.

Serket awoke shaking and in a cold sweat. She then rushed from her bed to the altar with a torch in hand, heading up the stairs. To her surprise, there in the corner was Isis, totally upright and in deep meditation. "Oh, Isis, I had a most terrible dream," cried Serket.

Isis was roused and startled. "What dream?" she asked. Isis noticed Serket searching around for something. "What are you searching for?"

"Blood," Serket exclaimed. "So much blood. I saw chaos and blood running down the altar. They were coming for the temple, hiding in the night—horrible figures with soulless eyes. I think they were coming to steal the sacred box of scrolls and scarabs." She was shaking like a leaf.

Isis placed her hand upon Serket's arm, and the oracle stilled. She sat down next to Isis. Isis thought a moment and then smiled. "No one will ever harm anyone in this sacred space," she said. "Not now that we have sworn the divine contract of sisterhood and initiation. This must have been a parallel of what may have happened if we had not created such a nest of purity and love, surely."

Serket sighed. She trusted Isis with all her heart, so she agreed. "I am so sorry," she offered, lying down next to the space Isis had created for herself. "I don't know what is creating this vision of fear."

"It is all good, my beloved sister. Now, sleep," Isis said, and she placed a rug for Serket to rest her head. "Tomorrow will be a day of rejoicing and greatness."

However, Isis was most wise, and the next morning as the women gathered for a new day, she made sure each of them was formally entrusted with a scroll and scarab. They were to be the guardians and watch over the magic brought forward from the Atlantean masters.

These scrolls and scarabs would be passed on through the priestess initiate line to ensure the sacred lineage was protected. If a priestess left or passed into the spirit world, she would entrust it to her dearest sister. That way, the magic would remain in Philae under the watchful eye of the current Isis.

☥

"And so it was. We lived in great prosperity for many generations and ushered in a new golden age of worship and scholarship in Egypt," explained Isis, coming out of the regression. "I was many times their leader, the high priestess of Isis. My soul was bound to that mantle, as were others for thousands of years, guiding the oracles and priestesses of the feminine temples and keeping balance with the priests. We were the constant in the ever-changing political landscape of Egypt.

"The secrets and knowledge passed from generation to generation, and we had even amassed a huge collection of scrolls and sacred texts from our oracles who would record the wisdom. The original sacred box remained in Philae, and at various times, we would share the scarabs or scrolls with those in need. We were guardians, but never owners or masters, of this precious magic. After many years, the knowledge of the scrolls circulated around Egypt and helped it flourish. This made us want to spread our knowledge, and we felt compelled to go to other places to teach it. One such place was at Delphi. We taught the women there how to channel the gods and bring forward visions of the future.

"However, it was a mistake to let the scrolls and scarabs leave Philae. They were meant to be kept together by the sacred eight priestesses who were chosen to be their guardians, but we wanted everyone to have the ability to create temples. Unfortunately, at times they were misused or copied. The scarabs acted as protective amulets, but they also were used as a way to decode some of the more dangerous secrets of the scrolls. Even after all this time, we don't fully understand the power of the scarabs and the scrolls. Our temple here in Glastonbury, our Sanctuary, was simply the next one in line to protect them, as they had been for thousands of years in Egypt's history before that. Part of our job was to use the eight scrolls and scarabs to create harmony on earth, where all living things can coexist without violence and death."

"Like the garden of Eden?" I asked. I had felt it was now the time for the questions. Isis remained in a trance.

"Yes." Isis nodded. "Precisely. Forces beyond our control have prevented this, but perhaps one day in one lifetime, this will happen."

"What did the scrolls contain?"

"Well, there were eight original scrolls, which spawned many others, written by priests and priestesses about certain aspects of each. However, the original eight each had a specific topic it covered. There was the Scroll of Magic and Prophecy, the Scroll of Creation, the Scroll of Light and Shadow, the Scroll of Protection, the Scroll of Goddess and Fertility, the Scroll of Truth and Integrity, the Records of Life, and finally the Scroll of Death and Resurrection. Using what we knew, we were able to create a utopian temple at Philae that was perfectly balanced. Each had a matching scarab to authenticate it and activate it.

"But that came to an end when Cleopatra VII, the most famous Queen of Egypt, died. When she fell, we all fell. Her feminine energy was tied to the temple. It was during her reign that I was to pass the mantle of Isis to a new soul, but I never got the chance. We were cursed when the temple fell, and we became fragmented. The eight of us were never all together again in another lifetime. That sacred bond that we had shared for so long was broken by our own shortsightedness and ego. During the final days of Cleopatra, many dark deeds and karmic curses were created, and many of us have been paying for it ever since. I think a big part of it was because we lost most of the scrolls. Or rather, I believe they were stolen or sold.

"Our souls were cast out of Egypt, and all of our subsequent lives were lived in exile, living and reliving over and over again the same traumas that stemmed from our fall. For over two thousand years now, we have all been reincarnating to clear the way back to the golden age. We have been wholly unsuccessful, battling between ourselves and betraying or slaying each other when we do manage to find some of our own. I pray for the timeline to present itself every day to release us all from this never-ending cycle, to help us create our temples and sanctuaries here on the earth again. But until we can all unite and release the karma from that Cleopatra timeline in one lifetime and resolve the trauma that has followed us, we won't be able to do that."

Isis paused a moment. "Now do you see why you see Emilee and Naomi? They have this karma, this unresolved trauma, between them from many lives that has yet to resolve." Isis opened her eyes.

"Is that why I saw Salem?" I asked.

"Possibly."

"And the oracles, were they part of that group, do you think?"

"I don't know," she answered. "Time will tell. But it is the oracles that see the vision and will, I'm sure, in time reveal themselves. They have a sacred proclamation and initiation that allows them to not only enter the Akashic records and Halls of Amenti but also change the course of history. Pharaohs who sought their knowledge had insight and great power."

Why, oh why, is that always her answer? "Time will tell" was still not great for me. All it did was give me nightmares and confusion.

I went to ask another question, but Isis signaled that it was time to stop and placed the scroll on the table. She reached over and stopped the voice recorder. She then stood and placed her hands together in a prayer. "Blessed be, Anna. I think this is enough to get you started." She signaled to my journal.

I had written three words and a page of questions. "I don't think my reporting skills are so good," I said.

"Nonsense. You were wonderful. Go back to the Guesthouse, Anna. Meditate, remember, and write from your heart. The heart and soul never forget. Think about what I have shared. Now, I think this should be all for a while; let's break the date at the coffee shop, and the next time we meet should perhaps be the weekend retreat. I will be at the Chalice Well to greet you on that Saturday morning, the seventh, yes?"

"Yes." I got up and thanked her for her time, and then I headed back to the Gables to snuggle into my bed and write. It was late afternoon, and I was exhausted but beyond excited. Finally, I had a story I could run with, and I had characters to explore. Ideas and images flooded my mind. I flew out of the Sanctuary and back to the Gables.

CHAPTER 12

The Gables was again quiet and still when I returned. Emilee had left a note on my bed to say she hoped all was well and that there was a salad in the refrigerator. She was attending a meditation group in town.

Perfect, I thought. *I feel as if I have been talking to people for days, and my voice is shot.* It struck me that even though I was learning so much, I was not taking the time to integrate, but I felt too drained to do anything about it. I shrugged off the thought, grabbed the salad, and retired to my room for the rest of the day.

☥

Having a past life regression was powerful, but I was still skeptical of why this would benefit me. After all, wouldn't it keep bringing up old wounds and fears that would disturb me for no reason? The story of the creation of the Temple of Isis felt so real when Isis told it. Good logic and reason told me it was because she was simply a good storyteller from whom I could learn a thing or two. However, something in my heart told me it was more than just a story that I was listening to—it was a truth so real that I felt it in my bones. I wanted so badly to believe in all of this, but something inside of me prevented me from truly letting go and believing.

After the day I had, I couldn't even begin to try unpacking what that blockage was, so I decided to rest on my bed and let my mind drift away to whatever thoughts it wanted to drift toward.

I was woken a few hours later by the sound of a cat crying. I pulled my stiff limbs out of bed and rubbed the sleep from my eyes. I ran down to the kitchen to find Wallis waiting at the door. That was strange because Emilee often had her in the kitchen so she did not disturb guests. I looked to the side, and all of the keys were on the stand, which meant the few guests who were staying were out for the evening.

As I opened the kitchen door, Wallis rushed past me and immediately went to the window that overlooked the garden. A sudden sense of uneasiness overcame me, so I turned on the lights. I figured I was just feeling a bit peckish, so I wandered to the refrigerator to see if Emilee had any sweet rolls left from breakfast. To my delight, she did, so I pulled them out and sat at the kitchen table to eat them.

I noticed that Wallis was still looking out the window and pawing at the glass panes, as if to ward off something outside. I got up and looked out the window, but I could not see a thing. "What do you see out there, girl?" I asked, stroking her back. She gave me a look and turned back to the window to hiss at it. It alarmed me slightly. I had heard that foxes sometimes roamed the hills and got into people's gardens, so I flipped the switch to the lamps outside the back. I couldn't see anything out there, which should have made me feel a little better, but I still felt uneasy.

The cat got up to stand near the back door, so I figured she needed to go out, like she normally did. But when I went to unlock the door, she hissed at me and nipped at my ankles.

I backed away and let her stand there, motionless and erect, like the guards outside of Buckingham Palace. I wasn't one to take an animal's warning, but in this instance, it seemed best to heed hers.

Because I was up, I decided to go back upstairs and write. I took my journal and favorite pen out of my bag and set myself up comfortably at the desk in my room. After taking a deep breath, I opened my journal and put the pen to an open page, ready for the words to flow out of me, but they didn't. I sat there for an hour staring at a blank page. I guess I was having writer's block, which was frustrating because I wasn't even a proper writer yet. Earlier, at the Sanctuary, inspiration flowed through me and I had ideas to spare. But now that I was at the Gables, my energy had dropped, and all words left me. I wondered if Lesley had put a spell on me. Perhaps she did not want me to write. *Am I even supposed to write this?* I pondered on this.

What is a proper writer? That answer came easily. *Someone who creates a stunning tale that affects people and makes them feel something, or someone who can write a story that sells books. Or is it both?*

Suddenly I felt very overwhelmed. I'd only been here a few days, and my plan was already blowing up in my face. Just when I seemed to figure out what I wanted to do, the winds changed, and I was back to square one. I couldn't be a writer if I couldn't write. What cruel fate was this?

I was venturing into this vastly exciting spiritual world that had so much to offer, and I couldn't figure out how to write about it. But maybe that wasn't the problem. Maybe it was that this world felt too close to me. I felt so vulnerable whenever I was around Isis or Naomi. Everything they had taught me or shown me thus far scared me because it felt like they were showing me the self that I wasn't ready to face.

Could it all be real, then? If I felt this affected by it all, how could it not be real? If it were just a story, I would be fine right now. *If it holds truth, then it is fact, recounting a series of historical events. But then, don't all stories hold truth? That is why we tell them. It isn't always the words, the characters, or the setting that holds truth; it's what they represent and what they make us feel. We all can find truth in a good story. That's the mark of proper authors. They tell a story in which everyone can find truth. They wade through the light and the dark and translate the ephemeral and fleeting notions of true being into words that capture what we all want to know.*

I was roused from my thoughts by the buzzing of my phone in my pocket. Sighing, I took it out and saw it was Lucinda calling. I picked up the phone, and we exchanged pleasantries. Then she asked me how I was feeling, not out of politeness but out of genuinely caring, in a way that was meant to get me to say what I was really feeling. Her tone and phrase actually made me feel emotional.

"I am a little overwhelmed, I have to say," I croaked, my voice going a bit hoarse with emotion. "I went to the Sanctuary yesterday and met—"

She interrupted, "Naomi and Isis."

"Yes."

"And how was that?"

"Well, that's the thing: I'm not sure. They did a past life regression with me back to Philae, you know, the priestess temple you mentioned in the class we did about goddesses. I thought it would be so beautiful, but it wasn't. It was dark, and everything was decaying. It left me feeling really confused, or rather scared. I wasn't prepared for all of that."

"What exactly did you see, Anna?" I noticed that she was now using my formal name. I had learnt that Lucinda used

Annie to address me sometimes as if she were treating me as a child, but she used Anna when I was one of her peers.

"I saw the death of Isis, or I felt it happen. I didn't actually see it; I just heard a scream and I knew it was hers. It was the scream you make when you are ripped from the earth too soon. She must have been murdered. I felt her presence, and then I felt it leave. Does that make sense?" The phone went silent for so long, I thought that the call had been dropped. "Hello? Lucinda, are you there?" I asked.

"I am," Lucinda replied. "Are you sure she was murdered?"

"Yes, although I couldn't tell you why or how. Again, I didn't see it happen."

"Then it has begun."

"What does that mean?"

"Nothing," she replied, changing her tone. "Anna, you are moving so fast, and I'm really proud of you. Remember, though, that this will be a little hard on your soul. It's a lot to take in. Whatever happens next will not be easy, and you will question everything, even more than you already have. You are to be given a great task, the most important one. You will come to figure that out, in time."

"What is it with you and Isis telling me I'll find out 'in time'? I wish you were here so you could explain this in person, because I have no idea what you are talking about."

"Well, I was thinking about going to the retreat weekend in June."

"Will you, please? I will be there, and I miss you terribly."

"For you, Anna, of course I will. I'm going to come down and join in sometime on that Saturday, and perhaps we can have a private dinner later in the day. You know, I saw Laura this morning, and she mentioned you had left some clothes and was going to post them. Perhaps now I will just bring them to you myself. Emilee and I told her she should come to Glastonbury herself to get away, but she seemed adamant about finishing up some spiritual business here."

"You saw Laura, and she spoke to Emilee?" I asked incredulously.

Lucinda didn't answer me directly and changed the subject. "Oh, well, I am very much ready for a break."

"Do you need a room here?" I asked. "You can always share mine, if you want."

"Oh, dearie, I would never put you out like that. Emilee will have a room available for me. I'll call and check with her later tonight."

"I think she's at a meditation group for most of the night."

"I know; we spoke earlier today. She's a bit of a night owl, like me, so I suspect she'll still be up for a quick chat when she is done."

"Oh, wonderful. It will be perfect if you come. Now I feel that everything is starting to come together!"

"Me too, Anna. Now, I must let you go. You need to be well rested for your meeting tomorrow." With that, we bid each other farewell and hung up.

How did she know about my meeting?

It was so strange that Lucinda, Emilee, Isis, Naomi, and even Lesley, to some extent, always knew what was going on around me but wouldn't tell me what it was. I felt as if I was missing from this secret club. It crossed my mind that Lucinda and the others probably knew Alice too. For the first time, I had a feeling of mistrust toward Lucinda. In fact, I had a feeling of mistrust toward all these women.

I pondered that for a while. It was like musical chairs; they all seemed to have a chair at this sacred table, and I was still looking for mine. Then this would be it. This would be my motivation. What did all these women have in common, and why had they crossed my path?

I tried to start some writing, but again putting pen to paper did not bring anything forward, and neither did my staring at the computer when I brought it out. I decided to put everything away and start fresh first thing in the morning. I looked for the small voice recorder to listen to as I got ready for bed, but it was missing from my bag. *Oh no. I must have left it on the table in the office at the Sanctuary when I ran out,* I thought.

No worries. I would collect it upon my return, or perhaps Naomi would find it and bring it tomorrow for when we meet. All I had to do was transcribe the audio, and that alone was a novel. As that thought came, so did a text from Naomi:

Sacred Traveler Cafe, tomorrow, 10:00 a.m., okay?

Thankfully this was one thing I did not have to wake up for in the middle of the night and worry about. I sent a simple "Yes, thank you."

I heard the cat meowing downstairs, and then she stopped. I suddenly got a shiver, so I decided it was time to go to bed. Something also inside me told me I should perhaps lock my door as well that night. Who knew what visions would now appear in my dreams?

The next morning, I awoke shaking and feeling such fear. This was not a dream I wanted to remember or write about.

All I could remember was being back in the temple again. I was in a long corridor with doors lining the walls on either side. At either end of the corridor, the lights were being held by the sinister figures cloaked in dark smoke. I had a feeling what would happen next. I ran from door to door, attempting to open one, scrambling to find just one that would open.

"Don't let them get you," a faraway voice called.

The figures were closing in again. I was trying to get away from them by running and trying to open the right door. Only one doorway appeared then: the old dark wooden one with the ankh symbol near the handle. As I tried hopelessly to open the door, I could hear a faint crying from the other side. It pushed me to keep at it, to make it open.

"Find her!" Again the voice was relentless with its advice.

The crying became louder, and I focused on getting the lock to break. I was so desperate to open the door that I forgot to look behind me. Suddenly, the shadows were right behind me. As I braced myself for their impact, I was blinded by a flash of green light, and then everything went dark.

I shook it off as best I could and got ready for the day. I went down to breakfast and saw that the dining room had some new guests. We made polite conversation. I hardly felt like eating, but I knew if I didn't, Emilee would suspect something—which, of course, she did. It was the weekend hikers and walking crowd, and they had different intentions for visiting Glastonbury. These guests did not linger over their meal and were up and out for a whole new day of adventures. They looked like I had when I arrived, which was only a few days ago: eager and fresh with anticipation.

Emilee found me staring into my coffee cup, alone in the room, so she sat down with me. "Bad dreams, Anna?" she asked.

"The worst," I replied in a hoarse voice.

"Ah, these are the nightmares. Why, it is no wonder! A dark presence surrounds us last night."

That would explain Wallis, I thought. "Can't you stop them?" I whined. "You are good with potions and elixirs. Isn't there something you can whip up for me? I swear it was so terrible, I think I'll not wake up from the next one."

"I wish it was that easy, ma chère." She touched my hand. "These are your dreams, your creation, and your reality. If you do not like them, change them, or try to listen to what they are telling you. Then go from there. Oui?" I smiled and agreed with her. "Why don't you help me clear table, and you can share your dream?" she continued. "This often sheds light on the situation and helps release real message from the dream."

As we cleared the table, I recounted my dream: the doors, the crying baby, the lanterns, the dark figures, and that green light. *What does it all mean?* Emilee said nothing and simply nodded and moved slowly about the room.

"I think this was a past life I was returning to," I said at the end.

"What makes you say that?" asked Emilee.

"Well, my first past life regression was at Philae, and that's where I seemed to be in my dream."

"Ah, I see. Did you have anything happen yesterday?" she enquired.

I was about to say no when I remembered Lesley. "Yes, actually," I responded. "Do you know anything about the Salem witches?"

Emilee had been stacking dishes at a table facing away from me, and her back stiffened at my mention of Salem. She kept herself turned away as she spoke. "Yes, that was a very sad and dark time," she said in a gruff voice.

"Do you think that had anything to do with it?"

"No, no. It was probably your talk with Isis."

"Well, then maybe it was just a dream and nothing more. I will say those dark figures were mighty terrifying, though. Do you think that was my past life?"

"Who can say?" She shrugged and walked back toward the kitchen with a pile of neatly stacked dishes.

I followed her. "Do you think you could have been there? Have you ever imagined that time in history?" She stopped in the doorway and looked sad. I suddenly felt uncomfortable; I should not have pressed her. She had been the kindest person to me, and here I was, questioning her and testing her. "I'm sorry, Emilee, that was not called for," I said.

"It's okay. You may ask those questions at the right time, ma chère, but not now. It is not right," she said.

I nodded. I understood and felt a little embarrassed about saying anything in the first place.

"Now, did you have somewhere you need to be?" Emilee asked. "Are you meeting anyone today, ma chère?"

"Oh, yes, I nearly forgot. I'm doing my first interview with Naomi!" She knew even though I didn't tell her. I was right: they did know what was going on around me and were talking about it to each other.

"Well, that's wonderful! You should go prepare," she said. I felt like a small child being told to go play. I placed my pile of dishes near the sink and ran back upstairs to get ready.

Time to get moving with my interviews and figure out the bigger picture of these women and their connection to me and each other, I thought. Now I could and would start to write. *Day one: time to hit the reset button.*

CHAPTER 13

I met Naomi at 10:00 a.m. at the Sacred Traveler Café, not far from the Goth's shop. She seemed calm and relaxed when she arrived, unlike the nervous wreck I must have appeared to be. I was so unsure of everything but excited at the same time. *What does Naomi have to tell me? Can she answer all of my questions? Do I really want all of my questions answered?*

"Let's go through here; this is where I sometimes meet new clients. It's open but private," Naomi said. She led me through a small, curtained area near the back of the room. It was simply decorated but very bright and cheerful, in contrast to the tarot reader a few doors away. The waitress followed us, stood outside the curtain, and wrote down our order.

Naomi ordered a pot of herbal tea and some scones for us and then looked at me curiously. "You want to know why I am in Glastonbury, of all places, yes?" I was startled by this, but I suppose I should have assumed that everyone around me could read my thoughts. "Not all of your thoughts," she continued. "Just the ones about me." She laughed. "Do you want to know?"

"Yes, I do, actually. Is it because of Isis?" I asked.

"Yes and no. Why don't I just show you?"

Oh no. Not another vision. I felt so sick the last time.

"Don't worry. This tea we are drinking will prevent the same nausea you had last time. Now, let me show you my story."

She leaned back into the chair, and her eyes glazed over as if in a trance. Then she broke out of whatever state she was in to look at me. "You are recording, yes?"

"Yes, I guess so." I began to fumble in my bag and realized I had forgotten I had left the voice recorder at the sanctuary. I pulled my journal out of my bag.

Naomi looked at me and shook her head, "Too distracting," she muttered. "Here, use this," and she handed me a small device. "It's perfect for recording voice and connects to the computer."

"Now, let's get back to work," she said and closed her eyes.

I came from a family of European travelers. My father was an Irish traveler whose family had been merchants and tailors for generations. My mother was a Romani traveler from northern Italy and was gifted in the magical arts. I believe my gifts came from her. Because Dad was an Irish traveler, her family disowned my mother because she broke tradition by marrying outside the group. However, that didn't stop my parents as they were in love, and they travelled around Eastern Europe until they settled in a quaint village in Czechoslovakia, as it used to be known.

My dad could pass as an ordinary citizen, but my mother's dark skin and hair gave her away, and the two of them wanted to have a child. My mother had foreseen dark forces that would interfere with women and their fertility in the future. So, they fled to England, where they had me. Years later, the government was hostile towards travelers and instituted a sterilization policy in 1973 for all Romani women.

We had a blessed and harmonious life for a few years. My dad worked as a tailor in town, and my mother ran a potions and herbal remedies business out of our caravan. We were able to live on some land of a local farmer. I remember helping her find honeysuckle and picking cattails for her. My dad would make me the most beautiful dresses out of the spare bits of fabric. These were some of the happiest times in my life. But, unfortunately, it didn't last.

It was the summer, and I had just turned twelve. I remember because it was hot out, and my mother was yelling at me for only wearing a tank top and shorts, saying that I was turning into a woman and needed to cover up more. A landlord of the shop my dad worked at took a jacket in to be tailored. When he came to pick it up, he searched the pockets and accused my dad of stealing the money that was in it. My father assured him that there was no money in the jacket when he received it and that he ran an honest business. The man laughed at him and said that gypsies didn't know how to run honest businesses, and he stormed off without paying for the jacket. When my father got home that night, he was upset over the encounter. My mother sent me out to fetch some lavender so she could make some calming tea for him. I was a curious child and always liked to take my time getting back so I could look up at the stars a little bit longer. When I returned, I could hear loud shouts coming from our caravan, so I hid behind a nearby tree. I heard my mother pleading with someone to stop and then a sharp slapping sound that quieted her. Finally, I heard shots crackle through the air. Everything was silent. I saw a man stumble out of the caravan and walk off toward the village. Later, I would find out that he was the man my dad had talked about earlier that night. He killed my parents over twenty pounds, which he later found out his son had stolen from him to have a night with one of the streetwalkers. It was devastating. My whole world was gone in an instant.

After my parents' death, I was moved into my uncle's flat above his dry-cleaning shop in London. He was my dad's brother, another black sheep. They were a humble and kind family, but I was constantly reminded that I was a guest and should be grateful for the attic room they had surrendered up to me. At sixteen, I decided to stop going to school; my mother had been insistent I go to school, but without her there, it seemed pointless. I worked in the shop my uncle owned, taking in dry-cleaning and laundry, and helping customers with their alterations.

After about a year, I had settled into an uneventful routine of it all there. The work was enjoyable enough, but I never quite felt fulfilled mending trousers, hemming skirts, and folding other people's underwear. One Sunday afternoon, a cousin of mine decided she wanted to break up our routine and dragged me to a tarot card reading. She said she was tired of hearing me complain about the humdrum of everyday life. We went all the way to the Golden Heart Pub in the East End, where the owner, Gina, gave the tarot readings. I wasn't the least bit excited for her to read my destiny. However, I had been in a rut for a year, so what could I do?

It turns out the reading was more meaningful to me than I ever could have imagined. She told me I was an oracle from Egypt. That stunned me because as she told me what my past life had been like, I felt like I was experiencing it. It was amazing! I began to have visions as she talked, and I saw these wonderful images of me in silks and jewels, standing in the sunlight.

Gina then told me that my life would be charmed if I, as I had in my past lives, started to work in the psychic arts. She sparked something in me, and I wanted to know more. Gina offered me tarot and astrology lessons in exchange for working behind her bar two nights per week.

Thinking on it, any outsider would think I got the short end of the deal, but I learnt so much from her, and it was truly an invaluable experience. And, hey, I can also make a perfect gin and tonic, which is a skill of the utmost importance. As time went on, Gina trusted me more with the tarot readings and would let me do readings for her clients. I helped Gina grow her tarot reading business, and soon enough, the cash I was making in a week was more than I'd earned in a few months at the shop with my family. I could draw astrological charts in my mind without a computer back then.

Eventually, Gina offered me a room to live in and to come on full-time. At that point, I decided to change my name to Dawn Starchild, a more fitting name for my profession. My business cards even reflected that with the words "Psychic and Astrology Services" emblazoned on the front in gold ink. She and I worked very well together, no matter how busy or noisy the bar downstairs got. We were always present with each other, impervious to outside influences. It was such a gratifying time in my life. But she had said mine would be a charmed life, and I yearned for that to start because I didn't quite feel charmed working in a bar.

I remember, on a particularly rowdy night, a big football match was on telly. After the third fight broke out, Gina said how sick she was of running the pub. It seemed the alcohol was attracting a darker energy around us than we wanted. I remember the corner of her eyes turning up in a smile at a funny notion. We were supposed to be psychics, yet we couldn't even see the bar fights in our own futures. So we decided that we needed to create our own futures. New buildings were going up around us, and everyone had a website. We were behind the times, but the phones kept ringing; I have to say our clients were very loyal.

It struck me that we should change the pub and turn it into a spiritual center. I had seen a vision of a place where people came for readings and healings and perhaps bought things such as crystals. We had been playing at this craft upstairs, and perhaps it was time to take it professionally downstairs.

We turned the upstairs into a series of small rooms for individual meditation and healings, and we attracted some very interesting yet gifted women who rented space. We turned the main bar into a sanctuary of sorts for herbal teas, and we served organic food. We started advertising on a website for psychic readings that one could pay for by the minute. It took a few years, but we gained a large following and even went international.

One day, a producer from a small television network came to us for an astrology reading. He was this tall, handsome man with the most wonderful smile. I must say, I was quite happy that I would be doing his reading that day. He asked me what I saw in his future. I told him that he would soon find a TV show to pitch to his network executives and that he would find great love out of it. The man flashed me a smile and told me he already knew what that was. He then asked if I had ever considered becoming a television psychic and astrologer. How could I resist? It seemed my charmed life was starting.

We went on to create a show that ran for quite a few years and won the hearts of many viewers. I even had special events at theatres in all the big cities, where I would connect people in the audience to their loved ones passed over into spirit. We made it onto mainstream TV with my astrology predictions, and I was the darling guest of the chat show hosts. My shows were often filmed, and we sold the tapes.

I suddenly realized that I had seen her before. Yes, my mother and I had watched her, and my mother had her shows on DVD. But she looked so different in her appearance. Not the Dawn Starchild I remembered.

I would read their minds and tell them about their past lives. It was wonderful at first. He was so kind and caring. You see, I turned out to be that love for him. He proposed to me during one of my live shows on stage, and we were married soon after. It seemed like we were unstoppable, and our miniature empire's reign seemed endless.

I had a psychic reading with Gina, and she saw that my husband and I were meant to be together; apparently, we had failed in the past lives in which we had connected. He and I had a sacred contract. I would be his oracle and provide a love that would heal his heart; he would be my protector, guardian, and true and faithful love. To succeed with my spiritual work and help others in this lifetime, he would be the one to provide the physical temple that I needed, and we would fulfill the Divine Feminine and Masculine contract we had always promised each other.

However, he started to change once we were married. He got really short with me and yelled at me for no reason. He would get jealous of anyone I talked to whom he didn't know, and he was possessive and controlling in public. I was forced to break all contact with Gina and sell my part of the business to her. She was dead weight, and he was the only one who really cared about me and knew what was best—or so he told me. I regret that now because he wasted the money she gave us, and I was now without any income outside of our marriage. But I continued on because I kept remembering the sacred promises and contract.

When the third series had lower ratings and the theatres were threatening to cancel the live show, he really started to lay into me. He blamed me for doing the same tired routine and for not being perky enough on air. The first time we got the poor ratings in, he slapped me in the face when I tried to console him. When I would try to suggest new segments, he would belittle me and make me feel two inches tall. And if I would push against his decisions at all, he'd beat on me until I agreed with him. He would shout, "Don't tell me what to do!" and he would often create a stir just before I was about to host an event or reading. This was to sabotage me, and I'm ashamed to say I allowed this because my love and faith in him was blind.

After that first time, he was smart enough to only hit me in places that wouldn't be visible on camera. I once had to do a taping with three broken ribs. God, it was awful. By the end of that series, he was controlling every aspect of my life, down to the food I ate and what I wore. He would always tell me that he was doing what was best for me and that he only hurt me when I hurt him. As I had reached and passed the age of thirty, he would bully me about my looks: the lines forming around my eyes, the silver sprouting in my hair, and the fat that had started to accumulate.

In order to keep him happy, I agreed to go on a strict low-carb diet and worked out with a trainer six days a week. Then he had me get some fillers in my face and a breast augmentation to make me more appealing. It wasn't enough for him; nothing I could do would make me look twenty again. He preyed on the young stagehands and assistants on the show—and I let him. At least he wasn't paying as much attention to me. It made me feel guilty that I was letting him take advantage of younger girls, but I needed a break from his constant control and abuse. The guilt was crippling and endowed my stomach with sharp pains, and I got horrible bladder infections.

After a year of this, I was so tired of it and just wanted out. When the network came to us to tell us that the show was being cancelled, and the theatres said the show was not a good fit anymore, I was more than happy to let them do it. He managed to get us one more series by blackmailing one of the executives. I grinned and bore it, but inside I was a wreck. I didn't know what to do. After the show ended and the theatre appearance contracts stopped, my husband decided he wanted to go on holiday with his friends to the Caribbean. I knew what they were going to do there, but I didn't really care because it would be the first time in years I would be alone without him around. It was the perfect time for me to leave, but I didn't have access to any of my earnings to do so.

It took all I had to call Gina, because she was the only one I knew who might help me. She took my call and let me tell my spiteful tale of woe. Afterward, she was very quiet, and I thought she would hang up on me, but instead she started to cry. She wept for me and for what I had been through. Gina could feel how broken I was and how much I desperately needed to escape, so she agreed to get me out. She told me to go to Glastonbury and find Isis, a priestess who was psychic like me and could help. Gina gave me some cash to get me there.

I should have left that day, but my husband called from his vacation and promised everything would change. He'd had time to think while abroad and had a new idea for a show, which would make me adored again. He said he knew he would never be faithful to me, but we were a great partnership and friendship, and we could live separate lives. He would take care of everything, and as long as I said nothing about his indiscretions, I could stay in my home. He said he would always love me and be my best friend, and we were bound through fate, so why not make the best of everything? I believed him when he said he loved me, and it gave me hope, but I guess his words and promises kept me as a prisoner. Yes, I saw the signs, but I ignored them because I really loved him.

Naomi then paused and took a moment to wipe away a tear. It was obvious she had loved this man with her entire heart and soul. I said nothing and let her continue. This was not the story I had expected, but something told me it was the one she had waited a long time to share. I nodded to let her know I was listening.

One afternoon, I had a really bad feeling. He was not due back for a few days, and he would normally phone at a certain time in the morning. I would wait for it, always being the obedient wife. When the call didn't come, something told me he was coming home that day. I was hopeful that he would have changed, but at the same time, I didn't want to be anywhere near him until he could prove his promises.

I was actually packing to leave when he walked in the door. He asked me where I was going, and I told him that I thought we needed to live apart until he could show me that he had changed. He said that he wasn't going to live alone, that people would talk, and that there was no way he was going to let that happen. He said we had a domestic agreement, and he could live as he pleased; we had agreed on that. I told him we didn't have to tell anyone, but I needed time away from him until I felt comfortable again. That really set him off. He said that he had done everything to make me feel comfortable and that I was being a selfish witch. Then he pushed me to the ground and started beating my face. I pleaded with him to stop and said that we could start again, that I would be better, and we would be greater. He liked this version of me and told me to fix him a drink, which I obediently did. As I passed a mirror on the way to the kitchen, I caught sight of myself, and then it hit me. I knew that I had to leave that night, and for good; otherwise, I would never leave and would probably end up dead. It dawned on me that I had lived up to my part of the sacred contract, but he never would.

I went to the kitchen, took out a glass from the back of the cupboard, and pulled out a bottle of scotch. I then grabbed a bottle of valium pills from behind the oven that Gina had given to me when she gave me the money to leave. "Naomi," she had told me, "If he gets out of hand, you give him this and escape." I'd brushed it off at the time but was now thankful I had hidden them. I crushed up three of the pills and mixed them into his scotch. I figured that would be enough to put him out long enough for me to escape.

I was right. He drank his drink and was out within an hour. It took me another hour to finish packing my things before I stepped out the door. Then I ran to the nearest phone booth I could find to call Gina. She immediately knew what I needed and drove over to get me. Without saying a word, she got out of her car, handed me the keys, and pushed some extra cash in my hand. I went to protest, but she held up her hand and told me to go and to call when I was safe. I'll never forget the kindness and compassion she showed me and her look of concern when she saw my battered face. She said nothing; she just hugged me and then walked away towards the nearest tube station to make her journey home.

I drove to Glastonbury, as she had instructed. I thought I had booked a stay at the Sanctuary, but for some reason I wound up at the Gables Guesthouse. I have to say I was in a bad way when I arrived. I hadn't had time to clean myself up before leaving, so I still had dried blood on my face. That housekeeper, your Emilee, must have been terrified by my appearance. Not only was I bruised and bloody, but I was all skin and bones with thin, straw-like hair. That's why I wear my hair so long now, because I never want to look that way again. I stayed there overnight, and I don't even remember what happened; it was like I was in a trance.

I left early in the morning, not wishing to face the embarrassment of meeting the housekeeper again. I have to say I felt such a great shame that a very kind and graceful lady such as Emilee should see me in such a poor state. When I finally arrived at the Sanctuary the next day, Isis saw my black eye and the cuts on my hands. The first thing she did was tend to my wounds and get me back to a healthy weight. She was a crafty one and showed me how to access my husband's accounts secretly so I could pay for things. Unfortunately, I didn't have time to take everything, but I took enough to be able to support myself for quite a while. He had hidden so many things. I found he had been moving our assets and spending our cash for years on his dead-end ventures—so many secrets. In the end, I let him divorce me and keep everything. I was too scared to fight back. I hid and just submitted, and I signed everything over to him. I lost a lot, but I gained my soul and freedom.

I also never wanted him to find me in Glastonbury. I loved being here and didn't want to relocate again, so I stayed with Isis and helped her in the Sanctuary undercover. I changed my hair and image and have been working there for almost three years now.

CHAPTER 14

W ell, that's my story," Naomi finished as she sat up straight and wiped her eyes. "I apologize for the tears. I must say I have not thought about that man in some time. But I am getting off track. I know you were interested in hearing more about Egypt."

I paused the recorder and placed my hand on hers; she didn't pull away. "Are you sure? We can stop for today if you want," I said gently.

"No, no. I want to help you."

I smiled. "Thank you. You know, I thought you looked familiar. I used to watch your show all the time while growing up. My mother and I always made sure we watched the part where you predicted the star signs and the month ahead. We lived by it!"

"Really? Hmm." A coy smile played across her face. "Well, then, this must be fate."

I had a feeling she was right. Something told me that none of what had happened or would happen was a coincidence. I pressed download on the recorder and set up another file to catch Naomi's enchanting Egypt story.

She relaxed back into her chair again, and I waited. At first she described something in the same words as Isis. I could tell it was rehearsed and she wasn't channeling anything. She described the beauty of the temple and the sunrise and sunset ceremony. It was so bizarre because I did not see her in this; it was as if she was observing something. My mind wandered because this was not her story. How she had described her growing up, her abusive husband, and then her escape to Glastonbury—that felt real. Isis had felt real. Finally, I stopped writing and listened.

"And that was how it was." She smiled and opened her eyes. "Did you enjoy that?"

I smiled, "Yes, it was really beautiful and was very similar to the story of Isis. Were you in the same past life as her?"

"You know, Anna, we have discussed that, and it always seemed Isis had several Egyptian past lives, whereas I felt I may have had only one."

"So you weren't there at the creation of Philae?"

"No, I'm not sure.

"I'm not sure, either," I replied. "But Isis called you the Oracle of Edfu."

Her face suddenly changed, and I saw a younger version of her but in white robes. I saw a temple, but it was different than the one at Philae they had described. Naomi stood up and turned to go order something from the waitress, and for a moment, I could have sworn she appeared bald.

While she was absent, I closed my eyes to see a large, pale stone building with large figures carved into the front. It looked as if the temple reached the sky, and the figures stood with spears in their hands. I saw a small child running—a girl, I thought, because I felt her feminine energy. I found it odd for her to be in a place that felt so masculine. I was not at all comfortable there. Then I felt very dizzy, so I put my head down on the table.

Naomi walked over a moment later with a new tray of tea and scones. She saw me with my head down and rushed over to me. "Anna, are you all right?" she said with genuine concern. "Don't go fainting on me!" I lifted my head up slightly to look at her. "Oh, my," she exclaimed. "You have gone white!"

I pulled myself completely upright and mustered a few words. "Yes, yes, I'm good."

"Are you?" she asked. "Why don't you have a cup of tea and a scone? It might make you feel better." I did as she asked, and truth be told, I did feel a lot better afterward. Sugar and cream seemed to be my new spiritual diet.

I looked up at Naomi and said, "Now, tell me about the female child raised in the temple, the one with the gifts—your real Egypt story. I don't think you were right to think you only had one life in Egypt. Please tell me about her. Who is she?"

Naomi, who had been sipping her tea, stopped dead in her tracks. "I never mentioned the child," she hissed at me. "Where did you hear that?"

"I don't know," I responded. "It just came to me, and I saw a small girl in a white robe."

"How do you know it was female?"

"I don't know; I just felt that she was. Her energy was completely different than the masculine energy I felt around her."

"So, what, you have been seeing this as I talked to you?"

"No, I saw a vision only when you got up from the table. I'm not sure what triggered it. The temple didn't look like the one at Philae; it looked more austere. I haven't been to any of the temples, but I don't think it was just my mind making things up, based on what you told me. It felt real. But these days, I'm not sure what reality is anymore. I really don't mean to press you, Naomi, but it seems important. Do you know who this child was?"

Naomi looked uncomfortable, which showed in the higher pitch of her voice. "Who have you talked to? Lucinda or Isis?"

"Neither. This is the first time I have seen the child or

known anything about her."

She paused for a moment and then cautiously spoke. "A few years ago, we held a ceremony and gathered priestesses from all over the country. We all joined hands, and there were a few of them who became overcome with grief."

"Grief?" I asked.

"Yes. They saw a small child, a girl. She had been removed from Philae."

"Was that normal?"

"No. The priestesses always stayed at Philae, except for the designated times during festivals when they visited other temples or other temples visited them. They all had protocols for visiting each other to bring alignment to the temples. Each temple had a certain gift, a ritual, and everyone respected the way they practiced giving it.

"The priestesses in the ceremony that day were grieving because, like you, they saw something that had been broken, and they said it started with a small child. The only children to visit other temples normally were the boys. They were born in Philae or Dendara at the female temples and then would join the male temples around the age of eleven or twelve years old. They were trained as priests and would step into the rituals of Horus. It was unheard of for a female child to be given over to a male temple." She paused, not sure if she should carry on, but it would appear I had caught her interest. "Tell me, can you see anything else?"

I closed my eyes and took in a deep breath. The visions of the child returned to me, and I described them to Naomi. "The child looks around five years old and really small for her age." I stopped to explore the vision.

"What else, Anna?" Naomi asked impatiently. "What does she look like?"

"She has long black hair and dark eyes. She seems very wise for her age but also a bit mischievous. I do not see her mother or father around; I think they are out of the picture, but I don't think she's an orphan, if that makes sense. It looks like she is practicing some fighting combinations, like martial arts or something. It's so sad. She's just a baby, really, and she's alone. It does not make sense." I opened my eyes.

Naomi swallowed and looked as if she didn't want to ask about more but knew she must. "What else do you see, Anna?" she said in a whisper. She looked straight at me, and suddenly I understood.

"You have a secret," I remarked. "That child...that child is you. That temple is Edfu."

"Yes," she said, barely audible.

"I need to look further." I did not even ask permission before I continued. My voice and manner changed, as if I'd been taken over. The normally strong Naomi sat very still, biting her lip nervously and unsure if she wanted more to be revealed.

"Okay, let me focus. I feel like I have a strong connection here and can get through," I said as I put down my pen and reached for the voice recorder.

Naomi grabbed my hand and stopped me. "Anna, this is my story. You don't know what you are doing; you have no training. Don't be reckless."

"Oh, of course." I intended to stop, but coming into contact with Naomi triggered a vision that I could not control. My awareness was back to that tall, foreboding temple. This time I kept my eyes open and allowed my focus to drift into a hazy state, and the visions became even stronger than before.

You are so happy at the age of five. You have all the love and attention of the Temple of Isis around you, but you aren't there. You have these people with you, but they behave more like servants than family. It is like you are a princess to them. Oh, yes, you are all from Philae, but you are in Edfu for some reason.

I see that you have two priestesses who take care of you and always attend to you. But you aren't an easy one, and you regularly defy them. You like to make fun of them, saying they know nothing because you can do what you want. And you think you can do as she wishes. I am not sure who you mean by *she*; it's a spirit or ghost, maybe. The priestesses look really nervous to be at the temple and are asking the high priest when they can all go home. Yes, I get a positive on Edfu Temple.

But he tells them he has made a deal with Isis, and they are all bound to the temple of Horus. He says they will not be going home. You all have private rooms or chambers, though, so I guess they aren't treating you poorly. The women still feel grief over the loss of their home temple. They create a small altar and temple to Isis and try to have you pray with them, but you refuse. You scoff at them and say that Isis is not the most powerful and that she should not be prayed to, that she abandoned them all. You look very sad at this realization. You know you can't count on her, and it wounds you.

I see you attending the same classes as the older priests. You are quick and fast with your answers to the questions, and your skills in rituals and magic are truly amazing. Some of the other priests are in awe of you, but most seem to fear you and say you are part of an evil eye conspiracy. The high priest is impressed, though, and takes you under his wing for more advanced instruction.

Now I'm seeing you older, around twelve and developing into a beautiful young woman, slender and athletic. You train with the other priests. You seem to have lost your playfulness, and there is an intense seriousness to you. You are always watching everything and everyone because you know that you aren't completely safe here.

The other priestesses have gone; I'm not sure where. The priest said they have left you and returned to Philae, but I'm feeling that they died in some unnatural way.

You still have your own chambers, but it is really lonely now. The high priest has been called away more and more to consult with the royal family, so he is not around to keep you company. You spend most of your free time crying in your bed and scratching prophetic images into the wall of your chamber. They are of eight oracles or goddesses; you believe these goddesses will save you, and all will be restored again. You like to talk to the drawings on the wall, giving them individual personalities. It's so sad. You feel that they are your only friends.

I have to stop. This is so moving, and I feel my heart in pain.

☥

"Move on, Anna." Naomi's voice was deep and intense.

I wasn't sure if she meant to stop or to go further in the story, so I did the latter.

☥

It's initiation day at Edfu, the day of the festivals, and it should be the day when the other temples visit to observe the rituals of Horus—even someone from the royal court visits. The hawks are released early that day before the visitors enter, and should they fly around the main courtyard, it would be a good omen. But they refuse to fly, and no one is sure why.

You prepare for the day and dress in your priest robes. When you are ready, you walk into the main courtyard. The energy in the temple is electric. There are many tests and trials to go through. I see you pushing past the other young priests in the courtyard. The high priest is not happy with your display of insolence, but the royal vizier in attendance seems intrigued. However, he scans the rest of the crowd and decrees that all must be here in this temple because the gods were gracious enough to allow them to be, but he sees no boy worthy of becoming a true priest of Horus.

He proclaims that they should all still be with their mothers and are not ready for such a great honor. The pharaohs of Egypt have been extensions of Horus's power for millennia, and as such, the priests are an extension of the pharaoh. He would never allow such poor stock to serve the royal family; he sees many who are unworthy and weak. He needs the sons of Horus to lead his chariots. The high priest is trying to reason with him, but the royal vizier tells him he has failed. He says the only one who could possibly serve Horus is the skinny twig of a girl standing in front of them. He tells the high priest that she is the only one who could become a true initiate that year. The high priest challenges his authority, but the vizier says he was given power by the queen to oversee this initiation and to take over if necessary. There is such a challenge for power in this temple. The royal vizier has other motives; he does not understand temple protocol, only power and ego. He needs to unseat the high priest and take power.

The high priest is then punished for his failure. The royal guards grab him, drag him into the center of the courtyard, and hold him down. The royal vizier declares that he will subject the high priest to the full wrath of Horus. He orders the other priests to bring out the large knives used to cut crops and the long whips used to control the horses. They are ordered to slash and whip his back until he bends to the will of Horus. He stands for so long, and for some reason, he keeps his attention focused on you. He has always been kind to you, even though you know he has held you captive. You feel great pain and sadness while watching your mentor being cut and whipped.

He has now finally fallen. The high priest knows it is his time to pass, and he crawls to the Horus statue to die there. He must get through the first gateway, and then his soul will go into the afterlife. Certain priests begin to step forward, but the older ones stop them. It's not that they do not wish to help, but they are afraid to, and they know that in helping him, they may interfere with the choices of the gods and attract the same fate themselves. Only the gods decide who may pass into the greater realms of the afterlife.

Even in his pain, he still keeps his focus on you. Unafraid of the royal vizier, you rush to him and try to help him to his feet, but he falls. He looks at you and then at the first Horus statue, and you know what you have to do. All the other priests step back, afraid to help him. In that moment, the sacred brotherhood is fractured; fear has arrived. To watch another fall and do nothing goes against everything these boys were taught in order to become priests of humility and honor.

You are now chanting something—what, I can't quite make out. Your chanting is louder and fills the whole courtyard. You are calling upon the mother Isis to carry his soul to the heavens. You then grab his arm and have him lean into you. It's crazy, but you look like you have super strength.

You get the high priest to reach the first large black stone of the Horus statue. You set him down gently, and his bloodied hands grasp the stones around him. The strength in him is all but gone, but he manages to utter one word before he dies: "Isis."

The temple is now in silence except for a lone hawk circling the courtyard and making the loudest sound. As the hawk circles, no one dares to move; this is a sign from the gods. You breathe a sigh of relief because this means his soul has passed to the gods. However, the royal vizier is angry that the high priest was helped and that you were able to summon the spirits of Horus and Isis when no male priest could. You have proven yourself to be a true servant of the temple but also a great threat if not controlled and made to bend to the will of the temple, which the royal vizier sees will be under his command. If he controls this temple, he gains greater power with the royal family.

The scene fades and it moves to a few days later. The temple is now reaching revolt. There are those who are now in competition to be the next high priest. A meeting of the council is called, and the elders and the priests of the other gods are summoned. It's strange because I think there should be more women there, but it's all men. You are the only woman there, sitting with the former high priest's second in command, a man with dark kohl around his eyes and a scorpion on his head. He has always been there for you when the high priest could not be. He protects you the best he can.

One elder priest steps forward and calls for the temple of Isis to help decide, as was the sacred bond and contract agreed many years previous, but the others shoot him down. You step between one of the priests, who tries to strike the elder and cast a curse in the name of Isis. The other priests shout and disagree. They say she has no power here. The royal vizier looks pleased with himself, and he glares at you and orders you to be removed from his sight by the younger priests. The elder priests are also removed, and I think they are killed. The assistant priest remains behind, co-opted into helping the vizier.

You are dragged away back into the temple. They take you back to your chamber and bind your ankles with chains. One of them whispers that you will never be free and will face all of the evil they can bring in the coming days. They finish by binding your hands as well.

Locked away, you lie on your bed, taking your comfort from the women on the wall. You call on them to bring you an army so that you can bring pain to your jailors. This room is where you hide your magic and call on the gods in many ways—ways that no one has seen before here on Earth.

The next morning, the royal vizier is declared the new high priest of Horus.

☥

"It's gone black now. That's all I can see," I said, opening my eyes. I noticed that Naomi had been crying and glaring at me with hatred, not unlike that of the young girl.

"I think you've had enough," Naomi spat out. "You see very well, Anna. You see *too* well. You see into the hearts and souls of people."

"I think I see their demons too. That's my fear," I interjected.

"Tell me," Naomi said with ice in her voice, "what demons of mine did you see?"

"Well, I'm not sure, but the ritual games, whatever they are, seem to be important, as does that wall. Something significant happens with that wall. I also see black cats guarding you. They are guarding you while you plot to escape. It's weird: every time a priest walks past your room, a mark on your wall disappears. I don't know why that's happening. There is so much hate directed at you and so much hate you are giving off. I don't think I can look at it anymore."

"No," snapped Naomi. "That's more than enough for today." She stood up abruptly, grabbed her purse, and stormed out. I wasn't sure if she was hurt, upset, or angry. Maybe she was all three. All I knew was that she left me to foot the bill.

I thought I was helping her.

I slowly gathered my things, placed some cash on the table, and left the café. I kept having flashes of the girl in the chamber and the images she created on the wall.

As I walked back to the Gables Guesthouse, it did not sit well with me how Naomi had just left. I felt the anger rise. I felt resentment, and then my mind wandered to how I could tell Isis and the others that she had asked me to the cafe, used me to gather her past life information, and then left for no reason and left me with the bill. That would be my revenge, letting them know she was no honorable priestess. I had to catch myself; this was not how I expected to think or feel. *Are these my thoughts, her thoughts, or something else entirely?*

"Excuse me, excuse me," I heard a voice behind me. "You overpaid us for your food and drinks!" I turned around, and there stood the young girl who had patiently waited on us. "I didn't realize your friend had paid in cash as she left." The girl stood with a twenty-pound note in her hand.

I felt my stomach do a somersault and felt shame cross over me. "My mistake," I said, color rising to my cheeks.

She held out the cash for me to take. I took a look at her and noticed her shoes were held together by tape, and her stockings had a run in them. She was just a young girl trying to make a living and needed the money more than I did.

"You know," I said with a smile, "that's for you." I pushed her hand back toward her.

Her eyes grew big, and she began to laugh. "Seriously?" She looked as if I were about to say it was a joke.

"Seriously," I answered, and I turned to be on my way.

I was ashamed that I had judged Naomi, but I was even more ashamed that I had thought to seek some type of revenge.

I knew I could be mean sometimes, as we all could, but I wasn't usually this easily triggered.

I decided to go to the Sanctuary to apologize and see if I could make amends. And I remembered I needed to collect the voice recorder. I was gathering my stories, but they seemed to be slipping away.

As I tried to make my way back to the Sanctuary, my legs began to feel heavy like they were made of lead. Something or someone was blocking my journey. I decided to wait until the weekend was over and I could clear my head and energy before I returned to see Naomi and talk about today's events. Monday would be a fresh week and a good place to start.

CHAPTER 15

Monday, June 2

I knocked for a while on the door of the Sanctuary, but no one answered. I decided to wait. I could hear the radio from the kitchen and knew someone was around, so I went around to the back door and looked through the window.

Lesley sat in the kitchen, reading a book and listening to a classical music station. I knocked loudly on the back door, but she willfully chose to ignore me. She ignored me until I called her name. Then like a sly cat, she turned her head and smiled at me.

"Anna, what are you here for?" she asked, opening the door a crack.

"Can I come in?"

"No, I'm busy."

"That's fine. Do you know where Naomi is?"

At this, she opened the door all the way. "She's not here. I think she said she was going to the Chalice Well. Something about collecting something from Alice, the lady who works there. Oh, by the way, Isis asked if you're still coming to the retreat this weekend."

"Oh, yes, of course. Do you know, by chance, if my friend Lucinda booked her place for the goddess weekend?"

"No idea. I've been busy with other more important things."

I decided it was time to leave; her tone was becoming a

little too uncomfortable, and it was obvious I was unwelcome. I turned to leave.

"Oh, and don't forget to be at the Tor on Saturday by 8:30 a.m.," she shouted behind me.

I turned back around. "I thought it was sunrise."

"Well, the sun will be up at 8:30, so ..."

"Fine, I'll be there just before 8:30 a.m., then. One last thing, Lesley. Can I use the bathroom?"

"If you must, but I cannot sit and chat. I've revisions to do." She left the door ajar and went back to the table to read.

I crept in, held my finger to my lips to signal I was not disturbing her, and walked quietly through to the hall. I was about to walk through to the bathroom when I heard hushed voices from the office. It was Naomi and Isis, from what I could tell.

I knew I wasn't supposed to listen, but at the same time, I had to know what they were talking about. I was worried they were talking about me—and I was right.

"Anna is out of control. She forced a vision out of me, Isis," said Naomi. "It's like it's some sort of game to her. She just wants to see how far she can push me. It's her ego, not her truth, that she's concerned with. I mean, come on. How much do we really know about her and why she has come here? Don't you find the timing odd? We are coming upon a pivotal time for the sisterhood, and she just happens to come to us right as we are preparing? I bet she knows way more than she lets on. How else could she do what she did?"

"Anna is uncommonly gifted, Naomi, and I thought we had discussed this yesterday and the day before," replied Isis. "There is no malice or ego in her actions. She is very new to all of this and doesn't know the extent of her power. Anna is here for a good reason, and we all knew this day was coming, Naomi, we called it in. She's going to become a key player in the events to follow. These stories are open to all the oracles when they choose to look; you know that. Oracles see everything when they wish to."

"Even if there was a good reason, she needs to control herself. We have our reputations to think about, and we do not want that whole recycled witch drama to show its face again."

"Ah, yes. Naomi, have you been particularly drawn to that timeline of late?"

"I guess, a bit. It started last week after I met with Anna. She's pulling out all sorts of unpleasant memories for me. I see them in my dreams and my meditations. They haunt me."

"Naomi, please be patient. The girl barely knew what she was coming into, and Lucinda should have prepared her better than she did. We are lucky she hasn't been scared off already."

"I'm just saying, Isis, we have been working through this for lifetimes, and the crucial time is arriving soon. You said yourself that some unknown force is attempting to work against us, and it all started around the time Anna arrived. Nothing is a coincidence. I can feel everything converging on the solstice. That means we don't have the luxury of time to properly vet her. If the mantle isn't passed in this lifetime, it won't be passed at all. The bonds of the eight sacred women will be fractured beyond repair, and what knowledge of the scrolls we have will be lost."

"I think you are being overly dramatic, Naomi. After all, you don't see everything in your future all of the time."

"Yes, Isis, but I see enough. She's dark and dangerous." I then heard her pick up her purse and keys. "I've always stood behind you and supported you, and I will now. I owe you my life. But I have to wonder if you are letting your judgment be clouded by your desire to pass the mantle. Just be careful and make sure you didn't let a snake into the nest."

I heard her walk toward the door, so I slipped quietly along the corridor and into the bathroom. From there I could hear the front door slam and her car start.

Once I felt it was safe, I slowly opened the bathroom door and attempted to escape undetected. I was not so lucky. I tried to tiptoe back to the kitchen, but Isis must have heard me and called for me. "Anna, can you come into my office, my dear?"

I slowly walked back and looked around the door. Isis was sitting at her desk, moving papers, and opening envelopes. She did not look at me when I walked in, for which I was thankful. I must have looked like a child who got caught eating cake before dinner. I didn't know what to do, so I stood in front of her desk.

"Are you okay, Anna?" Isis said, not looking up from her work and indicating that I should sit.

"I'm fine," I said, taking my seat. I hoped she couldn't see that my hands were shaking slightly. I prayed she would not ask me if I'd heard anything, because I didn't want to lie, especially if I was thought of as dark and dangerous. "I'm sorry that I pulled you from your work. I was trying really hard to be quiet and was hoping to see Naomi. She had to leave our meeting on Saturday rather quickly; she paid, and I did not have a chance to thank her. Then Lesley said she wasn't here, but I had to use the toilet, so I did that, and…" I tried to not stammer. I must have looked so guilty.

"You could have texted her," Isis said, not lifting her head to look at me.

I stayed silent.

Isis looked up and moved her chair around. She smiled at me, and I found I could breathe at last. "Naomi has ghosts, like most of us," she explained. "She simply needs to work through some of them. And she's a star rising, which means the drama will often follow her. Yes, she was certainly born to be a performer."

"Isis, I really want to learn, and I don't want to embarrass or confuse anyone, but this is all happening so fast, and I'm not sure why it's happening."

Isis stared at me for a while. She seemed to be mulling something over in her head. Then she suddenly threw her hands up in the air in defeat. "Okay, okay, I give in," she said in an exasperated tone. I wasn't sure whom or what she was talking to or about.

She rushed out of the room and returned with her scroll from the other day. Isis then gingerly unrolled the scroll and put it through the photocopier on one of her bookshelves. She carefully handed me the fresh copy, which was still warm.

"Study this. It will help explain, because it is the Scroll of Magic and Prophecy," she said.

In the other room, I could hear a phone ring. Lesley appeared a moment later at the door and looked surprised to see me there. She must have thought I'd left when Naomi had slammed the front door. "Isis," she said, "it's the woman from the tourist information office. She needs to speak to you about a permit."

"Oh, yes, Lesley, thank you. I'll take it in here. Anna, study what I have given you, and let me know your thoughts after the retreat this weekend. I may be a while, so let yourself out." She then took the phone and waved at me and Lesley to leave.

I followed Lesley out and placed the copy of scroll in my bag. "So you got the scroll. Aren't you gifted!" Lesley remarked. "It's very valuable, you know. You need to guard it with your soul."

I told her it was only a copy and made the mistake of asking if she had one. I got a nice glare for that one. I could not read this woman. *At first it's all smiles and sisterhood, and then it's as if she wants to put a knife in my back.*

As if she read my thoughts, her manner changed. "You know, I really am glad you are going to study with us. It will be nice to have someone around who is so powerful. Maybe you'll give Naomi a run for her money. Maybe you'll give *me* a run for my money." She chuckled. Lesley then ushered me toward the door and out into the garden. "Now, don't forget: 8:30 a.m. on Saturday," she reminded me.

Before I turned to leave, I asked, "Oh, before I forget, did you see the small voice recorder that was left on Isis's desk? I left it here the other day, and it had my story of Isis."

"No, sorry, I saw nothing. And remember, I had to clear the kitchen when you left. I'm not a servant. You know, Anna, next time you do work and study here, clear your own dishes." She turned and left.

☥

I felt as if I'd gone through three days in one, but when I reached the Guesthouse, my spirits were instantly lifted and my energy felt better. When I opened the door, I was met with the most delicious of smells, and the whole house felt alive as a result. I immediately went to the kitchen and knocked. Emilee shouted for me to enter.

On the kitchen table were pots, herbs, and bottles. Emilee was busy going from pot to pot on the stove, sprinkling something in one and stirring another. She turned around, wiped the sweat from her brow with her apron, and brushed her hands against it. She gave me a warm smile and motioned me over. "I'm making the potions and sprays for the retreat this weekend," she explained. She was so excited as she stirred the herbs into the large copper pans. "I've got rosemary, lavender, and rose hip over here." She pointed to one pot. "Oil over there, and in that bottle." She pointed to a beautiful glass bottle off to the side, "That's the blue lotus from Egypt for the ceremonies."

"Ceremonies?"

"Oui, this year is the time of the solstice and the eclipses; we have not seen a cycle like this in over two thousand years. We begin early on the sixth and seventh. June is the month of the greatest and longest light, the sixth is the day of harmony, and the seventh is the peace day before the eighth, the day of the Divine Feminine rising."

"But isn't the solstice around the twenty-first?" I asked.

"Yes, but the gateways and portals open early with the rising sun, and we begin to greet greater light each morning."

I was so confused but decided to allow the days to flow with no thought and judgment. "I can help, Emilee, if you like," I offered. Perhaps a little magic and potion mixing would do me some good. I looked over, marveled at this beautiful black lily on the counter, and went to pick it up.

Emilee rushed over and hit my hand with her ladle. "No, no, no! That's datura, dark and dangerous. Not for you, ma chère."

"Why would you have something dark and dangerous? And in the kitchen, no less!"

"It's good. I'm making a potion not to take, but to be burnt in the ritual. It does not grow here, so I had it shipped from a florist in London. But very poisonous, this one, not to touch without gloves. Now, Anna, sit down there. I will make something to eat for us, and we can chat while I make my brews. You can help by preparing bottles for me."

I figured that was a good idea as any and placed my bag on the other counter. My bag tipped to the side, and the photocopy of the scroll slid out.

Emilee stopped what she was doing and pointed to my bag. "What's that, Anna?"

"Oh, it's the Scroll of Magic and Prophecy. Isis wants me to study."

"She gave you the scroll?"

"No, a copy."

Emilee looked a little relieved. "And you have looked at it?"

"No, not yet. I was actually hoping you had books I could use to help me through it. I have a few days before the ceremony weekend, so I thought I would use my time wisely."

For the longest moment, she stood still. Then she wiped her hands and went into a back room which I had not yet seen or observed. She returned with an object wrapped in a worn silk cloth.

"This also has many of the secrets," she said, gingerly peeling back the fabric to reveal a small, blue scarab. "Please do not let this scarab leave the house. It was given to me by my grandmother and mentor. It has many answers for what you need."

"You mean they go together?" I asked.

"Oui, in many ways. But then to have them together, one has to be prepared for many steps forward in her journey."

Part of me wanted to say no to this special journey, but then what would Lesley and Naomi say when I deciphered the scarab and scroll and found out the story of stories? Isis would be so pleased and proud of me, and that would be such a powerful moment.

I promised Emilee I would guard the scarab with my life.

"Remember, it's not what the scroll and scarab say, it's how it feels," she said. "They are a mirror of you."

I was not sure what she meant and asked her to explain. She sat down and told me she needed a break from her potion-making.

"So, Anna, over history, there have been many pieces

of information and stories written. The sacred ones contain energy that, when you are open to understand it and are ready to embrace it, will unlock. When you judge it or compare it, so will you be judged and compared. If you curse it, then you will be cursed. The sacred artifacts manifest in many different forms."

I interjected, "Do you mean the scroll has consciousness?"

"Sometimes, because it was once a living thought, and now it's a living manuscript. Many rituals and great knowledge were passed between the generations, and then it was written. The Egyptians called to Thoth because he was the scribe, and his words were a powerful tool. The sacred scrolls are said to be from his personal library. Did Isis tell you of the Sacred Eight—the women, scrolls, and scarabs?"

I nodded and could barely breathe. I looked at the scarab and let my hand wander across the old etching on the back. "Then I guess this and I will just have to become best friends," I surmised.

She laughed. "Now, let's put your homework over there and finish up my treasures here. The guests for the ceremonies will arrive in the next few days, and Lucinda will not be here until late Friday or early Saturday morning."

"Okay." I pointed. "So potions over here, poisons over there, and soup and salad in the middle?"

"Exactly, ma chère. Now, let's get to work—and do not mix up the food and potions!"

☥

The next few days passed in a blur. Emilee would knock on my door and pass food through. I was engulfed with the scroll and scarab. It allowed me to read the text with perfect fluency—something I didn't think was possible. Just when I thought I had gathered a thought, something else would come forward. I was matching symbols with words and images with sacred teachings. I had no idea what to do with all the things I was seeing, thinking, and feeling, but I decided to go through with the collection of data and hope that this pleased Isis and impressed Naomi. Each time I matched something, I would have a short vision. As I learnt more from the scroll, I decided to push the visions further. By the night before the ceremony, I was spending half the day channeling. One thing kept coming forward over and over again: the emerald-eyed woman. She was ever present in my mind's eye, guiding me and urging me to find something more.

Friday, June 6

On that Friday, I realized I had a few missed calls from Lucinda, but I ignored them and continued with my studies. I knew I would be seeing her soon, and we could chat then. I was just getting back into my studies when Emilee knocked at the door.

"Yes?" I said.

"May I come in?" Emilee asked through the door.

"Oui!" I shouted.

Emilee came in and looked at me with a curious expression. "Ma chère, do you not have your mobile turned on?"

"I do; why?"

"Lucinda has been trying to reach you!"

"Oh, is that all?" I asked, looking up from my work. "I know she called a few times. I figured I'd just talk to her when she gets here later tonight or tomorrow."

"Well, if you'd pick up, you'd know that she's not coming."

"Not coming?" I stood up and turned to face Emilee. "What do you mean? I want her to share this experience with me!"

"Now, she does not."

"What do you mean? Of course, she does!"

"No. Lucinda had a dream and a warning to not come this weekend."

"What warning?" I asked, slightly panicked.

"I don't know, and she would not say." With that, Emilee left me alone.

I immediately called Lucinda and tried to reason with her. "But you have to come and see me and the work I'm doing!"

"And your writing, of course," she said.

"Yes, that too," I said dismissively. "Lucinda, I can channel for hours at a time now! I'm able to go back through past regressions I've done with other people."

"Is that so? And did you get permission from them to do this?"

"Permission? These are already visions I've experienced, like Naomi at Edfu. Why would I need permission?"

"Oh, Annie." She sighed heavily into the phone. "It is a violation that is felt every time you enter another person's past life. That poor girl must be feeling positively awful if you have been frequenting her lives. Not to mention it is extremely dangerous to be under for so long in another's life."

"Dangerous?" I scoffed. "How could it be dangerous? I am taking all of the necessary precautions."

"All the same, I don't like this newfound ego of yours, Anna. You need to slow down and take a breath." I could hear the disappointment in her voice. "And what about your plan in life, Annie?" Her tone softened.

"Oh, I don't know. I really think I could make it here, be successful, and give Isis all the help she needs—and perhaps even run the Sanctuary when she travels."

"You have been there just over a week, and Isis told you all this?"

"No, she never said anything, but she's slowing down, and I have a greater gift—" I stopped myself, but not quite soon enough.

Lucinda heard me. "A greater gift than whom, Anna?"

"Isis or Naomi," I replied before I could stop myself. "At least, that's what the woman said."

"The woman? What woman?"

I said, "The one with the emerald-green eyes. She comes in my dreams and visions." There was a long silence. "Lucinda, please. It isn't a big deal."

"Anna, let me meditate on this," she said and hung up the phone.

What is her problem? She was so frustrating, but I wasn't worried. I would manage on my own.

My sleep that night was so disrupted.

♀

I saw myself back in the Temple at Philae. It was just after dusk, so everyone was going about their evening business. The rituals had been finished, and the women were gathering in various groups around the promenade. I was drawn to a group of women speaking in hushed tones near the small temple of initiation near the water's edge. I tried to walk over to them and join them, but every time I was near, they seemed to move and float to another section. It was strange, but I saw Laura. She was coming to meet me, but as she got closer, she seemed to slip away. I wanted to reach her, but something was pulling me back. My feet were slipping into the floor, and I was crawling to reach the doorway that had appeared in front of me.

From out of nowhere, Lesley appeared and told me Isis had left, adding that I should leave, too. She was laughing and saying she would take care of everything. I asked her what she was taking care of, and she pointed outside the temple.

I went toward where she was pointing, and at the edge of the water surrounding the temple, I saw a boat had arrived. Seven dark shapes wearing dark cloaks climbed out of the boat. As they neared, I realized their faces were gray and gaunt, their eyes black and empty. They crept slowly toward me, and I was terrified. I turned to see if Lesley was still with me, but she was gone. Everyone was gone. I was paralyzed by something—not fear, but some strange force beyond my control.

The figures drew nearer, as they had almost every night for the last few weeks. I tried to run but sank into the sand. Unlike the other times, they reached me before I could escape. Their cold, thin hands groped for something on my body, attempting to pull me into their grasp. I screamed and felt my soul on the edge of shattering into a million pieces. As they pawed and tore at me, their hoods fell from their faces and changed. I recognized them from the vision Isis had shared. They were the seven women who had helped found the temple. Just as their hands had nearly choked my last breath out, I heard a voice say, "Don't let them get you, Anna." The hands retreated, and the last thing I saw was the emerald-eyed woman standing above me.

Saturday, June 7, 7:33 a.m.

The next morning, the morning of the ceremony, I awoke feeling the lingering effects of my nightmare. They quickly dissipated when I realized that today, I would get to put some of my studying to use and meet other like-minded women. I got dressed and went downstairs to have breakfast with everyone. When I entered the dining room, I was surprised to see that no one was there. Emilee came in to clear dishes and nearly dropped them when she saw me. "Oh, dear," she said. "What are you doing here?"

I looked at her, confused. "I am here to eat breakfast. Where is everyone?"

She shook her head at me. "Oh, mademoiselle, I am sorry. I thought you went early, so I did not wake you. The ceremony started at 7:30. You are late."

Panic started to rise within me. "No, I was told 8:30. I still have time."

"No, you do not. It was sunrise. You are late, and you need to go—now!"

I looked at her wide-eyed for a moment and then ran out the door. *I can't believe that this is the first impression all of those women are going to get of me!*

CHAPTER 16

I was late and very out of breath when I arrived at the Chalice Well for the ceremony. I had slowly tried to make my entrance, but the crow had returned and was trying to not only alert the group I was there but also wake the spirits of the land. My cheeks were burning red, and I was so embarrassed when I reached the circle. All the women wore beautiful robes and capes, and some even had golden headdresses. I stood in jeans, a jumper, and welly boots. I presented myself to the circle, much to the scorn of Naomi, and I mouthed that I was sorry and had been held up. She ignored me and continued to lead the circle in a prayer of gratitude. She stood opposite me; to her left was Isis, then Lesley, then Alice, then me, and then three other women I assumed must be staying at the Sanctuary. There were also a couple of women who had been staying at the Gables. The women from the Sanctuary had ignored me when I joined the circle and gave me disapproving looks when they thought I wasn't looking. Those from the Gables simply ignored me and looked down at the ground. I looked at Lesley, and she shrugged, mouthed "High priestesses," and rolled her eyes. I could feel everyone's anger at me. Suddenly I felt very small and insignificant. But no matter, I must rise above this. I was here to receive my gifts and to record another story for my book.

"Anna, declare yourself," hissed Naomi. In my newfound spiritual enlightenment, I had not been listening.

I looked at Lesley, and she looked away. I looked at Isis. "Say your name and where you are from," she offered.

"Oh, I'm Anna of York!" I proclaimed.

Naomi began to call the spirits of the earth and the four directions. She drew symbols with a willow stick she had in her hand. The ritual continued, and I began to feel really sick. I wondered if this was me or the fact that the three older women from the Sanctuary were still glaring at me. Naomi burned the incense, and the scents and oils that swirled around me were both earthy and exotic.

I was not really sure what was happening. My vision began to blur, and the pressure in my head caused me to feel faint. The familiar darkness arrived soon after, and I felt like I was sinking into the ground.

"Anna, Anna." I heard Isis calling me, and I began to come around. "Breathe, please, dear. Breathe, my darling," she cooed.

"Isis," I gasped. "I think I'm having a heart attack."

"No, you're slipping into a regression. Stop fighting it, and the dizziness and nausea will go away. Let it wash over you. Focus on what the records are trying to tell you. Now, what are you seeing?"

"This is the Scroll of Magic and Prophecy at work."

All I could feel was the ground, and I curled like a small child on it. Isis knelt next to me and whispered, "What do you see, Anna?"

"I see Edfu; it's dark and evil. I don't want to see that. I want to be here; I swear I do."

"I know, I know, but you're seeing the records of what came before. Now, please release the story, and we can all be free of it."

"The boys, oh, those little boys. They are training day and night, night and day. Sometimes they rest, but they never get to play. The smaller ones have to fight the stronger boys. Many of them die from their injuries. They all fear the older priests.

"The priests tell them that Mother Isis has sent them here and that they can only go home once they achieve the greatness they came here for. So they train, and many more fall before achieving greatness.

"Then I see the hole in the wall. Oh, my god, the hole! They have to crawl through a hole in the wall and face the demons. They lose their friends each day as the initiation trials continue. So many are lost. The temple grows more and more silent each day as another son of Isis does not return from the other side."

"Anna," Isis whispered, "slowly see the Akashic record but do not become part of it. Open your heart."

I did as she requested, and I found such a sense of calm and peace. I felt now as if I were floating almost like an angel, seeing the story now as just an observer.

At the end of the trials, the new high priest, the royal vizier, has gathered the whole temple to salute those who have returned to the heavens and the gods and to celebrate those who have survived and attained glory.

This high priest tells them that mighty Rome is seeking to take power over the fertile land of the Nile. Cleopatra and her sacred priestesses have lost their way, and their fall is coming. The oracle has seen this, and only Edfu can save Egypt. As he shouts the name of the oracle, I see a woman standing in black robes with a golden snake belt around her waist. She's crying, her eyes are red, and she's in such pain.

I tried to look at Naomi, but Isis was kneeling close to me, and she kept bringing my face back to look at her and saying to focus only on her. She encouraged me to carry on.

Oh, Isis, it's Naomi, and for every boy priest they lose, she pays a price. For every one that survives, she is saved from a cruel torture, and she feels the shame of the temple. She's in such pain, and she's mumbling and moving her hands. They don't know that she is cursing them, cursing every single one of them for what they have done.

She calls to the gods of darkness, and she calls to her true father. She calls him Set, for only he can conjure dark magic. She believes she's bound to this, but she's confused.

Suddenly, I felt a sharp pain in my stomach like I'd been kicked, and I cried out and held myself in pain.

"Breathe, Anna," said Isis. We seemed to be in a world of our own, but I could hear faint chanting in the background.

"They are coming, Isis, I see the circle closing in! The hooded ones from my dreams!"

"Who, Anna? The witches?"

My vision then shifted to an old village, the same one I'd seen many days ago when Lesley had first mentioned the Salem witches. They were all here again, cursing and pointing the finger. I fell into silence, unable to articulate what I was seeing.

"Where are you now, Anna?"

"In the courtroom. I'm watching innocent women get accused."

Suddenly I rose to my feet, fully coming out of the regression. "You did this! You did, Naomi!" I pointed at her, and the group stopped chanting. Isis backed away from me.

My words kept coming, and I felt as if something was speaking through me.

"You, Naomi, cursed them at Edfu, and then again at Salem. You called upon the demon god Set to create evil beings. You let the Divine Feminine die in the name of prophecy and magic. You told the high priest these trials were the work of the gods, and he believed you! You created the curse that will follow the oracles forever. You condemned us to lives ever searching and being alone without our soul mates and our hearts closed from being loved, locked into being servants without our gifts and insight. We were abused for our psychic sight and challenged and ignored in our wisdom!"

Suddenly, I felt the winds change around me and realized I was in the center of the circle above the ceremonial potion. Naomi now rushed to it and threw water over it, subduing the potent odors. It dawned on me that everyone was staring at me. Some were furious, and others were too shocked to do anything. I could not even look at Naomi.

"Dark oracle, sorceress," the women whispered.

"Take it back, Anna," Naomi said, now inside the circle. "Take it back. You have said many things in the last few days, and you will pay for any untruths you speak. Now take it back!" She turned to the other women. "This circle is broken. We will not be able to complete the ceremony today or tomorrow. We have a snake in our midst, and we need to get it out." She looked directly at me. "The dark and dangerous oracle without integrity will face her own path and the demons of the temple soon enough."

"Shadow oracle, dark sorceress," the woman to my left kept repeating to herself.

I was not sure what was happening.

"Witch!" cursed another one, and she pointed her finger at me.

"Isis, don't you see? She's here to thwart our plans and forcibly take the mantle from you! She has been channeling all week, peeking into my life without my permission. She is here to take our secrets!" exclaimed Naomi.

"No, I'm not, I swear!" I said, on the verge of tears.

"But you did," hissed Lesley. "We saw you expose Naomi, didn't we, ladies?"

I looked at Alice for help, and she looked down at the grass.

"You stole the secrets, like you are trying to do now," said the oldest of the women.

I began to shake. I found my head spinning, and then I saw myself traveling back in time. I saw myself taking sticks with faces just like these women's, binding red wool around them, and then sticking them into the ground. I fell to my knees and put my face in my hands. I looked up and saw Isis.

"You were late," Isis said, "and I had a vision that the priestess to join the circle late would cause trouble. I had prayed it would not be you, Anna. I trusted you, but you stole a vision from Naomi. You forced a vision!"

"I was last, yes, but not late."

"You were late. We started at 7:30 this morning."

It dawned on me the Lesley had told me 8:30 a.m. I had been played.

"You don't belong here," one of the women hissed again.

I looked at the other women around the circle, and then I looked at Isis. She was supposed to be my teacher, my mentor, and my friend. She had told me her secrets, and I had sworn I would share them in the book. This, I thought, was what she'd wanted from me: to write her story.

"The real Scroll of Magic and Prophecy has been missing for a few days now. Where is it?" Naomi demanded.

"Anna," Isis said patiently. "Did you take the original scroll?"

"No, just the copy you gave me!"

"But all I found was a copy. I only made one for you."

"I just have the copy. I don't have the original, I swear."

"A likely story," said Naomi. "I told you, Isis. I told you she was only going to cause trouble."

The other women whispered among themselves. Isis said nothing.

"Anna, we don't trust you, and you don't belong here," Naomi continued.

I felt as if my heart had been pierced by twenty daggers. I looked around for a friendly face, but I could find none.

"I think it is time to leave," Alice announced. "This area has had enough blood and pain over the years; we need no more today. We open to the public at 10:00 a.m., ladies. I ask you all to clear your belongings and whatever energy has passed here today."

Everyone nodded their heads in agreement.

"Yes," said one of the women, "leave her there. She has her own fate to work with." They all walked away and left me alone in the middle of the field.

It was a while before I could stand. I had not seen this coming. The only thing I could think to do was call Lucinda and pray she could help me make this right. She was correct, as usual: I had let my ego take over, and I had done horrible things as a result.

Her phone went straight to voice mail.

CHAPTER 17

I decided I needed another tarot reading. Things had begun to be confusing for me. I needed to know more about myself and how I fit into this dark nightmare. I couldn't possibly be this sinister force everyone was talking about. Sure, I had made a few mistakes, but it wasn't with ill intent. I couldn't go to the Sanctuary, and neither did I wish to return to the Gables because I didn't want to risk running into any of the women from the ceremony. I decided I needed some clarity and knew just the place to find this. I had thought this was to be a day of harmony, but now I was broken in two.

I went back to the small store where my Goth-looking friend was working to see if I could have another appointment. As I carefully approached the door, I imagined that the girl with the long red nails would be awaiting me and casting spells on me. I could swear she was also in my dreams sometimes. I opened the door, and to my surprise, no one was there at the counter. I could hear voices in the back and presumed they were on a break. I waited and glanced around the walls.

After about five minutes, it became obvious that no one was coming to greet me. I decided to ring the bell on the counter and shouted, "Hello!" After shouting three times, I decided to leave. Then I heard footsteps shuffling from behind the curtain. Suddenly the curtain was drawn back, and a strange man walked out. He was wearing white robes, and his head was shaved.

"Oh, my goodness," I exclaimed. I leaned forward to get a better look, and when I squinted my eyes, I could see this man was my gothic friend. "Wow, that is you in there."

"I'm so sorry," he said in a quiet voice. "We are closed today." He pointed to the sign in the window I had totally chosen to ignore. My assistant Lydia must have forgotten to lock the door this morning.

"Oh, I'm sorry, I was hoping for another reading. I'm Anna, by the way. Things have been so crazy the last few days."

He smiled and nodded his head. "Let me guess: the oracles?"

"Yes, the oracles."

He nodded his head slower and wore a rather thoughtful expression on his face. "I've been seeing them in my visions. I wondered if you were involved," he said. "I knew they were performing a ceremony, and even though it's a Saturday, I felt the need to close the store and see what magic came my way."

"But this," I said, pointing to his robes of pristine white silk. "What happened to the velvet suit and snake cufflinks?"

"Oh, this is the real me," he laughed. "The other is my alter ego, my dark side. The tourists respond much better to that. I trained in the theatre in secondary school but had horrible stage fright, so I never went into it professionally. I just liked playing roles; the person you met first, he felt like that was an old aspect of me, but the archetype he plays works."

"Mmm hmm. The past lives theme?"

"Well, kind of…Yes, actually, yes, it is! And you are part of this too now. I suppose it is time, then, to properly introduce myself. I'm Lucas. That's my real name. So now that we have been properly introduced, why don't you come on back?"

He went to the shop door and made sure it was locked this time. Lucas then walked back behind the counter and beckoned me to follow with a wag of his finger. I once again entered into the dark and eerie sanctuary of his. This time, however, the altar was lit with soft lighting, and the whole place felt calmer and softer.

"It's a reading you're seeking, yes?" he asked, sitting down in an oversized stuffed chair at the oak table in the center of the room.

"Yes, please," I replied. "I've had some weird experiences, and I'm not sure what my reality is anymore. And I want to know my part in this and what the oracle world means to me. I never asked for these visions, and I'm sure I never had the gift before I came here. I think they put a spell on me in some way, or maybe I'm cursed or being manipulated. I read in the Scroll of Magic and Prophecy that it's possible to hijack someone else's memories of their past lives." I realized my tone was forward and a little harsh, so I softened my voice. "Well, that's what I think I read and came to understand."

He sat silent for a moment, pondering what I had said, and then began to draw the cards. As he drew them, he explained what each one meant. "Five of Swords—it is hope and a dire warning; be aware of those who seek to create misunderstandings. Three of Coins—if you step up with your leadership, you will reap the rewards. Anna, it's time to step into your role here."

"But what is my role in all of this?" I asked, confused.

He continued, "The World—you're here to integrate what you are learning."

"But how?"

"Well, what comes to me is that you are beginning to see things." He turned the High Priestess card. "Ah, yes. You have been finding your skills, and this can help others. Now, see, the Ace of Wands—you will help others have new beginnings and clear their past."

"And do I need to be cautious?"

As if on cue: "The Tower—be careful of the tower; it can bring destruction. The Seven of Coins—but once the destruction happens, then the rewards will come forth."

"My book," I mumbled to myself. "My book?" I asked him louder. "I'm writing each day about all that I find. It's mainly past lives and how it's affecting those in the present time. The binding karmic drama we simply can't let go of sometimes."

"Yes," he responded thoughtfully. "Anna, tell the stories as spiritual lessons." I realized then that that was the real reason I had been called to Glastonbury. *But what is the oracle connection? Do I have a curse?*

My eyes lingered on the tower card, and for some strange reason, I reached out and touched it. "Oh, I'm sorry. I don't know why I just touched that," I said.

"It's okay," Lucas said. "Now, why don't you close your eyes and tell me what you see? I think looking back and within will help you."

"Okay, I'll give it a try." I leaned back in the chair and closed my eyes. He told me to be very calm and allow my senses to locate the messages. I was then aware of music, soft and gentle, playing in my ear. All I saw at first was the tower in my mind, and I began to feel cold. The images then shifted, and I described them as they appeared.

I'm in a boat, it's dusk, and we are floating on a river. There are people with lanterns lining the side of the channel. I think it's the Thames; I recognize some of the buildings around it, but they look older somehow. The people lining the water are wearing old English clothing—you know, like full, long skirts; lace-up boots; and the like. I'm wrapped in a cape and have many petticoats with the overdress made of fine silk. There are two women in the boat as well as the boatman. The women are crying because we have no idea where we are heading. I feel we have been captured and have no idea why. I keep staring at the people with the lanterns. I also see a priest on the river bank with a Bible, reading some prayer and pointing. I look ahead, and that's when I see it: the Tower of London.

The ferryman brings our boat to a large, corroded iron gate. He yells to the two guards, and they crank the gate open. Oh, my god—this is the Traitor's Gate.

The shock of the revelation took me out of my trance, and I began to panic. *What am I there for?* My brain was teeming with questions. Lucas must have noticed I had broken the trance and said, "Stay with the vision, Anna. Go back in. Find the vision; find your story." I leaned back into a comfortable position and went back in.

I see myself and the other women getting out of the boat and being led inside. There don't seem to be any guards around. Maybe we are being led to safety. A secondary gate opens, and we are all climbing the stone steps. It smells musty and damp in here. These poor women next to me look so worried, and I can't help but feel that way too. They are clutching each other like their lives depend on it. At the top of the stairs, I see two guards and a very regal-looking man with a set of keys. He calls us to follow him down a dark corridor. I cannot see their faces; it's as if they will not and cannot look at us. We are led to a chamber. The door is opened, and I see a woman dressed in very grand clothes inside. She rushes to me. She has dark hair with just a wisp of gray in the front. She tells me she's glad to see me and that I have to weave the spell. I'm confused and don't know what she means. The other women with me enter the chamber and sit down near the fire, but I can't see their faces because they are covered with hoods now. They begin talking to the other women who have appeared in the room, and they are pointing at me, but they all have covered faces. I'm sure I caught a glimpse of Naomi hiding behind one of the hoods they're wearing, but I think, *I do not want to follow that path and bring her into my awareness again.*

The room or chamber is not as I would have expected. It's large, with a striking four-poster bed, and around the room are other smaller cots. There's a table and chairs and a large fireplace. It's strange for prisoners. If this is the Tower of London, then it's not exactly a cell, but I let the thoughts go and focus on what comes to me.

The first woman I encountered on entering the room tells me to sit down and directs the man with the keys to leave. I hear him go, and he locks the door behind us. This woman looks familiar, and she reminds me of someone in her hair and her manner, but I'm not sure who she really is. She leads me to a table and sits me down at one end of it. A deck of old tarot cards with torn edges is on the table, which clearly means they have been used a lot. The woman asks that I use the cards and show her what the cards have to say. I'm afraid to touch them; it seems wrong to do that here. Her patience wears thin with me, and her insistences become more forceful. Finally, she commands that I do a reading.

At the rise of the woman's voice, a younger woman comes over and puts a Bible on the table. She reminds me of Lesley. The woman throws the Bible across the room. She indicates that it doesn't have the help she needs, but I'm not sure of whose help this is.

I have no idea what she's talking about, but at the risk of angering the woman again and alerting the guards, I begin to shuffle and turn over the cards. The cards are shape-shifting; at first I see strange markings, but they then appear like tarot images of current times. The first card I turn over is the Seven of Pentacles—someone of wealth is standing in our way.

Then the Lovers card comes up upside down—there is a loss of balance, or something is creating disharmony. The Tower comes up next—destruction. We are going to be destroyed?

The King of Swords—we must use our heads to figure this out and truth is on our side. Oh, and look, the king's partner, the Queen of Swords—we must clear our minds and focus on the task ahead. Now the last card, the Queen of Pentacles—she is telling us that we will eventually receive prosperity, but perhaps not in this lifetime.

The woman inquires about the Queen of Swords card and asks what is going to happen to her. I simply touch the card and give her a concerned look. The woman becomes hysterical. She shouts at me in French, "You promised, you promised! You told me I would be the high priestess!"

"The cards show their own fate," is all I can tell her.

"Did you see it? Did you see me? What did you see for me?"

She is frightening me, and I ask her what I should be seeing. It's strange because I tell her she can see just as well as I do. I tell her that her training with me has come full circle, and she must use her own vision. She obediently calms herself and then apologizes. As she goes silent, her insight comes stronger.

"They are coming for me and then for you," she warns.

"Who is coming?" I ask her.

"I dare not speak their names." She stops and touches her head. I see a flash of her being on the gallows, and now I feel a cold hand pushing her shoulder to kneel down, and I see a sword just sticking out of a pile of hay. I touch my throat. As I do this, she becomes very still.

"So you see it too, my oracle, my teacher? We both see it: the sword is coming for me?" Then she very calmly stands, takes the cards, mutters some words into them, kisses them, and places them in the fire.

I can't move. I ask her what she's doing.

"Breaking the circle, breaking our contract, veiling us all again," she explains. The contract? What contract? What is she talking about? Wait, what is going to happen to us all?

I suddenly heard a far-off voice say, "And now, it is time to return, Anna."

"What on earth was that?" I asked him.

"Remember, Anna, to put the storyline together! Only one woman died by the sword in the Tower of London: Anne Boleyn. That was her. Who can tell? But it would make so much sense. You know, she was famous for her thought on new ideas. She was the one who challenged the establishment, and for a while, she won. Her daughter, Elizabeth I, finished her work, the Book of Common Prayer, away from the dogma of the Church at the time. She knew the inquisition was coming to England in the future. Anne started the revolution for the Church of England, and she used tarot, astrology, and the spiritual arts to do so."

"But what is the connection to France?"

"Well, for a while, Anne went to the French court. The French and Spanish royal families were famous for their knowledge of the spiritual arts. I remember that was one of my most amazing past lives, working in the courts of Europe. Obviously, what she learnt in France would have included this.

The tarot readers of the day walked a fine line. They could bring great favor or face a cruel death." A question popped into his head. "Did you see anyone else in the vision?"

I told him I saw Lesley, and I caught a glimpse of Naomi.

"Why do you say you saw Naomi and Lesley?"

"Oh," I explained, "we were at the Chalice Well this morning, doing the ceremony, and Naomi began to talk of the bonds of sisterhood and the goddess energy. Lesley has been acting really strange, and she began to crouch down and hiss. It was very disturbing. Another woman had to ask us all to leave. It was really strange." I didn't want to share the real event because I was too embarrassed, so I gave him my interpretation of it.

"Not as strange as you might think. If these women were in that timeline of this past life circle of women, and if one who had been a high priestess of the day, which is similar to a queen, had faced death, then those left behind would have suffered afterward. If the sacred circle had been cursed or broken, as it seemed to say from your regression, it can be still affecting those women's souls today. Those women around Anne Boleyn all had a connection and purpose. The sad thing is when one dies, part of the sisterhood also dies."

"So I was an attendant to Anne Boleyn with other people I know in this life. How does that explain my greater part to play?"

"You have experienced the death of Isis, right?"

My face went white. How did he know that? "Yes," I responded. "At least from a distance. I didn't really see what happened or any of the events leading up to it."

"And you know that Isis is looking to find her successor to the mantle, yes?"

"Yes. I overheard her talking about it with Naomi."

"The solstice will help shed some much-needed light on

the situation. Then she has a window of time until the Lionsgate portal day on august 8th to complete the circle. Soon you will know exactly what befell Isis at Philae all those years ago, but all you need to know is that she was betrayed perhaps by someone within the Sacred Eight. From the sound of it, you have come into contact with at least two of them in a very significant way."

"You think that they are part of the founding of Philae?"

"I do, and I think others around you are as well. Everything is finally converging."

I wrinkled my brow. "Naomi said something like that. What do you mean?"

"The bonds of the Sacred Eight were shattered at the fall of Philae, and the next Isis was unable to take the mantle as a result. The souls of the eight have been searching for each other for almost two thousand years. But not all of them are needed to reestablish the Temple of Isis. I think that, perhaps, a new Sacred Eight is forming, one made up of the originals and newer souls, as a way to strengthen their sacred circle. Perhaps you were drawn here to find them and protect them as they carry out this most important sacred contract. Who knows? Maybe you are one of them yourself."

"Me?" I looked at Lucas incredulously. "One of the women who will refound the temple? That cannot be possible!"

"Oh, but it can." He nodded. "There need to be eight of you who were at some point initiates at Philae. That is all that is required to reestablish the temple. Part of your job, and those around you, is to find and crown a new successor for Isis. She is most likely already among us, if my readings are correct. So although undefined, you are connected to the Sacred Eight and have a role to play in founding a new temple."

I sat back again in the chair. I did not wish to share that part of my world yet, and I looked at Lucas and decided to change the subject. "Wow, that is amazing. But, you know, I feel you have a part to play in all this."

"Perhaps I do," he said mysteriously. "For some reason, I'm trapped here. I just can't seem to leave. My only escape is in the dress-up box; from there I can disappear."

I smiled slyly. "Ah, yes. I wonder if there is a costume in there for me."

"I'm sure I can whip up something," he said with an equally sly smile. I was then aware that his face had changed, and he wore dark kohl eye makeup and had a snake drawn over the top of his head. On his forehead was a scorpion. I shook my head. *There goes that déjà vu again.* I decided that this was not perhaps the right time to share that, so I smiled and asked about the payment.

"Nothing," said Lucas. "I think you will perhaps be doing some kind of reading or session for me in the near future." He handed me a business card that said, "Lucas Hammond, 750 8888."

"Call me when you figure this whole thing out. The full moon will be here before we know it, as will be the lunar eclipse." Something about the word *eclipse* made me shiver. "Now, Anna, it's time to send you home," he said, getting up. "I feel there is much work I need to do in the astral levels."

As I left, I felt exhausted, like all my life energy had been drained away. I had found a new friend in Lucas, but I had also opened up more questions than before. I felt my phone buzz in my bag, and I prayed it was Lucinda returning my call.

She had sent a text instead. "I think it is wise that I come to Glastonbury when there is less of a negative presence there. Have heart; you will figure out what is happening."

And just like that, I was on my own again to figure everything out.

CHAPTER 18

That afternoon, without anything left to do for the day, I decided to walk around and collect my thoughts. I found myself hiding all afternoon in the back of another café for lunch, which I could not eat, and then wandering back toward the Tor again for sunset. I sat down near the outer gate and replayed the day's events in my head. I didn't realize how late it was until I found the moon shining down at me from the center of the sky. I went back to the Guesthouse and tried to be quiet as I crept in. It was past 10:00 p.m., and I knew everyone would be in bed.

I snuck into the kitchen to grab a snack and found Emilee there. At first, I could swear she had on a long black dress and bonnet, but as my eyes adjusted to the dim candlelight, I saw that she was wearing a dark purple housecoat.

"Emilee," I said softly, "I'm home. Is everything okay?"

She looked over at me, and her eyes looked red from crying. She smiled softly. "Oui, ma chère. I am just remembering some past times. But tell me, how was your day?"

I sat down on the other chair. "Karmic drama," I sighed.

"Ah, yes. Ms. Starchild was created, I think, for drama and the reality TV. You may be her next aspiring actress."

"So you have encountered her work before?"

"Oh, yes," she said, "for many lifetimes—and not happy ones."

"You knew Naomi in a past life? Are you sure? Which one? I found out today that she was responsible for some horrible things. I just hope you weren't involved." I was so eager to hear, but then I thought I had better not because who knew what that would open up.

"All right, my friend, you are the eager beaver. Calm down, and I will share with you. It is time," she said as she motioned for me to sit down. As I did, I went to locate my journal, but she held her hand up. "No, this is private, please."

I nodded and watched as she poured herself a glass of red wine into an exquisite crystal glass. She poured from a bottle that was nearly empty, which meant she had been pondering this for perhaps a while. She motioned the bottle toward me, but I declined.

☥

About three years ago, not long after I had opened up the Gables to others for room rental, I never knew who would find their way to my door. It wasn't as simple as going on a website to book a room. I had left my card with the tourist information office and highlighted that I preferred single guests or couples. I'm not great with families; we have a lot of antiques in this house.

There was one Friday evening around the full moon. I always know that because often people would be walking past on their way up the Tor. At that time, we had wooden gates on the driveway. These gave way last year, so we switched to metal frames, which are easier to move and to see through. Anyway, I received a call around 5:30 p.m. from the tourist information office. They had a young woman who needed a room; they had called most other places, but they were full. I don't like last-minute bookings, but in those days I was glad of any booking I could get because there was a loan to pay. I told them yes and said that she should come up at once. I would open the gate, and she simply had to ring the bell on the front. I forgot to take the name. I simply trusted.

About twenty minutes later, the gate rang, and I answered. I called out and pressed the button for the gate to open. The light was on, which meant the gate was open, but no one came through. I waited and waited and had the strangest feeling. I was nervous. When an hour passed, I was relieved that the visitor had decided not to stay.

A little later, I remembered I had some mail to collect from the box at the front gate and went out. I opened the gate to step out, and there in the cold leaning against the wall was a woman. It was raining, and I was not sure who or what it was, but I felt scared. She looked at me, not saying a word. I asked her if she was the girl from the tourist information, and she nodded.

"Let's get you inside," I said. I looked for her luggage, but nothing was there. I tried to stay calm and told her to follow me. I walked back toward the house, completely forgetting about the mail. Once inside, she simply asked how much, and I remember she handed it over to me in cash. By the look of it, she had a whole bundle of cash.

I gave her room seven. I asked if she was hungry, and she shook her head. I asked if she needed a doctor because I noticed her hands had linen wrapped around them, and her hand kept reaching up to cover the side of her face. She thanked me and said no, stating that nothing could help this curse. I was used to this kind of talk in Glastonbury, but not from a stranger.

I put on all the lights, and I could see her clearly for the first time. She was in a great deal of distress. Her face looked bruised, and I truly thought she had been in a car accident. I showed her to her room, and again she said very little but simply mumbled. I felt this great sense of fear, but how could I ask her to leave?

Once she entered the room, she looked more relaxed, and she closed the door behind her and locked it. I stood for a while and heard the shower go on as well as the TV, so I left and went to bed.

Before I went to bed, I locked all the other rooms and the kitchen, and then I went to my room, locked the door, and put a chair behind it. Can you imagine owning a guesthouse and fearing your guests? But I guess it does happen. The next morning, I woke up and she was gone. The bedroom door was open, the keys were on the side table, and she had vanished. I went outside and looked for a car, but nothing was there, not a trace.

I went back to her room, and all was in order, however, it was very bizarre. There was salt on the carpet beside the bedroom door and on the windowsill. In the waste bin were lots and lots of red string. I had no idea what this was, and the other interesting thing was that Wallis had spent the night with me and would not go into room seven for a long while. Often when I book a day to clear the energy of the house, I will have the cat walk with me, and she lets me know which rooms need the prayer or the lavender spray.

Well, the next day I still could not get settled, so I called the tourist information office, and they said they had no details about the woman except that she had come looking for directions and a room at the Sanctuary, but the Sanctuary was full, so they had suggested me. Apparently, she had been booked the following day but had arrived a day early.

All afternoon, I could not settle, so I called the Sanctuary. Isis answered the phone, we had met on occasions over the years and at various ceremonies, but I would not describe her as a friend. I said that I was a little concerned for a guest I had staying with me, and I enquired if they had seen her. Isis asked me to describe her, and I did the best I could without sounding too judgmental, but to say the woman looked unhinged would have been kind.

"Ah yes," she said, "that would be Ms. Starchild. She's a witch. Best we leave that story alone." Then she put the phone down.

"So what did you do?" I asked.

"Well, I call Lucinda, your friend. We have been friends a long time. We once visited all the churches connected to Mary Magdalene in France. She was a pilgrim, and I was a translator. We were both connected to her work and her gospel—you know, the one that's not in the Bible."

I shook my head. Witches, and now the Bible? I was getting confused. "What did Lucinda say?"

"Well, she confirmed that Ms. Starchild was a witch, but she said that didn't mean she was a dark one. Salt is to protect, and the string can be used to unwind curses. They are symbolic more than anything. Obviously, Ms. Starchild had no physical baggage, but she did have a great deal of mental and emotional bags to carry." Emilee paused and looked at the clock.

I said, "I know it's late, but I have to understand. Please, Emilee?"

She continued with her story.

Lucinda came to visit me after that. She always came to visit on a goddess festival and solstice time. She helped me to clear room seven of negative energy. She confirmed that witchcraft had taken place, but more from a protection level than an evil one. She also thought that in some way, we knew her from a past life. Lucinda said she felt the spirit of this woman was connected to ours, especially because Isis had taken her in.

"But we know her on other levels," she said. I asked who "*we*" meant, and she didn't give me an answer. We all found our way to Glastonbury by chance, but it was all in divine order.

Lucinda had trained with Isis the previous year. I knew nothing of this. She was attending an event in London when she met Isis. They struck up a friendship, and Isis began to mentor her. That was a peaceful, pleasant time. Isis and Lucinda would visit the Chalice Well, and that is where they met Alice and me. We all crossed paths, and that was it. When Ms. Starchild arrived—or should I say Naomi—many things changed. Whatever Naomi was hiding from was mean and nasty. And even though she thought she had escaped this, it appears it followed her and all of us to Glastonbury.

As time passed, Lucinda became a regular and chose to stay with me. She said with Naomi always staying at the Sanctuary, there was too much drama around Isis. We began to meditate together, and that's when our oracle work really started to show itself.

One day, Naomi had crossed paths with Lucinda in a local café. For some reason, Lucinda asked about Isis, and Naomi ignored her. She called Lucinda a fraud. Lucinda was very agitated; as you know, she takes her work seriously. Lucinda returned home beyond upset that she had been embarrassed, and I decided to help her. It's so strange how we kept passing in events and places so long ago.

"So Lucinda and I did our oracle regression," Emilee explained.

"Oracle regression? What's that?" I asked.

"The oracle sees many things, like the books and stories of many historical times. You remember the Akashic records?"

"Oh, yes. I'm trying to understand the oracles and think I may have been one too."

"Ah, très bien, ma chère! Well, when any group of oracles or seers get together, they see the visions of a particular storyline. One will often start, and then it moves to the left. One oracle will often see, another feels, and another hears. You can piece the storyline together a little like a movie. The main thing is to not become emotionally attached to the moment. You can get caught in that timeline forever."

"Oh, I think that happened today," I said.

"Really? You did past life regression, or oracle work?"

"Is there a difference?"

"Well, it's similar. An oracle can see the past, present, and future. She sees everything. The past life regression, many can do; they are simply returning to a memory."

"Well, it's been happening a lot lately…it's weird. I have been around Naomi a lot in the last week, and I keep getting visions off of her. The women at the Chalice Well said I was forcing visions from her. I didn't even know what I was doing. I kept seeing Naomi connected to the Temple of Edfu and the Salem witch trials, which this woman called Lesley at the Sanctuary mentioned. She said you were there too!"

"Ah, well, I would not say *force*. You know not what you do! But they are not wrong. You were experiencing her past life. But not force, no, just…how you say, eager? No, uh, powerful without proper training. This is what oracle work is: it takes time and patience, which they clearly don't have with you."

"Emilee, tell me about the oracle work with Lucinda, please?" I was afraid that I was distracting her and also delaying her from sharing something with me that I really needed to know.

"Well, Lucinda and I were just starting to practice this art, and we needed help, so we called Alice."

"She can do this?"

"Oh, oui, she is a master Akashic librarian."

"Librarian? Wow."

"Who do you think works in the Akashic records? It is a massive library. We called a formal oracle vision."

"A formal oracle vision," I repeated.

"Oui, it's like a summons or gathering, and from the time we announce it, those called to the oracle vision all begin in small ways to see, feel, and hear things."

"Is that like spying on someone?" I asked.

She smiled a little, ignoring the question. "But as Naomi had performed witchcraft in my home, the karma needed to be relieved. The oracle vision was called at 11:11 a.m., and we all sat down that morning in the dining area and made sure that it was bright and that daylight was streaming into the room. This kind of work takes on another tone in the twilight times of day. We called in the spirits and joined hands, and I started the regression.

"I described Naomi briefly because at that time I had no idea who she was, and apparently she was a famous psychic astrologer with a successful following. I focused then on the vision of her until Alice and Lucinda were also telepathically connected. I was seeing the vision, and Alice touched her cheek, which meant she felt the energy, and Lucinda began to hear the messages.

"I first began to describe the vision of Naomi and how she was going about her day until she came home. It was then that Alice began to feel the pain. Lucinda repeated the cruel words from what we thought was her lover or husband. Then I felt myself go very small, like curling up, and Lucinda began to utter the curse words. By this time Alice was feeling quite dizzy, and we decided that we had enough information to see who and what was being cursed, and it had nothing to do with Glastonbury or me. Or so we thought.

"We were about to come back out of the meditation when Lucinda began to say the year 1692. She was deep in a trance, and Alice and I looked at each other. I told them that I would go back and figure out what was going on. I closed my eyes again and began to wander back to 1692."

Suddenly she stopped and sat up. "But, dear Anna, now I think it is late, and I have drank too much of this precious elixir." She laughed. "We can tell this sad tale another day."

"Emilee, please continue!" I begged. "Something tells me that if I can work out this connection of you and Naomi, I can unravel many of the curses that ail you two and perhaps others. Please, please tell me more."

She considered this a moment and then poured herself a tall glass of water. "Okay, ma cherie," she conceded, "but perhaps now I let you record this." I quickly grabbed my bag and the voice recorder from Naomi thankfully was still there.

I recorded it and later would script and translate it to put in my book. It was weird, because everything she said that day was a mix of English and French, but as she spoke, I understood everything, even though I hadn't taken more than three years of French in school years ago. Here is that translation in English of her story.

♀

Okay, I am relaxing, remembering, and going back to 1692. I close my eyes and open the Akashic record. I can see Lucinda, Alice, and myself back in the front room. Okay, yes, I see it all again and tell the other oracles all that I sense. I first see an old American house, and then a church, and then people walking around. Many people are wearing black and white and carrying

Bibles. Up ahead I can see a clearing, and I wander over the field, and there is a tree. Hanging from the tree was a woman.

"Salem," hissed Alice.

As we do with oracle protocol, we always stay a moment before going further.

"I feel cold and afraid," said Alice.

"I can hear whispers behind closed doors," said Lucinda. "There are those for and against us."

I see everything, but I want to know how this started. I decide to go and look further back in the timeline. I see a village going about its business. Then I see myself. I am happy, and I have a small daughter. She is so precious. My husband is just returning from a trip; something about being in Jamestown. He has a fever, but this soon passes once he rests. However, whatever he had has passed to my daughter. Before long, a few of the town's other children have a fever. My daughter is the sickest of them all. It is then that I see Naomi, and she has children of her own, a son and two daughters.

I'm very scared my child will die, so I consult the doctor, who tells me nothing can be done. I make arrangements to get some medicine from Tituba, a slave woman owned by the Parris family. We agree to meet in the woods. I get there early and see Tituba meeting with another woman. Tituba is handing her a green bottle. The woman turns, and I see that it is Naomi. I don't pay much mind to it. I wait out of sight and then get my blue bottle potion from Tituba. I pray with Tituba that my child will survive, and I am happy about that. I trust Tituba, and as I'm seeing her, her face shifts. I know her, and I trust her.

I move on further in the timeline. I now see Naomi in mourning; both her husband and son have become sick, and then both die. Naomi blames the fever my husband brought back, but this illness could not have killed anyone. It hadn't killed anyone else in the village. Around the same time, two young girls living near Naomi begin to show symptoms of sickness. They say the devil is within them.

♀

Now I see the trials starting. At this point, Lucinda begins with the chants and the prayers. She talks in tongues and describes what the girls are hearing. She begins to read out the degrees from the judges and the cries and fears of the townspeople.

Alice is now feeling the panic and fear, and she begins to sob. She asks me to stop, but I cannot. Lucinda is in a deeper trance by now, and to awaken her without the full story would leave her caught in a parallel story where she is trapped.

I have to carry on because the universe brought this woman to my door in present time, and we have a sacred duty to reveal the truth. I have a great sense of foreboding, but I can't help myself. I need to see what happens. I now know we had a past life karma. The universe and our souls are giving me the opportunity to clear this. I take a deep breath and go deeper into the storyline.

I continue to see the trials and each of the various women and children who are accused. Anyone who uses holistic or herbal remedy is under attack, and any family with a grudge brings forward stories that they have seen evil. They cast doubt on others before they themselves can be doubted. I also see that anyone connected to the moon rituals is gathered and imprisoned. Everything is in chaos and panic.

I ask my spirit guides to help me see where Naomi and I cross soul connection and karma. I am shown that I'm being formally accused by Naomi. She is telling everyone she followed me into the woods and saw me talking to Tituba. It's strange, but I see Tituba with a black face, then a white face. Naomi is saying I gave her coins and that I wanted to be in league with the dark ones. She tells them I belong to the dark ones, the ones who come at night in dark capes. They are the powerful ones; they come in our dreams and steal our souls. She is in fear.

And now my formal trial has started. I'm standing alone in the area for the prisoners. My hair and face are red, and I look to be in pain. I'm wringing my hands and am terrified.

Naomi steps forward and says I met with Tituba and left with a green bottle of poison, and that she sees my hands are like those of a witch.

"That is not true," I shout. "I had a blue bottle."

"So you had a bottle and you were there?" The judge is quick to jump in as others at the back of the room begin to scream. I realize I've been tricked, and this confession has sealed my fate. I feel helpless as they read out the verdict of witchcraft.

I'm not listening. All I can think about is my daughter. Who will care for her? Her fate will be a tragic one; I know it. Oh no, I wish she was coming with me—but I don't mean that. I don't want harm for her.

But they are bringing her toward me, and she is weak, starving, and neglected. She's also cursed because she was the one who survived. They are saying she carries the devil's mark because she's the daughter of a witch. They pull back her sleeve to double-check, and sure enough, there is a mark on her skin. She's crying hysterically now because she doesn't understand what is happening to us.

She runs to me, and as she does, people push her. I gather her into my arms and bury her head into me to shield her from this evil state of affairs. My husband has fled and disowned us; I see him creeping out of the courtroom. I cry to him, but he leaves. I'm abandoned without hope. He promised to care for and protect my daughter and me, but he flees like a coward. I nursed him back to health, he originally brought the fever, and now he leaves. I curse him to never find true love in his next lives, and if he should attract love, may he always be blind to it.

Emilee paused, and I found myself shaking. I felt like I was right there in the courtroom, watching her point at her husband and actually seeing the curse fly from her lips and wrap around him in a swirling cloud. My heart began to feel so heavy, and it was then that I turned off the recorder. Some stories of the past needed respect, and I wanted to be there for Emilee as her friend and not her therapist or a story hunter.

Emilee was openly sobbing at this point, but she continued her story.

They take us away and leave us in a dark, cold place. I see my baby die in my arms. I see her soul go with the angels to heaven, and she waves to me. I take small pieces of hay that we sit on and pull threads from my skirt. I tie each one around each stick and wind it around with my prayer. I call in the spirits and bind each soul to me so that justice may prevail in this or the next life.

My final vision is of me walking to the gallows, and I see Naomi watching me, but she looks at me with guilt and shame. All I can do is shake my head. I pray she carries this in her soul forever.

Emilee then came out of her story and looked at me. I asked her what happened to the oracle vision group.

"Well, Lucinda was the first to awaken. She said that was the most traumatic vision she had seen. Alice was a wreck. We all figured out that we had seen other people in that vision that we knew. Lucinda said she saw her friend Laura as Tituba in that lifetime, and she recognized one of the young women who accused her, but she couldn't place her." I could see this story had taken every scrap of energy she had to tell it.

"All right, Anna, I am done now. I take no more of this," Emilee said, heaving a ragged breath. She wiped tears from her face. I got up from the table and embraced her. I had felt so close and protective of her. I could feel her loss and how it affected her all these years later. "Yes, ma chère, I lost my precious child, but sharing my journey with you lifts a weight from my heart," she exclaimed, embracing me. "I think you are right to be concerned about what happened today." Emilee let go of me. "Be careful around Naomi, for she has caused much pain in many lives. Don't let her repeat that in this one."

"Why is it, then, that the women wouldn't listen to me? If she is so dangerous, shouldn't they be warned?"

"Those women today, they seem to protect Naomi at all costs. She is a star to them, a powerful force in our practices. Since coming to Glastonbury, Naomi has proven to be the most skilled of Isis's students, next to Lesley. She is heir apparent, closer to the high priestess than anyone. No one will cross someone so important to Isis. They won't listen to anything against her."

I took that to heart and thought for a moment. Suddenly, I realized something. "Emilee, what you just did was a regression into your own past life, but you shared it with me."

"Oui," she replied.

"You needed help your first time around?"

"Oui."

"You know, I think that happened to me. Earlier today, I went to the Goth—though his real name is Lucas—for a tarot card reading and it jump-started something in me. I had a vision of Anne Boleyn. I was on my way to the Tower of London to visit her as she awaited trial. The whole thing made me sick and dizzy."

"You were Anne Boleyn? Anna, is that true?" Emilee responded.

"No, that does not resonate, but I think I was someone very close to her, so close that she trusted me with her secrets. I think I was a teacher or mentor to her in spiritual or psychic arts. I know we were friends of some sort."

"What did you see after the regression?"

I told Emilee about the tower and the gate, and how I was able to easily move around. I told her how I'd touched on the messages from the tarot cards and felt the despair the woman had felt.

Emilee asked me how I'd felt when it was over, what the prevailing emotion was.

"I thought I should feel grief at the loss of my friend and my student," I explained. "But to be honest, I felt guilt more than anything."

"Guilt for what?" she asked.

"I think I was supposed to protect her."

Emilee bit her lip.

"What do you know? You know something, Emilee."

She paused for a moment and pondered whether she should share or not, but ultimately she decided to do so. "I've had Anne Boleyn come to me before in a ceremony. It is the most curious thing. She spoke in perfect French to me; it was très magnifique!"

"What did she say?"

"Vous devez protéger le temple."

"You must protect the temple?"

"Oui, parfait, Anna!"

"I'm not sure what that means, though."

"Anna, I think she was a priestess of Isis like us, like you, maybe. She went to Philae in a past life. She was trained in sacred arts like tarot and divination in the French court in her later life. It would make sense for the soul of a priestess to migrate to that. Perhaps the English court was her temple."

"How can we tell for sure?"

"I need to take you back to her, to her timeline before the Tower of London. Let's see where and how you come into this story."

I began to feel dizzy again. "Oh, Emilee, I don't know if I can handle going back again. I've done it so much today already."

"We must know what magic she knew and how it is affecting you here and now. This is très importante."

I was reluctant to do it again, but something told me that this would haunt me unless I looked, so I sat back in the chair and nodded my head.

Emilee pulled a blue bottle out of her pocket and handed it to me. "Here, drink. This helps with the dizziness and nausea more than any herbal tea could." I drank it quickly. The liquid was sweet and coated my throat. A warmness came over me all of a sudden, and I felt calm and focused.

I glanced at the clock on the wall; it was nearly midnight. I prayed we would have the answer soon so I could go to bed and hide under the duvet all day. After all, I certainly was not invited back to the gathering tomorrow.

"Anna, focus, please."

Emilee then led me down a sacred pathway and back in time. We went back to my past life and connected to the visions

I had had earlier today.

"Now tell me, what do you see, Anna?"

"I'm in an English garden."

"How do you know?"

"It's lined with bluebells and has neatly trimmed bushes. There are rows and rows of white roses and a few apple trees on the far side of the garden. The whole thing is enclosed by a large stone fence. I am turning around, and I see the large country estate.

I'm going toward the house, and there is a coat of arms above the door. I feel happy here, but there is something dark floating around in the water that is near the garden. An energy that's watching me."

"What is the connection to Anne Boleyn?" Emilee asked.

"This was her home as a child. It's a joyful place, where she was happiest with her brother and sister."

"Can you locate Anne Boleyn, though?"

"No. I have to go to another place and another garden, a great garden with a palace. Yes, now I'm in a different place; I'm at the Palace of Whitehall in Westminster, Middlesex. I'm wandering in the gardens, and the people passing me are in Tudor dress. They are all wealthy dignitaries with nothing better to do than gossip."

"What are you wearing?"

"I'm in a dark cape and emerald-green velvet dress. I can see that I have golden hair."

"Find where you need to be, Anna."

"I'm in the palace now, in a private sitting room. The walls are paneled with wood, and grand tapestries hang from them. I hear a woman crying, and people are running."

"Find the people, Anna. Where are you now?"

"I'm in a bedroom with a dark oak wood bed and beautiful

drapes. The woman on the bed is Anne. She is wearing a white nightgown that is stained with blood. There is blood all over the bed. She sees me and calls me over. I'm her friend, and she calls me sister. She's pointing at another woman in the room and telling her—no, she's screaming at her that this is her fault."

"Who is the woman?"

"I'm not sure. She is wearing a dark purple cloak that obscures her face. The cloaked woman is begging for forgiveness. She resembles Lucinda. Queen Anne is hysterical and says there can be no forgiveness. She tells the woman she listened to her spells and prophesies. She says that the magic to win her husband's heart was slowly fading. She tells the woman her witchcraft has cursed them all. The cloaked woman shows her a scroll with symbols on it and tells her that the planets and stars foretold a great prince would be born. She tells the woman that she saw Mother Nature giving a great prince. She has the scroll of the records of life; it holds the knowledge of destiny.

"Anne screams that it was years ago when she was told this, and all she has to show for it is a princess. She's telling the woman that she also said the king would be her loving husband forever and that they had sacred work to do. She says the king has moved to another woman's bed, and the golden age is slipping from their grasp. She calls the woman a false prophet and liar. She curses the woman to leave her sight and says that the blood of all is on her hands.

"The woman bows her head in shame and does as she is told. As she leaves, she tells the queen that the stars have declared this, and she must not lose faith. She talks about how her coven had moved the balance. That the queen paid a price in gold so that Lilith would favor the queen with a boy child above all others. Then she leaves.

"The queen looks at me. She tells me to do what I can to

protect them. She says to look in the mirrors and secret waters to connect to the spirits and pray for our souls.

"And that's all I can see." I sat up and brought myself back. "It's too much, Emilee. I do not understand. What does this have to do with anything?"

"I think," replied Emilee, "Anne Boleyn was told that a great prince would be born, and that is why she pursued the king in her special way. She did bewitch him in many ways to get this, but she never had a son. However, she didn't realize that the prince was a princess who would become a queen, Elizabeth I. Such was the time when they needed male heirs, but they had to make do with her.

"Nature is all about balance, Anna. What I saw was these women's fear. People do strange things out of fear. I think that Anne called on this woman—Lucinda, as you thought it was— to perhaps conjure up a spell to tip the odds in her favor for her having a boy. By taking away any newborn or infant boys in the area, she may have felt it created better odds for herself. Unfortunately, this came back to haunt this woman with karma, and I guess that created her fate."

"And that's true?"

"Who knows? But I think so."

"Did you see anything, Emilee?"

"Yes, I saw pregnant women being given gifts of elixirs for healthy babies by the cloaked woman who was in the tower with Anne. It was a health elixir for girls, but it forced a miscarriage if it was a boy. And this woman convinced Anne to finance this, but I don't think she was personally involved. I feel one in particular seems to cast spells on the others. It is as if she conspires against the queen but is her trusted servant also."

"And that woman is?"

"I'm not sure."

"Whoever she was, she was powerful enough to block any of us from seeing her identity. I think we were able to channel this because this is one of the points in history when the Eight tried to reconnect and break the curse. The problem was that not all eight were there, which caused them to fight and fracture."

"Oh, yes, the Goth said that. They were cursed."

"Oui, and spirituality was lost to witchcraft, and the sacred arts and wisdom were then hidden and only remembered through the use of the scrolls and books that I feel may have been altered, with their secrets abused."

"Like you shared with me, and like the scroll Isis gave me."

"Oui. Once, the wisdom was recorded in our souls, but as we lost our faith, we had to resort to written materials, which unfortunately left out precious messages. Also, our sacred scrolls were stolen by men who did not understand or feared us; their ego thus created our downfall and persecution. But we must remember in all these visions that we had a choice as women to come together: to heal the past, to trust like in the original days of Philae. But always we failed. We did not protect our sacred vow, and that was our real temple.

"You know, Anna, you are becoming an oracle, a keeper of the secrets of our people. We simply need to figure out who you are. Which one you are."

I looked down, not sure what to say, but a thought occurred to me. "Isis said that I was special, and I overheard her talking to Naomi about my abilities and needing me to help them with something."

"Ah, I see. You do have a unique talent for oracle work, and you were able to read the scroll right away."

"Yes."

"Anna, there is a reason you are here. You could be one of the Eight who will bring about the new temple, but what if you were the next Isis? People may fear you, but you bring a change for them that they cannot manage themselves. You force people to face their past traumas."

"That's crazy. I'm not the next Isis. I would know; I'm sure I would."

"Would you, though? Did you know you knew Anne Boleyn in a past life? And not only did you know her, but you taught her. Did you ever see her in a movie or book growing up?"

I shook my head, but then a childhood memory came to me. "No. However, when I was seven years old, I was taken to a hobby shop, where they had all types of plastic models, and I bought the Anne Boleyn one. I treasured her and painted her and thought she was so beautiful. Whenever I saw her shown in a history book, I always cried."

"What made you cry?"

"That's the odd thing: I never felt sad when she died. It was only when they would refer back to the small princess, showing her alone, that my heart would break. Perhaps that is my connection?"

"Perhaps."

"But I keep seeing all these lives of other people, people I seem to know today. Like, why Naomi and Salem? Why is that so prevalent and vivid? What does this all have to do with Philae?"

"Well," explained Emilee, "after the fall of the Temple of Isis, as you know, the souls of the priestesses who served there were cursed and scattered, forced to relive the worst manifestations of their past traumas. It was rare that any of them would find even one other oracle in the same timeline. Every so often, a few would manage to find each other, usually those who share the similar trauma. There is power in this.

"You see, their souls are all trying to find each other to break this cycle of trauma and resolve it. So when they find a few, they try to break out of the curse, but they end up creating more pain for themselves that they then experience in the next life. Salem was one such instance, as was the time of Anne Boleyn. In fact, Salem was the last time that many oracle souls found each other—other than now, of course. Timelines are converging on a larger scale than ever before. We feel it. But first you must discover what your part is. What you felt just now was guilt, not grief. This is the first piece of the puzzle, so to speak. The essence of your trauma is guilt."

"But how does that help me?"

"It might help give you a window into your life in Egypt. I am positive you had one there; I just can't sense it."

"You think I did?" I asked.

"Yes, others who served Isis were there. You being part of Anne's inner circle and court is not a coincidence. I do not know which one, but you are part of the new Eight and could be the new Isis. A new soul, one who had not been present for the founding of the temple, was supposed to take on the mantle every couple of hundred years, but that never happened. It is promising that you have not had a vision of you at the creation of Philae."

"Why?"

"The mantle should never be taken up by anyone from the original Sacred Eight. They shared a sacred contract with each other, and their souls bound to the roles they were assigned. A new soul is needed to renew their contract." Emilee nodded and thought a moment. "Oui, but everything changed when the Eight broke their contracts with each other. They may not even be with us anymore. It would take an extraordinary priestess or oracle to bring it back into harmony and balance. And you, Anna, you appear to have all the gifts bestowed upon the original Eight without being one of them."

"Oh, I don't know…Maybe. Look, this is all a bit overwhelming." I was sweating. I couldn't even begin to grasp what she was saying.

"I know it is. Why don't you sleep on it and go visit Alice on Monday, when the retreat has ended? She might be able to help you as she did before."

"She didn't help much today. She was the one who told me to leave."

"Do not take it personally. She is not one to stir the pot like me. Maybe that's part of her trauma, not speaking up when she sees wrong. She will help, though, I promise. Now take your record machine, go write and then to sleep. It has been a very long day."

Emilee got up, and I turned to ask her one more thing, "Emilee, are you one of the Sacred Eight?"

There was a twinkle in her eye and a smile on her face, but she said nothing. It seemed that maybe I'd found one more. I then excused myself for the evening, although, as I looked at the clock, I realized it would soon be morning.

CHAPTER 19

As I got ready for bed, my mind was racing after what Emilee had said. I prayed that on Monday Alice could help me make sense of this. Even though I now had seen dark secrets connected to Alice, she was someone I felt I could trust.

I was now beginning to wonder who or what I was. *Perhaps going home to York is my answer. I could stay with Laura, find a job, and live a simple life.*

I opened my computer to write down a few of my thoughts. I managed to write ten pages, but they were not well formed and were rife with spelling errors and poor sentence construction. I had had enough hits to my self-esteem today, so I closed my computer and got into bed.

If I'm an oracle, why can't I channel my own past? I thought. *I want so badly to be able to do this on my own.*

I sat up in bed and dimmed the lights in my room. I put on some meditation music and begin to think about how my past life regressions were achieved.

Yes, that's it. I'm going back to the memories, and this feels wonderful.

Suddenly, I sensed a cold presence in the room.

I'm seeing the figures in cloaks again. They are laughing and pointing. It seems to be all the historic times merged, and I see us all at different points. There is me, Naomi, Isis, and Emilee. Now Alice appears too. We keep going back and forth between light and dark. Sometimes we curse others; at other times, we are the cursed. No one seems to win this. Then a very large gray being enters my vision, but I can't see its face.

I brought myself back to the room and my reality. I was too afraid. I went back to my laptop to make a few notes on a clean page. Then I glanced at the time on the top corner of the screen; it was 4:44 in the morning. It really was time for bed. I closed my computer, turned off the lights, and crawled into bed.

The damp stone corridor is lined with wooden doors. All I have to do is find the right one. I sense them coming. Them. Who are they? I need to find the right door. I heard laughing, the laughter of a young girl. Where is that coming from? I can hear her in the distance. She must be at the end of the corridor. I need to get going—they are coming. I need to find the door.

They are getting closer.

I am running down the hallway, but I don't seem to be getting any closer. I keep trying to open all of the doors on the way, but none of them budge.

They are right behind me.

I am panicking, and I frantically pound and pull and scratch at any door I can find.

They are here.

The figures from before surround me and descend upon me. As they do, a door to my right opens. I run inside before they get me.

The source of the laughter lives here. She is one of the girls from Salem. She is the ringleader for all of the young girls who accused women of witchcraft. I know I know her from somewhere, but I can't see her face. All she has to do is turn around, and—

Sunday, June 8

I awoke abruptly to the sound of the doves on my window; they made such a gentle sound. I looked at my clock: 10:33 a.m. *Wow, I must have really needed the sleep.* I jumped out of bed, relieved to have survived the night, but a nagging feeling about that Salem girl perplexed me. Today would have to be my day to make everything good in the world.

I went downstairs to get breakfast. The guests from Saturday night had departed for home early now that the goddess retreat was in disarray; I had heard them banging on the stairs and complaining as they walked past my room. I prayed they would leave early, and they had, so now I didn't have to creep around to avoid them. But there was a great noise coming from the dining room.

"They came early," Emilee whispered to me as I entered the room. "Tourists from Italy, so they just laugh and eat, and eat and laugh" she explained. Wow, the energy had certainly changed. I simply pulled up a chair and began to people-watch.

Emilee seemed to be in a great mood, chattering away in Italian and bringing around fresh espresso every five minutes. Every time she brought more, they applauded and cheered. *A very different group indeed.*

Once I finished breakfast, I slipped out the door without

bringing attention to myself. Emilee had her hands full, and I didn't want to take her away from it.

I went back to my room and put all my books and the scroll into the chest of drawers. I decided I had to take a day of rest and find my own inner peace.

Monday, June 9

When I arrived at the Chalice Well, a different woman was at the gate selling tickets. I was afraid to ask her where Alice was; I still wasn't completely sure that she was on my side. Regardless, I bought a ticket and walked the grounds. I wandered back toward the Lion's Head Fountain for some sacred water so I could at least make use of my time. It was a shame I couldn't take a bath there; that would surely please the gods and clear my sins. I laughed.

"What's so funny, my dear?" a voice asked from behind me. I turned and saw that it was Alice. She sat behind me, where we had been the other day. She looked amused at my laughter. Maybe she wasn't too upset with me, and perhaps she was still talking to me. I sat down next to her and smiled at her.

"I was wondering," I teased, "if I needed to be covered in holy water to clear and cleanse my soul. I figured after Saturday, that might be best for someone like me."

"Ah, yes, because of your public disturbance at the ceremony. I am sorry you had to go through that. Do not take it too personally; the sisterhood has been fractured and distrustful of each other for millennia." She looked out over the grounds. "Do you know many died in the battles of war and religion here and around this area? This land is marred with blood and anguish, but over time it healed. So too will our dear sisterhood. This is the heart, a place destined to see the most horrible atrocities and the most wonderful miracles. It is all about balance, Anna."

"Yes, that is all lovely, Alice, but I know nothing about this."

"But you do, my dear. You cannot play an innocent child any more. And everyone knows you now. You have come out in a big way and have put a target on your back. They distrust you because you showed your power too soon. You can't control yourself yet, and that scares them."

"But I have no power."

"Did Emilee not tell you that you do? At any rate, they think you do, and I have to be honest, my dear, so do I."

How does she know about my and Emilee's conversation on Saturday night? Wait—I have to stop wondering that. They all know everything.

She continued. "You slip in and out of places and people's lives in this town. Not many can do that. You see what people hide, or what they do not wish to see about themselves. Perhaps you could use more care and have more finesse, but you must be a powerful oracle to be able to look into the souls of others with or without their permission. I've only witnessed Isis do this before you."

"Well, I have not looked at everyone," I tried to protest.

"Yes, but you could, without even trying!" She talked excitedly. "Whether they want to or not, they are opening up their hearts because of you. Stop with the false modesty and accept this part of you. You would do well to look in your heart, Anna. Look at your own records."

"I tried that last night, and all I saw were evil, caped monsters."

"Souls held by this old, nasty, powerful soul group."

"Ah, I don't like the sound of that."

Alice shook her head.

"But that's why I'm here, Alice," I continued. "I saw all of us in a circle."

"Who is the 'all of us'?"

"Naomi, Isis, Emilee, me, and you."

She looked at me, astonished. "So you *do* see, my dear. You have an all-seeing eye, and by my count it's a good one. That's, what, four or five of the eight?"

"But I can't see who is the evil one. I'm not sure if it's male or female, or if I even known them."

"Well, we shall have to see. At any rate, you have just told me that you have been in contact with five of the original Eight. That is the largest group of them that has been together since…" She paused, not wishing to carry on.

"Salem, I know."

She looked at me, her eyes full of tears, and I reached out and took her hand. She smiled, and we nodded to each other.

We then sat in silence for a while, and it felt so good not to have to make conversation. I knew I would eventually have to break this and talk about why I was here. Alice knew it too. But for a moment longer, we basked in our blissful silence.

"Do you think they all hate me?" I finally piped up, shattering our peace.

"Who, my dear?"

"The ladies from the ceremony."

"No, not hate, but they have trust issues. The last time a powerful oracle came, we all nearly lost everything."

"What happened?"

"It's not my story to tell, my dear." She paused. "Ask Lucinda. I don't think that you will cause harm."

I looked down at my lap. I was afraid to ask Alice this next question. "Do you think Isis hates me? I know she thinks I brought down the temple."

"No, dear, Isis does not hate you. She's just trying to accommodate everyone and do what's best for the whole group."

"*Accommodate* is an interesting choice of words."

"Now, you did not come here to talk about that. You came for information. And information is kind of my specialty. I think my story will help shed some light on what led to what is happening now. I witnessed the beginning of the end."

"You did?"

"Oh, yes, and I've preserved the knowledge for over two thousand years just to tell it to someone like you."

I was all ears, and I took out my phone and turned on the recording app. I remembered to ask permission this time, before getting started. "Is this okay, Alice?"

"Yes, my dear, perfectly fine. Like I said, I've waited over many, many past lives to let this go. Now, where shall we begin?"

This was Alice's story, and it was not easy to forget.

As Seshat's apprentice and oracle to Ra around 356 BC, I always resided in the temples at Heliopolis. I started as an initiate and student of the priests of Ra; there were only a few of us, and we were a mix of male and female. We would spend our days reading and learning from texts; we called them the texts of truth. They had been passed down to us for two and a half millennia. We originally got them from a place you now refer to as Atlantis. Yes, I know you thought that was a mythical place, but before the time of time, and before the tectonic plates shifted, we were blessed with a utopia for knowledge and learning and art. This place created, solved, and held all the secrets. Over time, these secrets were sent out into the world and then passed from generation to generation.

We priests and priestesses watched over the texts written

on papyrus scrolls and stored in sacred boxes, and from time to time we were allowed to study from them. Eventually, I ascended to the role of keeper of the scrolls.

We were the only temple complex in Egypt that had written down all of the information. The rest of the temples had to learn the scrolls orally, or they would receive only partial scrolls that left out vital information. I had trained many of the priestesses at the temples how to memorize the important information so that it didn't have to be written down. Once the other temples had enough information, we scattered the scrolls out in the desert and even cast some of them, sealed with resin, into the river in jars for the crocodile god Sobek.

One day, I was called to the high altar and told I was being considered for the initiation work connected to the Star Chamber Pyramid. You know that as the Great Pyramid. This was a very high honor, and it was even more impressive because I was a female. Even though I held an important role as the keeper of the scrolls and an oracle, I had never been allowed to actively perform initiation rites for other priests.

I was led to the pyramids to perform my rites of acceptance of the role. In those days, we took boats into side entrances of the pyramids. For many years, I had to be trained inside them, and then I would get to do what only a select few had ever done. The details of the rites and pyramid maps can never be disclosed, but know that it took me many years to complete them. At the end of it, I knew the chambers and the sounds and secrets of the pyramids better than anyone else.

One day a few years later, I was in the temple just outside the pyramid, praying in a sacred area connected to the Sphinx, when news arrived for me. I was told that a new initiate would be joining us and that he was entrusted to me for training. That had never happened before. We took only those picked from birth that showed the signs and star constellation birthmarks. But the elders believed that the time had come for a new order of priest that could go out into the world and make a real difference in it. We also had sometimes had visits from great prophets from other cultures. They would be accepted into the sacred halls and chambers of wisdom.

I waited for the next three days for the new initiate to arrive. Each day, I prepared and waited sunrise to sunset. On the third day, I was about to give up when I was surprised to see soldiers arrive on horses. There were three of them in wealthy clothes that royalty wore, and they carried swords. We had no weapons around the pyramids; it was forbidden. I think they were just as surprised to see me, being female with my head shaved and wearing robes that covered my body. They introduced themselves and were very adamant about where they would stay and what they wanted to do. They assumed they could just go into the pyramids, and the secrets would be revealed.

I had to persuade them that I would reveal all at the perfect time and that protocols had to be followed so that the gods would not be angered. They laughed, but they also realized I had the power that they desired, so they chose to stay and listen.

First of all, I sat them in a circle and lit the sacred oracle fire. This fire carried specific oils and resins underneath the wood to bring forward the prophecy messages. In the fire, they would have a vision that revealed their true fears. One saw a snake, one a sword, and one a man. I explained that this fear would be presented many times in the next three months. They must face and conquer their fears if they wished to carry on and read the sacred books and enter the forbidden chambers.

This seemed to capture their interest. After this, I told

them that their first training would be for the next fourteen nights, from a new moon till the full moon, and would be in silence; they would have only small meals and water. They were appalled that there was no wine and fine food and there would there be no other priests and priestesses to entertain them. They were children in men's bodies, and I tried to not be insulted.

At night, I was instructed to place each one in his chamber and lock the gate. This was very hard for two of them, and they complained to the point where it was downright abusive. But I had seen this in the fire and knew this was my fear being revealed. Of course, none of the men knew the others' fears, but I, being an oracle, had seen them all.

The new moon was soon past, and each day I would visit with lessons until the cycle was complete. I sat down with them on the morning of the full moon with a straw basket. I took off the top, and out slithered a cobra. I wore an oil that charmed the cobra, but to them it seemed that I could control the creature, and I had taught it to hiss and spit on command. The man who feared snakes recoiled at its presence. I carried on with my ritual.

Then I brought forward a dagger, which I informed them could cut the soul and spirit from a man—and if this dagger touched them and drew blood, they would be damned forever, living here on the earth plane without a soul. As I moved the dagger around, the second man shivered. Neither of these two men had been kind, so I didn't mind that they were scared.

The third man, however, had been respectful to me and had an energy about him of calmness, a regality. He was the true initiate that we wanted, and the man he feared was the man he was meant to be.

It was then time for me to lead a regression for each of them to have a vision of themselves in ten years from that date. The first two men were unable to connect, and I saw nothing for them. The third man was different and saw himself as a great ruler and purveyor of knowledge. He ruled over much of the Mediterranean, including Northern Africa. I told him I had also seen him as a great leader, but I had also seen how his work would endanger many secrets and souls. He needed to be careful and make sure to approach every decision with great care and thought.

It was clear from this that he would be the only one who could make it through the next step, so I told the other two men to leave. They looked at me, aghast, and demanded that I take them through the next step. I told them that if they could not connect to a regression, or progression in this case, then they did not have a future here because they couldn't see one. The men were extremely upset by this, but the third man gave them a look of warning, and the other two men left the temple. Once they had left, I asked the name of this worthy man, and he told me he was Alexander, Prince of Macedon.

Throughout the last few weeks of the initiations, Alexander had been very respectful with me and was a welcome addition to the temple. We had many stimulating intellectual conversations at night during meals, as well as philosophical debates in between training. Out of the three men, he was clearly the most respectful of the traditions of the pyramids. He was a fine student.

On the final night, I was to lead Alexander into the inner chambers of the pyramids to obtain the knowledge of Seshat and Thoth. They were the gods of the Akashic records: Seshat the oracle and Thoth the scribe. Both the feminine and masculine were required to bring through the greater, deeper wisdom. We prepared to enter, and I had taken my basket and my oils with me to complete the rituals and initiations.

As we were walking in, I heard horses neighing in the distance. The two men who had been dismissed were fast approaching. It was then that I realized I had been tricked. They were ambushing me in order to steal the secrets of the inner temples. I looked at Alexander with disbelief. He hung his head in shame and looked away.

"Did you doubt yourself, my prince?" I asked. "Did you doubt you could do this without force? Did you know that your knowledge would come through ego, power, and greed?"

He remained silent a moment longer and then said, "It is all I know: that when I conquer you and this structure, I will rule as you saw. I cannot achieve greatness without this. I will be a living god."

The men standing around us looked at me with evil smiles. They started at me and attempted to restrain me. I called to Isis and even to their gods for strength and revenge. To do so in such a holy place, I now see, cursed me. I thought Alexander would stop them, but he simply encouraged them.

Alexander told them that he would go into the inner chamber and take what he could; the other two were to get the location of other scrolls. They held me down and threatened to kill me if I didn't tell them. I told them that what they were looking for was not on a scroll. It was told orally to a priestess from another place, and she must have now fled as she heard my cries and their threats. I did not say that the priestess was me and that I had been about to share the Scroll and scarab of Truth and Integrity with Alexander. I now see Alexander was looking for the physical documents and forgot that the magic is always held in our minds and souls. They were furious at this, and one of them pulled out a sword to kill me.

Luckily, I had come prepared, and I pulled out a dagger from my belt. I threw it at the one with the sword, almost instantly killing him when my dagger went directly to his heart. I reached into my basket and tossed the cobra that was inside onto the other man. The cobra had no mercy for its prey.

It was at that moment that Alexander came out of the hidden chamber empty-handed. He seemed to falter at what to do next. Honor told him to kill me for killing his men, but he was intelligent enough to know that my death meant he would never get the information he needed. Alexander then told me to thank the gods for sparing me, but in our future meetings he would not show mercy again. He promised to return for what he came for after he had toppled the rest of Egypt.

Many years passed, and the Temple of Ra had been attacked multiple times by Alexander's forces in an attempt to retrieve the scrolls he still thought were hidden there. We held our ground for a long time, but on the eighth attempt, we fell to the Greek soldiers. The priests were imprisoned in the temple, and I was captured and taken to a place now known as Alexandria.

When I first arrived, I was taken into a small chamber of a large cave, where the other priestesses and oracles who had been captured from other temples were kept. Alexander had become obsessed with the Akashic records and the wisdom they held. The oracles were a strange mix of women; there was an equal number of old and young women. The older women did not speak, but the younger girls chatted nervously with each other.

Alexander was smarter than I thought he was. He had gathered an oracle priestess from each of the female temples. He knew that any one of them could be the keeper of the secrets of our scrolls. He also knew the legend of the sacred box of Philae, the box of scrolls and scarabs that was rumored to have come from Atlantis. I did not know whether the box still existed; I knew only that the wisdom had been copied or stolen many times, so who could tell where it all was now? Alexander had played a numbers game and covered his options. That must have meant that he had obtained the incomplete copies. He constantly asked for the Scroll of Death and Resurrection, which for some reason, was the most sought-after.

Not long after my arrival, the younger girls were taken out for questioning. They would come back an hour or so later with bruises all over their bodies and torn clothes. I could tell the guards were getting frustrated with them. I went over to the oldest woman and asked what was going on. I needed to know what scrolls Alexander had captured. As the keeper of the scrolls, I was never supposed to meet the others in case it was discovered that we had pieces of information that went together. The woman knew me, judging by the way she looked at me, and she smiled but wouldn't say anything, so I asked her about each scroll. She mostly shook her head at the titles I listed off, but she got really excited when I asked about the Scroll of Light and Shadow. It was a risk, but this was her scroll, which kept the balance in all of nature. She pointed to herself and to one of the younger priestesses nearby. She smiled widely, and it was then that I noticed she wasn't just silent but couldn't speak. In anticipation of being caught, the older women had all taken a vow of silence and had drunk a mix of hemp oil, arnica oil, and other herbs to freeze their vocal cords. They had all seen in a vision what had happened when Alexander tried to steal the secrets, and they had taken action. The guards were smart, though, and knew that the priestesses were in the midst of relaying that information to the next generation. The women had already seen their fate in the prophecy visions.

"They knew it would happen?" I asked.

"Yes. Some fates we can never escape, but they could protect the temple."

"I have heard that before. What does it have to do with this?"

"The temple is not just a building. It can be a belief or even a person or group of people. It is far more than us and mortal walls."

She continued.

After the fifth girl the guards took told nothing, they realized this secret code of silence and decided to wait. They knew that no matter what, the older priestesses would have to pass on the information to the younger ones out of a need to preserve our knowledge. The guards didn't seem to know exactly who I was, so I pretended like I had also silenced my tongue. None of the guards seemed concerned with checking my mouth, so I was safe for the time being.

For the next year, we all lived in that small chamber, communicating in sign language. It was awful. Through a small window, we watched as wagons full of precious scrolls would arrive, often covered in blood, which meant the priests and priestesses must have died to protect the items that were removed. We would watch the soldiers haul in more and more scrolls and books every day. It seemed that Alexander had amassed quite a collection of texts and relics.

Then came the saddest day: the day of a powerful lunar eclipse with an alignment in the stars. I knew it would be when the Orion constellation would be over the Great Pyramid, beaming its energy into the sacred chambers. When this happened, it was time for the ritual of passing the knowledge to the young priestesses. The elder priestesses all knew the timing of this; they felt it in their souls and would get into a circle and relay the rest of the information telepathically, the old priestesses to the new, thus forgetting it in the process.

The guards must have known something was happening because they were checking in on us every few minutes. I knew what the plan was. The guards would wait that night until the ritual was over and storm the chamber to grab the young girls before their throats and voices were silenced with the herbal potion. Then, they would be beaten and raped until they gave up the information. I knew there was no way we could keep this from happening, but there was a lunar eclipse that night, and we had to move forward. This night would have the power and protection of all the gods, and I knew how to call on them.

While the priestesses were all in meditation, I spoke for the first time in over a year and demanded to see the man in charge. The guard I spoke to seemed surprised at my boldness and forcefully dragged me out of the chamber. He led me down a long hallway into a secret passageway that led to an ornately decorated chamber full of marble and gold. He pushed me forward and left. The only other person in the room was a man hunched over a table, looking at a scroll. He turned around and revealed himself to be none other than Alexander.

"So you finally speak? It only took you a year," he said sarcastically. "I was beginning to think you may have cut your tongue out to be like the rest of your harpies."

I gathered up all of my courage and spoke in an even, measured tone. "Yes, well, I found I didn't have much to say until today."

"Of course you didn't. But now that you have, I am curious about what you have to say."

"I take it you know what is going to happen tonight? I thought you were out east fighting a campaign with mutinous soldiers."

Alexander clenched his fists and said through gritted teeth. "Yes, that's why I'm here." He then returned to his cool demeanor. "You know, it may not be in your nature to write things down, but the priests of Horus at Edfu keep excellent records. In fact, I was reading one of them just now. It is amazing how much they know about your rituals." He started to walk closer to me. "And it is amazing how much they know about you, Seshat's Keeper of the Scrolls." He smiled.

At the mention of my title, I flinched ever so slightly, and his smile grew. "So you know who I really am and what I can really do," I said. "Then you also know that you don't need those girls to get whatever it is you want."

"I suppose," he said. "But it would be so much more fun for me and my men to get it from them. There aren't many women around here, and my men have been very respectful of your priestesses so as not to disturb the process. I would hate for them to think it was all for nothing."

I shuddered at his words but refused to let him get a rise out of me. "That is true," I replied. "However, it would take you much longer to get what you want from them, and I know you have waited a long time already. So why don't you just tell me what it is you seek, and we can make a deal."

"A deal? Between you and me? Now, why would I ever do that? You killed my men all those years ago and pretended to be mute for a year. I can't trust you to give me what I want."

"Yes, you can," I told him. "The last thing I want is for those girls to be harmed. If one of them dies in your care, then the book she carries in her mind is lost to the world. You have amassed a greater collection of texts than anyone else on earth, You, of all people, know the value of information."

"Yes, I do. But to truly have the greatest collection of knowledge on this earth, I need to have books that no one else can get. I need every book. Live books would be something even the richest kings in the East could only dream of."

"But you don't need all of them. What if I told you that everything they know is already condensed into one large volume? You are nothing if not efficient, and twenty priestesses take up a lot of space and resources, plus the twenty you would need to bring in to keep the information passed down."

"You make a good point, oracle. Tell me, are you the one I need?"

I drew a deep breath at this. "Yes, I am. And if you promise to let those girls leave after tonight, I will stay here and answer any question you have."

Alexander thought for a moment and then answered me. "You would tell me anything? Even the most sacred of information?"

"By my honor and duty, yes, and what I do not know, I will call on the gods to show me."

"Then tonight, you will tell me how to create an invincible soldier, one whom no mortal man can defeat. A soldier who can contend on both the physical and spiritual planes."

I gasped. What he spoke of, very few people dead or alive knew. "How did you find out about the priests of Unal?" I asked.

"Through this." He held up a scroll that I knew to be about Unal, a product from a few priests of Ra and their fascination with the Scroll of Death and Resurrection. This Scroll of Unal was conjured from that evil timeline.

The priests of Unal originated from Atlantis. They were

not mortals, yet they were very powerful and magical. It was said that they were corrupted during its last five thousand years and fell to the dark side—hence the fall of Atlantis. Alexander wanted that magic and dark alchemy from Atlantis to rise with him again. He wanted to resurrect them again and be their master.

"Now," he continued, "what will happen is this: I will tell my men not to disturb the priestesses during the eclipse. They will go through their ritual in peace. During that time, you will come to me here and tell me how to create an army of Unal priests. If the information you give me seems fake, I will tell my men to rape and kill every woman in that chamber while you are forced to watch. Then I will kill you, and no one will ever have the knowledge of your temple ever again. Do I make myself clear?"

I was so dumbfounded that I could only nod. He smiled and called for the guard to come back and take me to the chamber. The women were waiting for me, and I told them what was going to happen.

Later, I watched them as they gathered in a circle that night, just before the start of the eclipse. I wished them well and waited for the guards to collect me. They came and brought me to the same chamber as before. Through the window, I could see the start of the eclipse. I told Alexander about the priests. "The scroll will tell you everything you need to know about performing the ritual and how it is activated, but it doesn't say who is needed to activate and facilitate it."

"So who do I need?"

"You need a female oracle who serves a masculine temple that worships the shadows in the light."

"But there are no oracles like that. Masculine temples don't have female oracles, except for the Temple of Ra, which is you."

"Yes, but I am not the one the scroll talks of. I may reside in the Temple of Ra, but I still serve a female master; ultimately, I serve Isis. The Scroll of Unal comes from our Atlantean ancestors and directly conflicts with the other Sacred Eight scrolls. It has no scarab that accompanies it, and is the only scroll with true shadow energy because it can raise evil on this land. As Seshat's keeper and because Isis is my true mistress, I am bound to the Eight and cannot go against them. You need an oracle who can, someone who serves as the oracle for a god of darkness—a contradiction. She will constantly be battling her dual nature. That is what is needed. Look, we don't always understand what the scrolls mean. They are notoriously vague. This Scroll of Unal once brought down the priests of Atlantis. One must be warned against its use again. I can tell you anything else, but not the true nature of this scroll."

"Fine." Alexander was angry, and he turned to the guards. "Go release the priestesses—and make sure that none of them make it back to their temples."

"What? No!" I screamed. "You promised you'd release them if I helped you!"

"And you did, in a way, but if they are all killed, then I'll be the only one in the world with all the information. I can't let someone else have that power, I now have you, and I will be your master."

That night sealed my fate. My soul was bound to Alexander's collection. Instead of being reborn at Ra, I was reborn at what would become the Library of Alexandria. For the next couple hundred years, I was reborn periodically with all of the knowledge and served as the living book for the Alexandrian Library. After the Great Library was destroyed in the fire, I learned that a few of the priestesses managed to evade capture and took up refuge at Edfu. One of them carried the secret of the Scroll of Unal.

In return for her safety, she wrote down what she knew of the creation of this super evil priest to those who gave her sanctuary, but she did not know the secret of the invocation of the god Set. Many times the priests tried and failed in secret to resurrect this evil species. After this oracle passed, female oracles were banned from visiting Edfu because the temple had such mistrust and disrespect for them. Priestesses slowly began to take on another role that did not include adviser.

I had lied to Alexander and not shared with him the final piece of information about the true Edfu oracle: she would not return to be born on this earthly plane for another 250 years, and this would be during a lunar eclipse to two people of divine lineage. Her true purpose would be to align Divine Masculine and Feminine, to create balanced temples here on earth.

Alice sighed and hung her head. I could sense she was weary. However this story was like a blockbuster movie. Something troubled me, and I thought back to my dreams. *The women on the shore had a baby. Was that who I was meant to find?* I shook off the thought and turned back to Alice, encouraging her to tell me more.

Alexander met his own demons as he travelled the world and found the karma of the women he slew following him in his nightmares. He was slowly poisoned to death and died a completely broken man with little dignity. After he died, the oracles who had been hidden joined together in a circle of sisterhood in a small temple to the goddess Sekhmet in Karnak temple to do a ritual, cursing Alexander in the afterlife. They then returned to Alexandria to work in the library, never revealing themselves but passing their wisdom in secret to a whole lineage of new oracle initiates. They were like a secret underground movement, committed and connected.

Every so often, an oracle of great power would return to help clear the curses and keep the temples communicating and in balance. They had secret hawks that would carry information and scrolls to Philae and Isis. This is how the Isis of the time knew everyone's business. This was a true sisterhood, and they did what they could. We librarian sisters are all connected through the heart and our psychic gifts.

It wasn't until 48 BC, when Julius Caesar was waging war with Pompey that this cycle broke. In an attempt to kill his enemies, Caesar set fire to his own ships. Unfortunately, he lost control of the blaze, and the library caught fire. The confusion sent messages of fear throughout Egypt, and the sacred bond of ritual and magic was broken. I managed to escape to the Temple of Isis, but I knew that this was the beginning of the end. The gods had spoken, and life as we knew it was about to implode.

She came around and looked at me. "And that, my dear, started a chain reaction that has carried on throughout the ages. Removing our voices, our wisdom, and our power was the most destructive and dividing thing. We managed to live in relative harmony until the fall, but it would have never happened had I persuaded Alexander to not kill the priestesses. His killing them and their cursing him started this cycle of evil, I think."

"It wasn't your fault. You didn't know what this would do."

"But if I had done nothing, all of the priestesses would have been kept alive, and the information they held could have still reached the other temples. My actions led to the halting of all the information and ultimately, our downfall."

I looked at her, realizing something awful. "Alice, did Alexander succeed in creating priests of Unal?"

"No, he didn't, but one of his successors did, or at least they were created under her reign."

"But the priests of Horus at Edfu did. That vision on Saturday—it was of the rituals for creating them, right?"

"Yes."

"And Naomi is the oracle of Horus."

"Yes, she was. She was the one we had been waiting for. But understand this: the circumstances that led her to do this were unavoidable. She had been tortured for so long that she figured it would be easier to do what they asked. Those priests at Edfu were supposed to protect her and support her. That way, her heart would have been open, and we would have succeeded in a golden age. The priests of Horus at Edfu ultimately failed her there. Then she failed the sisterhood, and the sisterhood failed Isis. It was like Alexander: when he had my trust, I would have been like his guardian angel. But greed took hold of him, and he cast me aside."

"I guess I can understand that. Thank you, Alice, for sharing with me. This has all been so exciting and amazing and inspiring. I can't help but think, though, that I won't ever be able to do what you did and discover who I was in Egypt."

"Anna, you need to stop doubting yourself. You can do it. You just need to have patience and take the time to practice. You are lucky, because you have quite the aptitude for this."

"I agree," said a voice from behind us.

CHAPTER 20

I turned around and saw Isis standing there behind us. I wondered how long she had been there.

"Not long," she replied.

"Oh, Isis, I am so sorry for what happened at the ceremony on Saturday. Truly, I didn't know what I was doing. And I promise I didn't take the real scroll, just the copy. Please forgive me, I—"

She held up a hand to stop me. "There is no need to apologize, my dear. It is I who should be apologizing; things got a bit out of hand. I did some meditating after the ceremony, and I think that whatever force is blocking us, or is attempting to, is still out there. You are not the source."

"Out there? What do you mean by that?" I asked.

"Well, as I am sure Emilee explained to you, there was a disturbance in the priestesses' timelines after the fall of the temple at Philae. They were cursed during the fall as a result of their actions leading up to it. They revolted against the high priestess, which is what cursed them most of all."

"So what really happened that made them revolt? Why was that so bad?"

"Well, Anna, I think Alice and I can show you if Alice is agreeable to helping me." Isis turned to Alice.

Alice, who had been very quiet this whole time, nodded her head and said, "Yes, of course; anything for you."

"This may be the timeline where the curse can be broken, but all of the souls must be found, and it must be figured out how the curse must break," said Isis. "But let's perhaps move to somewhere we can all sit and reflect."

"Yes," said Alice, "and I know just the place." She pointed to a location farther up in the gardens. We walked in silence, and my heart raced, but all was calm when we reached the sacred Chalice Well and sat around it on the stone wall.

Isis pointed to the well cover. "See this?" she asked. "The vesica piscis, the sign of the sacred union. I live in hope we can bring that into our worlds, and our unions can be restored."

Isis took a deep breath. "Now, my dear sister Alice, I pray continue."

Alice spoke.

Like I said, I had been bound to Alexandria and had reincarnated there again many decades later. Born a child of poverty, I was left on the library stairs, and the temple guardians knew me at once by the markings on my body. I was raised in the library and knew no other world. After I escaped the burning of the library, I went to seek refuge at the Temple of Isis at Philae. I served the high priestess, my precious Isis, for many years. She was kind and patient with me.

It was touching how each woman smiled at the other.

She always said she was waiting for me to come home to them. I hadn't known the comfort of sisterhood in many lifetimes, and it was a relief to finally be free of that burden and live with love around me.

Unfortunately, things in Egypt were not going well since the destruction of the Alexandrian Library. Julius Caesar had been assassinated, and another civil war had broken out between his successors, Octavian and Mark Antony. It was widely known that Mark Antony preferred Egypt to Rome; he had taken up with Queen Cleopatra and wholly adopted our way of life. But the war wasn't going in his favor, and he was getting desperate.

From here, Isis continued the story.

I was afraid that the priests of Edfu had gone into the shadows and were willing to help Antony by any means necessary. I had it on good authority that they had been in talks to enact the Unal priest ritual. The knowledge of this ritual had been passed down to all of the ruling members of the Ptolemy family, including Cleopatra. She loved Antony, and I knew she had told him about it. The priests of Unal are preternatural beings of unbelievable strength and magic. They are skilled in both combat and the mystic arts. If successfully created, they could turn the tide of the war in Mark Antony's favor.

Once created, these beings were nearly impossible to stop. I also knew that the priests of Horus at Edfu finally had an oracle strong enough to complete the initial ritual and create them. I sent Alice to go convince Cleopatra that it was not a good idea to create Unal priests; they would destroy everything and put the world out of balance.

Alice took over again.

I went to see Cleopatra in Alexandria and begged her to not go through with it. I told her what would happen. She didn't want to hear it.

"I have done so much for your high priestess and the other priestesses of the sisterhood. How could you ask me to not do the one thing that could save my love and my land from being overrun by Roman swine?" she asked in a high-mannered tone.

"You must understand, my queen," I said. "It may seem like a good idea now, but it goes against the balance and is an abomination to the gods."

"The gods have abandoned me. I can only rely on Antony and myself," was her response.

"I assure you that the goddess Isis has not. She is with you, but you must stop this from happening."

"It is too late, oracle. We have already given the order for the priests of Horus to conduct the ritual and bring forward these greatest of warriors. They are now ready and simply wait on my command. My royal vizier is there and is in total control."

I looked at her in complete shock. "Then you have to order them to be destroyed. Now!"

"How dare you order me around! I am your queen. *You* answer to *me*. As soon as I get word from Antony, they will be dispatched, and Octavian will be defeated. Antony and I will rule over Rome and Egypt and usher in a new era of culture and peace. We will rebuild the library Caesar destroyed and ascend into the heavens once we are done. I know you came from Alexandria; wouldn't you like to see your library restored?

You would have complete domain over it."

"That won't happen, I am telling you! Even if you use the Unal priests, you will not usher in an era of peace. It has been my duty for over three hundred years now to know everything about the magic and rituals of the temples. The Unal priests can only be controlled for so long. Their true allegiance is to the Sons of Set, a dark order of priests who want power and control. They will overthrow you and kill all of your people until they have created a land that is completely subservient to them, worse than anything a Roman could ever do. You can still send out an order to stop them from completing the ritual. I can tell you how to do it, and your messenger can tell them."

Just then, a messenger came bursting through the door with news from the battle. Mark Antony had been killed, and his body was being brought to their hiding place by Octavian. Cleopatra let out a sound I will never forget; she was beside herself in grief. She asked me to stay with her in the coming weeks as her counsel, and she delayed the decision on what to do with the priests until she found out what Octavian's plan was. That was a fateful day, and in many ways, he reminded me of a young Alexander: wise but ruthless.

Octavian came to her and said that he had full control of the coast and the major cities, including hers. Octavian assured her that he would let her stay in Egypt and rule as a governor. She reasoned that it would prevent any more Egyptian blood from being shed, so she agreed.

We got word from a spy the next day that Octavian had lied and was planning to move Cleopatra and her children to Rome in three days. She vowed to never be on display in triumph like her sister.

"Oracle," she said to me, "I refuse to be some war prize to an impersonator like Octavian; it is an affront to me and to

Antony. I would rather die than go to Rome again. Would you help me make sure of that?"

I knew what she meant, and I agreed to help. I found her a way to achieve her afterlife journey, and we made plans for her children. That evening I sat with her as we created scrolls of lineage for her children.

"My daughter by Antony will be safe from Octavian's wrath; he will most likely marry her off to rich senators. My sons, especially Ceasarion, will be at his mercy. However, my other child with Caesar is different. Octavian must never get hold of the child or know she exists."

"Where is she?" I asked. I had heard the rumors about her, but no one knew for sure.

"Safe for now, with your priestesses. I sent her off before all of this happened. That was many years ago, and I have never mentioned this to anyone except Isis. Now, can you help me with that?"

"Yes, of course. But what of the Unal priests?"

"You said you know how to stop them. I know now that even if I did send word, they would never get there in time. Go back to Philae and tell the high priestess about them. Destroy them if you can; tell Isis if she still holds the Scroll of Creation, that it has a potent spell to undo evil. I thank you for your service, oracle. You have been a great source of wisdom and comfort these past few weeks. Now, go. It is time for me to join my husband so that our union can be great in the heavens, as it seems to have failed here on earth."

I looked at her with tears in my eyes and left my queen. I managed to get out without the Romans detecting me, and I raced back to Philae as quickly as I could to warn Isis.

Isis continued.

And warn me you did. But unfortunately, the unrest had already started among the priestesses. I could feel it. I was still training a replacement but decided that we needed to push up her initiation. We needed someone strong to help us.

Alice took over.

But the other priestesses weren't interested in going through this process. One, in particular, was telling everyone how the trainee was ill-equipped to become the next high priestess, adding that she herself was more suited for the job. By that time, most of the Sacred Eight had returned to Philae in anticipation of crowning the next high priestess of Isis and renewing their sacred contracts. This usurper was able to get an audience with most of us and managed to win over some of us. It caused tensions to rise in our group; we had never disagreed on something so vital before.

The Hathor priestesses from Dendara and I were staunchly against this arrogant priestess and tried to protest, but our voices were drowned out by those who opposed Isis and her apprentice. They were angry with how Isis was ruining things and had let the temples fall and their sisters be captured by Romans. The ringleader promised she could restore the balance and repair their ruined relationship with the priests of Edfu. She, along with some and her most trusted followers, created their own circle of eight, the number needed to enact the mantle passing.

They devised a plot to kill Isis, the high priestess, before she could initiate a new one to ascend and bind their soul to the role. They were going to replace the current Isis with this usurper, someone more suited to their needs. She would bow to the masculine temples in the hope that balance could be restored in that way. The few of us opposed to the idea were powerless to stop it, and we were forced to watch while they took down Isis and her apprentice. It was the final nail in the coffin, our sacred contract was broken, and our relationship with each other was irrevocably damaged.

We all came out of the vision then, and Alice and Isis were both crying.

"So did they do what they said they would?" I asked cautiously.

"Yes," said Isis, regaining her composure. "And they paid the price."

"But what happened to the trainee? And the Unal priests? Were they stopped?"

"Unfortunately, those are not questions I can answer for you," she said with a sigh.

"So in order for these women, the Sacred Eight, to break out of this curse or whatever, they have to go through the ceremony properly?"

Alice and Isis both looked at me approvingly. Isis replied, "Yes, exactly. Your intuition is spot-on. Once the next high priestess of Isis is initiated, the original Sacred Eight will need to recommit themselves to serving the goddess Isis and the Divine Feminine, writing a new sacred contract with her and each other. Then we need to rebuild and protect the sacred temple."

I furrowed my brow. "But Alice just got done saying that

part of the Sacred Eight broke from the pack to help out this other betrayer. Won't it be difficult to convince all of them to help initiate your true successor? And more to the point, isn't that some major bad karma or something if they do participate?"

Isis nodded. "Even though the Sacred Eight were all supposed to participate in the mantle passing, they do not all need to be present this time in their physical form. As long as we have eight powerful priestesses and oracles who were at one time initiates at Philae to act in their place, we can still perform the ceremony. Those of the Sacred Eight who were loyal to me before will be there again."

"So that is why this other priestess formed her own eight: because she knew she didn't need all of the original Sacred Eight?" I questioned.

"Yes," said Isis. "But she would not have been successful because she wasn't my true heir, and killing me before I passed the mantle meant I would be reborn into a new lifetime as the high priestess to fulfill my destiny. This may be our last chance to get it right. I have to pass the mantle in this lifetime in the correct way, or we risk losing the temple forever." Isis's features hardened at this solemn confession.

"Something tells me that you might be able to help!" Alice chimed in cheerfully.

"I hope so, although something was off about this last regression story you have both told me," I muttered.

Isis raised her eyebrow. "What was off, my dear? Alice and I both saw what happened very clearly. Did you not?"

"No, not exactly." I struggled. "I saw everything clearly, except for Cleopatra's face. For some reason, she didn't show it to me."

Alice looked over at Isis, who was considering my words. "Yes, that is strange," she said absent-mindedly, and then she snapped back to attention at Alice's sudden interjection.

"Hmm, yes, Isis, she shows many of the signs."

Isis looked me up and down and agreed. "She does. Anna, as I think you can already tell, you are extremely talented in our ways. You know that I am to pass my mantle on, but I wonder, might you be the person to pass it to?"

I looked down at my feet. "Well, Emilee mentioned I could be, but—"

Alice interrupted, "Then it is settled!"

"Not so fast." Isis shot Alice a warning glance. "Anna is not the only contender. Lesley has shown great promise as well. It is too close to call at this point. They are equally matched."

"What about Naomi?" I interjected. "I thought she was your successor."

"No," said Isis. "She is to be the oracle of Isis at Philae, the one who aids the high priestess. She's already well aware of that."

"What if you are wrong about Lesley?" Alice continued. "Isn't it odd that we have two people equally matched? Lesley claims to have the lineage, but is she who she says she is?"

That was interesting. *Who is Lesley?* I was afraid to ask.

The two women continued to talk as if I were invisible.

"Yes, Alice, but these things are never so simple. I believe that in the coming weeks, we will see who the next Isis really is. I am not going to make any decisions now."

Alice looked like she wanted to say something but thought better of it.

I turned to Isis. "So does that mean that Lesley and I are going to have to engage in some cosmic battle or something to figure out which one of us is right for the job?"

Isis chuckled. "No, but as the solstice draws closer, your powers will grow, and one of you will unmistakably become my heir. She will be the one to build the new temple, bring the

Sacred Eight together again, and help all those other priestesses of Isis remember who they were and how loved they are."

"What if one of us doesn't?" I pressed.

"One of you will. It is fated as such."

I was amazed by what she was telling me, and it all finally sunk in that this stuff was real—and maybe I did have a part to play. Then I remembered what Naomi had said about me to Isis when they thought I wasn't looking: *She is dark and dangerous.*

What if I was the one in Egypt who suggested that the priestesses kill Isis? After all, the other women seem to really distrust me, and the priestess in the vision seemed to think she had a lot of power. Maybe all of those dreams I have been having are trying to tell me that I was the dark one, the betrayer of Isis. It then dawned on me that whoever the betrayer was at Philae was most likely the one at Salem.

"Isis," I piped in. "The betrayer at Philae—I think she is also the accuser in Salem."

"Really?" She looked at me curiously. "Do you know who she is?"

"No. I couldn't see her face, not in Emilee's vision or in Alice's just now, but I think that means something."

"I agree. Someone is working very hard to conceal herself from everyone's visions. That is a good sign. That means you are headed in the right direction. Keep on this path, Anna; I think you will find the answers we need. I can tell everything is going to converge here at Glastonbury."

Alice chimed in. "Yes, but if we fail to find everyone, and even one or two of us are missing, then that could have catastrophic consequences on subsequent lifetimes. It could push back a convergence another two thousand years."

"Understood," said Isis, almost curtly. "That is a possibility, but I don't think it will happen. Just to be sure, I will go into seclusion for the next week or so and meditate on this. In the meantime, Anna, I would like you to go to the Sanctuary every day to train and learn from Naomi. She will help you."

"Are you sure she wants to see me after everything?"

"Yes. We got it all straightened out. The real Scroll of Magic and Prophecy turned up, so there is no problem there. And Naomi knows you didn't mean to provoke a vision. She will train you. Now, I must go. I'm tired and have much work to do." She looked at me, and I swear her eyes turned golden. "Good luck, Anna," Isis said. "Be true to yourself and follow your destiny. Become the master oracle you..." She never finished her sentence and left.

I thanked Alice for her time and her amazing story, and then I went home to write about everything I had just learned. I still had so many questions. What had triggered the temple of Isis to create such anger in the priestesses? What had happened in Edfu? And why couldn't I see Cleopatra?

CHAPTER 21

I left the Chalice Well and was heading in the direction of the Gables when I realized that Naomi was still on my mind. It was as if I could hear her in my head, her voice and her tone. I turned around and made my way to the Sanctuary to see if she was there.

When I got there, I saw that for some reason, the door of the gateway had not been locked and was slightly ajar, which was strange. That served to tell me my intuition was correct and I was in the perfect place at the right time. It was late afternoon, and the gardens were so beautiful. I decided to sit for a while and rehearse what I would say to her. No one seemed to be around, and I was sure no one would notice. I took a moment to sit next to the Buddha statue and almost felt him come alive to give me instruction. Once I had my key points for conversation, I thanked my newfound friend with a "Namaste" and bowed with a gratitude prayer.

I then walked around the back toward the kitchen. I was confident with my speech. I would apologize but also try to explain to Naomi that this power struggle had to end, and she had to take responsibility for her actions in this lifetime and all others. Perhaps she was the key to the curse we were all carrying. But then I realized that was my ego talking, and I must stay on the real reason I was here: to ask her to forgive me and teach and mentor me.

I entered the small stone courtyard with the crystals laden in places to catch the light. To my surprise, Naomi sat very still on one of the benches. She looked lost in trance.

"Naomi, Naomi." I moved slowly toward her. She looked up at me, but her eyes were empty, and her soul was not present. She shook her head, and the life returned to her eyes.

"I wanted to apologize for the ceremony and ask forgiveness," I continued, "and I'm hoping you will still teach and mentor me." I paused, but she said nothing. Then I felt this overwhelming fear, like I was the child and she the parent. It was from this silence that my truth came. "Naomi, I'm out of my depth, and it scares me."

She raised her hand to stop me from talking. "Sit," she told me. "Sit and be in silence."

For a while I sat, trying to stop my thoughts and predicting what she would say.

"Silence, Anna, can open the doors."

I wasn't sure what she meant, so I decided to let go of my thoughts and focus on the large amethyst crystal across the courtyard. I felt a jolt of energy, and then it was as if I could feel everything. I felt Naomi and her pain. This time I did not see anything, but a sinking feeling was in my stomach. I leaned over in pain.

"Release this, Anna. This shame is not yours but mine," she whispered.

"Are you sure?" I whispered back.

"Yes, mine and mine alone. You need not bear it for me."

I didn't know what came over me, but I reached over my hand and squeezed her arm gently. "But you do not need to bear it completely alone. Not anymore."

Tears immediately sprung from her eyes and fell onto her red cheeks. She said nothing, so I waited until she was ready to share her feelings. But nothing came, and we simply sat in a quiet reverence with no need for anything. No questions, no answers, just a pure sense of balance and quiet.

After about thirty minutes, I felt she needed alone time and whispered that I was going into the house. She stopped me and indicated I should stay. "Now I'm ready," she said.

"I have been seeing the temple of Edfu and those priests, and I'm confused," I offered by way of explanation. "They all seem to blend in some way, and sometimes I see them differently in my visions."

Naomi sighed. "Yes, that's the truth. These were souls who did make choices in their lives and initiations to be either dark or light, or even sit in between."

"Sit in between? What does that mean?"

She paused before she spoke. "Wow, you really don't know much about this, do you? Okay, so the universe consists of light and dark, or rather light and shadow. The watchers, the record keepers, the oracles, us"—she pointed to herself and then to me—"we kept the balance and simply presented information to both sides. We kept the peace and the balance within the temples."

"But in Edfu, you tipped the balance?"

"Yes, my dear. I chose a darker path, and I presented a plan to the priests that was full of darkness."

"To create the priests of Unal?"

"Yes." She sighed impatiently.

"But I'm still confused. How does it fit in with Philae, the pharaohs, and the rest of Egypt?"

Naomi sighed again, slightly less annoyed, and she took out a large journal and pen from her bag on the floor. Again I felt like a small child, watching as she opened it to a clean page. "Look, I will write the key groups and how they all interacted on a map for you," she began. "At this time in Egypt that you have been seeing in your visions, the Ptolemies had been ruling for almost three centuries. Ptolemy III Euergetes commissioned a grand temple at Edfu dedicated to Horus. Horus had been worshipped there for millennia, but Ptolemy wanted one that did the god justice. Even though Heliopolis and Memphis near Cairo were the religious centers, Edfu played an important part in performing rites and rituals that served to protect Egypt and its people. The priests of Horus at that time were the male offspring of priestesses at Philae and Dendara and could only come from there."

"Why is that?"

"Philae is home to Isis, Horus's mother, and Dendara is home to Hathor, his wife. Only priestesses who worshipped the most important women in his life could bear children for his temple. All of the children would go to Philae and learn the ways of feminine worship and spirit. They were taught how to be strong and nurturing, as well as tolerant, loving, and respectful. Usually they would be versed in magic, potion making, and divination. Then between the ages of nine and eleven, the male children would be sent off to Edfu to start their formal training as priests of Horus. There were other temples as well, but to be chosen for the priesthood of Horus was a special invitation.

"Once joined with the masculine spirit, they would study martial arts, astrology, and the rituals for the Temple of Horus. Having the training of both the masculine and the feminine arts made them extremely powerful and effective religious figures in Egypt. The Ptolemies would regularly recruit them as spiritual captains and generals in their armies because of their advanced academic, religious, and combat training. The priests were also seen to bring good omens with them, like a hawk flying above them, signaling that Horus blessed their conquest. Does this all make sense so far?"

"Yes. So these were warrior priests, like superheroes?"

Naomi gave a small laugh at this. "In a way, yes, but they always acted for the betterment of the Egyptian people. They had good souls, even if their methods were something out of the ordinary for most priests of the day. They had been nurtured in their early days, taught to love and to respect girls and women. This created the balance, the infinity symbol, Divine Masculine and Feminine. They were also initiated into the feminine temples like the priestesses."

I drew the symbol with my finger in the air.

"Yes, Anna." She nodded. "And it was nothing about being with a partner—it was within the self. These little boys grew into great men: strong, masculine, and with open hearts. However, over time the Ptolemies, as pharaohs, grew more and more demanding of the priests." She wrote the word *Royalty* onto her paper. "They were going on increasingly riskier military campaigns against the Seleucid Empire in Syria and faced threats from the rising Roman Republic. They needed to know the weakness of the enemy. Under pressure, many of the priests at Edfu turned to an ancient form of worship of the cult of Set. He was a god who had largely been thrown out from the pantheon for killing his brother Osiris, Horus's father. It was sacrilegious to be worshipping the god that Horus fought against. They were desperate and believed Set could teach them magic and give them power that no other god could. But it came at a price: they would sacrifice their humility for ego and greed. For any of the priests at Edfu who weren't succeeding in their lessons, Set made their souls an offer they couldn't refuse. Many took it and have been holding on to his mantle of lust, power, and greed ever since. It still takes them down a dark path every lifetime. My ex-husband was one of them, and I feel he still is, although he has no awareness of this."

She wrote down *Set*.

"So those that chose to follow Set in secret called themselves the Sons of Set, and they became the secret favorites of the pharaohs. The Sons of Set gave them the advantages they needed in their wars and battles. That was, until the Romans showed their unwavering strength and vast military resources to the surrounding Mediterranean Sea. This was around 55 BC, the time of Ptolemy XII. He had to ally himself with the Romans in order to regain rule over Egypt after he had been forced to abdicate. He and his children knew that they needed something more than what the priests at Edfu could provide in order to keep Rome from taking control. The Ptolemies had long known of a scroll rumored to have in it a way to create superhuman priests with enhanced strength and magical ability. Remember, they knew of the stories and rumors about Alexander the Great. Therefore they charged the priests of Edfu to find it and create these beings at whatever cost."

"Did they find the scroll of Unal?"

"Yes. In fact, they had held a copy of it in their archives for centuries since the time of Alexander."

"And they couldn't make these beings sooner without you, because you were the oracle of whom the librarian had spoken?"

"Yes. I saw things in the Scroll of Unal that they did not because I remembered it being created during the times of Atlantis."

"Oh, so you were the child born on a lunar eclipse, then? Who were your parents?"

"I don't know. That information has never presented itself. The Scroll of Unal created these super priests who would upset the laws of nature and nurture, and who would disrupt the balance between the masculine and feminine spirits that always existed between the various temples. The priestesses of Philae and Dendara did everything in their power to keep the knowledge of the circumstances of my birth, and me myself, out of reach."

She sighed. "They did try to protect me. However, those priests who worshipped Set figured it out and got to me as a small child. They tortured me, Anna, until I broke down and did what they asked."

She wrote down *Unal*.

"Now, we need to channel our thoughts and see if there is anything to be learnt from this new information. Close your eyes, breathe slowly, and take your left hand and move it over the paper. Tell me what you feel when your hand passes over each word."

I moved my hand across the paper, and I felt many things.

"Hot, then cold...Powerful...Loving..." Then something stabbed me in the heart painfully, and I suddenly saw a flash of a priest in dark robes, his eyes black like coal, walking down a corridor. It chilled me to my core. I opened my eyes, unable to withstand any more pain or visions. I looked down at the paper, and my hand was over the word *Unal*.

"Ouch, that hurt," I said, putting my hand over my heart.

"Like a dagger?" asked Naomi. "You saw one of them, didn't you?"

"Yes."

"Good. You need to know the difference between the regular priests and the dark ones. It is always the emptiness in their eyes because their hearts are closed. They can appear vacant and will always project everything toward you that you fear. Now, take a deep breath and let the pain fade."

"What does this all mean?" I asked after a few more deep breaths.

"It means that we must be careful as we bring forward any more information. Someone or something is trying very hard to keep us from finding the whole truth. If I had to guess, I would say it was the priests themselves."

"How is that even possible?"

"One of the powers imbued upon them is immortality, but not necessarily the kind of immortality they wanted. The priests, as part of the ritual, promised their souls to Set, who chains it to the mortal world in a way that robs them of all humility and, eventually, a physical form. Their spirits can lie dormant for centuries or millennia and can be awakened at any time. Even without physical forms, they are still incredibly dangerous and volatile."

A lump in my throat the size of a golf ball formed. I didn't know whether I should tell her I'd seen similar figures in my dreams. *It couldn't have been them, could it?* But somewhere in my bones, I knew that it was them, stalking me and waiting for just the right moment to strike. I swallowed the lump and nodded.

"Those priests, the ones without physical form—can they enter dreams?" I asked.

Naomi regarded me with a curious look. "Yes, I suppose that is possible. Dreams are more real than we think. They are the bridge between the mortal and spiritual world. Why do you ask?"

"No reason," I quickly countered. "Just curious. Can I keep this paper?" I asked.

She gave me another questioning look but decided not to press me further. "Sure." She tore the sheet of paper from her journal. "Consider it our first lesson: how to tune into energy and read the spiritual maps."

I took the paper and stuffed it in my bag. Something told

me this was a key to learning more about the temple, the other scrolls, and hopefully our past life connections to them.

Naomi then took my hand and smiled. "I'm truly glad you're here again."

I smiled at her and replied, "Me too." It crossed my mind that perhaps we had been here before in this exact situation and conversation, just another time in history.

☥

After my talk with Naomi, I decided to go into the house and see if I could find Lesley to confront her about what had happened the previous Saturday. The house itself was in darkness, so I presumed that everyone was either retired to the bedrooms or out for the evening. However, as I entered the kitchen, there was Lesley sitting at the large table with a small candle lit, reading a book. If I was complete with Naomi, then perhaps it was time to address Lesley. I moved over toward the table, and even though she knew I was there, she never spoke.

When I was standing next to her, she looked up at me and went back to her book. "What do you want?" she asked.

"Two things, Lesley. The time for the ceremony—why lie about it? And why accuse me of stealing the scroll?"

"First of all," she said as she sat back defiantly. "First of all, I forgot the time. It was going to be the leaders of the ceremony at 7:30 a.m. and the other visitors invited at 8:30 a.m. Emilee was meant to also be a leader, but she cancelled the night before, which I think was a bad show on her part to not to tell you, but she must have gotten everything confused. So when everyone else arrived, we had to start. We couldn't wait for one person."

"And the scroll?"

"Well, that was the crazy thing. I'm a guardian of the scrolls. I have had this role in many lifetimes, even though no one seems to pay attention to that when you are around. I couldn't find the one you claimed to have a copy of—the Scroll of Magic and Prophecy. I had seen it out on Isis's desk a few days prior when you were there, so I put two and two together. I don't know you or the kind of person you are. It seemed like the most likely scenario."

"There is more than one scroll, and isn't Isis the guardian?"

She did not seem to like this question, but she answered, "So as a guardian, I have the right to accuse anyone to whom the spirit guides me. You had a copy, and I saw you taking another. I have been a guardian of the scrolls for many lifetimes." She was repeating herself as if trying to make it true.

I reminded her, "Lesley, Isis gave it to me in the office. She made a copy and gave it to me."

"I never saw that."

"Lesley, she gave it to me to learn from."

"Well, at any rate, I was also caught up in the negative energy you were doling out. Don't you remember? You were lying on the ground and accusing everyone of everything, making people afraid."

She was very skilled at deflecting back to my issues and confusing me. It was strange, and I felt that sinking, dizzy feeling again, so I decided to leave the issue and possibly address it with Isis the next time.

"You know, Lesley," I said, getting close to her face, "I think that you are jealous of my talent and worried that I am going to end up the next Isis, so you sabotaged me in order to make yourself look better."

Lesley stood angrily at my words. "How dare you accuse me of such a thing! I have no reason to sabotage your studies. I have been preparing for months, studying eight hours a day, in order to be ready to take over for Isis. Even if you studied for the next two weeks without stopping, you wouldn't even be close to where I am. Think all you want about being the next Isis, but I can assure you I wouldn't make you look bad to help myself. It is my divine birthright."

I sighed. There was no use fighting with her. She would never admit what she did. "Fine, Lesley. Let's just chalk it up to it being a strange day. Perhaps we leave it there," I said.

"Perhaps, Anna," she agreed. "Blessed be."

She went back to her book, which I guessed meant I was dismissed. I decided it best to leave, and as I stepped out of the kitchen to the courtyard, I expected to see Naomi, but she was gone. I opened the gate, closed it behind me, and headed home. My phone was buzzing, and I opened it up to see a text from Naomi. "Lessons start at 10:00 a.m. sharp tomorrow at the Sanctuary. Do not be late. N."

I replied, "Yes, m'lady," and went back to the Gables. I was so excited now that I could be trained and perhaps be an initiate again. I was not sure where these thoughts came from; all I knew was that my heart was happy. One thought did sit heavy in my heart: *Who is Lesley, and what is her divine birthright?*

For the next seven days, I visited the Sanctuary every morning at 10:00 a.m. for my lesson. Naomi never asked for payment, and I was sure a large bill would appear. Every time I saw Lesley poke her head around the door, I waited for the credit card machine, but it never came.

Naomi made me practice the regression and channeling every morning, and I practiced writing ritual scripts and protocol as well. Then in the afternoon, we would talk about temples and review the scrolls we had access to, some in visions and some studied by looking at images online. Isis had gifted us with copies of her private collection, the Scrolls of Magic and Prophecy, Creation and Death and Resurrection. I loved every minute. We created a chart with all the oracles we knew and the scrolls and scarabs we thought were in existence.

The days passed quickly, and I was now a frequent visitor to the shops and cafés that had once seemed so strange and mysterious; I was a tourist no more. Everyone I met was a joy, and life seemed as if it had turned to a new page. Everyone, that was, except Lesley.

Lesley made small talk and was polite but never interacted in a meaningful way, except to tell me of the amazing progress she was making and that she had been asked to lead a meditation for a group of women in town every week. She was also returning home to London soon and was going to make a TV series about psychics and spiritual practice, apparently.

One morning Lesley came in to say her book idea was being looked at by a publisher. I tried to ignore her. I wanted to say, "Pick a dream, Lesley, and pick your own." But before I could go to speak, Naomi opened the living room door.

"Time for class, Anna."

Monday, June 16

About a week later, the week of the summer solstice, Naomi opened the door, and there sat three women. "Anna," Naomi explained, "these are guests here at the Sanctuary. These ladies have all been connected to the temple of Philae, and they need a regression for them to remember."

"Three, all at once? That's wonderful—I can observe!"

Naomi shook her head. "No, Anna, you can lead."

The ladies said nothing but stared at me. "Isis is away, and Anna is her protégé in the temple arts," said Naomi.

The women relaxed a little and smiled. "I'm a little nervous of Isis, anyways," one said. "We met her in London when she was speaking at a conference, and we promised we would come to explore more."

"You are in amazing and safe hands, I promise," said Naomi.

"We also wanted to say we just love you and your show, Ms. Starchild," said another woman.

"Why, thank you. I'm starting a new one next year." Naomi could always turn on her star smile.

"Oh!" The ladies were a little starstruck, but I could see they had very gentle souls.

"Shall I do the music, Anna?"

"Yes, please." I nodded to her and took my place in the small chair in which Isis always sat. I had to admit I did feed a little off Naomi's star flair, and suddenly I became a star myself—Anna the Oracle.

As I look back, this makes me giggle, but at the time it was the encouragement I needed to help myself believe that all this was happening and real. I took a deep breath and told myself this was just a graduation test, and that Isis was somewhere watching on a small video camera.

"Then let us begin!" I said in a soft whisper. I felt as if I was giving a performance on the stage. I kept my voice and pace slow and led the ladies back to Philae to attend their initiations from a past life.

☥

When I was finished, the music slowly faded, and I looked around to see the ladies crying and Naomi smiling. One of them got up and came over to thank me. "You touched my heart more than you will ever know," she said. "Thank you. I needed to remember, and now I do. I feel whole again. Thank you."

After that, Naomi ushered them out of the living room and

turned to me. "Anna, take a moment to gather yourself. I'll be back with the sanctuary diary."

A while later, I thought she was not returning, but then the door swung open. "I called Emilee, and she has your room for another few weeks," Naomi said, taking a seat. "I hope that means you will stay to finish your training."

I nodded. "I will."

"Good." She held up the diary. "Now, that can be your diary, yes?" She pointed to my journal poking out of my bag. I nodded. "More people are coming, Anna, and you need to be ready. These are all the initiates, and for some reason, you and Isis have connected to them in various lives before. You are now also drawing them here. I predict that in the future, the phone here will be constantly ringing."

I was speechless. I had gone from failing Priestess 101 to leading them back to the place in their hearts, all in a few short weeks. "Naomi, do you think I could write their stories?" I asked.

"As long as you ask them first. Well, you can always change the names, I suppose." She winked at me. "But don't steal them—that's against the oracle code!"

"The oracle code? I do not understand."

"My darling, you will come to find the dressing-up box soon enough. In my day, when I was touring and on the stage doing my mediumship, I would come backstage and meet fans. One night I had three people declare they were Mother Mary, and two said that they were King Henry VIII. I heard their stories, and who can tell? But I know enough to say that we often get mixed messages, and for me to agree with them and call them that would be inappropriate. So we smile and listen, but we do not directly anchor their consciousness into a tale of ego. Oracles may tell a story to educate, but we never lie and claim to be something we are not. Get it?"

"Got it. Thank you." Just then, I fell silent.

Naomi noticed and asked, "Is something else troubling you?"

I nodded slowly. "Yes, I…" I hesitated. "Those dark creatures—they are still haunting my dreams, and I've been seeing this sign that reads, 'Traitor's Gate.' It has been troubling me for the past week or so."

"Ah, and you don't know what it means."

"No, I don't."

"Do you think it could be connected to your visions?" Naomi asked.

I bit my lip, still unsure.

"Well, let's take a look and see, shall we? I said I read in a history that Anne Boleyn went through another gate, but this seems as if someone is trying to give us a message."

We sat down, and she regressed me back to the vision at the Tower of London.

☥

I'm entering the gate, going up to the chamber with the bedroom, and seeing the women. But there is someone I can't see in the corner. Some are shadows, and some are real. The ladies are crying because one of their fathers has just been executed. The woman in the corner is winding thread around a piece of wood. She reminds me of you.

I'm drawn to stand next to another woman; I've seen her before. Yes, she's the queen. She's Anne Boleyn. She sees this woman with the thread, and she goes over and takes it from the woman. She is telling the woman that she betrayed them all.

The woman, I think, said she was trying to save them. She said she covered up for the murder of the children with the dark witch, and she has the word of Jane Seymour, who is to be the new queen, that Anne and Elizabeth could live safely. She has the word of the French courtiers.

The queen screams. She cannot live without her daughter having her rightful claim. Then she looks at me again. "Oracle," she calls me, "give me the fate of my daughter."

I turn the cards: Empress and High Priestess.

"She will live, my queen, and possibly marry well, as she will live a long and precious life."

The queen stops and looks relieved. She then tells me to leave and return tomorrow with more news.

☥

"Ladies, I have a call!" Lesley barged into the room and broke the trance. She stood there staring at us, waiting for one of us to deal with it, but Naomi and I were trying to reconcile what had happened.

"Naomi?" I looked at her. "Did you betray the queen? Anne was one of us. Don't you see we were meant to protect her? Were you the woman in the corner doing the curses?"

"Anna, you know nothing really about me," Naomi snapped. "Why do you always have to take it too far? Any one of us could be her. This is all in your mind."

"Like anyone here could lead a revolt against Isis," Lesley said with a smile.

"Who led a revolt against me?" Isis was suddenly at the door.

I suddenly felt too overwhelmed to continue. "I think I've done too many sessions. I need to rest." I excused myself and ran back to the Gables.

✹

Emilee, as always, seemed to know when my karmic drama show was about to erupt. She was watering the plants outside when I arrived through the gateway. "Anna, come inside so we can talk. You looked exhausted and confused."

We sat in the kitchen so I could tell her the story about Anne Boleyn.

"You know, Anna, I think she is trying to reach out from beyond the grave. They say she was the one responsible for the pain and suffering in the churches," Emilee explained.

"But they were corrupt."

"Yes, I know many were, but some were simply god-worshipping people, and some lost their lives for what they believed." She pointed to the Tor, which could be seen off in the distance in the sunlight. "Did you ever wonder, Anna, why you could not enter and walk up to the Tor? It's because it carries the curses of that time. This is something you and Naomi must heal. People died at that monument for something, and perhaps your souls were involved with it. The Tor was to be a temple space here in Glastonbury, but the Tudor times caused death and grief instead—something of which Naomi and others we know may be guilty.

"Anne Boleyn trusted her maidens and oracles, but in the end, some of them betrayed her. She was meant to create the golden time of sacred grace and free minds. Politics got in the way, and the women around her did not defend her temple. She was a high priestess of her day."

The doorbell rang, and Emilee excused herself to answer. To my surprise, Naomi followed behind Emilee.

"I know I'm the last person you want to see, but I ask you

both to hear me out. Ladies, if we can join in circle, I'd like to show you my truth now."

Emilee looked hesitant. "I don't think I want to. You cause me nothing but pain, Naomi!"

I turned to Emilee. "I know she has hurt you—for many lifetimes, in fact—but you should give her a chance to help you resolve this. That is part of lifting this curse: it's working through your past traumas and letting them go. We are juggling many timelines between all of us, and at some point, we need to start wrapping up these karmic scrolls we all have outstanding."

I stopped myself, aware that I was now beginning to sound like Isis.

Emilee still looked skeptical, but she softened slightly. "All right, I will try."

"Good," said Naomi. "Let's go to Salem."

CHAPTER 22

Naomi spoke.

I lived in a home next to a barn and other homes in Salem. I was a dutiful wife, always making sure the house was clean, the clothes were washed, and the food was cooked. I produced three children, a boy and two girls. I thought all of that meant I was the perfect wife and had gotten everything everyone always said a woman wanted. But the perfect life I should have had was anything but. My husband was moderately successful at trapping but would often go days or weeks without getting any good game.

After a particularly harsh winter, when I was pregnant with our eldest, our son, my husband yelled at me for serving cold potato soup for the third night in a row. He slapped my face and pushed me to the ground. Then he yelled that I was good for nothing and would probably give him a daughter anyway, so he kicked me hard in the stomach. It was a miracle that I carried the baby to term and gave birth. I think that kick really messed up my son. The following years, I had daughters, and for some time my husband would leave me alone because he was afraid I may lose him another precious son. After the third child was revealed to be a daughter, he did beat me for not giving him more sons. It was bad enough that the midwife thought I would never bear children again.

From then on, my husband would beat me whenever he got upset. My son did the same to me when he was old enough. Whenever his father would leave to hunt, he would take on the duty of berating and bullying me. I was at my wit's end but unable to do anything about it. Then one day, I came home from the market to find my son beating his sisters with his belt in the same way my husband did to me. I tried to stop him, but he pushed me away and laughed.

I decided to visit Tituba in secret. The Parris wife was always whispering about Tituba's involvement in the dark arts and how she had learned to charm her husband, and I thought that Tituba might have a solution for me. She agreed to help and told me to meet her in the woods to get a potion from her. We met just before noon, and she gave me a potion that would mimic the symptoms of the disease that had been going around the village, saying I should be mindful that in large doses, it could be fatal to my husband and son. I simply wanted them to be sick so I could nurse them back to health, and they would be grateful for me.

But while they were becoming sick, they began speaking in weird voices. When I saw them standing over my daughters one night, they had looks of evil and lust. I went back and took another green bottle from her. I set out to poison my son and husband over the next few days.

It was very easy to do. My husband always had me make him and my son a separate meal from the leftover meat from his kills. He said that men deserved the best cuts because they worked for them. My daughters and I were always left with the scraps. They never noticed the liquid laced with the poison I was feeding them.

They got sicker after a week and died another week after that. I blamed their deaths on the sickness and buried them on our property. Then I played the part of grieving widow. No one suspected a thing, and my daughters were safe at last. I was worried that Tituba might tell someone, so I tried to dispose of the green bottle by breaking it into shards and scattering them in the barn next door. Unfortunately, a few of the local girls found the shards and began to play with them, and they started to hallucinate and complain of feeling ill. They started to accuse people of witchcraft, and it was too late for me to do anything about it. I panicked when I found out Tituba had been accused. I knew she could name me as co-conspirator to gain favor with the courts, so I quickly accused the only other person who could corroborate her story: my next-door neighbor.

I didn't think that the trials would get as out of hand as they did. I never regretted anything more than watching you, Emilee, hang for my crime. Not long after, I was accused and put in jail. My daughters went to live with relatives in Virginia, but I died before I could find out what happened to them. My visions never showed anything either. It was as if that life had cursed everything and everyone.

Naomi came out of her regression. Emilee struggled to catch her breath as she said, "So we all died for nothing? We were all cursed because you were selfish? Naomi, you must have known what would happen."

"Emilee, this was a different time. We were all in a new world, and no one gave a damn about a trapper beating his wife and children! I wasn't being selfish. I did what I did for my girls, and I paid the ultimate price!"

"Yes, you sacrificed your life and my life for your two

children. You had no business getting me involved like that."

"I know, I know. I didn't expect anyone else to get involved. You have to understand that I never meant to hurt you. Is what I did really so awful? Is it so different from what you did? You used a potion to save your daughter."

"Yes, and because of you, she died in jail with me!" Emilee was crying hysterically now. She couldn't even look at me.

Naomi was about to respond when Emilee's words hit her. She slumped down in her chair and went pale. "I didn't know that," she said in a small voice. "I thought she went with your husband." She got up and knelt in front of Emilee. "Please forgive me," she said, taking Emilee's hands. "I would have never, if I had known. We have both been seeing this story since we met all those years ago in our visions. Yes, we have been standing on the edge of help and healing. Now is our chance to clear this karma and free ourselves."

Emilee calmed down, and she nodded and sniffled a bit. "Thank you for your sincerity, but I do not know if you can be forgiven."

I had been so focused on their exchange that I hadn't noticed the tears streaming down my own face. I looked at Naomi. "It's okay, Naomi. I know you didn't intend for it to happen. I know you have had a rougher time of it than most. Maybe you could show us. That might help Emilee understand."

Naomi turned to Emilee. "Would you allow me to show you? It doesn't excuse what I did to you, but I hope it explains how a person could do the things I did."

Emilee blew her nose in a handkerchief and gave Naomi the slightest of smiles. "All right, my dear, all right. Show us."

We formed a circle once again, and Naomi took us back to the beginning. "It is true I have suffered much abuse," she explained. "It wasn't just in Salem or in this lifetime, but every life I have lived. Lifetime after lifetime, and I don't know why. I know I've had lives with trauma, and I know I've spent many of those lives creating it for others.

"The first time I came here, to Glastonbury, I never understood why I came to this place first. When I walked in, I saw things, and it was like stepping back in time. I had been well-versed in the psychic arts and astrology for years, but the magic here was different.

"The night I stayed here in the Gables, I was visited by seven shadowy figures that were cloaked with their faces obscured. They came out of a boat—"

I finished her sentence. "At the side of the temple."

"Yes." Naomi looked at me with suspicion. "Then they just stood there for a while."

I piped in again. "Then they started moving toward you, slowly at first, but then they picked up the pace."

"Yes ..." Naomi trailed off, cocking her head to the side and giving me another strange look. "I'm sorry, Anna. How do you know all of this?"

"You were visited by them in your dreams. You said it was possible they could do that." I gave her an intense look. Naomi's eyes widened at the suggestion I was making.

Emilee looked back and forth between the two of us. "I'm not following," she said.

Naomi sat silent for a while and then explained. "Anna is talking about the priests of Unal. They lost their physical forms many lifetimes ago and now reside somewhere between the physical world, the mortal world, and the spiritual one. But, Anna, how did you know what they did in my dream?"

All eyes turned to me, and suddenly I felt like a teen being caught sneaking out of the house. I swallowed hard and attempted to answer in the most even tone I could, but my voice came out small and shaky. "They have been haunting my dreams for over a month."

Naomi raised her eyebrows at my revelation but made no other indication that she was surprised. "Well, that would explain what you and I experienced earlier with the map we drew with the names on it. The priests of Unal want something."

I had a sinking feeling. "They want to stop us from passing the mantle and restoring the temple. In my dreams, they are always trying to catch me, and I get the sense that if they do, I'm done for. Each dream had something to do with a different timeline I saw. Someone close to us must have summoned them and brought them into every timeline that the other oracles and priestesses were in. These are the dark forces we sensed earlier. I just don't know who did it or why."

"I don't know the why, but I might know the who," Naomi said.

"You know who brought them into other timelines?" I asked.

"I must have summoned them, and they attached to my soul somehow. They came to me and were in all of the timelines that you saw, which I was in, as well. I was the oracle of Edfu, remember?"

I got a shiver. Then the doors slammed outside, and Wallis ran in through the cat flap. "Just because you summoned them, created them, that doesn't mean you used them to inflict harm on us."

Naomi only nodded. All of the color had drained from her face, which now took on a pallid hue.

"Go on," Emilee urged her. "We have no guests to worry about. Only us three."

"No, there are now five of us," said Naomi. "Who else is here, Emilee?"

We heard the door open, and all three of us jumped. There in the doorway stood Lucinda, red hair glowing like flames. "The wind is wild out there," she remarked. Lucinda came into the kitchen, and Emilee ran over to her and hugged her.

"You came, ma chère!" she exclaimed.

"Yes, and I brought a friend." She pointed to the door, and Laura appeared. I began to cry. I had no words; they were all here, all of the women who loved and supported me.

"Ladies, sit down," said Emilee. We shuffled around the table, and the energy of the room shifted. Before, we had felt the darkness and sadness, but now we were surrounded by friends and sisters. Emilee began preparing hot drinks and food plates.

Naomi, who normally was in complete control, sat like a small child curled up in her seat. Wallis jumped up into her lap and snuggled, purring at her warmth. I sat close to Laura, and she patted my hand. We all took a moment to catch up with each other.

"Lucinda called me this morning," said Laura. "She said with the solstice nearly upon us, many things were shifting, and you needed our help. Do you need our help, my dear?" Laura looked at me with concern.

Lucinda stopped talking to Emilee, and then all eyes were on me.

"Yes, I do," I said. "I need all of you. We have been called here for a reason, and I think now that we are all here, it will become clearer." Then I didn't know what happened, but my strength and energy surged, and I had a great deal to share.

I was beyond animated in talking about the ceremony and the revelations about Alexandria and the libraries. The table was alive with conversation, and the food plates kept arriving with pots of tea. It was a true women's circle. The oak kitchen table came alive.

We lost track of time, and soon the clock showed 9:00 p.m. Emilee looked around the group. "Ladies, it is getting late. Would you all like to meet here tomorrow, and perhaps you can share the Edfu story, Naomi?"

Naomi nodded. "Yes, that would be perfect."

"No!" Lucinda's voice sounded across the table. "Naomi, I know this is hard, but the circle must be cleared, and by holding back on this past life, we lose another night. That's another night that we miss our perfect window and miss the chance to resolve the trauma of another lifetime. We are in the solstice cycle, in the eye of its storm."

Naomi said quietly, "I know you are right." She sat up in her chair. "Can we clear the table, ladies?"

At once we all stood and cleared the table. Emilee dimmed the lights, and the cat jumped down and sat guard near the door.

"I know, I know." Naomi smiled at her. "You never left me."

"The cat?" asked Emilee, and she went to lock the front door.

"Yes, the cat," she called out over her shoulder. "She has been with us in lifetimes before."

When we were all ready, Lucinda lit a candle. To my surprise, it was Laura who spoke first. She led the prayer and the call to the ancestors and spirits of the land. Then she began to chant the names of the Egyptian gods: Isis, Osiris, Hathor, Anubis, Nepthys, and Horus—she named them all. As everyone sat in silence with their eyes closed, I peeked through mine and saw a woman dressed in purple silk with gold jewelry. Laura had changed; she appeared to me like royalty, sitting so serenely.

Laura called on us all to hold space for a sister to share her truth, and may we be blessed to see hear and feel all that we needed to know and then help heal her pain.

We all sat very still, hardly daring to breathe.

"So I'll begin," Naomi offered.

Many of you know the story of my childhood as an oracle. I was brought to Edfu and witnessed the death of the high priest. There was so much competition within the temple, and the fear regarding Rome was all that was discussed in the temple.

The death of our high priest and the ascension of the royal vizier to the position caused an imbalance; it was as if the gods had rejected us or cursed us and the temple to never be the same. The royal vizier's ambition and avarice poisoned our temple, infecting everyone with whom it came into contact. His new role as the high priest of Horus at Edfu, and the trust of Cleopatra, granted him the type of physical and spiritual rule that made him the second-highest authority in Egypt.

I woke up early on the morning after he ascended to find two black cats guarding me. They were cat spirits of Bastet, who had sent them to me for protection. At first, the other priests made fun of them and tried to harm them—until one of them raised her claws to him. Because they were temple cats who had simply appeared in the night, the elders saw this as an omen. The cats were also trying to guard me. They could not be seen to help me, but in this way, they could create a level of protection.

Their omen was fulfilled when, one early morning, one of the cats was heard making a loud crying noise. This noise woke the temple, and many came out of their chambers to see from where the noise was coming. I too ventured out. One of my cats was missing, but the male was close by me.

We made our way toward the holy of holies, the high altar, and there she stood: Isis, all the way from Philae. She stood in her golden robes, all alone with no maidens.

The priests stood still, totally surprised at how she could

enter undetected. She turned and smiled at me. There at her feet was my black female cat. She said nothing, but she kept looking at me. The cat scurried off.

The elders and the high priest soon came running down the corridor. As they arrived, the cat crying became louder and louder, but we could not see it. Everything came in slow motion, and no one knew what to say or do. Suddenly, my female cat came out from behind the back of the high stone altar.

At first, it was dark and we could not see her. Her green eyes became visible, and there in her mouth she held a hawk—not a fully grown one, but one of the new chicks.

Isis spoke directly to the high priest. "It is time for me to take her home."

The high priest refused, and he stood defiantly looking at me and then at her. "She belongs here with us. She is a daughter of Edfu. Her father lived and died here."

"You mean you killed him," said Isis as her voice began to waver. "Such horrible misfortune on you, my lord."

"You were not here, and you did not know her parent. We are her family. Her true place is here."

I was stunned by the news. The other high priest had been my father? "Then this really was my home all along?" I said as I looked at Isis. "You told me when I was younger that I belonged at Philae. You said that it was my destiny to join you. You said you would protect me from all of this!" I was so angry, and my voice rose. "How dare you try to keep me from my father. You said I had no parents! My father died here, and I will follow him."

Isis her eyes filled with sorrow and tears. She nodded. "As you wish, dear child."

"Let the cat decide," shouted one of the elders.

Isis and the high priest stood and looked at each other again.

"As they wish. The cat will help you decide," said the new high priest. "This place has the word of Lord Horus, and he no longer needs a mother, for he is chosen by the gods and leads this land for them." The high priest then commanded everyone to walk into the courtyard. He stood at one side, and Isis at the other. I stood quietly with my cats beside me.

The female cat walked out into the sunlight at the perfect moment. She paused for a moment, holding the bird gently in her mouth, and the hawk began to cry.

After a moment, she moved slowly toward me and gently laid the hawk at my feet. She then stepped beside me. Without thinking, I picked up the hawk and held it in my hands. I could feel its tiny heartbeat, but otherwise it remained still.

Isis and the high priest looked at me, waiting for me to make my move. I slowly made my way over to the high priest and handed him the bird. "My lord," I said, and I bowed.

"Then it is settled," he said with a smirk. "Now, escort the lady Isis from this place. She comes to distract the hearts of men from their purpose and place on this earth plane. She will not defend the queen our pharaoh, and she will destroy our true destiny of obtaining power."

As she was led out, the temple priests started to shout, and some of the younger boys began to cry. They remembered the love of Philae still, and its gentleness. They remembered their sacred initiation before they'd left Philae temple. The older ones, when they saw this, struck the smaller ones to the ground; the older ones had chosen to forget this feminine love they once knew. Isis saw this but could do nothing. She clenched her hands into fists, and I could feel her anger. But she said nothing as she glided from the courtyard.

My heart began to feel pain, but suddenly I had a crowd of priests celebrating me, accepting me. All of their previous doubts about me had seemingly melted away, as did the memories of me being confined to my room in chains the previous day. I went over to the statue where my father had died. I could still feel his presence, and at once I felt this was where my family should be. The priests called me the oracle, and the elders greeted me with tribute. The high priest, however, did not look so happy. I felt nervous and wondered if I had made the right choice. But in that moment, I felt like I had a family and purpose in my life, like I was a celebrity now in that place.

After Isis was dismissed from my life, I returned to my chamber to find everything broken or destroyed. I could hear a group of young priests snickering across the hall. I didn't understand why they had done this; I had just openly declared my allegiance to this temple and proven my loyalty.

Naomi abruptly stopped. She was sobbing and gently rocking herself. She looked up at me and in between sobs said, "Anna, the next part is too painful. Please channel for me? You and I have a connection—that much is clear from all of the other times you channeled my story. You were right: I do need help bearing all of this, and I would be honored if you did this, this one last time."

I bowed my head low to her and looked up. "Naomi, I would gladly take on this task. Now, just to make sure, you are giving me permission, right?"

Naomi and I both laughed at this. "Yes," she said. "For the first time, you are actually getting permission."

We both laughed again. Then, I took a deep breath and took her hand. This gave me greater access, and I could hear, feel, and see all that she was afraid to tell. I told her story to everyone at the table.

After the day Isis came to visit her for the last time, the oracle, as she was now called, begins to see a change in the Edfu temple. The priests are becoming bolder in their interactions with other temples and their display of power. They would dismiss them or demand tribute, which was unheard of at the time. They start to advocate bringing back the worship of Set and establishing him as the true god of power. Any of the priests who are loyal to Osiris are secretly killed when they visit with messages and concerns. They are preparing for something, but the oracle could not quite figure out what. All she knows is that they have largely gone back to the same routine of ignoring her and locking her away.

She figured that after she accepted Edfu as her home, she would have a better life there, but that is not the case. Despite her allegiance, the high priest is worried that she will eventually overtake him, become the new leader of the temple, and restore Horus as the only patron god. She has power from Philae and Edfu being channeled into her, and she can read the walls of hieroglyphics easily, as well as the scrolls and records kept in the secret chambers; she is even able to correct the elders for their mistakes and inaccuracies. Having her there reminds the high priest that the priestesses still hold power and could thwart their plans. He is also haunted by the fact he was never initiated through a female temple as a child, so at any time his position can be at risk. The high priest decides that he will move to enact the trials for the priests of Unal. If they can be created under his rule, that will cement his position of power so that it can never be questioned.

The high priest summons the others and tells them that the oracle was the one they have been waiting for to enact the trials.

He says that they have to move quickly to get this done before Isis and the other temples realize what was happening. The high priest convinces them that Isis will call upon the oracle to help her, and because she is just a woman, she may foolishly reject Edfu and leave them.

The next day, the High Priest gathers together all of the boys who have come from Philae and Dendara. The trials demand the innocent and pure-hearted. The older priests force them to train for the trials day and night for three weeks, until the full moon.

Those poor boys are worked to death. The priests have little care for what happens to them. All they need are a few, the ones worthy enough to get through the ritual trials, which they do get. It is inhuman, what they have to do. Whenever one of them is struggling, the others have to beat him. Every three days, the strongest faces off with the weakest, and they fight until one of them is dead.

The oracle watches this happen and weeps for them. She can't stop the bloodshed and the death. At night, she hears them crying for Isis to save them. It breaks her heart. The priests tell them that their mother Isis and their birth mothers have sent them here and that they should not pray to her for help. A dark cloud enters the temple, and the message that women are weak and evil circulates through the temple walls. It does not help that the oracle is there. Any prior protection she received from the elders is eradicated, and the cats that have come to protect her have disappeared. The priests are openly hostile to her now, pushing her around and berating her with lewd and rude comments. A few of them even go so far as to beat her. Even the younger boys join in on tormenting her, throwing pebbles at her as she passes them. Her rising fear is palpable, and she knows that no one respects or fears the power she has.

After a week, the oracle stops crying for the boys. She stops seeing them as little boys. Something is changing inside her, and a darkness is taking over. Her white robes are exchanged for black, and she prepares to make these boys into great vessels of power to be what they desire. "Let them have the power they desire, and let them be damned," she repeats to herself.

At the end of that week, she marches into the library area and demands the Scroll of Unal and the Scroll of Death and Resurrection. These scrolls had been studied for many decades, but no one knows how to really use them. But the oracle knows—Naomi knows. She now gives them the power they crave. The irony is they can only obtain it through her own power, a woman's power.

"If you wish to be the heroes and the gods of men, then follow this path that I show to you, and you will have all that you wish for," she declares at a gathering that night. "And it will be done!"

Next, I see the trials being enacted. I see the hole in the wall. Oh, my god, the hole! The initiates have to crawl through a hole in the wall, face the demons, and return through another chamber at the far back of the temple. But some do not stand up to the challenge. Those standing in the courtyard are waiting and praying they won't lose their friends and brothers. But each day the initiation trials continue, and so many are lost. The temple grows more silent each day as another son of Isis does not return from the other side.

At the end of the trials, the high priest gathers the whole temple not only to salute those who have returned to the heavens and the gods but also to celebrate those who have survived and attained glory. His voice rings loud and clear in the courtyard as he addresses them. "Brothers, our mighty enemy Rome closes in on us and seeks to take power over the sacred land of the Nile. Cleopatra and her sacred priestesses have lost their way, and their fall is coming. The oracle has seen this, and only Edfu can save Egypt. We are its salvation, as ordained by the mighty god Set. Our bravest men have gone through the trials, and now we will have an elite group of unnatural warriors at our disposal who will stop at nothing to take what is rightfully ours!"

As he continues to shout, I see the oracle standing in black robes with a golden snake belt around her waist. She's crying, her eyes are red, and she's in such pain. I see her having an internal battle that torments her more.

Ah, I see now: she has correctly invoked the creation of the priests of Unal with these trials. She is torn. Horus and Set are fighting for control of her soul. She realizes she wants to save those boys, but at the same time she wants the satisfaction of knowing she is more powerful than the high priest. She cries out in anguish, but no one hears her.

She is taken to stand before the seven initiates, the only ones to survive—seven from many. They appear large with taut, gray skin covering their bulging muscles. The oracle looks into their black eyes and sees that they have no souls anymore. They have gone to Set. The oracle knows that they will destroy everything; she can see it. As a last-ditch effort to undo what she has done, she rips the snake from around her waist and holds it above her head. She calls out, "Isis, I no longer forsake you. Punish me if you must, but I beg you to first give me the strength to kill the abominations against the gods!"

As if by magic, the sky erupts in fire, and a lightning bolt crackles out of the heavens and strikes the snake. It catches fire and begins to writhe in her hands. She unfurls it like a whip and cracks it in the air.

She charges at the abominations with all of her might. Just as she is about to reach them, she feels a sharp pain in her shoulder and falls to the ground. As the world goes black around her, she can see the high priest descending upon her.

She awakens chained to a skiff being dragged by a larger boat. The oracle struggles against the chains and yelps out in pain. They changed her into a white robe, she notices, and she can see the dried blood from a wound in her shoulder. Someone from the other boat in front of her hears her moving and comes to look at her. To her chagrin, it is the high priest.

"Ah, yes. We might want to be careful. We wouldn't want to reopen our arrow wound." He smiles a sickening smile. The oracle's mouth is covered, and she cannot respond. "Oh, what's that? Did you want to say something?" He laughs. "You know, I knew this would happen. I saw it all in a dream. You think you are the only one with the gift of sight?

"It didn't matter that you placed the hawk at my feet. You will always have the heart and magic from Philae. You could never truly serve Horus and Edfu. It is laughable that you thought you could."

The oracle struggles again to say something.

"We are on our way to Philae. Now that we have the Unal priests, we no longer need to fear the power of Isis and her temple girls. The end for them is near; it's a pity that fool Isis won't know until it's too late." He laughs maniacally. "Just remember that everything that happens now, you are responsible for it."

When the convoy reaches the shores of Philae a few days later, the high priest decides to teach the oracle a lesson and parades her in front of the temple. He yanks her from the skiff and drags her by her hair upon the shoreline until he is in front of the doors, twenty meters away. "Isis!" he shouts, "Isis, come out here and face me! Come collect your precious daughter of Philae!" All of the priestesses come to the steps of the temple to see what is going on. "Come out, Isis. Your harpies are here. Now, where are you?"

The doors to the temple fly open, and Isis steps out. She walks slowly forward and says nothing.

"There's a good priestess," says the high priest. "You have been a thorn in my side for years, even before I took over as high priest. You are the only person in Egypt who is my equal and the only one who can stop me. Our power has been matched for so long, and no one has been able to tip the scale…until now. Your precious oracle here has helped us create a weapon that we can use to kill you all and take Egypt for ourselves. We will be the most powerful temple in all of Egypt. I will say, this one here gave us nothing but trouble, trying to call to you to stop us, but we prevailed. And now you will witness her punishment for going against us, and you will see a real display of our power."

He walks back toward the oracle and signals for a priest to remove her white robe and place an old sack cloth around her. "You, oracle, will no longer wear the robes of Edfu. We strip you of your title here." Then he has her hair on her head shaved in a rough fashion, which leaves her scalp bleeding. "Now, you will no longer have the hair and beauty of Philae. We strip you of your title there. You are no longer an oracle of Edfu, and neither will you be a priestess of Philae. You are nothing now, and you will be treated as such."

Then he gives a signal and the seven priests of Unal come out of the boat carrying a post. For some reason they are unable to keep their balance on this sacred land, and the high priest orders them back to the boat and has the other priests bring forward the large wooden beam. They stake it into the ground in front of Isis on the shoreline. One of them roughly grabs the oracle and ties her to the post. The priests are about to start taunting her when the high priest interrupts them. "Wait! Remove the cloth from her mouth. I want to hear her scream." They do as he commands. Then he nods his head, and half of the priests begin to beat her with crooks while the other half wait to whip her with flails.

The first blow strikes her arrow wound and elicits a blood-curdling cry that can be heard throughout the whole island. This only serves to spur on the priests. They hit her harder, and she screams out, "Help me! Please, high priestess, help me! Ahh! I am sorry! I am sorry!" She looks into the high priestess's eyes, pleading for her to stop them.

But as the crooks continue to fall upon her now broken body, Isis just watches, motionless. Her stoic look gives nothing away. The high priest suddenly calls upon them to stop beating her. The oracle thinks it is finally over, but then the priests with flails start whipping her. It is when this starts that Isis turns away, unable to watch any longer. The oracle realizes she will not be saved and gives in to the high priest. In a choked and raspy voice, she declares, "High Priest, conduit for Horus and a Son of Set, you are the one true ruler of Edfu and the temples. You are a god living among men, whose power knows no limits and cannot be matched by any other earthly being. Now, please, call off your priests. I have learned my lesson. I yield to you and am your humble servant."

He immediately signals the priests to stop hurting her, and with the last of her strength leaving her, she slumps down, still being held up slightly by the post to which she is tied. The high priest grins at this, and his eyes turn as black as the desert night.

Then he turns his attention to Isis, who has now resumed her original stance, and announces, "Isis, heed my warning. You will fall, like this one, if you do not do the same and yield to me." Then he addresses all of the priestesses who are watching. "You will all fall." With that, he turns around and leads his envoy back down to their boats and across the river to set up camp on the opposite shore. They leave the oracle there, bleeding.

Isis turns to her priestesses and addresses them with a strong and authoritative voice. "My sisters, this is a trying time for us all. The gods are testing our fidelity, and foreign peoples seek to rule our lands. Make no mistake, the high priest is not one of us. He did not grow up in the temples and does not know our way of life. Although he has succeeded in creating seven priests of Unal, he has failed to keep the balance between the Divine Feminine and Masculine. This will be his undoing."

She pauses and calls forward a woman carrying two scrolls and scarabs. Isis takes one of the scrolls and scarabs and continues addressing the temple. "With the help of the high priestess of Renenutet and the Scrolls and Scarabs of Protection and Creation, I proclaim this temple to be protected by our queen of the gods, Isis, and by Hathor, Renenutet, and Qetesh. I claim this land in perfect harmony with the River Nile, as I did at the founding of this temple, for the initiates of Isis, for the Sacred Eight she created, for those priestesses who serve her and the other seven women, and for the Divine Feminine. No masculine energy or priests, whether they be of Horus, Set, or Unal, can come within these walls. Only those with our consent may descend upon our land.

"But heed my warning. If you cross the threshold of the temple, you will meet the same fate as the oracle of Edfu. The high priest has shown a grave disregard for the life of holy women. He does not care how many of us live or die. Let the broken woman before us be a reminder. She is beyond our help now, but you all are not. As tempting as it may be to flee or to run and help this woman, I urge you to resist. The priests of Horus are bowmen of the highest caliber; they will shoot arrows at you, and they will not miss. Have heart and know that soon I will be passing on the mantle of Isis, at which time we will all be at our most powerful and in the best position to strike back." With that, Isis ushers the other priestesses inside and gives one more forlorn look to the oracle before shutting the doors.

Ah, now I know why the priests of Unal cannot go onto Philae. It is a land balanced in nature. The priests of Unal are not natural and can never set foot on such a sacred place.

$$\varphi$$

My vision is now shifting to three days later. The oracle has been outside, tied to the stake the whole time. Her wounds have become infected, but by some miracle, she is still alive. On the third night, a group of priests are sitting around a fire and excitedly discussing the events that have transpired over the last few days. They are taking bets on how long it will take the oracle to die. One of the priests suggests that they visit her to see if she is still alive. A group of them takes a boat to the shore and sneaks over to where she is tied up.

When they walk up, they see that she is breathing, and they decide to have a little fun with her. One of them grabs her and forcefully pulls her to her feet. She moans in pain but cannot speak or fight back. Another one comes up behind her and lifts up what is left of her tunic. The third one slaps her in the face and then puts his finger in her shoulder wound. She screams loudly at this and gathers enough strength to thrash around.

The priest puts his hand over her mouth and tells her to be good, and maybe they will give her some water. The three of them laugh at her. Their laugher is momentarily interrupted by a noise coming from down the shore, but they quickly dismiss the sound and return their attention to the oracle. Just as the third priest is about to hurt her again, a priest dressed in white comes out of nowhere and subdues him with a single blow to the head. With the strength and agility of a cat, he quickly pounces on the other two and brings them forcefully to the ground. They get spooked and run back to their boat to get to camp, not wanting to deal with their rogue brother. The priest in white turns briefly, and I can make out a strange marking on his bald head. I know he is familiar to me, but I cannot quite place him; it is too dark for me to clearly see his face. He quickly tends to the oracle and her injuries, untying her and helping her down in the process. The oracle smiles at him before collapsing in his arms. Then he sits with her, guards her as she sleeps, and chants to summon the gods for assistance.

Soon after this, a sandstorm appears, and although the temple stands strong, the high priest's camp does not. The high priest has no choice but to set sail in what is left of his boats; he returns with his prized warriors. He will wait for another day to strike back. The bald priest in white uses this as an opportunity to bring the oracle to Isis.

I see that Isis and a small number of priestesses meet him at the gate to retrieve the oracle. As they lift her and carry her, they already know her days are numbered, but at least she is home.

"I need to stop now. I'm exhausted," I said.

"Yes, yes, let's stop," said Lucinda. "I'm feeling dizzy so goodness knows how you all are."

I came out of my trance fully and looked around. I could

see a change in Emilee's face. She finally understood why Naomi had done what she had done, and she embraced her fully.

The other women sat around, and Laura moved to Naomi and held her. "Words cannot express what we all saw, heard, and felt, but we know that we would never want this to happen again. It's late, but I know this story is not yet finished. We will have to see, in time, what happens."

I said, "But wait—what about the other female?"

"What other female?" asked Laura. "I did not see another female."

"There was one. I felt her," I said.

"No, Anna, there were no other females there."

"But I'm sure I felt someone. It was like she was just out of frame the whole time."

"Sometimes the timeline gets crossed with others, Annie," Lucinda offered.

"Look, it's late, my dear," Laura said. "We are all tired and in need of some sleep."

"Yes, it is," agreed Emilee. "We should all retire for the evening. Naomi, room seven is open, if you wish to stay."

Naomi smiled. "I would be most happy to do that, thank you. For some reason, the Sanctuary does not feel like the safe space I need tonight."

"Lucinda, please choose your room. And you too, Laura. You will stay, oui?" asked Emilee.

"Tonight, we helped repair a lot of karmic damage and are that much closer to getting our temple back!" declared Lucinda. With that, Wallis jumped up onto the table and started to purr.

"Complete with temple guardian, I see," said Naomi.

We all laughed at that.

CHAPTER 23

Tuesday, June 17

I came downstairs the next morning to find Lucinda eating breakfast with Emilee.

"Lucinda!" I squealed. "I am still just so happy that you are here!"

"Anna, dear, I am so happy to be here as well and witness all the good you've done." She smiled at me. "You know, I didn't get a chance to tell you last night, but I've been taking phone calls from all the other priestesses I know. It appears that since you arrived in Glastonbury, everyone's Akashic records have been opening, and the stories are spilling out."

"Really? And you think I have something to do with that?"

"Perhaps," she said. "But have you not seen some strange things happening?"

"And you?" I hardly dared to ask.

She looked around and leaned in to whisper, "Well, the last few nights, my dreams were all about Egypt and the priestesses. I saw Isis leaving in a jet plane in one dream." I had held my breath because I wanted to giggle, but she looked so intense and serious. "Well, I wanted to go with her," she continued, "and I saw many others leaving with suitcases, boarding with her. But she sent me back to a hotel with my suitcase. I got into a clear glass elevator, and I watched her leave as it ascended up into the sky. Now, what do you make of that?"

"I don't know. I'll have to think on that." I grinned. "Perhaps we could do a session with you today, Lucinda."

She gave me a very strange look. "Perhaps." She laughed.

After breakfast, I decided to become invisible again. I could hear the noise in the dining room as the women gathered, and I went to sit in the back garden area of the Gables. I sat on a wooden bench, and Wallis jumped up and began rubbing herself next to me. The sun shone down, and I felt its warmth. The women's voices grew louder, but my thoughts became deeper.

Everyone I had come close to recently had a story to share about another, some good and some not so good. I had the words of Lucas, the Goth tarot reader, in my head again, reminding me that the time of the tower was approaching again. The Tower had appeared not once but twice, as a tarot card and as the Tower of London in my vision. Both spelled destructions, but for whom I wasn't sure.

I had felt that I was beginning to think, feel, and even daydream in other realities. Everything was blending together, and I was starting to have trouble bringing forward my own spiritual truth and my path; it felt as if I was distracted by everyone else's. After all, I was here trying to write a story.

I wondered if my curiosity and story writing were considered a breach of personal space to the women I had talked to. Or perhaps it was a breach of my space. *Is it dangerous? Will people be offended? Will I lose myself in the process? Could I be about to fall from the tower in which Anne Boleyn had been imprisoned?*

Lucinda made herself available to me over the next few days as we prepared for the solstice. Over meals, she would talk nonstop in a constant channel, and Emilee would smile and raise an eyebrow. I simply nodded to her that I was listening and at the same time was always reaching for my journal. I had noted that I had now gathered a lot of content and had been writing it up during the evenings. But I needed Lucinda's personal story, and I decided now was that perfect moment.

I looked at Lucinda that Thursday morning over breakfast. "So what's your story? What's your connection to these other women?" I pulled out my almost full gold journal and got ready to write. Emilee was pouring coffee and appeared to be frozen in time. She moved around in the dining room silently clearing up after the other guests, all the while glancing back at Lucinda and me in the nook next to the window. It was after 10:00 a.m., so we were late and the last to finish.

I could tell Lucinda was not used to being put on the spot; it made her have to focus and be grounded. "My story, my story..." She smiled and looked at Emilee. "I think I should start with my life in Egypt and connection to the Temple of Hathor at Dendara." Emilee walked over at that point and placed down the coffee pot. She and Lucinda shared a smile, as if they both knew what was about to set forth.

"Shall we go to the temple room?" said Lucinda with a glint of mischief in her eye.

The temple room? I had not been shown this, even after all these weeks, and I had not even heard a whisper of it.

Emilee stood silent as if to think, and then she checked her watch. "One hour, Lucinda," she said.

Lucinda agreed and leaped up with her breakfast dishes. "I'll clear up!" she said cheerfully.

"After you, mes chères," said Emilee, and she motioned for us to exit the breakfast room. I followed, clutching my precious journal and pen to my chest.

The ladies then turned in behind the pantry. They moved some large baskets that Emilee used to gather her herbs, and then Emilee unlocked a small door that led off from the kitchen. As we had entered the kitchen, Emilee had locked the door and placed a "do not disturb" sign on the front of it. I could hear Wallis moving around the kitchen, scratching at the fabric chair in the corner to show that she was present and on guard.

Lucinda stood back from the doorway and motioned for me to go through and into the secret room. It was like another world. Pictures of ancient Egypt adorned the wall, and in the center of the room was a small table with candles. The room was filled with cushions and chairs for relaxation and comfort.

In each of the corners, there were four large golden statues of goddesses, like the ones I had seen in the Egypt books, their arms outstretched with a different symbol on the top of each. On the back wall was a large image in beautiful blue and gold. It was round and had certain figures upon it.

Lucinda told me to sit down, and Emilee lit the candles and put on some gentle background music. "I need your help, Anna," said Lucinda. "I have shared with you some of my temple story and my initiations in my classes, but after that I am blank. Even Naomi could not see for me, and Isis will not. I thought in time you could help me see. I know I'm connected, but I don't understand."

I remembered not quite understanding her, but at the same time my logical brain began to question. "Okay, so you saw yourself as a child and then going through the initiations, the rituals? Then when you went to Philae, all was empty and dark?" I asked.

"Yes," Lucinda said with a nod.

"So what do you wish me to do?"

Emilee said gently, "We want you to look into the records and see. Lucinda may have curses blocking her from seeing, but you can see deep behind those veils. Look for her like you did for Naomi."

"Okay, I'll try," I said.

"We have faith in you, and I have belief in you," said Lucinda.

It was then that I noticed an image of a large stone relief above us. It was circular and had what looked like paintings of different animals all around it. "What is that?" I enquired, pointing to the ceiling.

"Ah, that is the Zodiac of Dendara."

"It's beautiful!" I said, and Lucinda and Emilee exchanged glances.

"Oui! And real one of it is in the Louvre, the museum in Paris, that is so dear to my heart." Emilee giggled.

"Is it connected to this? I feel it is."

"We aren't sure," said Lucinda. "We think it is, though."

I paused and closed my eyes and held up my hands to gather the energy like Naomi had shown me with the maps and the words. "Dear spirits, now open my ancient eyes within my hands, so that they are now open to the messages." I brought my arms down and rubbed my hands together. "Yes, they are open and talking to me. Yes, this piece is very important, a vital key to everything we have been going through!"

"Now, ladies," I said, "let's find out! I'm calling forward an oracle vision. Will you partake with me?" I held out my hands, and we connected in a sacred circle. I had Emilee count me down into the regression, and back to Egypt we went.

"Are you in the temple?" asked Lucinda.

"I'm not sure. It is a temple, but I don't think it is the Temple of Isis," I said. "I'm walking around, and it's a very busy place. Everyone is scurrying around, preparing for something. Oh, I overhear one of them saying that the queen is coming. It is Cleopatra, coming to meet the resident oracle there. But this does not look or feel like the Philae temple.

"There is confusion in the temple. The oracle has channeled the story from the cosmic heaven, and the information is for the queen only. The other priestesses don't understand why. People are moving very quickly, and there are the sounds of sacred chants and offerings being given. There are many special, almost holy areas in this temple, and I'm seeing an area where babies are born, and also where the elderly pass. It's as if all life cycles are respected here."

"We are in Dendara Temple," said Emilee.

"Yes," I replied. "I get a positive response to that, and it is the truth."

I now see a small room with a blue ceiling, and those priestesses look to be in trance, staring at the sky. There are a few of them communicating with the stars, asking for guidance. They have clay tablets, and they write down the constellations and the meanings. This is used to create the predictions for the royal family. It will tell of the future.

I'm now on the roof, and there are a few priestesses performing rituals, but I'm not keen on their energy because they look to be hiding something. A man is with them, and I'm trying to listen to what they are saying. He turns, and I see that he is the royal vizier who eventually becomes the new high priest of Horus. I don't like his energy, and he whispers secrets that seem to bring fear and scandal. They divide the temple and the women.

The women are complaining that they have not been allowed

to go the festivals in Edfu and that Isis and the temple of Philae are to blame. They feel that the temple, their sacred temple of Hathor, is being ignored and overlooked. The royal vizier is agreeing with them and telling them that change is coming and that there will soon be a new high priest of Edfu who will create change for the greater good of the gods. He tells them Isis is not who they think she is. He says she has broken her sacred promise to protect the Divine Feminine. He whispers that someday she will ban the sacred union between the priests and priestesses. They will lose the men they love and desire. He is very psychic and tells the tale of how, in the future, Isis will witness the beating and humiliation of a great oracle and will turn her back on her, leaving her to die on a stake outside her temple.

Those who see clairvoyantly visit the high altar, and they see this vision in the future and proclaim the royal vizier to be of truth and integrity. But there are so many secrets and lies; I can't tell who is genuine.

He tells them to send offering to the god Horus, and also to Set for him to take away the impersonators from the temples of Egypt. These are not the true Divine Feminine creators but women who work dark magic. He carries around a box, which he tells the priestesses contains the spells of love and magic. The priestesses desire this above anything else.

I don't like this energy and move away. It makes me feel unsteady. It's like he hypnotizes everyone.

I see a girl in the corner, and she's listening. She's hiding, so I feel she is spying on them. They don't see her; no one sees her. But I do.

I follow her. I can't see her face, but she seems familiar too. Now I hear a woman's voice. Ah, it's Lucinda's voice, and the girl hears her too. She goes toward it.

I am following the girl down the corridors. She goes into

the small high altar area, and she begins to whisper all that she has heard. I see the oracle of the temple praying, and the high priestess is chanting and creating offering to the gods. She stops and looks at the girl, and then she commands her to leave. It is Lucinda! Lucinda, you are the high priestess of Hathor at Dendara, and I think the oracle is Laura!

♀

I stopped and opened my eyes. It was like the entirety of my energy was being drained from me. Emilee looked at me sympathetically and handed me some water, but Lucinda showed me no such mercy and told me I must carry on.

"This is further than I have ever gotten, Anna," she exclaimed. "I've never made it into the inner chamber. You have to press on." She glanced around the room, and I noticed she was trembling something fierce.

Emilee placed her hand on Lucinda's arm. "You were a chosen one, Lucinda. Never forget that."

Lucinda placed her hand over Emilee's and nodded in agreement. Then they both looked at me and said in unison, "Carry on, Anna."

Emilee spoke up. "But, Anna, you must go alone. This is a powerful story I feel we need to hear and not see." She looked at Lucinda, who nodded.

"Anna, you do not need any other oracle or one who sees, because you can connect to all the levels of information and vision. You have access to the whole Akashic record," whispered Emilee.

Again Lucinda simply nodded and smiled.

I tried to relax back into the chair, but my eyes were drawn to the large disc of the zodiac. I could make out individual symbols and people depicted on it. I tried to focus on the hieroglyphs, but it made me dizzy. That was all I needed to put myself back into Lucinda's past life.

I'm back at the high altar, and the rituals continue. First they chant, and then they burn incense and inhale it. The suspicious girl is still around, spying on them. I see Lucinda throwing oils and herbs onto the fire, and with each one she makes a declaration, a prophecy that a young scribe sitting nearby etches into a clay tablet.

But something is wrong today. Lucinda begins to wail loudly, and it's as if she has seen something so terrible. Suddenly she picks up the water and throws it onto the fire. There is a strong smell of roses that punctuates my nose. Lucinda announces that the temple must be purified, but I don't know why. I'm trying to see the girl who was spying on them, but I still can't see her face.

Lucinda leaves the altar, and I am now following her. We enter a smaller room, and there is a group of priests and priestesses. They have clay pots and tools. Ah, yes, I see now: they are creating the zodiac. But this time it's on the floor. Lucinda sits down on the floor and begins pointing at different tablets above her in the ceiling.

Now one of the priestesses from the star chamber with the blue roof enters, and she sits on the floor. Everyone has these clays tablets, and I'm not sure what they are for. Okay, now Lucinda is pointing to a certain point of the zodiac, and one of the artisans is listening very intently but looks surprised. They ask her again and again if this is true, and she solemnly nods. They now appear very quiet, and with heads bowed, they attend to the work. The priestess from the star chamber whispers to Lucinda.

I'm trying to see if anyone else is there. I can't see, but I can feel them. Oh, wait—I see them coming into focus now.

The royal vizier in the corner, the one connected to Horus, is here. He's just standing there, smiling. I do not trust him; he should not be here. He fancies himself a priest, but he is a false priest. I see the artisans placing new images onto the zodiac. "Predications and prophecy," the artisans whisper. Now they are placing drapes of thin fabric over the zodiac to hide this new information.

Now I am in the high altar room, and it is a few days later. Everybody is in a frenzied state, running around and making preparations for the new queen's arrival. I can see out from the roof that Queen Cleopatra's envoy is arriving. She has just begun to rise to power but is challenged by her brother. She is coming to gain the blessings of Hathor and Isis to bring power and prosperity to her.

Her procession is very grand. She has colorful chariots pulled by horses, with camels carrying beautiful silks and woven baskets. There are exotic animals wearing elaborate costumes, carrying gold and silver trinkets. It is truly an amazing sight.

While she makes her way from the east, from the west an equally large, but far less grand, procession of priests from Edfu make their way down the Nile. The high priest is directing them from the front. I see that he is Naomi's father.

I can see the other priests are carting a large statue of Horus on a large skiff. It's strange; he looks to be racing to be there before the queen. He arrives on shore, attended by a young priest, a man robed in white with the mark of a scorpion on his head. I do not know why I didn't recognize him before, but that is Lucas, the Goth! He is the priest who helped Naomi!

The royal vizier is asking that the priestesses of Hathor bow to him, and when they refuse, he becomes very angry. Lucinda balks at this. She can't believe that he would even ask. I feel such confusion, and the looks on the priestesses' faces show such fear. For some reason, everything seems out of sequence. I'm confused. The protocols are all messed up.

Lucinda, the high priestess, holds her own and allows the Edfu priests to carry the statue into the temple. Then she has the initiates bring out an offering. The high priest approaches Lucinda, and they clasp hands then and turn in unison to wait for the queen's procession to get to the temple entrance. There is a palpable tension between the high priest and high priestess, but neither is willing to address it. They simply wait in silence.

Finally the procession stops, and the queen is led forward on a throne by two footmen adorned in lapis and gold and set down in front of the two religious officials. As she is helped down from her throne, I can see how truly beautiful and regal she is. She's wearing a simple white dress that cuts off at her thigh—the only simple thing about her—and a large gold collar with onyx stones arranged in ascending order, radiating from the center of the collar outward. Her long, black hair cascades down her sun-kissed shoulders, and the dark kohl around her eyes creates a piercing effect. I am absolutely captivated by her.

She stops in front of Lucinda and the high priest and nods to both of them. She is glad to have both of them there to advise her and help her accept the mantle of queen. Cleopatra tells them that she seeks predictions from the high priestess and advice on power from the high priest. She asks to meet with each of them and expresses her gratitude. She tells them she welcomes their advice but warns them she will also seek the wisdom from the libraries and oracles of Alexandria and the visions of Isis in Philae. The high priest looks confused that she would treat him as a lesser power to women and oracles.

Lucinda smiles at the queen, who waves her hand to indicate she wishes to be taken to the high altar to consult with the oracles of the temple. Lucinda will be first because this is her domain, and Cleopatra will go to the high priest afterward. Now he really looks like he is ready to protest, he should be before any woman. His ego has taken over but then he realizes he is talking to a queen, and he bites his tongue. Lucinda leads Cleopatra by the hand, and they walk in unison into the temple.

When they reach the high altar, they both kneel to pray to the statue and the goddess. After this, Lucinda asks the queen to visit the birthing chamber in order to be advised on her future heirs. The women in the birthing chamber remove her dress and anoint her stomach with sweet-smelling oils. After a series of prayers, they tell her she will have healthy and strong children, but they will come from a false king and a true one.

The queen seems somewhat relieved by this news, but she worries what it means for her kingdom's future if she is going to have two lovers who would be kings. She tells the women that she praises the gods because she feels a sense of unrest, especially from the priests of Karnak, the political seat of Egypt; her family; and now the high priest of Horus at Edfu. Then she asks to be taken to the zodiac. She has followed its progress closely from the oracles of Alexandria.

Lucinda now explains that they have started to create some of the new images and that she must warn the queen of two major eclipses. One will be connected to Isis and the other to Horus. She indicates that Cleopatra should follow her to the room with the zodiac. I follow, and now I see Lucinda pulling back the fabric cover that was placed over the stone tablets. The queen kneels down to study it, gingerly tracing the symbols and pictures with her fingers. The queen asks Lucinda to explain what they mean. I watch as Lucinda takes incense and inhales blue lotus oil. She then sits down, bows her head, and channels what it is the queen needs to hear.

In a trance, Lucinda tells of what she could see in

Cleopatra's world and life to come. The true king will come into the queen's life with a greatness that rivals that of Alexander. He will eventually fall, but his legacy will live on with her. They will have two children together; one will become a pharaoh, a king, and the other will obtain the highest honor the gods have to offer. The child will take up the mantle of a God and their living conduit on earth.

She tells the queen that for this all to come to pass, she must read and be guardian for the secrets of the Scroll and Scarab of Records of Life. To command this scroll, the queen could rule without her brother and make Egypt a great power. She tells the queen that the scroll is hidden in the zodiac images and that this scroll reveals all the records of life and therefore all the secrets that one holds in one's soul. The zodiac represents the astrological charts of the soul, and the scroll can reveal its wisdom. The queen tells her that Isis has also promised her the Scrolls and Scarabs of Protection and Creation. She whispers to Lucinda that many of the sacred scarabs will soon be within her possession.

I don't really understand this, and neither does Lucinda. What I do see is that these scrolls and scarabs must be passed to one of the queen's daughters, the one who will become the Isis of her time; this will bring the heirs and legacy of Cleopatra to surpass any other ruler in history.

Lucinda carries on and relays what she has been seeing in her visions, saying that the Sons of Set are rising at Edfu. They have begun to gather the secrets from the child oracle, the one who serves a masculine temple, the oracle of Edfu. She alone can use the Scroll of Unal to enact the trials. The Sons of Set will use this in a battle with the priests of Horus. This will cause the priesthood of Egypt to turn from Horus to only the cult of Set. The battle will either spell destruction and the end of the golden age of Egypt, or it will herald in the days of balance, prosperity, and peace for many lifetimes. The eclipses will start the cycles of time, and the libraries and oracles of Alexandria will show the way.

When Lucinda finishes, the queen seems unconvinced and asks Lucinda to confirm what she said was true. She asks Lucinda about the powerful man in Rome and whether she should pursue him. Lucinda advises the queen to be careful of inviting the Roman legions into their lands; they will not respect the temples. Cleopatra thinks Lucinda is lying to her and has her own agenda, and I cannot figure out why. Lucinda senses it too on some level but can't quite figure it out. Lucinda then explains again that the priests of light and shadow in Edfu are gathering forces. They are in conflict due to the child oracle brought from Philae to Edfu and her messages. The queen asks about the child oracle, and Lucinda hangs her head. This is the conversation both women should be having but do not.

Laura the oracle of Dendara has foretold of a child born to a high priestess and who be protected. Lucinda at this time is unsure if this was to be her or another High priestess, as pregnancy is strictly forbidden.

Lucinda switches back to telling the queen about her reign and her future children. Cleopatra should be ready to usher in historic changes for her people, but she must be aware of who she is and who she is becoming as a person. Then she tells Cleopatra about her first child, a boy who will be immortalized on the walls of temples with her. This, Lucinda knows, appeals to the queen's vanity and desire to be a famous ruler. Lucinda figures it is enough to satisfy the queen and distract her from the more harrowing news that has befallen her.

The zodiac and other information are of little interest to the queen now, and she dismisses Lucinda as only being able to comment on womanly things. Cleopatra then calls for the high priest of Edfu to come to her so that she can get an understanding about her true destiny, beyond bearing children. The snub is clear to those around her, and a few of the priestesses present whisper about it. I wonder if this is part of the mistrust that happens. This is the seed placed where women see the high priestess, another woman, as less than a high priest and a man.

At the queen's request, Lucinda quickly covers up the zodiac and takes her back to the high altar. They come into the room to find the high priest performing a ritual with the royal vizier. This is the person who whispers to the other priestesses, the one who is like a viper in the nest. I can feel the power shifting and a new force being exerted; something about it feels deeply dark and sinister. The ritual calls on the Scroll of Magic and Prophecy. The high priest produces a scroll and lays it out in front of the queen, and he encourages her to incant the words with him. Lucinda and a few other priestesses are watching from the outer chamber. A few of them are crying over what appears to be a loss of their own power and trust with the royal family. This should never have happened. It's strange they do not seem to have the scarab.

I paused and brought myself back to the current moment. Emilee and Lucinda were sitting with their best poker faces on, eyes wide open and mouths expressionless, listening. I smiled, nodded to them, and closed my eyes again. I was afraid of what was to come, but the story was finally unraveling, and the players were showing themselves.

It's now a few years later, and the temple of Dendara is very quiet. The women have splintered into small groups that are often at odds with each other. They all have their little meetings and whisper nasty rumors about other women. When the groups do interact, they can be extremely cruel to each other. There is a growing group of them who believe they are the Daughters of Set and that one among them is the true high priestess of the temple.

The lack of trust among the groups has thrown off the oracles' abilities to bring forward information that holds truth and integrity; what information is coming through is confusing, but no one can figure out from where it is originating. The royal vizier has returned to Alexandria but regularly visits Dendara to further sow seeds of distrust and deepen the rift between them and Philae. He says that their own high priestess is keeping things from them and not allowing them to grow and fully use their power. He calls for Lucinda to be banished for being derelict of duty.

Lucinda feels her grip on the temple weakening and appeals to Queen Cleopatra for help. She argues that she must remain high priestess of Dendara because her prediction about the son has come to pass, and as promised, the image of her son is carved into the temple. Cleopatra acknowledges this but states that she cannot help because she doesn't want to get involved in the politics of religion and has to focus on diplomatic relations between Egypt and Rome. She says that she has been in close contact with the priests of Edfu and trusts them to handle whatever unrest is happening in the temples. Lucinda attempts to protest, but Cleopatra stops her, reminding her that although she did correctly predict her child's birth, she was unable to show her anything of value when it came to ruling Egypt.

Cleopatra's trust in the priests of Edfu has emboldened them to exert more influence over the other temples. They are regularly visiting Dendara to copulate with the priestesses there as they wish, an act typically reserved for the times of festival— but the priestesses of Dendara have also stopped producing children. Many of the unions are not sacred unions, which will not create a child fit for temple service. They do, however, still honor the ways of Philae temple and follow the protocols. This is something of a point of contention for the Dendara priestesses, now never getting the same honor of bearing children of Edfu like those at Philae. Lucinda attempts to stop this from occurring, but with no success. The priestesses who have turned away from her have overruled her, and the new high priest of Edfu will not grant her appeals for him to stop sending priests. Isis learns of this and attempts to block them, but she decides instead to restrict their access where she can. She greatly decreases the number of priests allowed at Philae, to help compensate.

I'm seeing Lucinda standing on the roof and petitioning to the gods. Power is slipping through her hands, and she needs help reestablishing order. When she finishes, she looks down and sees a small legion from Rome approaching, bearing the queen's insignia on their shields. Lucinda rushes down to meet them at the gate. They inform her that they are there by order of the queen to retrieve gold for the war effort and to move the Scroll of the Records of Life that is hidden in the zodiac to Alexandria.

Lucinda informs them that they are welcome to their gold but that it would be impossible to take the scroll; it was sealed in the zodiac relief and cannot be taken out. The leader of the legion gets angry at this and demands that Lucinda show them. He orders his soldiers to throw spears at it and attempt to break it as they think the scroll is buried behind it.

I am now seeing Lucinda running to a back chamber, where the original scroll is located, they have not mentioned the scarab so she seeks this in her private chamber, but it is missing.

She has broken her vow to always be truthful, but in her vision, she saw this day come, when the Romans would begin to take the scrolls and use them for themselves. They would seek the scrolls rather than the oracles for their information, and should this occur, all the oracles of Egypt would be doomed and damned for their gifts.

This sad prophecy was starting its cycle, as has been shown from the eclipses. She decides to hide the scroll in a sacred urn filled with snakes used for high priestess initiations. Only a worthy high priestess can place her hand in the urn to retrieve what lies inside; any other person will be bitten by poisonous snakes and die in seconds. Just at the moment she puts the scroll in the urn, the royal vizier, who had tagged along with the legion, sees her. He knows every turn of this temple and has followed her for many years, waiting for this perfect sinister moment. He grabs her and the urn and drags her by her hair back to the zodiac room to inform the Romans of her treachery.

The royal vizier warns the Roman general that the urn is filled with snakes and they need to be careful when breaking it. The soldiers attempt to break it but are unsuccessful. The general suggests they simply open it and lure the snakes out, but the royal vizier advises against this. He tells them that only a worthy high priestess or equivalent can put her hand in without being bitten and dying.

The general then asks, "Royal vizier, surely you are worthy enough to retrieve the scroll? Why don't you try your hand in it?"

He looks hesitant and responds, "Well, General, I would,

but it seems foolish for me to risk my life when we have the high priestess right here."

Lucinda takes this opportunity to challenge the royal vizier. "But is it not you who always comes around my temple and declares yourself a man of great power? You have been attempting to take it away from me for years, and this would be the perfect opportunity for you to have unquestioned authority!"

"Yes, it would," he concedes, "but this urn is typically for womanly worship. I am not a woman."

The general says, "But you are well versed in temple worship and a servant to your queen, are you not?"

"Yes, but—"

"But nothing. Your queen commands you to do it. If you do not, I will execute you for treason," the general declares, because he too wishes to show the power of the man above the woman.

The royal vizier swallows hard and nods his head. Lucinda opens the urn with a smirk on her face, knowing that he will not succeed. He slowly lowers his hand into the urn, holding his breath as he does so. To Lucinda's shock and horror, the royal vizier pulls out the scroll, unscathed by the snakes. He holds the scroll high in triumph. The general quickly retrieves it from him and places it in a box for safe keeping.

The royal vizier addresses everyone present. "As you all can see, I am the true ruler over Dendara. You have been fooled into thinking the false high priestess is your commander. I am now and forever the ruler of Dendara. You will bow to me out of respect." He points to Lucinda. "And you will be stripped of your title and leave this place at once! From this day forward, I will appoint the high priestess who suits my needs and wants!"

Lucinda looks shocked but she sees he is holding the scarab of the records of life in his other hand, this protects him and she flees the room. It's heartbreaking. I see her crying in her chamber in shame and then sending word to Philae that she is coming. In the meantime, I see the general congratulating the new ruler of Dendara. The royal vizier asks for a favor: he would like the general to send a few of his men to follow the false high priestess and kill her before she reaches Philae. He knows that she could rally some support there, and he doesn't want to his new authority challenged. The general agrees and dispatches a few men to follow her.

That night, Lucinda must formally give up her title and leave the temple. Everyone gathers outside to watch. They form two rows on either side of the path leading to the entrance at the temple wall. Lucinda appears at the top of the path dressed in her ceremonial gown of red, a gold headdress, and jewelry. As part of the forced abdication of her title, she must remove one item of dress with each step she takes until she has them all removed. She starts by removing her headdress made of gold and sapphire. Then she must hand over her mantle with the sacred feminine symbols on it. She continues her shameful walk, removing her rings, earrings, and sacred cartouches, which bear her name. They are trampled on. A crowd of priestesses and soldiers jeers at her, and many spit on her as she passes by, but just as many stand behind them weeping in emotional pain.

Lucinda was their mentor and teacher and was very loved. They whisper promises they will search for her through all the next lives to find her and follow her again. They hold hands in silence as she passes, and they communicate with each other with their eyes. "Always and forever we will find our temple again," they say.

By the time she reaches the end of the path, all that is left on her body is a dirty white tunic and her symbolic ankh necklace. She stands in front of the royal vizier with tears in her eyes as she is forced to hand over her most prized possessions. He smirks at this and then orders a cloak to be placed on her. Lucinda must wear a dark cloak to signify that she is unworthy to be looked upon by others and seen as a human being. He informs her that now she has shed all relics of the temple, she will not be recognized by it and faces death by snake should she return. Two priestesses then grab her by the arms and forcefully throw her out, closing the gate behind her.

Lucinda takes one last look at the temple that shunned her, that had been her home, and then sets out for the river, broken and in despair. However, when she reaches the boat, she has no time to grieve. The oracle of Hathor meets her there and is helping her rig up her decoy boat so that she could escape safely, without the new high priest's men following her.

Lucinda goes to leave, but the oracle stops her. She tells Lucinda to claim the box in Alexandria. It's very confusing because I can't see a box or its purpose, but the oracle is adamant that Lucinda must seek it out for all their sakes. However, the box comes with a warning, and if for any reason she is captured, she must throw the box into the Nile and let the gods claim it. Lucinda promises and then goes to hide up shore, out of the sightline of the temple or any approaching boat. She watches the boat she was meant to be on sail away. Oh no—I also see another priestess wearing a dark cloak on this boat, another soul sister I feel is going to protect Lucinda, I think it is Emilee. Then I see another boat with Roman soldiers following it. This other priestess's fate is doomed.

Lucinda waits until they turn a corner before getting in a smaller boat hidden in some brush. She charts a course north for Alexandria, safely out of harm's way.

I came out of the trance. I couldn't go on any more. Lucinda was silently crying, and Emilee held her close.

"I left them," she sobbed. "I left them and my temple. How could I do that? I should have just put my hand in the urn. Even if the Romans had the scroll, at least I still would have been in power and there to protect them, and Emilee you sacrificed your life for me."

"Lucinda, that was a long time ago," Emilee comforted her. "Anna, I think that is enough, and it's past an hour. We don't want to see any more."

"But I do. I'm now also seeing Laura there. She was my second in command, my oracle," said Lucinda. "I also need to know what it was that was so important about the box. I think I know, but I need to be certain."

"Lucinda, I don't think I can look. I'm so tired," I protested.

"Then let me look," said a voice suddenly from nowhere. It belonged to Laura, who was standing in the doorway.

"Welcome, dear one," said Emilee, and she moved to find a place for Laura to sit down.

"Don't worry," Laura said as she patted my hand. "Now let me look at these records for the answers you seek, Lucinda."

I had never seen this side of Laura before, and I looked at her in disbelief.

She explained. "You didn't think you could get into the records of the scrolls without gathering attention, did you? I am the oracle for Hathor at Dendara and guardian of the Scroll of the Goddess and Fertility, for Pete's sake. I know when someone is looking in my records. So I must be present. I have aided dear Isis and Lucinda for centuries in these matters. Here is my scarab, the one of Goddess and Fertility, to help guide us."

She placed an exquisite blue scarab onto the table. "Besides, Emilee, my dear, when one is doing this kind of work, it is best to also lock one's back door, if you don't want surprise guests!" We all had a laugh at that.

"Then tell what you see, dear oracle," said Lucinda, and Laura obliged.

Okay, let me see…Ah, yes, I see Lucinda near the Luxor temple. She sails by in a small boat. She is cloaked and travels now with ferrymen who appear harmless and very poor; the Roman guards who are now appearing at every temple door pay no attention to them. She stops for sanctuary in the smaller temples. It appears that she managed to keep safe her scarab with the insignia that gives her protection. Each elder of the temple recognizes this, and they provide safe space as she shares with them that the cycle of prophecy has now started and that she must reach the oracles of Alexandria. The journey is harsh, but Lucinda carries on.

I'm seeing the port at Alexandria now. With nowhere to hide, she decides that the library will be the best place to go. The city center is crawling with soldiers, and Lucinda decides that it will be best to wait until nightfall to venture to the library.

Oh, what horrors, though. Lucinda, I see you heading toward the library. You see all sorts of light radiating from it in the distance. You come upon the library to find it is burning down. Everything is burning to the ground.

A singular oracle runs from the building. She is the one who had assisted with the building of the library, Seshat's

Keeper of the Scrolls—our very own Alice. She tells Lucinda that the oracles, who held the wisdom and the magical scrolls, were locked inside. They were the ones who were taught the secrets from the current oracle of the great pyramid. They have been outspoken since the child oracle was taken and held in Edfu, and now they have all perished along with the promises and prophecies.

What is important is that she tells Lucinda that they were waiting for her. They received a secret message when she left Dendara, and they have been watching every night in secret. Each night an oracle would wait near the secret tunnel and gateway with the box, to be given to the woman in a dark cloak who bears the insignia and scarab of protection. She carefully hands the box to Lucinda.

All is now lost, and Lucinda can only sit by the water with Alice and watch the library and the others burn. They can hear the screams from inside. "All that is left is me and this box," Alice tells her. "The gods have saved me, so please take me with you."

"They will rise again," Lucinda says, pointing to the library, "for it is our legacy, lifetime after lifetime, to rise and protect the scrolls and ancient libraries of wisdom."

It's as good a time as any for her to open the box, because it might help the hopeless situation. There are three things inside: a papyrus of the zodiac, the Scroll of Truth and Integrity, and a scarab that bears the symbol of the ankh of life, of creation. She places the scarab of protection into the box. In time, this box will come to be filled with all eight of the scrolls and scarabs—essential if they ever need to found a new temple. But now that the Alexandrian Library has fallen, Lucinda and the other oracle can only make their way to Philae temple and seek refuge.

The years pass, and in the fall of 44 BC, Lucinda receives a secret message that Cleopatra will be returning to Egypt soon and will be in need of a safe place to give birth. Hang on—that can't be right. This child is not one of her known children with Mark Antony. Ah, I see. Cleopatra has conceived her second child by Caesar in Rome, just a month prior to his assassination. The message Lucinda receives also says that the queen and the child are in danger and are being pursued by Roman assassins. Lucinda then gets a vision of Cleopatra and Caesar and that they have met together in secret so that Caesar can sign a document stating that he legally recognizes this future child as his legitimate heir and successor—something he could not do for their first child, Caesarion. They have consulted an Oracle in Rome who has predicted this child is destined to be favored by the gods to bring forward a golden age and they believe it will be another male child. This is just a few days before Caesar is killed. He knew that it was possible an assassination may be attempted, and he wanted to make sure that he had an heir who could unite Rome and Egypt and create the most powerful empire in the known world.

Lucinda sees that Cicero has found out about Caesar's new heir. He knows that if Cleopatra has her baby and delivers Caesar's new will to the Senate, Octavian, Caesar's previously named successor and child by adoption and not blood, would have to yield to this new child. Although Julius Caesar was in no uncertain terms Cicero's enemy, he still preferred Octavian to Mark Antony, who immediately started to take great liberties with executing Caesar's will. Cicero has already sent word to Octavian, requesting that he return to Rome from Apollonia immediately so they can deal with Cleopatra before she can leave Rome.

The queen consults the priestesses at the Temple of Venus Genetrix, who allow her to pay tribute to Isis and perform pregnancy rituals to Hathor. Cleopatra knows that she cannot challenge Caesar's public will until her child is born, but she knows that staying in Rome could prove fatal for her and her child. One of the priestesses at the temple suggests that Mark Antony might be sympathetic to her cause because he has essentially taken over for Caesar after his murder and will want to retain his newfound power for as long as he can.

Lucinda's vision now shifts to seeing Cleopatra and Mark Antony meeting in a secret chamber in that temple. She explains to him that she and Caesar had conceived a child a few months before his assassination during the time of the Lupercalia festival. She says that he promised her that this child will be recognized as his legitimate heir, unlike Caesarion. He made her a commitment, and Cleopatra shows Antony the papyrus with Caesar's insignia on it. She says that Cicero is moving quickly to bring Octavian back to Rome to challenge her child's claim.

Mark Antony listens intently to her and agrees that they have a problem. He is no more eager to have Octavian ruling than she is. Mark Antony says that he will have his spies look into it and provide her with protection until they can get it sorted out.

It only takes a few days for Mark Antony to find out that Cicero intends on having Cleopatra assassinated before she can give birth, and Cicero plans to send more of his men to track down and kill Caesarion. Cleopatra is deeply disturbed by this news and is at a loss for what to do. Mark Antony explains that he has a plan to keep them safe. She will leave Rome before the end of April and head back to Egypt to have her baby in secret. Her people will send word to Caesarion's caretaker in Alexandria and get him into hiding for a few months, until Cleopatra can have the child. Then she should declare Caesarion her co-ruler, forgoing any claims to Rome and taking the target off of his back. Mark Antony will remain in charge in Rome and keep Octavian at bay until the child is old enough to rule, and then Antony will transfer everything back to the child.

The queen is amenable to the idea and thinks this must fate because it will aid her children in obtaining the greatness they are destined to have. She sends word to Egypt and gets Caesarion to safety. Antony knows that Cicero is waiting for Octavian to arrive in Rome before he will make any move against Cleopatra, but with his arrival only weeks away, Cleopatra must leave as soon as she can without being detected by Cicero's spies. Mark Antony and Cleopatra ready two identical barges and move to send them out on two different days in two different directions. This splits Cicero's men up and keeps them occupied while Cleopatra slips out a day after that on another boat and heads south back to Egypt to hide until the birth.

Lucinda realizes, in a vision, that Cleopatra will eventually be heading to Dendara for this sacred birth, and she has no idea that the royal vizier has fully taken over a few months prior and the new usurper high priestess is his puppet. Lucinda sends word to her most trusted priestesses to meet Cleopatra outside of Dendara and safely deliver her baby. I, Laura will be one of the ones to meet her.

By the time the queen reaches Dendara, it is September, and the temple complex is busy celebrating her son Caesarion's ascension to joint ruler. It is the distraction we need to help her. The queen's handmaiden arrived a day earlier, telling us where along the shore to meet them and to be ready. On the night of Caesarion's celebration, three priestesses and I meet up with Cleopatra's barge. Lucinda was sent a vision of when and where to be, but there is no guarantee she will get there at exactly the right time.

When we come upon Cleopatra's convoy, we find out that she is not yet in labor, and it will need to be induced. We have hidden all of the necessary herbs, linens, and tools to do this. I have my attending priestesses cook up the herbs into a drink and give it to the queen to start the process. We pray with the scroll and scarab of the Goddess and Fertility to bring forward a safe birth.

Luckily, it only takes a few hours to kick in, and she is soon lying on her back and attempting to push out her child. Lucinda shows up toward the end of it and helps me deliver the baby.

When the baby comes out, she doesn't cry, and a shooting star crosses the sky overhead, as if to tell us it was okay. We hand her to Cleopatra, who takes the child lovingly into her arms. She whispers to the child that someday she will be a queen like her mother, but she will be far better and rule over more people than Cleopatra ever has. The scene brings tears to our eyes. I look over at Lucinda, who has a sad look on her face.

She goes over to Cleopatra to speak with her. "My queen, this child is blessed by the gods. She is destined to become a conduit for them."

Cleopatra frowns at this. "A conduit? No, she will be my great pharaoh and rule over Egypt and Rome. It is already decided."

Lucinda sighs. "The prophecy states that you will have two children, one a king, the other taking on the mantle of a god. Your son, Caesarion, was named your co-ruler today. That makes him a king."

"No, that is only temporary. I am planning on sending him to Thebes to study there. My daughter is the one who will be the true king—or queen, in this case."

Lucinda seems unsure of what to do next. "I know that you and I have had our differences, my queen, but I foresaw this.

The second child is to be the conduit for a god, not the first."

Cleopatra furrows her brows. "But she is in a better position to take power. It is her legal birthright. I have the document to prove it!"

"I know this is difficult to hear. But she is meant for one of the temples, not a royal court. Close your eyes and call for Isis; she will show you."

Cleopatra looks like she is going to protest, but she humors Lucinda. Her eyes snap open a minute later, and tears stream down her face. She looks up at Lucinda. "You were right. Isis showed me that my daughter is to become her apprentice. When she is old enough, she will take on the mantle of Isis and re-unite the temples, she could be the oracle of her time."

Lucinda gives her a sad smile; she is highly attuned to the queen's pain. "She will bring order to chaos, renewing and restoring the sacred contracts between the priestesses and Isis and between themselves. She will protect our people and do so much good for them." Lucinda hesitates before saying the next part. "And I need to take her back to Philae with me."

Cleopatra openly weeps then, realizing that she will never get to watch her daughter grow up, and that her daughter will likely never know who her parents are or anything about her royal lineage. This child was born from so much love and hope.

When her tears have slowed, she looks down at her baby, who by some miracle has slept through all of that. Then she looks back up at Lucinda. "Yes, I understand. I know she will be safer with you than with me anyway, what with Cicero's men still after me. Could we just wait until morning, though? I want to hold my daughter for just a little longer."

☥

We came out of the regression and sat quietly, thinking on

what we had discovered, which we had never expected. There were two sacred children, two girls born at a time that changed many things, and perhaps they were meant to stop the fall of the temples. One thing I knew for sure was that Naomi must be one of them, but who could the other one be? It was also interesting that they were both girls and were both destined to possibly rule the physical and spiritual worlds.

Then I saw a flash of green eyes in my mind. I had never been able to see her face clearly, never known who she was—until now. "That child," I said, looking at everyone with wide eyes. "I've dreamed of that child before, and of Cleopatra. She is the emerald-eyed woman who has been visiting me in my dreams, telling me to find her. It's time to visit Isis and really obtain some answers," I said.

I looked at Laura, Lucinda, and Emilee. "It's time, Anna," they said in unison.

"Truth time. Go to her. Blessed be to you," said Laura.

I picked up my phone and sent a text to Naomi. It asked if I could have a session with Isis the next day. I prayed she was in town and open to seeing me. She replied almost immediately, telling me to come in at 11:00 a.m.

"I'm in at 11:00 a.m. tomorrow," I informed the other women.

"Then you will need this," said Lucinda. She walked over to one of the bookcases and took out a box that was on the shelf. It was old and wooden, and as she handed it to me, I saw it had a golden ankh symbol inlaid on the top. As I held it in my hands, my heart began to beat so fast. I was tempted to lift the lid but stopped myself. It was not mine to open.

CHAPTER 24

Friday, June 20, the summer solstice

The next day, I knew there was more to the stories, and I wanted to know more about those priests of Unal. I was also curious about the girl I had felt and seen in Edfu and at Dendara. No one else seemed to see her. It was as if she was a shadow and did not wish to reveal herself. I wondered if she had been in the Tudor timeline. I tried to write down all these questions but kept saying to myself that they were not important. I had so many doubts.

Wow, my golden journal was just about full, so perhaps this last story and part of the jigsaw puzzle would come from Isis, and I could find out my part and role in all this confusion. I checked my phone: it was 10:30 a.m. already. I had to make haste and not forget the box.

♀

I had no need to announce myself because the gateway was on the latch, and as I arrived just before 11:00 a.m., the doors were all open. I walked into the Sanctuary foyer. Isis was waiting for me in the living room. She looked anxious, she was pacing and pulling out books, and she had a scroll.

"Is that the same scroll you gave me?" I asked. I sat down and decided it was not time for the box to show itself.

"Yes and no," she replied. "This side of the scroll is the copy I gave you, but there is also a story on the back of the original."

"May I see?" I asked, walking up to her and examining it. "The Dendara Zodiac. Look here: there is the marker of Isis and the eclipse. But I don't understand why it's here."

"Do you remember my story of Philae? The beautiful one with the sisterhood?"

"Yes." I did not want to say that I had still not found the voice recorder.

"Well, there is more to tell."

We sat down, and I was very still as she placed the scroll on her lap and smoothed it out.

♀

In 66 BC, the ancient wisdom temples of Egypt were in their golden lifetime. The system and connections between the priests and priestesses were harmonious and in balance. The Egyptian royal family understood their importance and was showered with abundance.

However, across the waters, Rome was becoming unsettled, and the energy of ego, power, and greed was beginning to seep through the Nile and into the hearts of those once so pure and connected with the alchemical mysteries of the universe. The relationship between the priests of Horus at Edfu temple and the priestesses of Isis at Philae were about to face challenges after hundreds of years of living, loving, and working together.

In 54 BC, I was still a young high priestess in that lifetime and had only fully reassumed my duties as required by the mantle of Isis a few years prior. I remember so vividly a new priest of Horus coming to the festival that year. He was unlike any man I had ever seen before. We had caught sight of each other across the courtyard. He was most strong and athletic, with his head shaved and held high with great power of knowledge and wisdom. He had a tattoo on his head and a yellow sash around his waist, indicating that he would become the next high priest.

Something in me stirred at his intense gaze. My heart stopped, and though he held my gaze only a moment, it felt like blissful eternity. I was not the elderly lady you see here; I was young and vibrant, with piercing eyes. That night, he entered my dream and my chamber—something no man had ever been able to do. He whispered words I never forgot about a time before and a time after, when we would be together.

The next day, he was chosen to walk into the small temple to pray with the elders and was immediately sent back to Edfu after that. I remember that as he left, his shoulders looked heavy, and there was a hawk that circled him. Then it turned, as if he commanded it, and stayed with our group at Philae. One day the hawk left, and I felt lost to my beloved, but still he entered my dreams. I knew I would never seek another man in this lifetime. I was bound to his soul.

He returned the next year, much to my joy. I chose him to help me with the rituals so that we could have time alone together. There was never any hesitation in our actions; we were certain that our union was destined to be, regardless of the rules saying we couldn't. For the rest of the festival, we spent our days celebrating and our nights together in my private chamber.

I fell pregnant, something that was forbidden for my position, and I had to have the child in secret. I could not openly declare the child mine because and I would have been cast out and lost my position before I could pass on the mantle. I knew my time was limited as the high priestess of Isis, but I couldn't let this corrupt the will of the gods.

The only people who knew were my handmaiden, my love, and a young priest who was shadowing him. We had a part of the temple blocked off where I could keep the newborn hidden from all of the other priestesses. To protect my child, I was also hidden, and this created unrest and disconnection from my fellow priestesses. I did what I could, but the fact that temple life was not running as normal created some tension.

Unfortunately, I could not keep her there forever, so when she was a few weeks old, I had to give her up. I managed to have her taken by my trusted handmaiden down to the water, and it was made to look as if she had been a child left in the high grasses by the gods. She was then brought before me, and my oracles examined her. They said she was the oracle born to help change the focus and course of Egypt. I decided it would be too dangerous to keep her at Philae, lest someone figure out who she truly was. I broke protocol and sent her away when she was old enough to safely make the journey.

My love was now the new high priest at Edfu, so he indicated that he could take her and raise her there openly without anyone questioning his authority. We agreed that we would not tell her who her parents were so no one could use that information to hurt her.

You see, news had already reached Edfu that a child was born with the markings of a powerful oracle, and I knew that pretending she was a stray child who was found on our doorstep would be best. I knew at some point they would take her. This had been prophesied during the times of Alexander the Great, when he had been searching for this power.

During Alexander's reign, Alexander continuously searched for an oracle who could start the trials, convinced that what the librarian had told him was false. None of the ones he found was gifted enough to give him the Unal priests he desired.

He had been told the child would be born in auspicious times and of divine lineage, and this child would open the doors between the heavens. This child, *my* child, would be born of both shadow and light. I prayed that she would always choose the light.

"Like during an eclipse?" I asked.

Suddenly, Lesley opened the door and said, "The Fosters are here, Isis, and they want to see you and be shown to their rooms." I had forgotten she was here, and in true Lesley fashion, she was as inappropriate as ever.

Isis looked at her. "Can't you do this, my dear?"

"But they want you, not the servant girl," Lesley whined.

Isis looked frustrated but got up anyway. "Then let me assist," she said.

While she left the room, Naomi put her head around the door. "Can I join?" she asked.

I paused before speaking to her. It must have been a long time because she gave me a strange look and raised her eyebrows at me. I snapped out of it. "Of course. Come on in." I was not sure what to share; my mind was racing as I began to pull the puzzle together.

Naomi turned to me. "What did you see, Anna? I know that you can see more than us."

"I'm not sure." I changed the subject. "Naomi, when you showed me the priests of Unal in your last regression, and we figured out they were the figures haunting my dreams, it got me thinking. I know you helped create them, but I don't think you had anything to do with them appearing in other timelines. You tried to destroy them, and then before they could do anything more to you, you were safely on the ground of Philae, where they couldn't step. What if someone else called them here, into our sisterhood? What if they were using the priests to hide their activities? They could have been using the Scroll of Light and Shadow to move in between timelines without being detected, and they used it to keep the priests of Unal tied to us!"

Naomi regarded me for a moment and pondered my words. "So," she eventually said, "we perhaps need to look at the initiation trials again and what happened then. All we know is that they went into a hole, and only a few came out. We need to know why they decided to forsake Horus and turn to Set."

We both looked at each other, and in that moment we saw many sad and evil events of the world: boys born into the light but coerced into the shadows by their own mentors.

Isis then returned. "That girl is all drama. The Fosters are two beautiful people from Wales who come every year. Thankfully, Lesley will be gone soon." I felt a little uncomfortable about this and wondered if Lesley had heard.

"Isis," said Naomi, "Anna and I would like to be regressed together to look at all the priests of Horus at Edfu. They seem to be the key to all of this, and I think that when we look, we will see it was one temple with many masters."

I wasn't listening to what she was saying. Instead, I was staring at Isis and Naomi, realizing that I saw a connection between the two of them that needed to be known. As Naomi settled in her chair, Isis looked straight at me, and I heard her telepathically tell me to wait. *Patience and temperance, my dear beloved.*

"As you wish, ladies," replied Isis. She began with the regression and asked us both to open our hearts and go back to the temple to see the trials. Naomi was first.

More is coming to me now than last time. Those boys, that anger I felt toward them—it wasn't real. I never enacted the trials out of spite or revenge against them. It was forced out of me by the high priest. Why would I forget that?

I see myself being held in my chamber until I begin to channel for the new high priest, who was the royal vizier. The royal family has issued a decree that the priests are to be trained in the ancient ways. The high priest has told them that he holds the signature of the oracle and the books of wisdom, and that he will turn his superior priests of Edfu to those of Unal.

The temple has various groups and factions: Horus priests and the Sons of Set. It's strange because the Sons of Set were forbidden during my father's lifetime, but this other high priest allows them to openly practice. The Sons of Set wear dark cloaks to signify their allegiance to him. The high priest himself encourages the priests at Edfu to convert to this cult of Set, and many go along with it. Those who don't are cast aside as weak. In truth, I think this started long before my father was killed.

The high priest demands I channel the trials. He commands me to a sacred star chamber with blue on the walls and stars on the ceiling. He won't allow me to leave until I enact the ritual of the trials. He visits me every day for five days, attempting to get me to do his bidding. I can't stand the man. He tells me I am to blame for my father's death and the deaths of all the priests who refused to follow him.

On the fifth day, somewhat delusional from lack of food and water, I laugh at him. "If a man seeks to be bestowed with the gifts and abilities of the gods, then he must pass through the eye of Horus into the other worlds and return. Your artisans have been trying to create the Unal sacred chambers in this temple for many years but are always missing the key. It takes a true High Priest who can command them—something you are not. Trained in the streets, not the temples, were you."

"You insolent girl," he sneers. "I am the high priest of Horus, and I am the ruler of Dendara. Despite what you might think of how I run things here or came to be here, I am in charge now."

"Oh, I don't think anything of you."

"Funny," he says with a hollow laugh. "But it doesn't matter. You were fated to do this, so just make it easier on yourself and tell me what we must do." He then pulls out a water bowl and begins to drink from it. He looks at me with a smile and stops, wiping the water from his face that had fallen on it. I am so thirsty. He knows this.

"So," he says with a smirk, dangling the water in front of me. "I'll ask again: what do we have to do to enact the trials?"

Thirst overtook me, and I croaked out the answer as quickly as I could. "The trials are this: The initiates must complete them in pairs. Only one of two can advance. They must race in the courtyard, scale the walls to the Lion's Head, and release the water fountain. Then they will follow the flow of the water to the inner chambers. These are the true Unal chambers of initiation.

"There they will find the room where the Eye of Horus lives and cross its threshold. Once there, they will go through five chambers to gain access to the final room, which is said to have a direct connection to the spirit world.

"There is first the Room of the Serpent, then the Room of Shards, the Room of Herbs and Potions, the Pit of No Return, and finally the Room of the Brother. They will have to pass a test related to the theme of each room in order to gain access to the next. They are harrowing at best, and most of your boys won't survive."

"What happens in the final room?" he asks.

"They will come face to face with Set himself, and he will judge who is worthy of joining the priests of Unal. If you are deemed worthy, he will rip all that is weak in your soul out of it and replace it with his magic and strength. I can create these rooms if you send me your architects and builders."

The high priest smiles at this and hands me the water bowl. It is empty.

☥

"Oh no, no, I can't go any further." Naomi was taking short, shallow breaths.

"Why can't you go further, my dear?" asked Isis.

"They changed it. They changed the rooms, and they changed the protocol."

"Can you see, Anna?"

"Yes, I can see," I said. A jolt of electricity flowed through me.

"Anna, tell us what happens."

☥

I see Naomi bringing the trials forward, and she knows they are cruel, but she tries her best to help the poor, young boys. She gives them potions that heighten their senses and give them increased strength. Naomi is trying to help keep the boys alive as long as possible, so that they can escape if they want to. There is a secondary shaft that leads out of the complex in the fourth room that many use to get out and escape. Oh, see, Naomi? You were trying to help them, you really were!

The high priest figures out what is going on and has the shaft sealed off. He chains up Naomi in her room to prevent her from interfering any further. The high priest calls upon a priestess from Dendara to help him control the oracle. She has taken over as high priestess at his command. This priestess, whose face I can't see, specializes in manipulating visions and minds; she was using the Scroll of Light and Shadow to obscure truth and reality. She visits Naomi, the oracle, and gleans her secrets. She forces the oracle to submit and to continue issuing the rites to the initiates. The high priest also has the priestess force Naomi to prepare a tonic that will give an advantage to the initiates he deems the most promising.

After months, it is determined that god Set is not happy with the tests taking place in the chambers, because not one initiate has pleased him enough. But I can't see what they changed in order to make him happy.

"I do," said Naomi in a very deep and calm voice. "I'll show you."

Another test must be put in the last chamber. The priestess has forced the information out of me. In order to take on the mark of Unal, one must face the fear of the gods and take the life of an innocent. For each trial, they place a small boy in the final chamber in the dark. Outside the chamber, an elder sat.

When the priest neared the end of the trial, he would be faced with the innocent child. The voice of the elder would give him a simple choice: save the child and drop out, or kill the child and progress. In the first few weeks, the child would be saved, and the initiate would be banished.

The high priest was getting impatient, so he changed the rules: kill the child, or die. It only took another seven days before the initiates who made it the last chamber chose to kill the innocent. Those who killed received the mark of Unal and went into the final room. Only seven ever made it fully through the final initiation and therefore were the chosen ones. Many priests did kill the child and then killed themselves in shame, however they would pay for this crime for the rest of their eternal lives.

By the time Isis became aware of what was happening, dozens of men and boys had been killed. She refused to send anymore until the trials were shut down permanently, and she completely closed Philae to any outsiders. It was of little comfort to me because I had already helped so many get killed. Even for those who were not chosen to be a priest of Unal, I had still inadvertently made them mark their souls with the blood of innocent children. I had corrupted everything that was sacred and holy about the priesthood.

"Enough," I suddenly said. "I can't hear anymore."

"Oh, Isis. I never created that. I could not, I would not," Naomi sobbed. "Not the innocents…and all those priests."

"I know, I know," Isis comforted her. She held out her arms to Naomi, who burrowed herself into Isis's warm embrace.

I piped in. "I knew there was someone else there. That priestess has been manipulating our timelines for over a thousand years. She made it seem like you were the one doing it because you were born of light and shadow!"

Naomi shifted slightly in Isis's arms to look at me. "What do you mean, I was born of light and shadow?"

"You know, like during a lunar eclipse! The child born of royal divine lineage, able to navigate both masculine and feminine energy!" I figured out in that moment that I had said too much.

Naomi was extremely interested in what I had to say now. "The oracle who could enact the Unal trials. But I was born on a lunar eclipse. How do you know that?"

I looked at Naomi and then at Isis, whose expression was unreadable. I looked back at Naomi. "Well, that is what I saw with Isis right before you came in."

Naomi still looked a little lost, but I could tell she was starting to piece some of it together. "I was born on a lunar eclipse to parents of royal divine lineage. Who or what bestowed in me the ability to practice both feminine and masculine worship? My father was the high priest of Horus at Edfu, so then my mother would have to be..." She trailed off, and her eyes got wide. She suddenly got up. "Wait a second. There is only one female counterpart to the high priest of Horus who is equally divine."

"Yes," said Isis, tears forming at the corner of her eyes. She got up out of her seat as well and went to Naomi.

Naomi's voice was small then. "Did you have a child, Isis?"

Isis took a deep breath. "Yes, I did. I sent her to Edfu when she was still very young."

Naomi turned around to face Isis, unshed tears forming in her eyes. "You told me that no one knew who my mother was."

"I know." Isis sighed. "I know, sweetheart. I couldn't tell you. I couldn't tell anyone. They would have taken you from me or done worse. I am so sorry, Naomi."

Naomi stared at her for a moment, tears freely and silently falling from her eyes. "You mean all this time? It was you?"

Isis nodded her head. "It was me. I couldn't claim you until the passing of the mantle had gone smoothly. But things are different now. I am here for you, darling, I'll be her for you until the day I die."

Naomi smiled at this and rushed into Isis's arms. They hugged for what seemed like an hour, crying into each other and letting go of almost two thousand years of loneliness. There wasn't a dry eye in the room.

Isis spoke first. "I am so sorry they forced you to do those things. I should have never let you go, the fates be damned!" Isis was more emotional than I had ever seen her, almost unhinged by her emotion.

"It's okay," Naomi said in a soothing voice. "I'm sure they would have tried to get their hands on me either way. At least this way, you got to protect the temple a little bit longer."

"Yes, I suppose so." Isis sniffed. "Your father was supposed to protect you, though, and then he went off and got himself killed. That stubborn man. If he had been around, the trials would have been done properly, and Set would not have been the patron god of that ritual."

"Wait, they had a choice?" Naomi asked.

"Well, sort of. Set was always the god who imbued the priests with their powers, but Horus was the one who would judge them. When the Sons of Set took over, they tipped the balance between Set and Horus, giving license to Set to do as he wished with the judgment. Originally, the priests of Unal were supposed to be the gatekeepers between worlds in the times of Atlantis. They helped to pass information between the spirits and people. The high priest of Edfu and Set turned them into monsters. The trials were corrupted by them. You know that the Scarab of Light and Shadow actually gave the holder a vision of the real protocols that would be enacted in the final room; the priest would be addressed by a woman's voice. She would calm the child and reassure the priest of his purpose and humility. Both could be saved when they listened and trusted her. They never used the scarab."

Isis's words helped bring a lot into focus. I realized that we weren't just restoring our bond but restoring all balance in the temples. I could now see we really needed the scarabs and scrolls to help us create that balance.

As Isis and Naomi continued to reconcile, I was haunted by the way the universe operated to bring us through timelines. Seeing them again like a family, mother and child, made this past month feel like a dream. For now a healing had occurred, and a connection was made between the worlds and timelines. We were not done healing, but we had come together enough to give ourselves a chance to fix what was happening. Our circle of eight women would crown a new Isis soon, and then we would attempt to create a new temple together.

Naomi roused me from my thoughts and asked me to show her what happened to her after she reached the temple at Philae. It had been an exhausting day, but I knew she needed the closure.

♀

You awoke in a small chamber in the inner temple. Isis was there, tending to your wounds. You tried to talk, but your mouth was still dry from the desert air. Isis seemed to sense what you wanted to say. "You're welcome. And I am here because you need help, and it's my job to protect you. Now, I haven't done a very good job of that, but I want to make up for it. Soon I will have the time to care for you properly, and we can be together like I always wanted."

You were confused by what she was saying. You thought, *Why would she need to care for me? And where will all of this time be coming from?*

Isis answered again, "Your first question is a harder one for me to answer, and I think that would best be done in the temple. As to your second question, I will be stepping down soon as the high priestess. If you can, I would love for you to be there."

You noticed that she had brought you to a place that seemed so familiar yet foreign. It wasn't as grand as the Temple of Edfu, with smaller doorways and columns. Somehow that felt more like home to you.

I was about to continue when Isis spoke. "You were broken, just like the first time you came to Glastonbury. I saw your head shaven and cut. And the bruises. They had been beyond cruel in that temple to you, far worse than I could have ever imagined. They had broken all of the decrees in the scrolls we had in Philae. The goddess had been destroyed in you, which meant she could be destroyed in all of us. What's worse, this had also occurred on sacred land both at Edfu and on the island of Philae.

"When you arrived that day in Glastonbury, I had full recall of our past life. I saw myself carrying you into the temple and working with the healers. Every woman who came into contact with you developed fear in her heart. Our brothers, fathers, husbands, and sons in Edfu had let this happen, and who knew who had taken part in the abuse? I knew our temple was over that day."

"I saw myself holding you in my arms as you died, Naomi. A child so gifted and rare and so precious from the gods." Isis hung her head in shame.

"So for two thousand years, you have been trying to heal from that?" asked Naomi.

"Yes, and to build a new temple. I wanted to find the perfect place for the Sacred Eight to come together and start anew. We may not all be here yet; you, Anna, and Lesley are not from that initial group of eight, as far as I know. We can still create a new temple and bring forward the new Isis. I spent my past lives searching the world for the perfect place where all my daughters of Isis could be safe. I prayed that you all would follow and come here with your past traumas resolved. It's only now that I see you had to come here to do that."

"Then that's what we should do," I said. "We cannot dwell on the past, but we can heal and clear for the future. Isis, we need the Sanctuary, we need the stories, and we need the oracles and priestesses to remember who they are. We are no longer broken-hearted and ignored or abused. We will find those scrolls and the scarabs and unlock the secrets and mystery teachings once again. The Temple of Isis will be once more, and our sisterhood will be fully restored. I just know we can do it."

Naomi gave Isis a big, knowing smile. "You see? I told you she was special."

"Yes, my dear, you did," Isis agreed. "This is a solstice to celebrate. Now, let us gather everyone and give thanks and grace for the sun and the light we share today. No more talk of the new high priestess; that will happen in time. We have a temple to build ladies, so let us get to work!"

We all stood, and I pushed my box under the chair; something told me now was not the time. That evening, back at the Gables, I brought the box back with me, wrapped it in a white scarf, and placed it at the back of my closet.

CHAPTER 25

July came and passed, and suddenly it was August. After Naomi and Isis's breakthrough, I decided to stay in Glastonbury and work at the Sanctuary more and more.

It seemed like the perfect choice for me in the moment. My dreams were still haunting me, but I had learnt in meditation how to address my fears, and they were showing up less and less. I was still worried that the priests of Unal would show up to take me. I hadn't dreamed about them since the solstice, but I could still feel their presence. They were waiting for me in the shadows of my mind.

Part of my new job was helping to track down the rest of the scrolls and scarabs. I knew that we could never reclaim our temple fully until we had them all. As of August, we only had the Scroll of Magic and Prophecy and its scarab, the Scroll of Death and Resurrection, the Scroll of Creation, and the scarab of the Goddess and Fertility. Isis guarded them all, however now Lesley and I were allowed to visit and study from them. I wanted to find them all, but I found myself taking over more and more of the duties of Isis. She was slowing down, and her health had been fading. Naomi was in London more often now, so she couldn't help out as much either. Word of our work had reached many parts of the world, and those who felt a longing and connection to Egypt found a safe space in our teachings and work. This meant that more and more people came to see us.

Isis pulled us aside one day and told us that now we had resolved the past, it was time for her to move on. She said that it was time she retired and spent the remainder of her life with her daughter. The new Isis was about to be revealed, and she would pass on the mantle in the coming weeks. Naomi shared this sentiment and said that she and Isis would be spending most of their time in London for the launch of Naomi's new show. They would travel one more time to Egypt with the group that September. The trip kept being postponed. But like Isis said, "Everything is in divine order."

With no one left to run the Sanctuary, it seemed that Lesley would be doing it—unless someone else stepped up. She had had decided to stay longer, had expressed an interest to run and manage the Sanctuary, and knew the most about the day-to-day operations, which I have to admit she was really good at. It was not something any of us wanted or were really qualified to do, so there didn't seem to be another option. Any further discussion would have to wait until after the Egypt trip, which was not far away, during the week of the equinox.

On August 2, I came down to breakfast to see Emilee sitting in the kitchen. On the table were two small envelopes, one addressed to me and one to her. I sat down at the table and looked at Emilee.

"She called it," Emilee explained.

"Called what?" I asked.

"A gathering on August 8. The eighth hour of the eighth day, in the eighth month of the eighth year of the new millennia."

I held up the envelope and inspected it. It was made of a

heavy stock linen paper, had my name written in swirly cursive script, and had a gold wax seal on the back, stamped with the symbol of an ankh. I carefully broke the seal and took out a crisp ecru note card that was branded with the same swirly cursive script.

You are cordially invited to attend the initiation of the new high priestess of Isis at the Sanctuary, on Portal Day, 08/08/08 at 8:00 a.m.

We will unite to anchor in a new day of connection to the Divine Feminine and begin to claim back the sacred relics of our priestesses. We honor your linage that you and your ancestors have protected these through many lifetimes.

I put the invitation down and looked at Emilee. She gave me a smile. "Well, I guess we are going to this celebration!"

This would be the first time I would be going to a Sanctuary ceremonial event since the incident at the Chalice Well. It made me feel a bit nervous, but I knew that things would be different this time.

Friday, August 8, 2008, Portal Day

I made sure to get to the Sanctuary well before the time on the invitation, on the off chance that Lesley had been the one to write them. I placed my belongings in the entrance, and in silence I went to the courtyard that held the large crystals. I stood in the circle in the spot that felt best. The morning air was crisp, and I could see far across the countryside. The morning mist obscured the Tor slightly, giving it a shimmery appearance, like a mirage. One by one, everyone else filed into the circle: Isis, Naomi, Emilee, Lucinda, Laura, Alice, Lesley, and I were there. We looked at each other, and I realized how much we had grown and learnt recently, and how much more we had to learn from each other.

Isis looked radiant, all in white with all her fine Egyptian jewelry. Next to her on a small table was a wooden box. She gently opened it, and there were the three papyrus scrolls and two blue scarabs.

"Ladies," Isis implored, "if you have brought any other precious relics with you to add to this box, please present them now."

Naomi stepped forward first and declared, "I have the scarab of Protection; it was given to me many years ago when I lived in London." She placed the scarab gently into the box.

"I hold the Scroll of Truth and Integrity and its accompanying scarab," declared Alice. For some reason, she handed them to me and told me to place them into the box.

As I did, something was not right. "Isis, it's the wrong way around," I explained.

"Oh no!" I heard Lesley gasp. She was about to disrupt things.

"No, not quite right," I said, furrowing my brow in concentration. It only took me a moment to understand that the scrolls and scarabs needed to be placed in a balanced position, and the matching sets needed to stay matched.

"See," I explained, "this scarab must go here. There, we now have two full sets."

"Good work, my darling," said Isis gently. "I knew someone would know what to do."

"But it won't fit everything," Lesley objected. "That's only four across! She is messing it up!" I could hear the whine in her voice and a change in pitch that made her sound nervous.

Isis was getting irritated with Lesley but remained stoic in her appearance. She asked, "Lesley, do you have something to offer the box?"

Lesley relaxed and gave a triumphant smile before striding up to the box. "In fact, I do. I have the Scroll of Light and Shadow. It was gifted to me many years ago, and I think it should act as an omen of my true purpose here today." She pulled out for her pocket a small and beautifully wrapped papyrus.

Isis took it to authenticate it. "It is real and powerful. Here, Anna." She handed it to me.

"Show me how that works, Anna," said Lesley smugly.

I took a breath, and then all become clear. I went to the lid of the box and laid the box flat. I then pulled at the lining in the lid, which came away easily, revealing another four slots. I held out my hand, took the scroll, and placed it gently into the lid portion.

I turned to Isis and said, "I'll find the rest, I promise, Isis. I'll search for all these sacred things. I'll bring them here, and we will all be home again."

"I know," she nodded. "Thank you, Anna. Now, ladies, if we can begin, please? Emilee, will you light the fire?"

Emilee went over to the small fire pit in the center and lit the flame.

"Ladies, priestesses of Philae, and Mother Isis," Isis began, "here you will witness my final stand. Soon I will be in other lands, but I stand here to welcome you home safely. It is time that I pass the mantle of Isis onto the next soul. It has been two thousand years in the making, and today, with her ascension, we will be rid of our curses and usher in a new golden age of prayer and spirituality. We have had two worthy candidates come forward thus far; now they will go into their final regression and see who was the child of the last queen of Egypt and was destined to take my place. Ladies, please sit down and begin to channel. Let the memories wash over you..."

And just like that, I was back on those fateful sandy shores, which I now knew to be those of the Nile. I was right in front of the emerald-eyed woman and the other woman in the black cloak. I recognized her now: it was Lucinda. I began to think this was not a past life regression and I had now entered my dream. I felt as if I were in a parallel universe.

I watched the two women argue about the child. Lucinda said, "I know this is challenging for you, but it is already midmorning. If we don't leave now, we risk running into more ferrymen, and that could be disastrous if they see the child!"

"I know," countered the emerald-eyed woman. "I know. I just want to be with her a little bit longer. I want her to know how much I love her before I have to let her go."

They went back and forth a few more times, but finally she allowed Lucinda to take her baby. As Lucinda left to go to her skiff, she turned, smiled at me, and gestured for me to look inside the wicker basket. I saw a small infant with dark hair and tanned skin like her mother. She had been fast asleep but awoke when I peered over her. She had green eyes like her mother, but there was something more familiar than that there. I looked up at Lucinda for guidance, but she only smiled and winked at me. Then she got on her skiff and departed.

I turned back to the emerald-eyed woman, whose eyes were still red from crying over her child. She was facing away from the water, as if seeing her daughter leaving would break her. When she thought it safe to look back again, she spoke quietly. "You look different."

I nodded. "A lot has changed since we last spoke."

"Yes, I can see you coming into your own. You look less lost than before." She smiled a sad smile. "I am glad."

There was a pregnant pause before she spoke again, this time in a voice so small that I had to lean in to hear her. "Did you find her?"

I frowned. "My queen, I apologize, I did not. I thought I had. I thought she was the girl given to Edfu, but I was wrong."

Her head perked up at these words. "My queen? So you know who I am?"

"Yes, you are Cleopatra Philopator, the last true queen of Egypt."

"Ah, so that Dendara priestess was right: my kingdom will fall to the Romans."

"Oh no, I'm sorry. I probably wasn't supposed to say that!"

"No, no, it's quite all right, my dear. You should know by now that time is a bit in flux, and we always know a little more than we should. Do not worry; I won't let it affect my rule." She winked. "But tell me, will I at least die honorably, when the time comes?"

I nodded. "Yes, most honorably."

She spoke with the upmost regality of her position, but I could see the unshed tears brimming in her eyes. "What will become of my daughter? Will she be safe, after I'm gone?"

I faltered at this. "I...I don't know. I'm sorry." I bowed my head in shame.

She tilted my head upward with her hand and spoke with a gravelly voice laden with emotion. "Now, now, you need not worry. I know this life wasn't meant to be her golden one. I do believe the one she lives now is."

"What do you mean?"

"Well," Cleopatra continued, "she has worked so hard to help those of the Sacred Eight and others around her find their way and make peace with their lives. She has helped Isis reconcile with her child. Above all, she has shown great courage and kindness in the face of horrible forces. I could not be prouder of her."

I furrowed my brow at this. I knew everyone now, and she wasn't describing any of them.

Cleopatra cupped my face with both of her hands. "Oh, Anna, can you really not see?"

"See what?"

Cleopatra chuckled. "I suppose we are most blind when it comes to seeing ourselves. You have all the gifts to help souls heal their karma that wraps around them and binds them. You bring the temples into harmony; you had the gifts then, but the timing was wrong. Now in this time, you can fulfill your destiny." We locked eyes for a moment, and then each shed a few silent tears together.

Just then, I knew what she meant.

I was the first to come out of my regression. "It's me," I said quietly, and then I looked up at everyone else. "It's me! I was to be the next high priestess of Isis!"

Isis smiled at me, and I looked around the group. I saw so many connections to my heart through these women who had shown me their hearts and allowed me to find mine. I saw Lucinda, the woman who had started it all and facilitated my journey to Isis not once but twice. I saw Laura, the woman who took me in and showed me what true kindness was. I saw Emilee, with her fiery spirit and her knack for knowing just what to say when I was down. I saw Alice, the wisest woman with the most unique sense of style I had ever known. I saw Naomi and Isis, the two women who pushed me to expand my horizons and hone my gifts. Even Lesley had provided me with useful information and an opponent to force me to get better quicker. We all linked hands and formed a circle. It was time to start.

"Wait," shouted Lesley. "I have a greater claim!"

Suddenly there was a loud sound from a car backfiring, and the clouds came over to cover the sun. Then wind was picking up, and I felt a coldness wash over me that I had only known in my dreams.

"Hold tight, ladies," I shouted over the wind. "Focus on the fire in the center! Emilee, if you please?" Emilee stepped forward and poured the incense onto the flames. The smell was sweet and floated around us.

Lesley began to cough, and she fell to her knees.

"Do not break the circle," shouted Isis, even though Lesley was kneeling. "We are one, remember, always and forever."

I began to chant some of the words from the scroll that I had translated. "Oracle sight, see all before me. Oracle of the light and dark, bring your wisdom to me. Let me see, let us all see! Call forward the gift of magic and prophecy. May we all see and align with this wisdom!"

☥

Suddenly, I am back in Egypt, in the temple of Edfu; its tall, majestic columns and Horus statues give it away. I see the festival procession arriving from Dendara and the delegations from Philae. The courtyard has both priests in white and black robes, and the area I thought would be a place of prayer is now filled with weapons and chariots.

I see Lesley now, and she's moving around the temple. She stands in front of the weapons and the animals in cages and gives them blessings. She's showing the priests the sacred powers of Unal. She is the one who can slip through the walls and veils between the temples. She carries messages and manipulates the visions of others. She is invisible to all of those without innate psychic powers, and she has read all the Sacred Eight scrolls. She has copied them and uses her power over others with them. But never do I see a scarab, which means her information is missing key elements. It's like the priest of Unal who needed the voice of the priestess to guide him.

Now she is meeting with the delegations from the female temples and showing them the strength of the men. She tells them that these priests will protect them, that they can overthrow Isis and surrender the temple to the high priest of Edfu, and that she has the magic that she can teach them to do this. My path is now blocked, and all I can hear is Isis scream. I see the priestesses leaving the high altar with knives; they run, ashamed of their actions. Their minds and hearts have been corrupted.

☥

I then saw her in all the other lifetimes, like a flashback, but this time I did not declare my story. I invited my sisters in the circle to see as well.

"Ladies, look with the oracle sight. I give you all the blessings," I shouted. I opened my eyes and saw each of the women now observing the timelines from Egypt's creation, the fall of Philae, Cleopatra, then through the ages of the Tudor reign to the Salem witch trials and to present day. They saw it all and, as all of them came to the realization, they opened their eyes and saw Lesley for who she truly was.

We all looked to Isis, but she stood still and silent. We held hands so tight, with the wind still whipping around us. They then turned to me.

"Ladies," I urged, "we must hold this circle and bring back our temple. Lesley has seen all the scrolls in her lifetimes. She has used the Scroll of Light and Shadow to manipulate our visions and hide her involvement. However, she is still part of this circle, and in time we will heal with her and resolve this trauma."

"Well, screw that!" Lesley shouted. "I am not sticking around to restore some weak temple that couldn't hold it together the first time. The Sons and Daughters of Set are far more powerful, and we will restore our temple. Then you will all be done for! You will never be whole again, and the Temple of Isis will be gone forever! If any of you had any brains, you would leave with me and join Set!"

Alice and Laura were on either side of her and tried to hold her in the circle, afraid that she would ruin it if she left.

"No, Lesley, we don't need you." A deep voice and a new energy appeared to have entered our sanctuary. "We only needed eight initiates of Philae for the circle. You haven't been a part of this circle for many lifetimes. The gods have judged you, and you will not make it to another lifetime. Go; you have no power here."

Lesley was suddenly thrust out of the circle. She ran as fast as she could to get away. As she did, she ran through the gateway and down toward the road.

We heard a screech of car brakes. Then the wind died down, and all was still. We slowly let go of our hands, and for a moment, I didn't think anyone took a breath.

I looked to see who the presence was, and I was delighted to see Lucas, my tarot Gothic advisor.

"Ladies," he proclaimed, "I was with you all then, as I am with you now. As a small boy in my past life, I was an initiate of Philae. I made my oath to Isis to serve the temple. I am sorry, Naomi, that I could not do more." He walked over to her and put his forehead to hers. They stood so still, and I saw him again as the high priest of Edfu's assistant and her as a young oracle.

He had been her protector at Philae.

As they exchanged this gentle healing, we all stood. It gave us hope that the men in our past, present, and future could regain a balance and help us to hold our temples again.

Naomi smiled at him and said, "That is all right. You did all you could. I am glad you are here now."

Each of the women smiled at him, and I continued. "Mother Isis, watch over your initiates. See us assisting others in this world at this time. Protect us and allow us to move with our hands, heads, and hearts. Greet everyone from thy heart and see thy one true, eternal self."

"And now, one more vision, Anna," called Alice. "Emilee, place down more incense."

As Emilee placed the incense onto the fire, I took a moment to retrieve my blue bottle of water. I knew she meant for me to see my final story, my completion.

"Hold hands, ladies—and gentleman." I smiled at Luke.

"Please share, dear Anna," called Naomi. "We see through you now."

I closed my eyes and saw the truth.

I'm back in temple and seeing Lucinda bringing the baby girl. She has the star mark. She is presented to Isis, and Isis takes her to the high altar. The oracles agree to raise the child, and she will be a great oracle and priestess.

Before she leaves, Lucinda hands Isis a scarab—the scarab of creation. "You know whom this child belongs to, and you know the danger should anyone reveal who she is," said Lucinda. "But if you or she needs help, then she is to have the scarab to protect her."

Isis accepts the scarab. It is the sacred scarab from Dendara that was always in the royal most high queen's possession for her to watch over the children of the land.

I see the child growing, and she has great beauty and wisdom, as well as a heart that is beyond open and kind. Her work is not grand or powerful. She is not destined to be a high priestess of this temple. She chooses humble work, and delights as she takes care of the nursery and trains the young initiates to walk like priestesses. But she is never formally initiated; she is told that her family may return for her and that she must not be bound to the temple. She knows she may be an orphan by now because no one has returned for her, but she has gratitude every day that she was brought to the temple stairs and received with love.

She knows that she was not born into the temple and listens as all the other priestesses talk of their blood relatives and the temples to which they belonged.

She cannot understand why the elders or Isis include her in their conversations, or why she is allowed to sit on the floor of the high altar and listen and help as they prepare for ceremonies.

I'm moving on in time now. The temple is changing, and the young girl senses danger. As Isis adores her and treats her like a daughter, when the temple falls, she runs to warn Isis.

When the priestesses attack Isis at the high altar, they hear the thunder and become afraid, and they run. The young girl is the only one who enters and tries to help.

She's crying as Isis hands her the scarab. "You will understand one day, and you will return. Always and forever."

I'm looking at the girl's face, and I see it's me.

☥

Lucinda stepped forward and brought me back. "Anna, where is the box I gave you?" I looked down at my bag, pulled out the box, and removed the scarf.

Alice and Lucinda spoke in unison, "Now, Anna. It's time."

I carefully opened the box to reveal the aqua scarab of creation. I turned it onto its back, and my fingers traced the images of the sun and moon—creation's sacred key.

"The royals decided and gave permission for a temple to be built with this scarab," I said. I held it up toward Isis.

"Yes," she agreed. "That one was the scarab required to create a temple, and it was always given to the high priestess. Anna, it was prophesied almost two thousand years ago that someone would reunite great temples of learning. But the time was not right, and we fell out of balance. But now, you can slowly spread the message of spirituality and higher consciousness again."

I placed the scarab on my heart and then gently kissed it. Then I placed it carefully into the box which Isis held and closed the lid. I rejoined the circle and nodded to Isis that I was ready.

"Everyone, are you ready for Egypt?" shouted Isis. "Everyone, join hands to Egypt. Are you ready, Anna? Egypt is calling, as well as your initiation to help you step fully into your soul's path."

I looked at her, and with a mischievous smile, I nodded. "To the temple. I'm ready."

CHAPTER 26

One Week Later

Things had been a whirlwind since that Portal Day. After the gathering, we all seemed to part with a knowing of our place in the world. Mine was now living and working at the Sanctuary. All of us, that was, except Lesley. Her dramatic and hasty exit was disregarded when she realized she had to return to the Sanctuary for her things. She came back the next day to fetch them. I was now in charge of the Sanctuary, so I was tasked with helping her move out.

"Lesley, can I help with anything?" I asked, standing in the doorway.

She didn't look at me but muttered under her breath, "Yes. Order me a taxi and tell them it's to the station at Castle Cary. I'm going back to London tonight. Oh, and I'll be needing my scroll back."

"As you wish," I said, much to her surprise. I went downstairs and lifted the scroll from box in the office of Isis—soon to be my office. I picked up the phone and called our driver friend.

"Are you sure, my dear?" Isis spoke softly, having come around the corner. She had been watching through the door.

"What? The taxi or the scroll?" I asked.

"Both."

"Quite sure. And it's a fake, by the way."

"Which one?" She laughed. "Lesley, or the scroll?"

"Both!"

"How do you know?"

"See?" I rolled the edges of the scroll. "Banana leaf, not papyrus."

Isis laughed and gave me a warm clasp on the shoulder.

Minutes later, I went back upstairs and handed the scroll to Lesley. A few moments later, the taxi driver honked its horn outside. She said nothing to me, and we stood there in silence for what felt like hours.

"Ready?" I smiled and lifted up her bulging bag. "Don't worry; I'll have everything else packed up and sent on."

She looked as if she was about to argue, but Naomi appeared behind me. "Time to fly, dear one," Naomi said with a playfulness in her voice but a stern look on her face.

Lesley was still scared of Naomi, so she simply grabbed her things, and we escorted her out.

"The temple is always open for you, Lesley," I said as she walked past me.

She stopped and looked at me. "I know, but this should have been *my* temple."

"Perhaps, but you could create another. There is plenty for us all."

She gave me a terse look.

"Well, maybe someday," I said with a shrug.

Naomi and I watched her go through the gateway, and we heard the car drive away.

A few days later, Lucinda, Laura, and I were clearing Lesley's room of negative energy and curses. Lucinda and Laura had decided to stay in Glastonbury for the time being to help me adjust to my new role and run the day-to-day business of the Sanctuary.

While we were moving the bed, a box fell out. There were all the copies of scrolls and the voice recorder, as well as letters from editors. It was as if she had taken every secret we had shared and stolen it. It turned out she had been trying to use our work and our stories for her book and even a screenplay.

"I know exactly what to do with this," said Lucinda, who handed me the voice recorder. Then she took all the paper downstairs and burned them. "That is cleared!" she declared, her red hair shining and her green eyes flashing. I was glad they were staying in Glastonbury. I now had nothing to return for in York, although I had to smile at what Lucinda had chosen to share with me about my former boss.

"You know, Natasha, your old boss came to see me before Laura and I came on August 8," Lucinda said while sipping a drink. We were having dinner at the local Italian restaurant—pasta and gossip.

"Natasha? Really?" I asked. "That is so weird."

"She came to the spa one morning," Lucinda explained. "Said she needed spiritual help. She said she was locked out of her bank accounts and couldn't access any of her money. Her ex-husbands had cut off all of her funds. She said she was there because she felt someone had put a curse on her. The poor girl at reception had to put up with her babbling hocus-pocus. I had to step in because the young girl was terrified.

"She told me she had watched the Dawn Starchild show from the 1990s, one of the old ones that talks about how when you lose everything, it can be because of a curse. She said they were DVDs from an old employee."

"Mine!" I shrieked. "She stole them!"

"I guessed that, so I told her she must look through everything and make amends, and that this was her time to start again."

"Did you do tarot?"

"Not really; she was not in a listening frame of mind. What could I do?" Lucinda shrugged. "So finally I told her she would be queen of her castle again, and all spells could be reversed. I waved my hands around and said spooky words."

We laughed until late that night. It was good to be surrounded by friends.

Life in Glastonbury became lighter over the next few weeks, and I had to say these were my happiest and most fulfilled of days. It was as if a dark cloud had lifted. My diary was always full of Glastonbury experiences. There were so many women we were helping, and it was rewarding. They were all finding out that they were once powerful priestesses in our sisterhood. It became my duty and mission to help any woman who came to me seeking help.

In addition to that, my other duty was to the sacred box of scrolls and scarabs. Lucas came by often to read and discuss them with me when he wasn't escorting Naomi around the country on her new show. He had become a celebrity in his own right, always being photographed wearing some new extravagant ensemble. Lucas also helped me figure out that that the seven priests of Unal were trapped in between worlds and haunted me because I was to be the new high priestess. Lucas thought that they believed I could save them.

Isis lived full-time with Naomi in London. Her health continued to be touch and go, but Naomi paid for the best care out there. This caused another delay with the Egypt trip, but it would now take place during the December solstice, and I prayed that the auspicious date would mean Isis would be well enough to go.

Without them, I quickly needed to find more people to work at the Sanctuary with me.

Laura decided that it was time to retire herself from her sacred contract in York with her husband David. She sold all her properties and moved to Glastonbury. She bought a beautiful cottage just up the road from the Sanctuary and helps me out part time. A picture of her beloved husband hangs on the wall but he's at peace I am sure.

Lucinda decided she too needed a change of scenery and decided to move into the Sanctuary with me and work there full time. I still find that I miss my room at the Gables, but Emilee always keeps it open for me just in case. She decided to expand her potion and elixir business and now runs a very profitable online store. Alice continues to work at the Chalice Well, but she also helps all the requests for research material we have been getting since she created an online database for our artifacts and other sacred texts.

We all try to get together once every few weeks, not wanting to neglect our sacred contracts with each other. I am so in awe of these women (and gentleman) and all they have accomplished in such a short time. My favorite moments with them are when we get together and talk and share, remembering our past lives and sacred connections.

My dreams have now become a gentler reality and not the nightmares of darkness.

Last night was my most profound yet.

☥

I saw myself standing in the back garden of The Sanctuary. A small gate appeared within the thick hedges with three stone steps leading to it from the stone courtyard.

I walked slowly towards it thinking I should be wearing suitable shoes, when to my surprise I looked down to see old boots of black leather with multiple thick crisscrossed lacing going up the fronts.

As I reached the first step I found myself in a long velvet gown of heavy purple fabric that touched the ground. I lifted it carefully so as not to fall as I mounted the steps to the small black wrought-iron gate.

I lifted the latch while holding steady my gown, and found myself in the thick dark green hedge growth. I moved slowly, so as not to catch my gown on the brambles. I could see the light ahead and suddenly I was at the base of the Tor hillside. No homes or signs of modern life. The grass felt soft as I walked slowly towards the circle like pathways that created various tiers towards the top.

"I remember being here," I said out loud.

"We knew you would come," a voice from behind me whispered.

I turned to see the woman I had seen in my vision many months ago. Her hair was still jet black but it was straight and cut into an ancient Egyptian style.

She wore the same dress as me, but carried two staffs. They were the same height and type of wood, but had different markings. She handed one to me, and as I held it, it felt familiar and I connected to a strength that made my spine raise up and I felt so much taller.

"Who are you?" I asked, looking behind her to see if there were more.

"We are you," she smiled, "guardians, priestesses and oracles. We come to the temple each night to bring our light and watch over the dreams of others.

We have been waiting for many years, watching as you all have been returning home, returning to the temple. The sacred temple of the heart.

The woman lifted her staff to point to the top of the hill, and once again I could see the large stone monolith lit by the moonlight.

"The new age is coming now. I see this". I looked at her and smiled.

She nodded and smiled.

"Now will you come?" Again she held her hand out to me, and this time I took her hand.

Her fingers, small and delicate held a strength in them, that cleared any sense of doubt or fear.

"I will, I will follow," I said eagerly.

"Then come my sister," she smiled. "There is so much more to explore."

On waking that morning, I had jumped out of bed and ran to the back of the garden to try to find the sacred gateway but it just was a flat stone wall with a solid hedge.

I must have woken the house as Lucinda shouted at me from her window.

"Annie have you lost your senses, what on earth are you doing?" she called down to me.

I had a reality check and saw that I was standing in my pajamas and slippers with scarecrow hair.

"Nothing. Just thought I had lost something," I had stammered back.

I was bursting to share my dreams and find this new sacred passageway at the back of the garden, but then I decided to hold my ego, instead enjoying the vision for myself on the condition that one day I would understand.

I had run back in before anyone else had seen me and thought I truly was a lunatic.

On a Sunday afternoon in early December, I was sitting with Naomi and Emilee in the courtyard of the Sanctuary. Naomi was on a break from filming and was at the Sanctuary to help us prepare for the Egypt trip. We were talking about how many had found their way to our door and how many were yet to come. Emilee looked at Naomi and asked how many of these priestesses she felt she'd trained or performed a ritual with over the lifetimes.

Naomi laughed and responded, "Well, it must be in the thousands by now."

They looked at me, and Naomi asked, "And you, Anna, how many?"

"Oh, I don't know," I said. "But I am sure I helped the ones who mattered and heard the call when needed."

Oracles, yes, I helped and guided them all at some point in time and will do so again, I thought. I would keep that secret safe for the time being.

At that moment, my phone rang. I opened it and saw the number was international, but I answered it anyway. "Hello, this is Anna."

A very deep masculine voice said, "Anna Harris, you were referred to me recently, and I think you can guide me. We knew each other in another life. I'm a keeper of the Scrolls of Amenti and the Sphinx in Egypt. We need your help."

End

About the Author

Amanda Romania is a visionary international author, specializing in sacred Temple work, spiritual mentorship and empowerment.

As a master Akashic Record Oracle and Librarian, Amanda is able to open the veils to the mysteries of the Akashic matrix and cosmic realms and the etheric database of knowledge containing all the records of our incarnations. She is able to assist in developing our skills to further enhance all of our unique spiritual gifts, and leads us towards next generation ascension consciousness and greater understanding of true spiritual purpose.

For the past 20 years, Amanda has, led tours to the world's major sacred sites including Glastonbury, Central America, Egypt, and beyond.

Join us on a journey into the mystical realms to examine the past, present, future, the lives between lives, and the effects of our karmic choices on future timelines. Join us on the path of the oracle.

Amanda lives with her family in the heart of Sedona, Arizona. Learn more at **www.amandaromania.com.**

Visit us at **www.floweroflifepress.com**

www.ingramcontent.com/pod-product-compliance
Lightning Source LLC
Chambersburg PA
CBHW020836030726
47496CB00001B/250